KINDREDS

a novel

B.B. RUSSEL

GREEN WRITERS PRESS *Brattleboro, Vermont*

Printed in the United States

10 9 8 7 6 5 4 3 2 1

Green Writers Press is a Vermont-based publisher whose mission is to
spread a message of hope and renewal through the words and images we
publish. Throughout we will adhere to our commitment to preserving
and protecting the natural resources of the earth. To that end, a
percentage of our proceeds will be donated to environmental activist
groups and social justice organizations. Green Writers Press gratefully
acknowledges support from individual donors, friends, and readers to
help support the environment and our publishing initiative. Green Place
Books curates books that tell literary and compelling stories with a focus
on writing about place—these books are more personal stories, memoir,
and biographies.

Giving Voice to Writers & Artists Who Will Make the World a Better Place
Green Writers Press | Brattleboro, Vermont
www.greenwriterspress.com

ISBN: 978-1-7336534-6-6
cover illustration: TK

Printed on recycled paper by Bookmobile.
Based in Minneapolis, Minnesota, Bookmobile began as a design and typesetting production house in 1982 and
started offering print services in 1996.
Bookmobile is run on 100% wind- and solar-powered clean energy.

For Grandma Anne

KINDREDS

GURNEY SPECTATOR NEWS
November 1, 1966—Tuesday Edition

CARNIVAL VANISHES

Set to run for another week, Carnival Nolianna up and vanished this morning from Hayward Field, near Potato River Falls, Wisconsin. Without a word from its owner, Mel Singer, hundreds of patrons are left with unused tickets. The carnival was scheduled to run until November 6. Anyone with information regarding this disappearance, please call the local police.

Chapter 1

❧

Twenty-two months and seventeen days.
Lilah repeated it in her head over and over again.

Twenty-two months and seventeen days until she turned eighteen, could move out of foster care and back into the house she'd shared with Grandma Pea for the last eight years. Her heart hurt each time she thought about leaving the only home she could truly remember.

A loud, hard knock interrupted her rumination.

"Lilah Jane McCarthy, open the door! I'm freezing out here!" yelled Mrs. Reed from the other side of the wooden front door.

Lilah let out a sigh and glanced through the peephole. She glared at the heavyset case worker. Wearing a short-sleeve, white button-down blouse, heavy, white winter boots, and a thick wool scarf but no coat, Mrs. Reed was a conundrum at best. Never smiling yet always boasting about how happy she was to find homes for foster kids, Mrs. Reed was about as fun as getting wisdom teeth pulled, without the drugs.

Lilah opened the door and a sharp, cold gust of late-autumn Ithaca wind rushed in, along with Mrs. Reed. An undoubtedly early winter was predicted for all of western New York, and Ithaca was no exception.

4

"Seriously, Lilah, let's go already! I told you yesterday that I'm on a tight schedule," Mrs. Reed huffed, arms crossed. She teeter-tottered from foot to foot, like a toddler who had to go to the bathroom. "I hope you have all of your things. It'll be awhile before you can come back here."

Lilah nodded and closed the door. Thoughts of all the times she and Grandma Pea had closed that door to take their nightly walk popped in her mind. Pea would let her lock it and then she'd put the key with the daisy keychain in her left front pocket of her white cardigan, patting the pocket to make sure it was safe and sound. Lilah felt all the air go out of her lungs.

"I'm all set," she replied. "I have everything right here in my bags. I don't need much. I've taken care of shutting off the water, and Mr. Gray from next door has agreed to keep a watch on things and forward any mail to the lawyer until I can come back."

"Well, good. I know this is hard on you, but it's for the best. Your Grandmother Penelope wanted you to have a good home."

Heat spread like wildfire across Lilah's cheeks. Mrs. Reed had no idea what her Grandma Pea would've wanted.

"Now hurry up and get your stuff. I'll be *waiting* at the car."

Without wasting another second, Mrs. Reed abruptly opened the door and rushed out as quickly as she'd come in.

Lilah stuck out her foot to block the door from banging into the wall and knocking pictures down—as Mrs. Reed had done several times in the past few days whenever she blew in or out.

Lilah hunched forward, a silent scream caught in her throat. She could feel the veins in her temples pulsate, and did all she could not to punch the pinky-beige wall beside her. Her thoughts raced, but she knew in her heart that resistance was futile. Ever since Grandma Pea had died two days ago, she'd asked politely to stay in her house, and then when that didn't work, she'd argued and pleaded. Each time, Mrs. Reed had said no.

Taking in a deep breath and holding it, Lilah straightened up, grabbed her stuff, and exited the house. She pulled the heavy, wooden oak door behind her with her one free hand, then turned and locked it before walking toward the car. Trembling, it took all of her strength not to drop everything and run back toward the house. Instead, she balanced her belongings in her arms and batted flyaway strands of long, frizzy, orange-red hair away from her eyes. The unruly wind made her hair get bigger by the second. All it took was someone to breathe heavy and the puff would begin. Her hair really had a life all its own.

Mrs. Reed waited in the middle of the driveway next to the state-issued, oversized, beige sedan, motioning her hands in circles and indicating for Lilah to hurry up.

A pang of sadness clanged in Lilah's stomach. She may actually have liked Mrs. Reed under any other circumstances.

"COME ON ALREADY!"

Okay, maybe not.

"All right, all right," Lilah muttered under her breath and walked toward the sedan.

"Hurry up!" Mrs. Reed repeated, walking to the trunk and opening it, never losing eye contact.

"I'm coming. I just had to lock the door!" Lilah shouted so that she could be heard over the wind. Mrs. Reed was deaf in one ear and refused to wear a hearing aid.

"Just put them in and let's get a move on." Mrs. Reed pointed to the trunk.

Lilah did as she was told and then let herself into the car. As she sat on the cold, leather-back seat, her eyes stung. Mrs. Reed plopped down in the front and glanced at Lilah in the rearview mirror while she started the engine.

"Well, you really should like this new family. It's not every day that a foster family is quick to take in a sixteen-year-old," Mrs. Reed said, shaking her head before turning her attention to driving. "Though I wish you'd dressed a little better for the occasion, Li."

"Li-*lah*."

"What?" Mrs. Reed replied, and glanced back.

"Nothing." Lilah shook her head. There was no use in trying to correct Mrs. Reed because she didn't really care what Lilah preferred. Her job was to listen, but she couldn't hear, literally or figuratively. To her, Lilah was just another kid without a family that she had to place. Lilah wondered if she even was a real social worker. Mrs. Reed totally lacked in the communication-skills department. Each time Lilah had tried to talk with her over the past few days, Mrs. Reed had shut her down. Lilah was invisible in the world of adults.

Turning her head to stare out the window, Lilah caught a glimpse of her hair in the reflection and the pit in her stomach widened. Attempts to tame her mane were point-less. She'd let it grow out when she turned fourteen, and after two years, her hair still did whatever it wanted. Even Aiden hadn't had hair like hers. He'd gotten their mom's beautiful black hair and tan skin—at least that's how she remembered him. So much had happened since her family died eight years ago. Grandma Pea had taken her in with-out question, but this time, there was no one left. Lilah's heart ached, and she wished somewhere there was a place she belonged.

"The couple you'll be living with has had dozens of foster children through the years. You never know . . . you aren't too old to be adopted!" Mrs. Reed said in a singsong voice. "Foster care isn't as bad as people think it is."

Lilah admired her useless optimism.

"Well, it's only a couple of miles away from here. Hopefully the gray sky and storms will lighten up soon.

Did you know that earlier this month the United States hit three hundred million people. . . , " Mrs. Reed jabbered on.

Lilah nodded to make Mrs. Reed think she was listening and stared out the window. Reaching up, she touched her mother's ring on her necklace: *twenty-two months and seventeen days.*

Mrs. Reed pounded the brakes like they were cockroaches frantically scurrying to escape. Lilah jerked forward and back.

"Oops. Thank goodness for seatbelts!" Mrs. Reed chuckled over her shoulder.

Pain shot up Lilah's neck. How Mrs. Reed ever got permission to transport children was a true mystery.

"Well, here they are, Li! Your new family." Mrs. Reed hopped out of the car.

Still shaken, Lilah looked down at her trembling hands and clutched them together. Holding her breath, she turned her gaze to the dreary neighborhood where they had stopped. Each of the three-story, 1960-something houses was so close together that someone could lean out their window and touch their neighbor's house. They were all painted different shades of dingy brown-gray with overgrown half-dead bushes in small, suburban-sized yards, and discarded toys lying all around. The wind had died down long enough for plastic wrappers, old containers, and random newspapers to haphazardly scatter across several lawns.

A deep-seated ache erupted in her bones, and everything in her just wanted to be back in Grandma Pea's tight-knit, well-cared-for home and neighborhood. She bit her lip.

Mrs. Reed caught Lilah's eye through the car window. She motioned for her to join. There was a small group of people who appeared to be waiting for the bus. No one looked at each other, or seemed to even acknowledge their arrival, despite Mrs. Reed's chattering.

Lilah looked away from the group and blinked several times.

The car door opened and Mrs. Reed yanked Lilah out by the arm.

"Really, Lilah, don't you think you could at least get out of the car? Stop being difficult and come meet your new family!" Mrs. Reed said through gritted teeth and gave a quick head jerk toward the small group of people outside the car.

Lilah reluctantly got out of the car and shuffled forward a few steps. She stopped and looked at her new foster parents.

Mrs. Reed hip checked Lilah forward a few more steps. "I know this is difficult for you, but *please*. Have some manners and greet your new family. They're *very* excited to meet you."

Lilah looked at the couple and the three younger boys who stood behind them. She tried to smile. No one moved or turned their eyes to even look at her.

"Hi," Lilah managed to squeak out.

Raising a bushy, unkempt, gray eyebrow and turning his gaze slightly, the man spoke. "I'm Abe Anderson. This is Eva, my wife. Call her Eva. That's Caleb, Eddie, and Brody," he said flatly, pointing at the woman and three boys under age ten next to him.

Abe's long, wispy beard covered most of his face, except for his dark, expressionless eyes. Eva was a five-foot-tall round woman who had gray eyes that matched her hair, which was pinned into a mess of curls around her portly face. She looked at Abe and flashed a quick attempt at a half smile. Her wrinkly skin sagged, and despite her best attempts to look interested, her deadpan stare indicated her true feelings. Lilah guessed Eva was tired of taking care of kids who weren't hers, or having new kids come in and out—or maybe she was just tired of waiting for the bus on the wrong curb. Lilah wasn't sure.

"I'm Lilah."

"Well, ain't you unusual? That hair of yours sure is something!" Abe said with a straight face, and stared directly at her for the first time. He ran his hand down his beard and looked Lilah up and down. "You sure must turn into a lobster during the summer."

An intense heat rose in Lilah's cheeks and she looked down at her feet. Her lily-white skin, covered by a million freckles, had been the butt of jokes since she could remember.

Lilah heard Grandma Pea's voice in her head.

Just remember, Lilah, the ugly duckling who turned into a swan. You, my dear, are a swan. Someday you, and everyone else, will see it.

Unfortunately, today wasn't someday. Today, Abe was just an ass.

While no one was watching and without a sound, all three boys, dressed in dirty blue jeans, ratty, once-white Nike sneakers, and gray sweatshirts, grabbed her belongings and darted toward the house. All three had the exact same short, black curly hair clipped short and tight to their heads. They all looked alike and about six to eight years younger than her. She'd never lived with anyone younger than her before. The day had just gotten more interesting.

Abe coughed, causing Lilah to turn her gaze back to him.

"So you've your own room on the third floor. It's small, but private. Eva'll go over the house rules with you later once you get settled. You'll find her in the kitchen whenever you need her. It's where you'll be, too, once you get settled in," Abe said in a monotone, and then added, "We're happy to have you here."

Abe moved his gaze to Mrs. Reed. She beamed ear to ear.

"Well, what do ya say, Li?" Mrs. Reed asked, and stepped

in front of Lilah. "How 'bout if we all go on inside and get acquainted?" Mrs. Reed took Abe's arm.

Lilah stared at Mrs. Reed. It was like watching a chameleon change to adapt to its new environment. Mrs. Reed was either horrible at reading people or really liked mirroring Abe.

"I've a very busy day scheduled. I have two other children who I have to take places today. It's just the saddest of circumstances . . . ," Mrs. Reed explained as the three adults walked up to the house, leaving Lilah alone, standing by herself in what was supposed to be a new, welcoming chapter of her life. So much for that.

Out of the corner of her eye, Lilah caught sight of the curtains swaying in the front window next door. Had someone had been watching them? The hairs on the back of her neck stood up. *At least someone is interested in my being here,* she thought.

Lilah stood alone on the curb and watched as her new family disappeared inside 7061 North Navy Way. She made a note of the house number she'd be living at for the next twenty-two months and seventeen days. Turning eighteen couldn't come soon enough.

Chapter 2

❧

Screech . . . clang . . . clank!
Lilah sat straight up in bed and glared upward toward the deafening noises.

"What the hell?" she said aloud, and scanned the small, unfamiliar room. Cracked yellow ceiling paint hung, suspended, threatening to fall and expose the brown, discolored wall beneath.

Where am I? She placed her hands up to her face and rubbed her eyes. For a blessed moment, she'd forgotten. *Right. Abe's house.* Dropping her hands back down, she let her shoulders slump and darted her eyes around the room. The clock flashed 6:52 p.m.

Screech! The noise of metal on metal erupted again and then stopped. Lilah growled and jumped up, tripping over her left K-Swiss sneaker and falling shins-first into the lopsided, purple chair in front of the matching wooden desk.

"Damn it!" she yelled. *That's twice in the past few hours.* She rubbed her shins. Sitting down for a moment on the chair, she looked out the medium-sized window at the end of the new-to-her twin bed. After Mrs. Reed had high-tailed it out of Dodge, her new foster family left to take the younger boys to see their family. With nothing to do,

Lilah decided to unpack, though it only took a few minutes due to her minimal number of belongings. She plastered her Indigo Girls album poster for *1200 Curfews* next to Ani Difranco's *Not A Pretty Girl* on the wall in an attempt to cover most of where the yellow paint had disintegrated. The tiny, closet-sized room was barely big enough to hold the metal-framed twin bed, the purple hand-me-down chair, wooden desk, and small, upright dresser. Thankfully, she wasn't claustrophobic.

Screech . . . screech! The high-pitched noise consumed the air again.

"That's it!" she yelled. Lilah jumped up, stepped forward, and thrust open the window. Three different colors of paint peeled off in her hands, and a gust of cold air whisked in the room. Grabbing her raggedy, cover-torn copy of *To Kill A Mockingbird* off the shelf, she wedged it between the window and sill and exited the window onto the narrow, rickety set of stairs that ascended to the roof. Rust on the metal handrails felt jagged under her fingers. Chips of grey paint were missing from the third story siding. Lilah's hands trembled at the sight of the ten fire-escape-looking metal stairs that narrowed toward the top. Her legs shook and stomach tightened with each step up. She kept her eyes focused straight ahead as she made her way up the stairs and hoisted herself onto the black roof. In front of her there was only a small section of open roof, with two tar-covered peaks jutting out from the bedrooms on either side of her below.

Lilah shuffled forward until she was between the peaks on the flattest part of the roof. Lilah sighed and scratched her head. She was all alone.

Shrugging her shoulders, she turned to go back down to her room when she noticed the tiny lights illuminating the sky above her. Letting the beauty of the night sky take over her senses, a moment of calm enveloped her. *Even in the darkest of moments, the light shines through*, Grandma Pea's voice resonated deep inside her. She always had a way of helping Lilah see the good. Tears welled in the corners of her eyes.

"Ca—hmm," a deep voice cleared his throat from behind her. Lilah jumped. She swayed and stumbled forward toward the edge of the roof.

A large, strong pair of hands grabbed the back of her faded University of Michigan sweatshirt and pulled her backward. In one full motion, she flew back and crashed into someone a good foot taller than her five feet three inches.

The person didn't flinch.

Lilah took a few small steps forward and steadied herself. She spun around and looked up into the heart-shaped face of a guy about her age. His close-set blue-gray eyes locked onto hers. He stayed quiet and Lilah watched his long brown eyelashes blink several times.

She stood perfectly still, taking him in. He didn't move. The night breeze blew his slightly too long tawny curls across his forehead. His linebacker-like frame blocked her view of the stairs she had come up. Squinting her eyes, she examined his chestnut-colored face. A lump formed in her throat.

A half smile crossed his thin red lips and a dimple on his left cheek appeared. His faint brown stubble accentuated his chiseled jawline. Lilah felt a churning sensation in her gut.

"Wow, you sure know how to make an entrance, don't you?" he said.

Lilah glared at him and held her breath. She wanted to pounce on him and push him backwards. "Seriously? You scared the crap out of me. What are you *doing* up here," she yawped, doing her best to stay still.

The guy's smile faded. "I'm sorry. I didn't mean to startle you—"

"Well, you did! I could've fallen off the roof!"

He opened his mouth to say something, and then decided against it. He closed his mouth and just looked at her, almost as if he was waiting for her to recognize him or something.

"Seriously, what the hell? I could probably hear you three streets away!" she said, even though she had no idea if there were even three streets in the neighborhood.

The guy's eyes widened. "I come up here sometimes. I live next door," he said cautiously, and pointed to the peaks that blocked the view of a house. "The metal ladder from my room sticks sometimes, and I have to tug on it to get it free. It's the only way up. It's really loud. Sorry."

Lilah shuffled a few steps to her right and peered around one of the peaks. Two wooden planks stretched between the houses, and a black metal ladder from an upstairs bedroom extended upward to the adjacent roof.

She stepped back and made eye contact with him again. "Okay, but if you live there, why are you over *here*?"

His shoulders relaxed. He smirked like a kid getting caught with his hand in a cookie jar. "I like the view better over here," he said, and took a step toward her. A flash of fervor swarmed her body. She looked down at her sneaker.

"I'm Joseph, but everyone calls me Jo-*ey*," he said, emphasizing the second syllable.

She stopped breathing and looked up at him.

"Wait, what?"

"I'm Joey," he said, and a wrinkle between in his eyebrows appeared.

"Jo-*ey*?" she said, repeating how he'd said it. He nodded. Lilah swayed forward, the night sky beginning to spin. She shook her head. "No. No way . . ."

His smile widened a bit. Her heart galloped.

"Yes, Joey."

She steadied her footing and focused hard on his face to stop the spinning. "But . . . you can't . . ." she said, her sentence never fully forming. "Impossible." Words caught in her throat and her mind scrambled.

He waited and leaned his head forward a bit.

"Joey? Aiden's best friend?"

Joey uncrossed his arms and leaned in slightly.

"You? The kid who basically lived at our house and always stole my chocolate cookies? *That* Joey?" she whispered. The lump in her throat turned to a boulder.

Joey's smile brightened and the hint of a deep-set second dimple appeared. "Yup. And to be fair, Aiden always made me give him half."

The thought of her twin made her head spin again. *Eight years. It's been eight years.*

"There's no way," she said again. "That was eight years ago . . . how did you get *here*? We lived in Connecticut."

Joey took a step toward her, his smile fading.

"About a year after the accident, after you moved away, my mom died from cancer. My stepdad brought me to New York with him. It's a long story, but basically he decided he didn't really want to be a parent anymore so I ended up in foster care."

Lilah heard the words, but they still didn't resonate.

"I never knew what happened to you other than you went to live with your grandmother," Joey said, and then added, "I've always wondered what would've happened if they hadn't gotten into that accident."

"You and me both." A sudden pain erupted in her stomach. She drew her arms around her.

"My foster mom, Danielle, told me about you yesterday and I had to see for myself. I didn't believe it until I saw your hair from Danielle's front window," he said through a coy smile. He tilted his head downward a bit without losing eye contact.

Lilah reached up and touched her hair. She cleared her throat and closed her eyes quickly to prevent the tears that threatened to escape. "It's impossible."

Joey touched her arm.

She let him.

"I wouldn't have believed it either," he said. "Not in a million years—and yet here we are."

Lilah searched his face for something. She wasn't sure what exactly she was looking for. A memory? A sign that it really was the boy who'd teased her and made Aiden laugh harder than anyone? But how could he be standing in front of her now? It had been eight years since the accident.

"Remember how we used to race up that hill? Your monster dog always beat us up to the top even though he started way after us," Joey recalled, his eyes crinkling at the corners.

Lilah lips turned upward.

"What was his name? Boo Boo? Boxer?"

"Bubba," she replied, smiling. "Well, that's what Aiden and I called him. Mom and Dad rescued him and named him after some town they visited in California on their honeymoon. We were so little when they got him, so we just called him Bubba."

"I've never seen a bigger Great Dane in my life," Joey said, leaning in toward her.

Hesitantly, Lilah shuffled toward him and let him hug her. Sobs escaped her throat and he held onto her until she let go and backed up. She turned away from him and wiped her cheeks with the back of her hand.

"Hey, it's okay," Joey said, and touched her on the shoulder. Tears continued to escape her eyes, and she batted them away again.

"No, it's fine. I'm fine," Lilah choked out. "It's just that my Grandma Pea died a few days ago and this all just feels so surreal."

A gust of wind blew a few of Lilah's long curls in front of her eyes. She reached up and tucked them behind her ear, giving her a better view of Joey out of the corner of her eye.

"Wanna sit for a few minutes?" he asked light-heartedly, his eyes sparkling against the night sky.

Lilah turned her head and stared at him. She shrugged.

Joey took a step and crossed in front of her. He sat down near the front edge of the house and let his long legs dangle off the side of the roof while staring off into the night. Lilah followed and sat next to him, allowing enough space in between them so they wouldn't touch.

Lilah stole a few glances at him and her stomach flip-flopped each time. Eight years ago, he was a chubby kid who always hung out with Aiden and teased her. Now he looked different, yet also so familiar.

They sat in silence for a few moments, allowing only the sound of wind between them. Lilah needed a few minutes to allow the lump in her throat to decrease in size.

"So, what's the deal with Abe?" Lilah asked, trying to distract the overwhelming heaviness consuming her.

"Well, I'd like to say you hit the jackpot, but you didn't. Abe's basic, and pretty much an ass. Stay clear of him and you'll be fine. Eva's okay. Just not a lot going on upstairs," he said, and pointed to his head.

Lilah half smiled.

"Abe and Eva move around a ton, but they've been taking in fosters forever. They usually have three or four at any time. About a year ago the boys came to them when their mom got picked up for drugs. And a girl named Emma left about three months ago. They haven't had anyone new since."

"Emma?" Lilah asked, and raised an eyebrow. She wondered how many foster kids had come and gone—but more, she wondered if Emma had come up on the roof to meet Joey.

"Yeah, she lived with Abe and Eva for only a little while. She kept to herself mostly. I didn't talk with her much. She never came up here."

"What about the boys?"

"Eva adores them, especially the youngest, Brody. Caleb and Eddie are always getting into something, and Abe's always mad at them. Eva loves them and protects them from Abe. They'll leave you alone, though. All they're interested in is playing football, cartoons, and Eva's cooking. She's an incredible cook," Joey answered and gave her a wistful smile.

"Good to know," Lilah said, and her stomach growled as a reminder that she hadn't eaten much over the past few days. With all of the sudden changes, she'd lost her appetite. It was overwhelming, not only did she have to move away from Grandma Pea's, she was giving up the only school she'd ever gone to. Even though she'd always felt like an outcast there, she learned to keep to herself and fly under the radar. Between being made fun of her wild orange hair, and being the kid without parents, she found solace in books and a few friends here and there. Now she'd have to start all over again.

"So are you going to school tomorrow?" Joey must have been reading her mind.

Lilah let out a sigh. "Yeah, I guess."

Joey laughed. "Wow. That's changed. I thought you loved it. You always used to hang out under that oak tree flipping through some book. Aiden and I couldn't tear you away to even play toilet tag. I remember, we tried and tried."

Lilah smiled. "I don't mind school really, and I still love to read. I just don't want to have to explain . . . you know," she said, still not able to form the words. She slumped. It was bad enough having to start at a new school in mid-October, two months after everyone else, it was worse having to explain the reason why.

"Well, if it helps, you aren't the only foster kid at school. There's a bunch of us," Joey said with a shrug.

Lilah shifted her weight, unsure if that made her feel better or even worse.

Joey reached over and touched her hand. She remained still, but found herself wanting to tell him more.

Taking a deep breath, she decided to take a chance and open up a bit to him.

"After my parents died, I always dreamt of them coming back to get me, that it was all just a big misunderstanding. Do *you* ever wish you lived a different life?" Lilah asked, and turned her head to look at him.

Joey sat forward a bit. "Only every day," he said with a sigh. "I remember as a little kid wishing I could live with your family. Your parents were always so fun to be around. And then one day, you were all just gone. I cried for almost a year."

"Me too." Lilah's stomach turned. "I really hate the idea of starting over again."

Joey squeezed her hand. "I get it. At least I'll be there too."

Lilah forced a slight smile. She reached up and touched the ring on her necklace with her free hand.

"That's pretty. Where'd you get it?"

Lilah felt a rush of heat up her back and neck. She tucked the ring under the collar of her shirt. "Oh, it's a ring my mom gave me," she said, and looked off into the distance.

"That's cool. Wish I had something from my mom to remember her."

Lilah's heart sank a little. "Yeah. Aiden had one that matched. They fit together. Just like we do, I mean, did," Lilah's voice dropped, realizing what she'd said. It was still hard to accept that they were all gone. Lilah swayed slightly under his gaze. Her heart pounded and a warm, tingly sensation spread like wildfire across her entire body. Years had changed them both, and yet, somehow, her heart recognized him. Lilah wasn't sure if it was the connection to him or her past, but in that moment, she didn't care. The pull toward him was second only to the one she'd felt for Aiden, yet different. She wanted to know so much more about him—what had happened to him, what he remembered about her family, what he remembered about her. And yet the words didn't seem to come.

Her eyes met his. They were kind and intense at the same time. Her face felt like it was on fire.

"So, do you go the gorges very often? I spent most of my summer there swimming and hanging out when I wasn't mowing lawns. You know, Ithaca is *gorges*," Joey said.

"Yeah, I've heard that once or twice," she said, and let out a quiet giggle.

"How come I haven't seen you there, or even in school?"

"I go . . . uh, I went to St. Josephs, and most of the trails are on this side of town. Plus, I'm not a huge fan of the outdoors."

"Too busy reading?" Joey teased.

Lilah smiled.

Joey leaned over and bumped her shoulder a bit. Warmth spread up her back and neck.

Suddenly, a high-pitched train-type whistle sounded and made Lilah and Joey both jump. Lilah leaned slightly forward and squinted off into the darkening night sky. It was hard to see even past the front walk of Abe's.

Joey popped up to his feet. "Uh, sorry, I gotta go. I wish I could stay, but I can't tonight," he said. In two strides, he was on the other side of the peak. Then he stopped. "It's been really great talking to you, Lilah. I'm really glad you're here." His smiled widened and both of his dimples showed.

Lilah looked at him and tilted her head.

"And hey, how about if I wait for you before school and we walk together, okay?" he asked not waiting for her answer before making his way around the peak. She heard footsteps on the wooden plank between the two houses and then the screeching sound of metal on metal as he made his way down the ladder attached to his house. She leaned to the side and watched him make his descent, passing his bedroom window. For a second, she wondered what it looked like inside, but shook her head at the ridiculous thought. The sound of his feet hitting the ground brought her attention back to him and was the last thing she heard of him, and then silence.

A slow tingle rose up her arms and into her shoulders. Where was he going in such a hurry? His sense of urgency was palplable and yet he offered no explanation. His sudden departure was downright strange. His promise to walk her to school was nice though.

The garage spotlight came on, illuminating him long enough for Lilah to see him stop, look up, and wave at her. She waved back before he turned and took off in a graceful jog. She watched until his shadow disappeared into the night shadows.

The warmth of Joey next to her dissipated, and chills ran up her spine. She wrapped her arms around herself. So far, nothing about foster care was what she had thought it'd be.

Chapter 3

❧

A hard knock at her bedroom door jarred Lilah from her sleep. She hadn't had a chance to talk with the family last night because no one was home when she came in from the roof. Relieved, she'd decided to just go to bed, though she felt a pang of guilt for not waiting up. She had fallen fast asleep with thoughts of Joey racing through her mind, the exhaustion of the last few days finally catching up with her.

"Lilah, it's time to get up for school," Eva called from the other side of the door. "I let you sleep as long as you could. You may need to hurry so you aren't late."

Lilah's stomach clenched at the sound of Eva's sugary voice. As much as she wanted to like her, there was something about the luckwarm greeting yesterday that just didn't sit well. She turned over in her bed and looked at the clock. It was 7:25 a.m. *Damn it.*

"Um, okay. Thanks, I'll be down in a few minutes."

The sound of Eva's heavy footsteps cascaded down the stairs. Without a moment to waste, Lilah jumped out of bed. Stepping over a few of the books on the worn shag carpet, she grabbed her distressed jeans, faded Led Zeppelin T-shirt, and gray sweater. She got dressed as fast as she could. Sitting on the edge of her bed, she threw on her black high-top converse and reached for her notebooks and pens to stuff in a backpack. She pulled her hair into a loose braid and twirled a few curls on the side of her face with her finger. A pit formed in her stomach. Her thoughts raced. *What if I missed Joey and I have to go alone? What if no one talks to me? Worse, what if everyone notices me? God, this day is going to suck.*

Tears started to form in the corner of her eyes. She knew that if she allowed herself to cry and focus on all the changes that had happened over the past few days, she would need to crawl back into bed. The hope of seeing Joey was the one thing that took her mind off of Grandma Pea and having to start over. Lilah shook her head from left to right, the weight of her braid grazing her shoulders.

Nope. Not today, she told herself. *Keep it together.*

She finished getting ready, looked in the mirror, and then added a hint of mint lip gloss. She forced a smile across her lips. She grabbed her bag and headed downstairs.

Eva was waiting at the bottom step in a pink velvet robe with embroidered roses on the lapel and a mock turtleneck. Leather moccasins covered her feet. She held a newspaper and brown paper lunch bag in her hands.

"You look nice. I'm sorry we didn't get a chance to get to know each other a bit last night. Our meeting went longer than we planned, and then the boys begged to stop for ice cream at Purity's. Brody just loves the cookies and cream," Eva said, and for the first time, Lilah saw a genuine smile on her face.

"Oh, that's okay. I was really tired and fell asleep kind of early," Lilah replied.

"All set for school? Do you have your notebooks and pens?"

Lilah turned slightly so Eva could see her backpack, and nodded.

"Well, I hope you have a good day, dear. The school is just down the block. Take a right out of the driveway, and follow the rest of the kids walking. You go down the end of the street, turn left, and it's just down a bit. You'll see it."

Lilah's breathing shallowed. The clock by the front door read 7:42.

"It's okay, you have a few minutes," Eva said, opening the front door and holding out the brown sack. "I put some yogurt and homemade granola in a bag for your breakfast. You'll have to get up a bit earlier next time if you want to eat in the kitchen with the rest of us."

"Oh, okay. Sorry. I didn't realize how late it was," Lilah said. "Thank you for the yogurt, Eva." She took the sack even though she hated yogurt—she didn't want to be ungrateful. Plus, she was hungry.

Lilah stepped out of the house onto the white wooden porch with cracking paint, stumbled down a few sand-colored cement steps, and stood on the old blacktop driveway. The late-October sun was peeking its head through the gray, luminous clouds, warming the air. Every year Ithaca's weather was fickle at best. Today, the sun was a welcome change.

Lilah scanned the street for Joey. She let out a sigh and slumped her shoulders. *All alone again.*

It took four-and-a-half minutes to walk to the large brick building with a green-and-yellow hanging banner across the main entrance that read "Ithaca High School." The school was bigger than St. Joseph's, the private Catholic school where she'd gone the previous two years . Enrollment at St. Joseph's had dwindled as more and more families relocated to the newly built homes on the other side of the gorges and went to IHS instead. Lilah was always glad there were fewer students at St. Joseph's. She knew everyone and everyone knew her. Now she had to not only find new friends, but also find her way around the massive high school.

She made her way to the front door and into the main corridor with Kelly-green lockers, yellow linoleum floors, and random bulletin boards with juxtaposed papers advertising clubs and afterschool activities.

Lilah walked down the unfamiliar hallway filled with groups of people talking and laughing. The smell of bleach mixed with dirty gym socks permeated the air. A sigh of relief escaped Lilah's mouth, and the tension in her shoulders lessened—no one noticed her. She followed the yellow signs to the main office from the front doors and got her schedule.

"Lilah," the woman behind the desk wearing horn-rimmed glasses called in a blithe and high-pitched voice as Lilah opened the door to go and find her homeroom. "Feel free to stop back in if you get lost, or ask a teacher for directions. It isn't easy being the new kid," she said with a large-toothed smile. "Have a good day, and welcome to Ithaca High!" She turned slightly and gave a quick thumbs up. The woman was way too chipper.

Lilah walked out in the hallway, staring at her schedule. Taking a few steps forward, she bumped into someone.

"Hey, maybe you should look up and watch where you're going," a low, sultry voice responded.

"Sorry, I, uh . . . ," Lilah looked up and stared at a boy with the longest black eyelashes and biggest green eyes she'd ever seen. He had high cheek bones, a pointed chin, and a tiny scar under the corner of his left eye that made Lilah wonder how he got it.

Pleased, his lips curled into a smirk. His devilish grin made her stomach flip. Clearing her throat, she tried to compose the butterflies fluttering in her stomach. "Sorry. I didn't mean to bump into you."

"Sure," he said, and leaned back against the metal locker. His voice was cool and confident like Ryan in *The OC*. He seemed independent in a bad boy kind of way, the kind of guy who Grandma Pea warned her to stay away from.

His shoulder-length brown hair curled loosely around his perfectly proportioned, olive-brown face. Lilah guessed he'd hooked up with a lot of girls. He didn't seem like a one-girl kind of guy. Lilah drew in a quick breath. Why would she even care if he had a girlfriend? She shook her head and looked down at her paper.

"Do you know where you're going?"

Lilah slowly raised her head, noticing the muscular body beneath his button-down white shirt. His sleeves were rolled up a few times to show off his strong forearms and black leather cuffs on his wrists, and a black tattoo on his right forearm. She couldn't make out what it was.

"I'm Sebastian. You must be Lilah, the newest foster over at Abe's place. Joey told me all about you," he said. He reached out his left hand with a thick silver band on his middle finger and swiped his hair away from his face.

Lilah's stomach tightened, and she shifted from foot to foot. Sebastian smirked. He waited a moment and then started again. "What's your first class? I'll walk you."

"Uh, no thanks. I can find it myself," Lilah said.

"Take a chill pill," he chided.

"Really, it's—" without letting her finish, he reached out and swiped the schedule out of her hand. He glanced down at it and then returned his alluring gaze to Lilah.

"I'm happy to do it. So, how do you like staying at Abe's? I stayed there a couple months before I moved into a house a few blocks away . . ." he said as he walked away.

"Seriously, thanks anyway, but I don't need your help. Can you please just give me my schedule back?" Lilah said loudly and stuck out her hand for him to give it back. Her patience was running thin. He really wasn't helping her feel comfortable in her new school.

Brrrrinnng.

Sebastian turned and looked over his right shoulder, still smirking.

"Uh oh," he said, and pointed upward with one finger. "That's the second bell. One more and you're late. Better hurry up."

Letting out a breath she didn't realize she had been holding, Lilah reluctantly followed him. He was about as subtle as a bulldozer. She fell into step behind him, waiting for the opportune time to swipe her schedule back. He walked in front of her and she couldn't help but notice how good his tight black jeans looked on him. Despite the pit in her stomach, a slight smile crossed her lips.

Seeming to read her mind, Sebastian stuffed her schedule in his back pocket and looked over his shoulder at her. His smiled widened.

Brrrrinnng.

He stopped in front of classroom 317.

"Here you go. I'll get you after your math class and take you to your next one. Have a good first class, Lilah," he said, and then added, "And welcome to Ithaca High." Sebastian laughed and walked away down the almost-deserted hallway. Doors were being shut, and the once-noisy hallway was mostly quiet except for a few hurried footsteps of students scurrying into classes before being marked late.

Lilah turned away from him and entered the classroom. The heat on her face radiated down her neck and back.

"Welcome to Algebra Two," a female teacher with black glasses, white skin, and springy, silver curls said with a straight face. "Find an empty seat. We're working independently and getting ready for midterms. Go ahead and look through chapters one to ten, and let me know if there's anything in there that you didn't cover at your old school. We can set up an appointment for after school if you want to review it."

"Ok, thank you," Lilah said in a hushed voice, hoping no one would hear her other than the teacher. She turned and walked in between two aisles of desks. Luckily, everyone in the class was already working on problems in their workbooks. A few looked up and made eye contact with her. Most just ignored her.

Lilah found a seat at the back and opened her book. It was all review to her, but she was glad for the distraction. The period passed quickly, and her math teacher never bothered to introduce her to the class. They reviewed a few problems during the last couple of minutes, and Lilah was thankful not to be called on. Class let out and, as promised, Sebastian was waiting.

"How was math? Stimulating, I'm sure," Sebastian said through a perfect, white-toothed smile.

Lilah walked up to him and held out her hand. "Can I have my schedule back, please?"

"Nope, but thanks for asking," Sebastian chuckled.

"Seriously, give it back," she said. "It's nice of you, but I can find my own way."

Sebastian turned and walked away again. "Now that wouldn't be very hospitable of me, would it?"

Lilah wasn't sure if she should be annoyed or flattered. Her stomach flip-flopped.

"You'd better hurry up, your next class is across the school," he said over his shoulder. Lilah followed him, sure to always be at least two steps behind.

This pattern happened for the rest of the morning. Sebastian talked at her while they walked each time, but never really waited for Lilah to respond. He didn't care if she was annoyed with him, and when she asked for her schedule back several times, he just smiled and told her she could have it at the end of the day.

By the end of fifth period, she'd had enough.

Frustrated with the lack of interaction and response to a lecture on the constitutional foundations and what led the colonists to declare their independence from Great Britain, her history teacher, Mr. Loncey, let the class out a minute early. Lilah walked across the hall, placed her back up against a locker, and waited for Sebastian to show up.

He arrived seconds later, a Cheshire-cat grin spread across his face.

"Can I ask you something?" Lilah said.

"Sure."

"What's wrong with you?"

Sebastian threw his head back and laughed so hard his curls shook. "Nothing's wrong with me. *You* just don't appreciate when people are being nice," he said, and walked down the hallway.

"This is getting old," she all but yelled, standing on her tippy-toes. Sebastian kept walking. About thirty other students milled around the hall, all moving in the same general direction. Lilah knew she was going to lose him if she didn't follow, but she was tired of following him like a lost puppy.

"Better hurry up. It's lunchtime and I'm starved. Today is turkey cheese boats. They're really just turkey and cheese on hot dog rolls, but they taste okay. Stay away from the salad bar though. Ezra Lanon found a worm in his salad last week," he said without turning.

She stopped walking and looked behind her. Her stomach tensed, and while a part of her was starving, the bigger part of her wasn't sure she could handle being in a lunchroom with a bunch of strangers. Joey hadn't shown up anywhere, and only one or two people other than teachers had even said hello to her the entire morning. Shoving her hand in her pocket, she searched for money to magically appear so she could buy lunch.

Suddenly, Sebastian was at her side. He grabbed her free hand and dragged her forward.

"Don't worry about not knowing anyone. You can sit with me. And we get free lunch. All us fosters do. It's on your schedule. Just give them your name at the end of the line," he reassured her and read her mind all at once.

Thankful for the information but pissed that she had to hear it from him, Lilah sighed.

KINDREDS

"Don't be such a chicken," he said, and pulled her along, never letting go of her hand. Lilah tried to wiggle her hand free and her palm became quite sweaty. When they got to the double doors where at least a hundred students sat talking, eating, laughing, and hanging out, she forgot about her hand and sized up the large, florescent-lit room filled with people. A lunch lady in a blue apron, brown Velcro shoes, and a hairnet covering her dyed-copper hair cleared trays, making small talk with some of the students. The noise of everyone talking and laughing was almost deafening. Lilah's eyes darted up and down the yellow and green cement walls and long, industrial-type gray picnic tables lined up in rows. She couldn't see Joey anywhere. The smell of fried bologna, cleaning supplies, and honey arrested her nose. She shook her head slightly.

"Smells yummy, don't you think?" Sebastian said, and wrinkled his nose. He slowly released his grip on her hand and she let go. "Come on, we got this."

Lilah forced a smile and followed him. As much as she didn't want to admit it, now that she was used to his slightly annoying company, being with Sebastian made her feel a little less out of place.

She moved through the food line without issue, just as Sebastian promised. Looking up, she saw Joey at the end of one of the tables. Pressing her lips together, Lilah let out a little growl. His absence all morning annoyed her. Realizing she was looking at him, a smile crossed his lips. Forgetting about Sebastian and her frustration, she walked up next to Joey and sat down. Sebastian stopped at the other end of the table for a minute to talk to a group of people, never taking his eyes off her.

"Hi," Joey said. His midnight blue T-shirt accentuated his eyes, making it hard to ignore how hot he was.

"Hi yourself. You *are* here today," she grunted, a little harsher than she meant to. He'd promised to show her around and then flaked. Was that the type of guy he was?

Joey's smiled disappeared.

"Sorry. Danielle reminded me this morning I had to make up a gym class before school, so I had to be here early. I ran into Sebastian on my way to school, and he said he'd show you around."

A frown formed on Lilah's lips. "So you stuck him on me?" she said, lowering her voice so only Joey could hear.

A look of surprise crossed his face.

"Wait, what? No, I didn't stick him on you. I just asked him to let you know I couldn't meet up with you. Why? Did he ditch you or something?"

"No, nothing like that. Let's just say that he took his job very seriously."

"Shit. I'm sorry," Joey said and looked down at his hands.

"Nah, really, it's fine. It worked out okay, for today. Sebastian isn't that bad I guess—"

"Hey, everyone, this is Lilah," Sebastian said, coming out of nowhere as if on cue. He put his hand on her shoulder.

Everyone at the table looked up. Some smiled and a few muttered hello. Two girls, both with long blond hair and perfect makeup, frowned and began whispering to one another. The rest of the people at the table just returned to their conversations and their food. Sebastian put his tray down next to Lilah and proceeded to hold court, entertaining everyone at the table with some story about a dog and the mail person. Lilah picked at her food, but couldn't take her mind off Joey. She wanted to confront him about why he'd ditched her, but he was engrossed in Sebastian's story like everyone else so she had to wait until later. The bell signaling the end of lunch interrupted her thoughts.

Sebastian stood up.

"Are you ready, Lilah?" he said, looking directly at Joey with a sly smile crossing his face. Lilah's stomach clenched at his words, but she stood up anyway. She turned, looked at Joey, and shrugged, stepping back from the table and grabbing her tray to throw out most of her untouched lunch.

Sebastian turned around to move closer to Lilah and knocked into a short, stout lunch lady with a plastic cap over her silver hair carrying a tray full of half-empty milk cartons. Milk poured out all over the tray, table, and floor.

"Oh shit. Sorry, Mrs. Fielding!" Sebastian said, and covered his mouth with his hand.

"Language!" she scolded, and then added, "It's okay, just grab some rags from my cart and   help me clean it up. Happens all the time."

Realizing this was her chance, Lilah discarded her tray and slipped out the cafeteria doors. Walking briskly, she headed straight to the office to get a new schedule before anyone could stop her. She was done being a damsel in distress. It was time to get back to doing what she wanted.

Chapter 4

❧

𝒯HE REST OF THE DAY went off without a hitch. She managed to stay clear of Sebastian and brought her backpack with her to her last class so she could go straight to Abe's when the final bell rang. Señora Ellen was impressed with her Spanish and suggested that Lilah move to the advanced section with the seniors. She told her she would consider it and thanked her for the suggestion.

When the bell finally rang, Lilah made a beeline for the exit, keeping an eye out for both Joey and Sebastian. Neither was anywhere to be found, and she was over the entire day. Being the new kid sucked and she had no desire to see anyone else.

Making her way back to Abe's, she walked in the front door and heard Eva talking on the phone. Not wanting to bother her, she went straight up to her room to put down her backpack and take a few moments to herself. Once in her room, she clicked on the radio and P!nk's "Who Knew" filled the air. Lilah took off her converse and lay on her bed, looking at the purple lettering on her Ani Difranco poster and wishing she were back at Grandma Pea's. Despite her age, Grandma Pea loved listening to Ani with Lilah while she did her homework. There weren't too many eighty-somethings like her.

After a few moments, she heard footsteps and a knock on her door. Lilah stood and answered it.

"I hope I didn't disturb you. Would you help me with dinner, dear? I'd love to have a chance to chat and hear about your first day," Eva asked timidly, standing in the doorway.

"Sure, Eva. I'd be happy to. I heard you on the phone when I came home and didn't want to disturb you," Lilah replied. A pang of guilt erupted in her stomach.

"Oh, no worries, dear," Eva gave Lilah a half smile that was difficult for Lilah to read. It was hard to tell if Eva was truly interested in knowing how Lilah's day was or if she felt like she had to ask. Either way, she didn't want to make Eva upset.

Lilah put on her converse again and followed Eva downstairs to the sunlit kitchen at the back of the house. It wasn't huge, but it was homey. The gray laminate counters were piled high with dishes, bowls, and brightly colored fall vegetables—and a sweet cinnamon aroma filled the air. Lilah's mouth salivated.

"It smells great in here, Eva," Lilah said, and went over to the white enamel sink to wash her hands.

Eva smiled. "Thank you. There's nothing better than the smell of home cooking."

Lilah agreed with a quick head bob. When she finished washing up, Eva handed her a black-and-white checkered towel that matched the floor, backsplash, and cushions on the mismatched wooden chairs. All around the room there were various jars, bowls, and even more knickknacks than Lilah had noticed before, in all shapes and colors. None of it matched, but it still seemed to go together. Eva motioned for Lilah to sit at the table.

"Thanks," Lilah said, and picked up the potato peeler. Eva placed a glass of milk and a freshly baked sweet roll next to her arm.

KINDREDS

"Just don't tell the boys you had one before dinner. They'd never let me hear the end of it," Eva said. Lilah took a bite of the roll. It tasted like powdered-sugar heaven in her mouth. Eva was being very kind, though Lilah couldn't help but feel a sadness in Eva that somehow mirrored her own.

"I'm sorry we didn't get a chance to talk much yesterday. It must have been such a difficult day for you. We wanted to give you your space."

Lilah looked at Eva. She could see the pity in her eyes.

She swallowed hard. "Thanks," she squeaked out. She knew Eva was being nice, but she could save her pity. "The sandwich you left for me last night was really good. Thanks," she said, changing the subject.

"Oh, I'm glad. I wasn't sure if you'd eaten. I didn't want to disturb you when we got home. I figured you'd come and find me if you needed something."

"Thank you," she replied and turned her eyes toward the potato she was peeling.

"I saw Joey come in from school earlier. I was wondering if he was going to walk you home. Danielle said he was asking about you," Eva said, all in one breath. "I didn't know the two of you knew each other from when you were little! Danielle told me all about it this morning. How romantic," Eva said, and glanced at Lilah.

Lilah continued peeling potatoes.

"I called her to see if Joey could help the boys fix their bikes before Abe gets home. I don't know how they managed it, but all three blew tires on the exact same day. Joey was nice enough to agree. He's really handy. The boys are over there right now getting them fixed."

Lilah remained quiet, not taking the bait.

"Don't get me wrong. Abe's a good man, but he has a temper when it comes to the boys and them breaking things. Boys will be boys. They play hard, but Abe forgets that and only sees the mess they leave behind. It's easier sometimes just to hide the mess."

Heat radiated up her back. The expression "boys will be boys" made her blood boil.

Rather than rock the boat, though, Lilah forced herself to not think about Eva's naïve statement, or Joey, for that matter. She took a bite of her roll and sipped her milk.

"So, Lilah, Danielle says you haven't always lived in western New York? Is that true?"

Lilah swallowed hard. "Um, no—I mean, yes . . . I moved to Ithaca to live with my grandmother when I was eight. I lived in Connecticut before that. That's where I knew Joey from."

"And you lived there with your parents?"

Lilah felt the lump form in her throat. "Yes. And my twin brother, Aiden."

Eva stopped stirring whatever was cooking in the large pot on the stove and took a step toward Lilah. Lilah saw the look again in Eva's eyes.

"So, what about you, Eva? Have you always lived here?"

Her question caught Eva off guard. Eva opened her mouth to speak and then closed it. She turned back toward the stove.

"No. Abe and I have lived in several places. We like to move around and see different parts of the country. I think Ithaca is my favorite though. I just love the gorges and the glorious fall colors."

Lilah held her breath and silently prayed Eva wouldn't ask any more about her family.

"Have you spent much time in the gorges?" Eva asked.

Lilah let out a sigh of relief. "Nah. I'm not much of an outdoors person. Plus, our side of town didn't really have the same access to the trails like yours does, though I never really took much time to check it out," Lilah said, almost verbatim of what she had told Joey.

Although she'd lived only a few miles away with Grandma Pea, she'd never spent much time in the infamous gorges in Ithaca. Lilah knew thousands of people flocked to the area each summer once the college crowds died down to hike and swim in the beautiful waterfalls. Grandma Pea liked to walk around the block after dinner with her, but that was about it. Lilah didn't care for swimming either, so when her friends invited her to go to the gorges, she didn't really see the point. She was just as happy for any excuse to stay inside and read.

"Oh," Eva said over her shoulder. "Well, I think you'll like it just fine here. For the most part, Abe and I are pretty easy. As long as you help out a bit here and there, we won't bother you much. I hope you'll like staying with us for as long as you choose."

"Thank you, Eva. I appreciate that," Lilah answered. "I'm finished with the potatoes. Would you like me to set the table?" Lilah stood up and placed the peeler in the navy-blue bowl that had held the potatoes before they were peeled. She took a few steps and placed the bowl in the sink.

"That'd be great, dear. The plates are up there," Eva said, pointing to the cabinet to the left of the sink. "And the silverware is in here. Go ahead and just leave the plates on the counter, though. I can serve from in here tonight." Eva moved across the room and opened a drawer with the utensils.

"Okay," Lilah said, and gathered up what she needed. She placed the plates on the counter and then stacked the silverware, paper napkins, and cow-shaped salt-and-pepper shakers into her hands and went into the dining room to set them on the table.

When Lilah finished, Eva called to the boys in the back-yard through the screen porch door. "Dinner's ready, boys. Wash up!" she said.

Caleb, Eddie, and Brody all scampered in through the

back door, racing each other for who would be first to the sink. They had black dirt and bike grease on their hands, arms, and faces. It was the first time Lilah had seen the boys interact. They were all elbows, arms, and hands. They bumped into each other every which way they turned.

Eva watched them and laughed.

"Oww, Caleb, you stepped on my foot!" Brody howled, and jumped back. A blue Yankees baseball cap covered most of his eyes. He wore a gray T-shirt with the Lucky Charms leprechaun on it.

"Move over, you jerk," Caleb said, and pushed Eddie, the middle-sized one with two missing front teeth, out of the way with his large hand. Caleb stood almost a foot taller than Eddie and was like a puppy that hadn't grown into his paws yet.

"All right, boys. That's enough," Eva scolded.

She went over to the sink and pushed Caleb over with her hip to make way for Brody to go first. Brody was the youngest and the smallest by far. Eva's over-attention showed her obvious soft spot for Brody. He didn't match his brothers in height or weight. In fact, Lilah guessed he was underweight and small for his age.

"So, what's your deal?" Caleb asked, and turned to Lilah.

"My deal?"

"Yeah, ya know. Is your mom a drug addict too?"

"Caleb! Manners, please," Eva said.

Brody and Eddie giggled. Caleb shrugged. "Whatever, I'm just trying to start a conversation. Isn't that what you told us to do if she ever emerged from her room?"

Eva's cheeks reddened. Lilah laughed.

"All right you three, let Lilah be. She's part of the family now for as long as she wants to be."

"I'm six," Brody said, and came up to Lilah. "Do you like to play football?"

"Um, no, not really. . ."

"Do you like to ride bikes?" he tried again, his eyes wide.

Lilah looked into Brody's sable eyes. She really didn't like to ride, but didn't want to squash his attempt to find something in common with her.

"Sometimes, I guess, but I didn't bring my bike with me."

"Oh, that's okay. I bet Joey could find you one. He can do anything. He fixed our bikes so Abe doesn't get his panties in a bunch. That's what Eva calls it when—"

Eva coughed. "Okay, you. That's enough repeating things you aren't supposed to. Let's go ahead and eat," she said, trying to change the conversation.

The boys threw the hand towels on the kitchen table and looked at Eva.

"Hey Eva, where's Abe tonight?" Brody asked, batting his eyelashes. "I didn't see his car in the driveway."

"Oh, he's at the lodge for his monthly meeting. I don't expect him home until late. We're on our own for dinner." She paused, and the boys all froze. Eva let out a little laugh.

"Can we eat in front of TV, pleeeease?" Eddie and Brody said in unison.

"Abe never lets us and Sponge Bob is on," Caleb added, looking at Lilah and not missing a beat.

"All right. You can eat in front of TV, but if there's *one* spill or one speck of food dropped on my floor, you'll never be able to eat in there again. Got it?" Eva replied.

"Got it!" the three said, and they all hugged Eva at once.

The five of them made their way to the small dining room with dark-red walls, a rectangle cherry dining table, eight matching antique cherry chairs, and a red, green, and beige oriental rug. It was cluttered, but cozy. The boys piled their food as high as they could on their plates and dashed into the living room to watch their show.

Eva laughed. "Those boys are a mess of trouble, but darn if I don't love them," she said, and filled her own plate with food.

Lilah smiled. She picked up a plate and piled on chicken, beans, and potatoes.

As soon as they sat down, the phone in the kitchen rang. "Well, darn," Eva huffed. "I've been waiting for Shelia to call about the pies all day. That woman can talk! Go ahead and just eat. I'll clean up everything when I'm done on the phone." Eva rushed out of the room and left Lilah by herself.

Lilah looked around the room and a feeling of sadness swept over her. She'd actually enjoyed the thought of having dinner with boys and Eva. It had taken her mind off of all the other stuff. She even contemplated if she should join the boys, but decided against it. It was obvious to her they really hadn't thought to include her, and the last thing she wanted to do was be where she wasn't wanted. It was a reminder that she was once again alone, invisible to others who chose not to consider how she might feel. Lilah felt her bottom lip quiver. Trying to avoid the tears that were soon to follow, she abruptly got up carried her food up to her room. If she was going to eat alone, she'd rather be in her own space.

Up in her room, she settled in on her bed and read *To Kill A Mockingbird* for the twentieth time while she ate. It was one of her top-five favorite books. When she was done eating, she sat back against her pillow and tried to get comfortable.

She picked up and put down the book several times. Biting her lip, she kept trying to read, but couldn't concentrate. Tears streamed down her face. She longed to be home again with Grandma Pea, watching *Jeopardy* and sitting together in the pastel-pink living room. It was Pea's favorite color and Lilah hated it. Now she regretted ever hating anything about living at her grandmother's.

The heavy pressure in her chest made breathing hard. An ache crept up her back, turning into a pulsating pain at the base of her head. She closed her eyes and just let the tears come. They flowed heavily at first, and she curled up in a ball on her bed. Eventually, the tears subsided and she fell asleep for a bit.

Clang, clang, clang . . . Screeeech . . .

This time, the noise was a welcome sound.

Chapter 5

꙰

LILAH SCANNED THE ROOM and sat straight up in bed. A bolt of excitement mixed with anger erupted from deep inside her. As much as she wanted to spend time with Joey, she also hadn't forgotten that he was MIA most of the day.

Should I go up? Do I even want to see him? So far he hasn't kept his promises, and he seemed a bit oblivious to how difficult it is to be in a new school without knowing anyone. Lilah knew she was going to go up and see him, but tried to restrain herself from being too reactionary. She failed.

The clanging and screeching stopped.

Lilah stood up, fluffed her messy ponytail, ran her finger across her teeth, and opened the window. Taking one step at a time, she made her way up the shaky metal stairs. Joey waited at the top, looking down at her. All of her indecision dissipated when she saw him.

He took her by the arms when she reached the top and steadied her while she stepped onto the roof.

"Hi," he said in a low, calm voice.

"Hi," Lilah whispered. She cleared her throat and tried again. "What's that?" she asked, and pointed to something wrapped in tinfoil in Joey's hands.

"This is only the best piece of chocolate cake you'll ever have. Eva dropped it off at Danielle's earlier. I brought you the last piece," Joey said.

He took the foil off the plate and then held up a fork. There wasn't one ripple in the chocolate frosting or the layer of thick milk-chocolate frosting in between the two cake layers. Lilah wondered if all Eva did all day was bake, not that she was complaining.

"Want it?" he asked with a sly smile. Lilah stuck her hand out.

"Never mind. Now that I think about it, I'm going to keep it," he said and held it up above Lilah's head, turning his body away from her.

Lilah reached out and grabbed his arm. A giggle escaped her lips.

"Fine. You can have it this time, but just know, I don't give the best chocolate cake to just anyone," he replied and handed her the plate and fork.

Without speaking, Joey moved over to the edge of the roof and sat down. Cake in hand, Lilah followed. She sat down next to him and dangled her legs over the edge of the roof. Her preference would have been to remain on the middle of the roof, but she didn't want Joey to think she was a scaredy-cat.

Joey looked down at her and sheepishly grinned. His eyes sparkled in contrast to the black sweater he'd thrown on over his T-shirt. Lilah fought the impulse to reach out and touch his arm, thankful for the plate in her hands to stop her.

"Am I forgiven for not being able to show you around school?" He leaned toward her and the outer part of his thigh touched hers. A shiver ran up Lilah's back.

"Yeah, it's fine. Everything's been such a roller-coaster. I didn't mean to take it out on you," she said in between bites of cake.

"It's okay. I know what it's like to be the new kid. I'd hoped I could spend more time with you," Joey said.

Lilah's skin prickled. "Me too," she said, and took another bite. "It's been a really long day." Lilah wanted to ask him where he'd been all day and that the one thing she was looking forward to was spending time with him. Instead, she just continued to eat.

"Totally," he responded in a calm, understanding tone. Lilah felt a warmth wash over her.

She finished the cake, put the plate behind her, and prayed she didn't have cake in her teeth. Turning her head the opposite direction, she avoided looking right at Joey just in case.

They sat together in silence for a few minutes, their feet dangling over the side of the roof.

"How was your first day *really*?" Joey asked.

"Fine." Lilah really didn't want to get into it. She was disappointed about earlier in the day and was just plain tired. All she wanted was to be comforted, but had no idea how to ask for it.

"I'm sorry I couldn't see you more. I really did plan on meeting up with you."

Anger erupted in her gut like a rattlesnake being poked at in a cage. "Is that why you stuck Sebastian on me?" she blurted out.

Joey turned to look at her, his blue eyes wide and clouded.

"Like I said before, I swear I didn't mean to stick Sebastian on you. He heard about you from his foster mom, and this morning I ran into him. I asked him just to say hi. I had no idea he was going take your schedule."

"Oh, he told you about that?"

"Yeah, so uncool. I thought he'd be nice to you—not bug you all morning," Joey said, and his shoulders slouched. "Most girls love to get his attention like that."

"Well, I didn't love it. I had to follow him all morning until I could get to the office to get a new schedule." Lilah could feel the tension rise up her neck. There was something about Sebastian that attracted her to him, but also scared her a bit. She wasn't able to read him and really didn't know what to believe about him.

"Sebastian really was just trying to be friendly. He's moved around a bunch and been in a bunch of schools too. Being a foster kid is hard. I don't think he meant any harm. I could talk to him again if you want," Joey said.

Lilah stared out into the distance.

"I promise I didn't ask him to follow you around school. *I* wanted to be the one to show you around," Joey said, nudging her shoulder with his.

The knot in her stomach untwisted a bit. "So you didn't just blow me off?"

"No. Of course not." Lilah was beginning to believe him.

"Okay. I guess Sebastian wasn't *all* bad. It did make it easier to get around school. I just don't like someone else making choices for me," Lilah said.

"Noted," Joey said, and took her hand in his. His touch felt natural. She felt a slow, shaky excitement creep up from toes. It baffled her. She'd only held hands with one other guy she dated for two months her freshman year. Nothing felt natural about holding his hand, and kissing him was even more awkward.

Joey interlaced his fingers with hers, and their hands fit perfectly. She tucked her thumb inside between his palm and fingers.

"So what do you do for fun?" Lilah asked, trying to turn her attention from his touch.

"I used to play basketball, but once I moved in with Danielle, I stopped. I tore my ACL playing in a pick-up game down at Buttermilk State Park. That pretty much ended any hopes I had of playing in college."

KINDREDS

"Oh wow. I'm sorry. I actually remember you and Aiden playing basketball in our driveway for hours." A bittersweet feeling erupted in Lilah's stomach. She'd thought more about Aiden in the last two day than she had in the last two years. He was always with her, but no one else ever talked about him. Joey made it easy to remember her brother.

"Yeah. Neither one of us were very good, but it was fun to play. I'd hoped to get a scholarship, but now I don't think college is in my future," he said, and looked out in the darkening sky.

"You don't want to go to college?" Lilah asked.

"Nah, but I'm guessing you do, " Joey said in a low voice.

Lilah couldn't quite get why this would bum him out. A lot of people go to college. "Yes, I do. I promised Grandma Pea that no matter what happened, I would get my degree. I've always thought I'd go to either Cornell or Ithaca College, but now that she's gone, I don't know where I want to go."

"So you'd leave Ithaca?" Joey asked and turned his face toward hers. His blue-grey eyes seemed more grey than they had earlier in the day.

"I guess. I mean, I haven't really thought much about it. I do know I want to get a degree in English and focus on literature." Lilah felt like she was missing something, something Joey wasn't saying. Why would it be such a surprise that she wanted to go to college? Didn't a lot of people their age want to go to college?

"Want to know something I haven't told anyone?" he asked in almost a whisper and leaned toward her so his face was close to hers.

"Sure," she replied and held her breath.

"I actually want to work at a carnival instead of going to college," he said, and vertical wrinkles appeared between his eyesbrows.

"Seriously? A carnival? Like with rides and concession stands and games? You're kidding, right?"

Joey sat back and turned his head away from her.

Lilah stopped and stared at him, wishing she could take back her reaction.

"No, actually, I'm serious," Joey sighed and wouldn't look at her. "I wouldn't expect you to understand."

Lilah scrambled for the right thing to say.

"I'm sorry. You surprised me, that's all. It's not something people say every day, you know?"

Joey shrugged.

"Really, please tell me about it," Lilah pleaded. "I didn't mean anything by it."

Joey reluctantly turned his head back toward her, but didn't return her gaze. He looked out into the darkening night sky. Lilah held her breath and waited for him to speak.

"It's just that I suck at school. Now that basketball is out, I don't care about college. I'm used to moving around and I kinda like it."

"But, a carnival?" Lilah asked calmly.

"I remember going to a carnival as a kid and being curious about all of it. I'm interested in everything from the setup to how the rides work to the takedown. All the workers know each other, and from what I can tell, they become like family. It's kind of a natural place for a guy like me. I don't have any family, so it'd be like joining one," Joey said, and then added, "I thought *you* might understand that."

Lilah felt like she'd been punched in the stomach. Somehow her question had turned into something much heavier than she wasn't expecting. She wasn't sure what to say. "Um, uh, well, when you put it like that, I guess. I've never considered it. I guess it's like a trade school, only you'd learn as you go." Lilah felt like a weight was on her chest. She wasn't sure what she was saying or if she even believed in what she said.

"And the best part, no school," Joey added. "I know it sounds crazy. Maybe someday I can explain it more. College and regular jobs just aren't for everyone. Not everyone's booksmart like you."

Joey turned his gaze back to hers. Taking his free hand, he placed one of her flyaway curls behind her ear. Lilah's insides eased a bit, though a million questions filled her head. "Have you ever thought about going to a trade school or business school first to gain skills and then join?" Lilah asked, her practical side still wanting to convince him there were other options.

"No. I know I want to join the carnival. I knew as soon as I went."

Lilah suddenly sensed that they weren't talking about when he was a little kid anymore.

"When—"

A high-pitched whistle pierced the air.

Lilah turned her head to look into the darkened street below, wincing from the noise. Several floodlights came on in the empty street below. Lilah leaned forward a bit and squinted. A tall shadow several driveways over appeared, but nothing more. She couldn't quite pinpoint where the sound was coming from.

Joey leaned over and brought his face close to Lilah's cheek. A tingly sensation erupted all over her body.

"I've gotta go. Sebastian's waiting for me. I promise I'll walk you to school tomorrow though," he whispered. "That is, if you're okay with it."

Lilah looked right into his eyes and she felt the bubbly sensation of goosebumps explode up her arms, though she was a little confused why he had to leave, again.

"And yes, I will be there this time. No excuses," he said with a genuine smile.

"Yeah, okay. Where you guys going?" Lilah asked, hoping this time he would invite her to come with.

"Some of the guys are playing cards at Sebastian's tonight. His foster parents are out of town. Maybe you can come with me the next time when other girls will be there."

Lilah nodded, though she had no interest in seeing Sebastian again anytime soon. She would have liked to spend more time with Joey though. Strange that he had to leave as soon as the whistle blew—for the second night in a row. It was a weird way to signal someone to play cards. Maybe it was just a coincidence? Her instincts told her there was more to it. Maybe a party that he didn't want her to know about?

Joey dropped her hand, got up, and walked around Lilah. He started around the peak to the planks and stopped. His face glowed, illuminated by the stars and moon above.

"Hey, Lilah?"

"Yeah?" She turned her head toward him.

"I'm glad we found each other again," Joey said, and disappeared.

Lilah's heart skipped a beat. Losing Pea was the one of the hardest things in the world, but somehow Joey was healing a tiny part of her.

"Me too," she whispered.

Chapter 6

᚛

Early on Friday, Lilah stepped outside into a crisp, fall morning. The bright, red-and-orange leaves had appeared almost magically overnight, and the cool air whipped through her sweater. She'd taken a few extra minutes the night before to get ready for the morning, in hopes of spending more time with Joey. Sleep had evaded her. Her mind had been too focused on all the things she wanted to ask him. It was a nice distraction from feeling so sad.

She stepped into the street and heard Joey behind her.

"Lilah, hey, wait up!" he said, and threw his black backpack over his shoulder. The sound of his voice and the sight of his alluring smile and gray-blue eyes stirred something in Lilah's insides.

"Good morning," she said, and felt her face flush.

Joey smiled a little wider.

"Sleep well?"

"Mm-hmm." No need to let him know she hadn't.

"How was the card game?"

"Uh . . . good," Joey replied and looked away from her. He fell into step with her and their arms touched every so often. A warm sensation arose in Lilah each time it happened. Her thoughts raced. The late-autumn sun peeked in and out from the clouds above their heads, mimicking Lilah's uncertainty for the day ahead.

Lilah let out a sigh.

Joey reached over and touched her arm. He slowed down their pace a bit to talk.

"You okay?"

Lilah shrugged. She wasn't quite sure what to say. Day two of a new school, Joey not keeping his promise yesterday, Sebastian lurking at every corner, and then Joey ditching her again last night were about all she could take.

"Sebastian and I were telling everyone last night all about you and they all want to meet you."

Lilah snorted. "You and Sebastian were talking about me?"

"Yeah, why?"

"Just seems like I can't escape him," Lilah replied and tensed her jaw.

"He's not so bad. He comes off strong at times, but he's really funny and always knows how to have a good time," Joey said, and then added, "Is that what's got you upset this morning? You're thinking about Sebastian?"

"I guess," she responded, knowing that was part of it. "I mean, he's been on my mind some. I don't know how to read him."

Joey reached over and took her hand. She was glad for the warmth. It may have only been October, but the brisk winter winds were strong. Lilah wasn't a huge fan of the seasons changing to colder days and darker night. She was always cold come winter. But Joey warmed her from the inside out.

"I, uh—I mean, yeah, for the most part he's harmless. He asked a ton of questions about you."

"Me? Really?"

"Yeah, why? Is that surprising?"

"A bit, I guess. I'm just not used to anyone noticing me."

"Why not? I would think you'd get all kinds of attention from guys," Joey said, and blushed.

Lilah faked an uncomfortable smile. She really wasn't used to any attention from anyone other than Grandma Pea.

"The thing with Sebastian is . . . ," Joey stated, trying to change the subject, "he's got a wicked temper. Most people just find it easier to just give in to him than cross him."

"Why, what happens if you cross him?"

They stopped for a moment, and Joey leaned his head toward hers. His eyes darted all around them to see if anyone else was around.

"Just take it from me, he likes to be in charge. The rumor is that he got into a fight the second day he came to school last year with Timmy Wheaton. I wasn't in school that day, but everyone was talking about it. Timmy's the biggest kid in school and always picks on everyone. He's also a national wrestling champion three years in a row, so he does whatever he wants. He started making fun of Sebastian's hat and Sebastian laid him out," Joey whispered. "No one's messed with him since."

"Oh," was all Lilah could say.

He squeezed her hand. His forehead wrinkled and the smile dissipated.

"I'm sorry if he bothered you. I'll talk to him. He really isn't as bad as he comes off; he really can be trusted. I know lots of girls like him."

Lilah shrugged. Something in Joey's tone seemed different. "Don't worry about saying anything to Sebastian for me. It's okay. I'll work it out."

"Only if you're sure," Joey said. Lilah nodded. They turned and quickened their steps toward school. "Lilah, don't write him off. He's not so bad. He has a lot of connections for kids like us, and actually, he's a lot of fun if you get to know him," Joey said, like he was trying to convince himself and her at the same time.

Lilah was just about to ask him what "kids like us" meant when they arrived at school and the bell rang.

"Oh, crap. We're late. Sorry, Lilah!" Joey said, and dropped her hand.

A shakiness overcame her, and her heart started to pound. She didn't like how short their walk had been and that there was no time to adjust before classes started. They both rushed toward the door.

"No worries," she lied.

Joey smiled at her and gave a little wave before he was lost in a sea of other students hurrying to class. Lilah rushed to her first class. She made it as the last bell rang. Luckily, the rest of the morning passed without incident.

After third period, Lilah hurried toward the library for her free period. Wanting to catch up on some reading, she was thankful for the chance to be alone. She rounded the corner right before the library, and that's when she saw Joey and Sebastian standing face-to-face at the end of the hall.

She stopped abruptly and took a step back. Peering around the corner, she hoped they didn't see her. She strained her neck forward to listen.

Sebastian was a few inches taller than Joey, though Joey was definitely more muscular .

"Look. She isn't like us. Leave her alone," Joey said in a strong, deliberate voice that Lilah had never heard before.

"No," Sebastian snarled.

Without warning, Joey shoved Sebastian into the locker. Sebastian stumbled and fell down. Lilah felt all of the blood rush out of her face. She raised a hand to cover her mouth to stop herself from yelling at them.

"Watch it, Joey. You're close enough to join. Don't do anything stupid to blow it. And remember, you don't get to pick. I do," Sebastian said.

What in the world were they fighting over?

Dropping her hands to her side, Lilah shuffled forward a few steps and stared at them both.

They both saw her at the same moment. Joey hid his outward anger and helped Sebastian up with a friendly punch on the arm.

"No hard feelings, man. She can join the band if she wants to," Sebastian said. He brushed himself off and then they both gave her a half smile.

"Joey and I were just talking about Nala, who wants to join our friend's band. I'm sort of their manager, so I get to decide who joins. No big deal," Sebastian said.

"Sure, man. Nala. No biggie," Joey said in a low voice, not making eye contact with her. "Not sure why I got so angry. Must be hangry or something."

Lilah could see the deception on Joey's face. His eyes grew darker in color and his brow furrowed. It was obvious they didn't want her to know what they had been talking about, so she just went with it.

For the first time since they'd met, Sebastian wouldn't look at her either.

"Wow, Nala must be really good if you two are fighting over her. I'm just headed to the library. See ya both later."

She brushed past them without looking back and ran into the safety of the deserted library. The large metal doors clanged behind her and the bleach-blonde, thirty-something librarian looked up and put her finger to her lips.

"Sorry," Lilah mouthed. She found a secluded wooden table in the back behind the stacks and pulled out her notebook. Ever since she'd moved to Grandma Pea's, she'd written down what was going on inside and around her. The words helped her make sense of what often didn't seem plausible or to remind herself she wasn't crazy. Both Joey and Sebastian made her feel a little unsteady; she didn't know if she could fully trust them, and worse, if she could even trust herself.

Chapter 7

ॐ

WRITING HAD ALWAYS just been a part of Lilah's life. From a young age, she would sit next to her mother at their small kitchen table, a pencil in hand. Sometimes her mother would give her words to spell, other times she would just write whatever she felt. It was a way to get out everything she held in. Plus, it made both of her parents happy. She wanted nothing more than to make them proud. After they died, writing became her one true friend. The words on the paper made what she was going through real, and sharing them, even if just on paper, helped her cope. Grandma Pea was always so respectful of the notebooks upon notebooks she had in her room, and Lilah never worried about her reading them. They were her heart and her mind as one. Pea knew that, and never once discouraged her from writing it out. Now that her whole world was upside down, the only place she truly trusted was within those cardboard covers.

Not wasting a minute, she wrote everything down that she'd just seen and heard in the hallway between Sebastian and Joey. As the words escaped the end of her pen, the pit in her stomach dissolved and the tension in her shoulders released. When she finished, she let out a big sigh and read what she wrote. Something about their interaction just didn't sit right. Joey never mentioned being musical or being the manager of some band. Lilah was pretty sure he would have mentioned it when they were talking about hobbies. What was so important that Joey would lie to her? Who was Nala and why were they fighting over her? Did they really think the best way to get a girl was to make the decision for her? While her notes helped soothe her insides, it did nothing to answer her many questions.

Trying to distract herself, she flipped open *Wuthering Heights* in the hope that Catherine and Heathcliff could distract her.

She heard someone approach and looked up.

"Hey, good looking," Joey said, and winked.

Lilah looked up at him and tilted her head quizzically

"I was already late to gym class, so I decided to skip it and come see you."

"Shh. There's no socializing in the library," the middle-aged librarian whispered through pursed lips.

"I'm very sorry, Mrs. Jenkins. Can we get a pass to go to the courtyard, please?" Joey said in a sing-songy voice. He smiled coyly and took a step closer.

Lilah stifled a giggle. She'd overheard girls talking in the bathroom about what a hard-ass Mrs. Jenkins was. So even she knew Joey was barking up the wrong tree.

"Okay, but Joey, hurry it up. You know I don't like to break the rules," Mrs. Jenkins said in a hushed, girlish voice.

Lilah gasped. Mrs. Jenkins handed the pass to Joey, and he thanked her.

"Hurry up, Lilah, before she changes her mind," he whispered, and signaled for her to follow him. She grabbed her books and walked behind him.

Hand in hand, they dashed down the yellow hallway that led to the courtyard, Joey leading the way. Her heart almost leapt out of her body.

They made their way down the hall and through the brown metal doors to the courtyard. The pimply security guard was more interested in whatever he was reading than them. He grunted and waved them in without even looking at their pass.

The day had warmed up a bit from the morning and the sun peeked through the luminous rain clouds, warming some of the ground it kissed. The courtyard was almost empty. Typical to Ithaca in the fall, the threat of rain had kept everyone else inside. They sat at a dark-gray picnic table that wasn't visible from the main door. Joey flashed his dimples and Lilah's shoulders relaxed; she was thankful that Sebastian hadn't followed her today. The thought of him made her eyes roll.

"Why did you just roll your eyes?" Joey asked.

"No reason," she replied. "What's the security guys deal? He couldn't even be bothered to look up when we walked in." She steered herelf and Joey away from her wonderings about Sebastian.

"At least we don't have to worry about him interrupting us," Joey said with a laugh.

Lilah slowly drew in a breath. She was avoiding asking what she really wanted to know. Her insides trembled, but she knew she wouldn't be able to forgive herself if she didn't ask.

"So what were you and Sebastian *really* fighting about?"

Joey raised his eyebrow. "The band. I told you. Can we just talk about something else for now?"

"Sure," Lilah replied. "Who's Nala?" A nervous giggle escaped her mouth.

Joey laughed. "You don't let things go, do you?"

"Nope. So who is she?"

"Nala's a friend of ours. Last year when Sebastian first came to town, she was really into him. They met at some open mic night at one of the local pizza joints, Mikey's, where she was singing. He liked her for a few days, but then he lost interest in anything other than her music. Since then, he's been trying to start a band."

The story sounded plausible.

"I do all the lighting and sound stuff for him," Joey continued. "I'm sorry you saw us arguing. I don't usually lose my temper like that."

"Okay. It just seemed like there's more to the story. Are you interested in Nala?"

"Nah. Nala is cool and all, but she's totally not my type." A smirk crossed his lips, and he raised his right eyebrow again. Lilah couldn't help wonder what Joey's type was, exactly.

"Why? Are you wondering what my type is?"

"Um, uh, no," she replied and shifted in her seat. "I was just wondering what your interest in her is, I mean, if not as a girlfriend."

"Well, Sebastian seems really set on having Nala join his band. And let's just say Sebastian can be very persistent, and from what I know of him, he doesn't change his mind easily. I just don't think he knows enough about Nala to make up his mind about her. He disagrees," Joey said, and looked away for a moment, breaking their eye contact.

"So whatd'ya have on your schedule for the rest of day?" he asked, and returned Lilah's gaze again.

"I have music and then writing workshop. I can't sing though. Mr. Mason put me in the back of the room yesterday where I can mouth the words. Guess he agrees with my assessment."

Joey laughed again. "Oh, so there are things you aren't good at?" he said.

"Of course. There's a long list of things I'm not good at."

"Name three," Joey challenged.

"Whistling, sitting up straight, and juggling."

"Oh, poor you! How will you possibly get into college if you can't whistle?" Joey teased.

"And cooking. That's four."

"Seriously? Those are what you came up with? You're so lame," he teased.

"Fine. What are yours?" Lilah asked, and leaned forward across picnic table. The fluttering erupted again in her stomach the closer she got to him.

"School, homework, and going to class," Joey said.

"Those are all part of the same thing, doesn't count."

"Sure it does," Joey replied.

"Cheater," Lilah teased. "Seriously, though, why would you think I don't struggle with things?"

"Cause as soon as Abe and Eva heard about you coming to the house, all they talked about with Danielle was what a great student and how talented you are. It was like they knew you, though they swore they'd never met you. It must've been in your file," Joey said.

"File?"

"Well, maybe I'm wrong, but they said Mrs. Reed told 'em all kinds of things about you and that you've the most potential of any kid they've had in a very long time," Joey said. "Plus, I think the fact that you're a girl helped Eva be excited. I guess I don't mind it either."

The pounding of her heartbeat intensified.

She shelved a mental note—Eva already knew about her, yet last night had acted like she knew nothing. Was she just trying to give her chance to open up? It seemed a bit odd. Shaking her head a little, she tuned into what Joey had said. "So you don't mind that I moved in?" Lilah asked, and looked at Joey.

"Mind? I'm glad you're there. Ever since Emma left, it's been a little lonely on the roof," Joey said.

A pit deep enough for the green monster of jealousy to stir opened up inside her. She inched back a bit from the table. "Emma? Oh, so you and Emma *were* close." Lilah asked.

Joey's eyes sparkled and the corners of his mouth turned upward. "Got ya. Emma and I didn't really talk. I just wanted to see how you'd react." Lilah's cheeks burned and the green monster neutralized.

"Emma was a free spirit. No one expected her to stay around long." Joey paused for a moment and then continued, "Ya know, living at Abe's isn't all bad. I've been in over six foster homes since my mother died. And I never knew my dad. Everyone that stays at Abe's has good things to say about them," Joey said.

Lilah waited for him to say more.

"As for me, my other homes just didn't work out. A lot of people take in foster kids for the money, though there isn't much of it. Some of the homes had six or more kids, and we all had to share rooms. I would've been happy to stay at Abe's if they'd had room. Instead, Danielle took me in. Eva still invites me over when Abe isn't around. I figure if I can have her on my side, I won't ever go hungry," he said.

"Eva seems nice. A bit lonely though."

"Yeah, she always wanted children of her own, but wasn't able to have 'em. She likes being a parent, but Abe's never wanted to adopt. I think he likes the extra paycheck and figures if he can have the money and Eva gets the kids, it's a win-win situation. I heard them arguing once about adopting the boys. Their mother is giving up her parental rights, but Abe's against it. My guess is they'll live with them until they age out of the system, but who knows. Eva doesn't say anything, but I know she worries about someone wanting to adopting them once they're free."

"It must be tough for her, especially living with Abe," Lilah commented.

"Abe isn't all bad," Joey assured her.

"I guess. He kind of creeped me out the first day when he made some comments about my looks. He only talked to me when he knew Mrs. Reed was looking for him to say something."

"Yeah, Mrs. Reed is an odd one too. It's funny, though. Abe rarely says the right thing. He usually says whatever he wants, but the day you got here, he was on good behavior. He contained his inappropriate self well from what I heard Eva tell Danielle," Joey chuckled.

Lilah giggled. "Could've fooled me."

"But the thing was, he was ecstatic before you got there. I don't know how to explain it. It's just him, I guess. I think he has a chemical imbalance or something," Joey said.

"That's just what people say when they can't figure out what's wrong with someone. Maybe he's just an ass," Lilah said.

Joey laughed even harder and said, "Maybe."

"I know you haven't been in foster care before, but take it from me—Abe really isn't that bad, and it's a nice house. You got your own room, there aren't a lot of rules, and for the most part, Abe will leave you alone. It could be a lot worse," Joey said.

Lilah believed him. He had no reason to lie to her.

Joey took her hand into his. "Hey, seeing how we live right next to each other, promise me that if anyone tries to bother you that you'll tell me. We have to stick together. It's how we can make it out without too much baggage, okay?" Joey said

"I promise," she said, and she meant it. "But you have to make the same promise. If anyone bothers you, you have to tell me, got it?"

"Got it," Joey agreed with a laugh.

"I'll never forget that day I found out about the accident, when you went to your grandmother's. I think that day was almost as hard as losing my own mother," Joey said, turning serious. "How come you weren't in the car with them?"

Lilah drew in a breath and held it. She wasn't used to anyone asking. "I went to play at a friend's house. My parents were killed instantly, and my Grandma Pea said the people that found Aiden followed behind the ambulance to the nearest hospital, but he died shortly after he got there."

An awkward silence arose between them. Lilah turned her head from him and tears stung the corner of her eyes. She squeezed her eyelids together to prevent them from escaping.

"Do you have many memories of them?" Joey asked in a quiet voice.

Lilah turned her eyes back toward him, but couldn't bring herself to look at him.

"Not really. Every once in a while I'll remember some random thing about my mom, like the way she smelled, or I hear my dad's laugh, but other than that the only time I can really feel them is when I dream."

"I don't remember ever meeting your grandmother," Joey said.

"I didn't meet her until the day she took me in. She and my mom didn't get along," Lilah said and bit her lip. She hadn't planned on talking to Joey about this, but he seemed so genuine in his interest. After all, he lost them too.

"Did you get along with your grandma?

Lilah smiled. "Yeah. I think she understood me better than I did. I miss her a lot."

Tears stung her eyes. Joey squeezed her hand.

"I'm sorry all that happened to you. It must be so hard," Joey said, shaking his head.

"It has been, but being lonely is something I think I got used to early on. Now I'm okay with being alone, at least most of the time. Pea left me alone when I needed it."

"She sounds pretty cool."

"She was. For the most part, I've always kept my feelings to myself. Pea always said to be careful who I share my heart with because I feel things deeper than most people."

Lilah looked directly in Joey's eyes, searching for something she wasn't sure of and yet wanted so desperately.

"I get it. It's hard to find someone to understand what you've gone through," Joey said, and squeezed her hand again. "I know we don't know each other very well, but I feel like we're connected. I've never opened up to anyone so quickly, but it's easy with you."

"It's a bit weird, honestly. I like you and knew the moment I saw you again," Lilah blurted out.

A grin appeared along with his left dimple.

"I like you too. I've really missed your family. Having you here now *is* like we're connected somehow."

Lilah nodded in agreement and the pounding of her heart quickened.

"I saw you through the window when Mrs. Reed pulled up and I wanted to talk to you so badly, but Abe told Danielle not to let me come down," Joey said.

"That's weird. I wonder why not." Lilah shifted in her seat, the thumping of her heart subsiding a bit.

Joey shrugged. His hair waved a bit in the wind and his cheeks reddened. A chill ran down Lilah's spine, distracting her from thinking about Abe any longer.

"So tell me three things most people don't know about you before we have to go inside," she said, and shifted in her seat. She had to change the subject. Her emotions were all over the place and her heart wasn't sure how much more she could take.

"Sure," he replied. "Let's see . . . I've never owned a pet. I like the band NSYNC . . . and I've never had a girlfriend."

Lilah drew in a quick breath. Joey's eyes widened and a sheepish grin crossed his face.

"Okay, your turn."

Lilah looked off in the distance for a moment, trying to ignore the fluttering in her stomach and the happiness that had sprung up in her heart.

"All right. My favorite ice cream is Creamsicle—the orange-and-vanilla kind. I want to be an author someday, and my father's favorite nickname for me was Carrots, which is one vegetable I will not eat to this day."

"Carrots? I don't remember that," Joey said.

"Yeah."

"Carrots. It fits, though your hair really isn't orange like when we were kids, it's redder—darker. It's pretty," Joey said. Lilah blushed and looked down.

"You don't like compliments much, do you?"

"Not really. I used to get teased a lot for my freckles and looking different than everyone else in my grade. That and I can't always tell when people are making fun of me, so I just assume everyone is. It's easier."

"That's horrible," Joey said. "Why would you think everyone is making fun of you? I think you're beautiful."

Lilah shrugged, unsure how to reply.

"I don't think you give yourself enough credit," he said. "I know Sebastian thinks you're pretty too. He told me."

"Yeah, well, I'm not so sure about Sebastian. He makes me uncomfortable. Truthfully, I just don't make friends that easily, and he seems like the type to make friends *really* easy, if you know what I mean."

Joey belly laughed. "Yeah, he definitely gets the girls."

"Jealous, are we?" Lilah asked, and batted her eyelashes

Joey's face reddened. "Nah. It just goes to his head and makes it difficult to be in the same room with him at times."

"True that," she joked nervously.

"I'm really glad you're here," Joey said. He leaned in across the table.

Fire spread from Lilah's face down her neck to the rest of her body. She leaned in over the table, closed her eyes, and moved instinctively toward him until she could feel the warmth of his face. Their lips met. They fit together perfectly. A surge of happiness exploded in her body. She couldn't believe this was happening.

Brrrrriiiinnnnngggg! They both jumped back at the sound of the bell. Lilah giggled unexpectedly, and Joey looked toward the courtyard doors.

"I guess we'd better head inside. Thanks for hanging out with me," Joey said.

"I'm glad you came and found me."

"How about if we meet out front after the last bell and we can walk home together?" Joey said.

"Okay. I'd like that. I have to run to my locker before music. I'll see you after school, okay?" Lilah said all in one breath, the tingle of his lips on hers still lingering.

"Okay, see ya, Carrots," Joey said, and turned to walk to his next class.

Lilah floated to her locker with a smile plastered on her face.

Chapter 8

❦

MUSIC CLASS WAS UNEVENTFUL and passed quickly. She made her way across the school and walked into Ms. Denton's writing workshop class right before the bell rang. On the chalkboard were directions for the class that read, "Please get in with your partner and work on your manuscript for Perform-a-thon."

The last class on a Friday afternoon was always the worst. It didn't matter that it was writing, her favorite subject. Lilah just wanted the day to be over so she could see Joey. Overall, it had been better than yesterday, but still not like her old school. At St. Joe's, she knew everyone, had a small group of friends, and was mostly left alone. Here she wasn't even sure if the teachers cared that she was new. Most hadn't bothered to ask her if she needed time to catch up, evaluate what she knew, or even introduce her the others in the class.

Lilah looked around the class and her eyes settled on the young blond woman not much older her who had to be Ms. Denton. She sat at the large metal grey desk grading papers. The rest of the desk and chairs were arraigned in pairs throughout the room. Ms. Denton wore her hair in a messy bun that Lilah guessed was much neater earlier in the day. Looking around the class, Lilah noticed everyone else was already talking loudly in pairs.

"Excuse me?" Lilah asked. "I'm not sure where to go. I don't have a partner."

Ms. Denton raised her head and smiled warmly at her. "Oh, you must be Lilah. I'm going to need you to go to Room 513. It's just down the hall, around the corner, and on the left," she said all in one breath. "The students are working on their projects for Perform-a-thon."

"Aren't I supposed to be in your class?" Lilah's could feel the heat rise up her neck and into her face. Was she in the wrong the place? Was anyone looking at her? The last thing she wanted was any more attention.

"Oh, no, I mean, yes. You are in this class, but today I need you to go down the hall. I have another student who's without a partner that's going to meet with you so you both can start on your piece for judging in December."

"Judging?" Lilah looked at her, crossed her arms across her chest, and raised her left eyebrow. She had no idea what Ms. Denton was talking about.

Picking up on Lilah's body language, Ms. Denton held up her pointer finger and then, in a booming voice, yelled toward the rest of the class, "Alright everyone. I know you're working, but it's too loud in here, let's quiet down." Ms. Denton obviously had a much bigger personality than her small stature would indicate. Lilah liked her already.

Ms. Denton turned her attention back to Lilah. "Okay, well, do you know anything about Perform-a-thon? Has anyone told you anything?"

Lilah shook her head no.

"So basically, every class that enters Ithaca High is assigned a classic book to read in their freshman year. Then, in each subsequent year, the entire class is assigned a project to complete about that book."

This was sounding right up Lilah's alley.

"Your class was assigned Romeo and Juliet."

Lilah leaned forward and let her arms relax at her side. She loved Shakespeare. And it helped that she had read it several times.

"Ok, so from the look on your face I'm guessing you're familiar with the book."

"Yes."

"Good. Last year your classmates were required to use their creativity to bring the story to life. Some created board games, others a soundtrack to go along with the themes of the book, one group dressed up like the main characters and performed the play throughout their day in the hallway between classes, several created mini-sets using shoeboxes, one group created a series of costumes to be put on display in the art hallway . . . you get the gist."

Lilah's skin tingled. She loved nothing more than reading, and creating something around a book sounded so enticing. "That's really cool. So, what's the assignment this year?"

"This year students are modernizing the book to present day and are to rewrite the ending. The best play will then be performed by the drama club and the authors will each receive a five hundred dollar stipend they can use toward college applications. We have a very generous alumni association that believes in making college a priority."

Lilah licked her lips and bit her upper lip as her excitement grew. College had always been her and Pea's goal. If she won, she could use the money for the application fees. She'd be one step closer to making Pea proud.

Ms. Denton opened her left desk drawer and rummaged through some papers. She pulled out a small packet stapled in the corner.

"Here's the information if you want to read through it. Why don't you head down to room 513 and you and your partner can work out the details," Ms. Denton said, and then added, "Let's talk in two weeks after mid-terms about what the two of you decide."

"Ok. Sounds good. Thanks, Ms. Denton."

"Welcome."

Lilah took the papers out of Ms. Denton's hand and made her way to room 513. Much to her surprise, no one was there. Lilah's shoulders dropped. It was just her luck that her partner wasn't there to meet her. Deciding she could start on her own, she sat down at a blue and grey Formica table and began to read. She used her yellow highlighter to underscore the most important details of the project.

"Well, well, well," Sebastian's voice came from in front of Lilah. "You just have all the luck."

Lilah froze and just stared at him. Her stomach dropped. Sebastian stood with his chin jutted slightly upward, a broad grin on his face, and his right thumb in one of his belt loops.

"We have to stop meeting like this," he teased.

How in the world was this possible? Her entire class was over five hundred people. How did she get paired with him? "Did you arrange this?" Lilah asked and pressed her lips together.

Sebastian smiled widened. "We're just meant to be together, I guess," he said, and plopped down in the booth across from her.

She felt a flash of irritation and giddiness at the same time. "What happened to your partner? Did you get a lot done?" Lilah asked, trying to focus on the moving forward.

Sebastian laughed. "Nah. I was partnered with Milo. He's a Navy brat and staying with grandparents while his mom was deployed. He went to live with her now that she's home."

Lilah scrunched her eyes and decided not to ask if any of that true. "Okay, so how do you want to split up the work?"

"I don't," he replied.

"What do you mean you don't?" Lilah sighed. He was not going to make this easy.

"It's not due for a coupl'a months. No need to work on it."

"Seriously? We have to rewrite the whole play. It's going to take a lot of time to do that."

"Not worried about it. And you shouldn't either," he said smugly.

"Why not?"

"It's just not that big of a deal."

Lilah looked directly into his eyes. She could feel her insides tightening and tension growing in her neck. "It's a huge deal. We could win money for college."

"Not going, so no need to work on it."

Lilah clenched her fists. "Well, I'm going to college. You're my partner, and I want to work on the project."

"Oh, so you want to spend time with me?" Sebastian baited her. "Why didn't you just say so?" He puffed out his upper body and a smirk appeared across his cherry red lips.

Lilah felt a rush of uneasiness erupt in her chest. "No, that's not what I said. Why are you twisting my words?" She tapped her fingers rhythmically on the table.

"I'm not twisting anything. You said you wanted us to work on the project together. I'm okay with that. I know it's hard not want to spend time with me."

Lilah rolled her eyes. He had a way of annoying her with his over-confidence that was strangely entertaining.

"Ya know, we could hang out more if you wanted to," Sebastian said, leaning in.

"How about if we just stick to working on the project," Lilah said and looked down at the papers in front of her. The annoyance was turning into something else. Could she really be attracted to him? No. He had to be like this with every girl.

She blew her several wild strands of hair away from her face and peered up at him. He continued to stare at her.

"Whatever. Don't touch me. You're such a jerk," shrieked a girl from somewhere in the hallway just outside the door. A locker slammed shut.

"Come on, babe. Don't be so dramatic," an infuriated male voice said, and the sound of something hitting a locker pierced the air.

Sebastian stood up and crossed the room in a few steps. Lilah was right behind.

In the hall, a guy in a blue Polo with a popped collar and jeans stood with his back to them, and a petite girl with pin-straight brown hair wearing frosted lip gloss, lace up jeans, and a pink popcorn shirt stood motionless up against the lockers. Lilah noticed smudged black mascara on her cheeks and puffy red eyes from crying.

"Hey, dude. What's your problem?" Sebastian said and placed his hand on the guy's shoulder.

At the touch of Sebastian's hand, the guy whipped around and gaped at him; he was only about five and half feet tall, and Sebastian towered over him. Lilah could see from his tense face muscles and clenched fists that the guy was barely containing his anger.

"I said, what's your problem," Sebastian growled in a low voice. A flash of recognition crossed the guy's face and he shuffled back a few steps away from the girl and Sebastian.

"We're just having a conversation, man. No biggie, right babe?" the guy asked and glanced at the girl.

She didn't budge, but looked directly at Sebastian. "No, we weren't having a conversation. You were just going off about how stupid I am for believing you that you aren't cheating on me when I saw you with my own two eyes!" the girl blurted out. "And then you pushed me into the locker."

Sebastian stood up straight with his shoulders back and brought his fist up to his other hand.

"Seriously, dude? You pushed her? Maybe you and I should go outside . . ." Lilah's heart beat quickened and an urge to get in between the guys exploded throughout her body. She took a few steps forward and placed her hand on Sebastian's back, not that she was sure what she was going to do. Lilah glanced at the guy and jerked her head to the side, indicating for him to leave. She then turned her attention to the girl—she was ogling wide-eyed at Sebastian and Lilah swore she could see her falling for him almost instantaneously. Sebastian never took his eyes off the guy.

"Nah, man. It's fine. I was just leaving . . ." the guy said and scampered down the hall.

"Are you okay?" he asked the girl gently, all signs of anger gone and only concern in his voice.

The girl wiped her cheek with the back of her hand and stepped forward. She reached out and touched Sebastian's arm. "I am now. Would you mind walking me to my locker to get my stuff?" she asked. "That is, if your girlfriend doesn't mind?" Lilah opened her mouth to answer, but Sebastian was too quick. "Nah, she doesn't mind. I'll catch up with you later, babe," he said and winked at Lilah before walking off with the girl, a smirk on his face.

Lilah stood motionless and watched them walking away, trying to process everything that had just happened. A mixture of feelings arose in her. She was glad Sebastian had stopped the guy from hurting his girlfriend, but she also was taken back by his willingness to fight without much thought. Lilah didn't think anyone should ever use force against someone else, but was also pleased that Sebastian had put the guy in his place. If Lilah didn't know any better, a part of her was also attracted to Sebastian, and a part of her really scared.

Chapter 9

AFTER DINNER, Lilah decided to help Eva in the kitchen. The boys and Abe disappeared in the opposite direction when they were done eating. Lilah was more than happy for the distraction from her own thoughts. She was contemplating whether or not to follow Joey and the whistling tonight—if it happened—and it was a bit unnerving. She wanted to just ask him, but every time she did, he was so vague. His answers left her with more questions than answers . . . and the nagging sensation that he wasn't being honest with her.

"So what're your plans for tonight?" Eva asked Lilah, handing her the plates with food on them to be scraped into the trash.

"I don't know. Nothing I guess. I haven't really given it much thought," she lied. She'd thought a lot about the weekend and Joey. Joey met her briefly after school, but he'd said he couldn't hang out until tomorrow. He wouldn't give a reason why. She'd spent the afternoon up in her room writing about the afternoon's events and coming up with ideas for Perform-a-thon. In her version, Juliette would save both herself and Romeo, she just had to figure out how. Just because Sebastian was being an ass about it didn't mean she couldn't work on it.

"Oh well. Maybe you and Joey can spend some time together getting to know each other a little better this weekend," Eva said. She glanced over at Lilah for a reaction.

"Yeah, maybe, I don't really know what he has planned." Lilah shrugged her shoulders and scraped the last bit of food into the trash can. She prayed Eva bought her act.

"I appreciate you helping me clear the table, dear. Why don't you go and watch TV with the boys? I can finish up in here," Eva said.

"Okay, thanks, Eva. Thanks again for dinner. It was delicious."

"You're welcome. And Lilah . . . ," Eva said and turned toward her, "make sure you stay warm if you decide to go up on the roof or anything tonight. It's getting cold out."

"Uh, okay, thanks." *Damn.* Eva was on to her. So much for being covert.

"Good night, Lilah." Eva returned her attention to the remaining dishes. Lilah could hear her humming "Sweet Caroline" as she walked out.

Lilah looked out the front door at the darkness setting in on the way to her room. Her heart beat quickened, causing her arms to shake. Running up the stairs, she prayed she hadn't missed Joey if he'd gone up to the roof, though she doubted he had. She burst into her room and threw on several layers of clothing, along with her running shoes knowing she was going to have to go down the ladder instead of up this time. The rain had come in, and she knew much of the ground around the neighborhood was going to be wet. Right before she opened the window, she grabbed a winter hat to keep her head warm. She just hoped Joey hadn't left Danielle's yet.

She opened the window and threw her first leg over the windowpane when the whistling sound infiltrated the air. It sounded like a high-pitched train whistle trying to alert people something was coming. It was so strange because the train tracks were on the other side of town.

"Damn it!" she said aloud and smacked the window pane with her left palm. She'd hoped to catch Joey before the whistle blew to ask him if she could come with. Now she had to follow him. It felt devious, but curiosity had gotten the better of her.

She climbed out onto the wet, cold, metal stairs and closed her window, leaving only a small gap between the window and the sill so she could pry it open when she returned. She looked down and her whole body swayed along with the metal stairs. Bile rose in her throat and her foot slipped, causing her to tighten her grip. Going up the stairs toward Joey the last two nights toward the open sky seemed much less dangerous than going down into the darkness. Plus, she had no idea where Joey was going or who she was going to find him with. Not knowing who he was hanging out with made her stomach hurt. Holding onto the stairs more tightly with one hand, she placed the other on the chipped paint on the side of the house. The jagged pieces of paint dug into her hand, causing her to wince.

She stood still for a few moments and heard Joey next door.

"Okay, thanks, Danielle. See you later," he called over his shoulder.

Lilah squinted, trying to see him. He walked out onto the front porch, and Lilah heard the slam of the wooden front door.

Joey hurried down the steps and into the darkened night. Lilah's hands tingled. Following him without talking to him first wasn't exactly what she'd planned. Trailing him without his knowledge made Lilah feel a little unsteady. She really wanted to trust him, and what he told her, but he'd already disappointed her when it came to school. Plus, the story he told her about managing some band just didn't sit right. Lilah needed to know for herself if he was who she remembered him to be, even if it meant she had to follow him.

Without another thought, her decision was made. She descended the remaining stairs and dropped to the ground, trying not to make too much noise. When her feet hit the wet pavement below, she froze and scanned the area. No one was around. Puffing her cheeks, she let out a quick push of air.

Catching some movement out of the side of her eye, Lilah watched Joey's shadow advance down the street, and she took off at almost a run. Following him at a safe distance wasn't easy given his much longer legs, but she he was able to catch up and fall into place a ways behind him, careful not to be seen.

Joey continued toward the whistling sound.

The pavement was wet from the rain, and Lilah took each step cautiously so she wouldn't fall. She quickened and slowed her steps as needed in order to avoid being detected. She'd seen people in the movies secretly tracking another person and they made it look easy, but it wasn't. In a million years she never thought she'd have to resort to following Joey to find out what she wanted to know. The whole idea of it made her sick to her stomach, yet, here she was.

Footsteps sounded from behind her. Fearful she'd be seen, she ducked behind a blue car parked in the street to get a better view of where he was going. Her heart raced as rain drops pelted the hood of the car.

Joey walked to the end of the half-lit street, turned the opposite way from the high school, and went behind the last house at the dead-end street. The large red brick house sat next to a nature trail that led down to the gorges. Lilah knew this because several kids at lunch had boasted they would go there on their free period to smoke.

Lilah squinted and wiped away the droplets from her forehead. She could see four shadows up ahead standing at the start of the tree-lined path, waiting for Joey.

She moved toward the end of street, ducked behind some bushes on the side of another parked car, and waited to see what they did next. A shudder ran down her back. Her sweatshirt was soaked, and water seeped into her socks. The winds had picked up, and random plastic bags flew back and forth across the street as the rain fluctuated between heavy and light. Lilah looked down and realized she was standing in a huge puddle. The water seeping in through the canvas caused her feet to feel like icicles. It was almost enough to distract her from wondering where everyone was hurrying off to and why he hadn't invited her. Was it some kind of party? Were they going to get drunk around a campfire or maybe smoke some weed? She never asked Joey if he was into that kind of stuff and just kind of assumed he wasn't because she wasn't. Assuming was probably not the best idea given she didn't really know him yet, and she hated being an ass. At her old school Lilah had gone to a couple of parties, but she didn't really care for the taste of alcohol, and having a hangover sucked. She shifted forward.

"Hey, man," Sebastian's voice came from in front of her. She hid behind a small maintenance shed that was labeled "Cornell University, School of Agriculture." Lilah stopped contemplating all the possibilities of what they were doing there and just listened.

Her stomach felt queasy. *Figures Sebastian would be here.*

The group had stopped at the top of a wooded trail that went down to the gorges where now six others were waiting. Realizing about half of the people waiting were girls, Lilah pressed her lips. Taking a deep breath, she tried to settle the rattling in her chest.

The group stood next to a small green sign outlined in white to the left indicated the path. It was a one of many strewn throughout Ithaca that visitors and avid hikers followed to get to any of the several waterfalls.

"Hey," Joey said. His voice was light and airy.

"Okay, let's get going. We don't have much time," Sebastian said, and disappeared down the darkened path, crunching sticks and dead leaves as he progressed.

Lilah watched as each of the shadows disappeared down the trail after Sebastian, and then she hightailed it to follow them.

Despite the winds and rain, the moon peeked out from behind a storm cloud and lit her way. What she wasn't expecting were the gnarly, knotted roots springing up every few feet, which made it difficult to navigate without falling. The knotty, brittle branches snapped beneath her feet. She tripped several times, each time falling onto uneven broken branches, which scratched her every time she got up.

The temperature was dropping fast, causing her to pause several times to catch her breath and rub her hands together for warmth. Each time she scanned the trail to make sure no one had heard her, thankful for the wind that covered any noise she made. The group ahead of her didn't waste any time and moved quickly.

After about fifteen minutes of walking, the group finally stopped in front of a magnificent waterfall. Turbulent, freezing cold water gushed down over the rocky ledge. Moonlight bounced off the falls, causing it to glisten. It was one of the smaller gorges in the area, but no less beautiful. The *Ithaca Journal* had done an expo on it last summer, calling it one of the hidden gems of western New York.

Lilah made her way forward step by step, careful not to trip or make any sudden movements. She ducked behind a sprawling oak tree about fifteen yards to the right of the falls for a better view.

Crouching down, she placed her hands on the uneven grooves and ridges of the tree to steady herself. Peeking around the large trunk, her breath caught in her throat. At least fifty other teenagers were gathered in one tight group in front of the waterfall. Her mind raced and she leaned around the tree as much as she could without losing her balance, trying to figure out what they were all doing there. But the pummeling water prevented Lilah from hearing anything.

She scrunched her forehead and strained her neck to see if she recognized any of them. Water from the oak dripped on her head and face. She sneezed. Lilah's heartbeat stumbled over its own rhythm. Had someone heard her? A sudden stab of terror tightened in her gut and she waited on baited breath for someone to point her out.

After a moment passed, no one responded and her muscles relaxed. She changed positions to try to avoid getting any wetter than she already was. She leaned up against the tree and strained again to listen.

"Hey, Sebastian, it looks like everyone is here. Can we keep going?" a tall guy with a lopsided mouth and big ears she didn't know asked.

"Yup. Go ahead and start up!" Sebastian yelled. The crowd cheered. Each person paired up and swiftly walked through a small pool of bluish-green water, past the main waterfall, and up a small, camouflaged trail nestled between two overgrown maple trees, whose verdant and thick branches shielded most of the opening.

Once everyone moved through the water and toward the footpath, Lilah stood up straight and moved a bit closer. She watched as one by one the group started up the trail. There was no way to see beyond the beginning of the trail due to the dense trees that overshadowed the path. Lilah sneezed again.

"God bless you," Sebastian said from behind her.

Lilah jumped. "Shit."

"Well, that isn't a nice thing to say to someone that you're following. I was wondering if you were ever going to join us. Why didn't you just walk with Joey?"

"You knew I was following you?" Lilah's heart sank. And here she thought she was being all stealthy.

"Of course. You're a loud walker. Plus, I saw you jump

80

down from Abe's while I was waiting for Joey. You could've just asked to come, ya know," Sebastian grinned.

Lilah rolled her eyes and felt her face flush. She teetered back and forth, unsure of what to do next.

Sebastian started walking forward and then brushed past her, turning slightly to talk to her. "Well, are you coming or what?" Sebastian asked, and held out a hand.

"Where are you going?"

"Come find out."

Lilah held her breath, nodded, and took his hand.

"Ya know, I would've been glad to escort you. All ya had to do was ask," he said. "Joey didn't think you'd want to come. I told him he was wrong."

Lilah's ears perked up, wondering what he meant by that. She opened her mouth to ask, but when she stepped forward, she tripped over a tree branch causing her to tumble forward. Sebastian let go of her hand, grabbed her, and threw his arm around her to steady her.

"Thanks," Lilah said.

"You're really graceful."

"Shut up," she muttered, though her lips turned upward.

"See, you do like having me around," Sebastian said, not missing a beat.

They crossed the pool of water and waited for the few stragglers to make their way up the trail. Joey had already gone up.

"After you, my lady," Sebastian said in a cheesy voice. He moved over slightly, and Lilah started walking toward the thin dirt path where the others had gone and then stopped.

Sensing her hesitation, Sebastian moved in front of her. A sliver of moonlight showed through the trees, and it was enough to see the wrinkles of concern on his face.

"Are you sure you want to follow them?" he asked.

"No," Lilah said, being honest. She didn't like the idea of following a bunch of strangers up a dark path at night to go who knew where. They were a bunch of teenagers she didn't know and the only reason she was there was because Joey was being so mysterious every night.

Sebastian's facial muscles tensed. "It's okay. I'll take you back," he said, and took a step toward her, blocking her from going up the rest of the trail. Lilah's mouth suddenly felt dry and an overwhelming sense of dread overcame her. She really wanted to know what everyone was doing and where they were going, but she didn't want to have to rely on Sebastian, again. She had to make a decision. Stay in her comfort zone and go back to Abe's, or allow herself to take a chance.

"No, wait," Lilah said, and Sebastian paused. "What's up there?" she asked, leaning her body against his to poke her head around and see the dirt trail again.

At her touch, his chest muscles tightened. Lilah's heart-beat sped up. She gazed upward hoping to see Joey, but all she saw was darkness through the trees.

"Go see for yourself," Sebastian replied. She raised an eyebrow and looked up at him.

"Just trust me. It's totally worth going in to find out," he said coyly.

Lilah dropped her shoulders back and stood up straighter. "Trust" was not a word she'd used to describe what she felt with Sebastian.

Sebastian looked at her and waited, and Lilah inched forward around him. She took a deep breath and started up the darkened path again. It went almost straight up, par-alleling the waterfall. The rocky dirt terrain was tough to navigate, and Lilah slipped several times. Sebastian's strong grip steadied her from behind and never let her fall.

As she ascended, the dirt path narrowed, and at first, Lilah had trouble seeing in front of her. On either side were large pine trees that narrowed in around her as she walked. The pines guided her forward, and as she moved, the darkness began to give way to a glimmer of light. The trees changed from dark green pine-needled branches to colorful leaves of various hues of reds and oranges, almost like that of autumn the more she ascended. The air around her faded from cold to a spring like temperature. Lilah felt a warmth on her face and more light appeared with each step up. At the steepest part, at the top of the trail, the trees gave way to large, overgrown sunflowers and the brightness of the sun at mid-day in summer. Up ahead there was a clearing where she could hear voices. It looked a bit strange, almost as if she were looking through a bubble. Shadows danced in front of her, but she couldn't make out what or who was on the other side. She opened and closed her eyes a few times to try bring everything into focus.

Curosity overtaking her hesitation, she quickened her step and made her way past the flowers. Sebastian was close behind. *What could possibly be giving off so much light at night? And why was it getting warmer?* Lilah was stumped.

With a few more steps, the shadowy bubble disappeared and she was able to see clearly.

Lilah placed her sneakers firmly on the flat, clay-red dirt. Squinting her eyes, she looked up, trying to see what was producing the blinding light. Placing her hand up to block the brightness, she took several steps forward. Dropping her head back down, she scanned the large group of people milling around in front of her. No one was drinking or sitting around a campfire. Several small groups of people her age stood excitedly talking in the field and disrobing from their winter gear. She continued walking toward the groups and her eyes adjusted more to the light.

With each step closer to the center of the field, her vision cleared and she gazed beyond the heads in front of her. Stopping a few feet from a group of girls she didn't recognize, Lilah rose up on her tiptoes and leaned forward. The hairs on her neck stood up when she saw it: a massive red and white carnival tent with multicolor string lights all around the outside loomed in front of them. Things had just gotten a whole lot more interesting.

Chapter 10

☙

LILAH HAD ONLY BEEN to a carnival once in her life. When she was six, her parents drove her and Aiden to a nearby town that was holding a Fireman's Carnival. One weekend every summer, in order to raise money, the local fire departments would get together and hold a fundraiser that would bring in people from surrounding counties. Lilah couldn't recall a lot about it, but she remembered being happy just to be with her family.

Blinking several times, she took it all in. She thought for sure she'd find everyone partying in an empty farmer's field. It was anything *but* empty.

Needing a moment to gather her thoughts, she tilted her head downward to inspect the dry, compact dirt and matted hay and grass mixture beneath her feet. Clouds of dust settled on her once white K-Swiss sneakers. In front of her was a carnival, but how in the world was that possible when just a few seconds ago they were at the gorges? Lilah had never heard of a carnival visiting Ithaca, let alone being in a hidden field at night.

Needing to see more, she shuffled forward, moving left, right, and left around small groups busily talking and laughing. She made her way to the front and stopped at the heavy metal chain holding back the approximately sixty or so of them waiting to be let in.

Sebastian followed close behind. She glanced over at him and noticed his shit-eating grin and then turned her attention back to the massive red and white striped tent perched in the middle of the field. Scattered all around it were smaller multicolored carnival booths adorned with neon signs and a smattering of abandoned amusement park rides of various shapes and sizes. A large, brightly colored red, yellow, and green Ferris wheel consumed the sky about two hundred feet beyond the massive tent.

Way off in the distance beyond the roped-off carnival grounds, Lilah spotted several barn-like structures she guessed were once part of the original farm. But how could there be a carnival in the middle of a field and that she knew nothing about? It just didn't add up.

"What is this place?" Lilah stuttered. Sebastian placed his hand on her shoulder and she turned slightly.

"I told you you'd never believe me. Pretty rad, huh?"

Lilah nodded. Heat covered her body, and sweat formed at the small of her back. Like many around her, Lilah stripped down to her T-shirt. She held her hat and outer layers in her hands.

Sebastian waited for her to disrobe before saying, "I know, it's a lot to take in." He put his hand back on her shoulder.

"It is," she replied and swallowed hard. A million questions swirled her head.

"Lilah?"

Joey's voice came from somewhere behind her. The deafening noise of the crowd made his voice seem farther away than it was.

"Lilah!" Joey called louder.

Lilah turned and faced the crowd, causing Sebastian's hand to fall away. Joey's face emerged and he made his way toward her, his eyes crinkled at the corners and dimples showing. He wore a maroon short-sleeve T-shirt and matching trucker hat, and held his winter coat in his hand. He zigzagged through several groups noisily conversing, walked right up, and scooped her off the ground.

"I can't believe you're here!" he said, and squeezed her tight. "What are you doing here? Did Sebastian invite you?"

"Um, uh . . . ," she stuttered, trying to catch her breath.

Joey put her down gently and released his grip a bit. He pulled back to look at her and their eyes met. Lilah's stomach dropped.

"I, uh . . . I . . ."

"She followed *you* here," Sebastian answered for her over Joey's shoulder. She and Joey turned to look at Sebastian.

"You followed *me*?" Joey said, and looked back at her, his gray-blue eyes clouded over.

Lilah eyes darted between the two guys. "Uh, yeah, I did. I wanted to know where you keep disappearing off to," she said, and looked down at her feet.

Joey gently put his hand under her chin and lifted it to look into her eyes. "I would've brought you here myself if I thought it was the right thing to do. I just didn't think this was something you'd be into," he said.

Lilah's heart raced.

"I am glad you're here," Joey said, leaning forward to brush his lips against hers.

"Ah, um," Sebastian coughed.

Joey backed away and they both looked at Sebastian. It was easy to see from Sebastian's scowl he didn't approve.

Joey put his arm around Lilah's shoulder and pulled her closer to him. "Did you know she was coming here?" he asked Sebastian.

"I knew she would eventually. I was surprised she followed *you*, but I have a feeling she's full of surprises, huh Lilah?"

Lilah shrugged. She wasn't sure what Sebastian was getting at.

He continued, "I saw her following us. I was going to invite her. I mean, it probably would have come up when we worked on our project together." Sebastian smirked.

"What project?" Joey said, turning to look at Lilah and dropping his arm a bit from her shoulder.

"I didn't get a chance to tell you. I was assigned to work with Sebastian for the Perform-a-thon," Lilah remarked, her stomach twisting.

"Not that it matters now," Sebastian declared. Lilah tilted her head and looked between the two guys, unsure what he meant.

"It's all good," Joey said, and looked at Sebastian.

Lilah bit her lip. It was obvious she was missing something, or maybe a lot of things. It was also clear that as much as she wanted to be with Joey, she also knew deep down she had to manage Sebastian. His constant presence seemed to be an omen that Lilah just couldn't ignore, though she wasn't really sure why. Regardless, she turned her attention toward Sebastian and the carnival.

"What *is* this place?" she asked, and looked around again.

"It's awesome. You'll see," Sebastian asserted, and stepped closer to Lilah.

Joey pulled her in closer, leaned down, and whispered close to Lilah's ear, "Lilah, this is what I was trying to tell you about the other night. Now you can be part of it with me."

"Welcome to Carnival Nolianna, Lilah" Sebastian said loudly with a wide grin, and held his arms out wide in front of him. He really didn't like when she gave Joey attention over him.

"How is this even possible?" Lilah muttered. She didn't get it. And why was she the only one of them that didn't understand?

"This place rocks." Joey proclaimed.

Lilah examined the field in front of them. They stood in front of a rope under a large archway with an oversized red, white, and black canvas with the word "Welcome" written in cursive. The massive field stretched beyond what the eyes could see. Several smaller tents in rich hues of red, burgundy, rust, and yellow were scattered throughout the field, adorned by rectangular signs with names like *Milk Toss, Push 'Em Up, Chance Your Luck,* and *Guess What?* Amidst the smaller tents were a brightly colored roller-coaster, concession stands, bumper cars, swings, twirling teacups, and various other carnival rides.

It looked pretty normal, only there weren't any adults or little children mulling around. The only people she saw were other teenagers her age. This baffled her, and she made a mental note to keep looking. Several droplets of sweat formed on her forehead and upper lip. She clandestinely wiped them off with the back of her hand. The temperature had to be somewhere in the eighties, easy.

"I'm so glad I wore a tank top this time," a girl with two long black French braids, amber skin, and a crooked nose said, as if reading Lilah's mind. She stood in the group next to them. Lilah made eye contact her and two other girls standing huddled close together, anxiously pacing side to side next to her, in step with one another. They all smiled and nodded at Lilah.

"Hi, I'm Rosa, that's Gracey, and that's Luna," said the girl with the black braids, and she pointed to the girls who stood next to her. Lilah had never seen any of them before.

"Lilah," she replied, and then added, "It's definitely warm."

"Tell me about it. Last time I came, I wore a long-sleeve shirt. That was a mistake," Gracey said, chewing on her half-painted pink finger nails. Her pixie-cut pale yellow hair spiked around her petite head.

"Last time?" Lilah asked.

"Yeah, last night," Luna said with a high-pitched giggle, shaking her head so that her chin-length blue hair swung from side to side. "First night here?

"Yes," Lilah replied.

"I wonder when we're going to go in." Rosa said and they all looked ahead at the field. Several others threw their winter belongings into a large heap behind the group.

Lilah felt a gentle touch on her arm.

"Wanna put your stuff in the pile?" Joey asked.

Lilah let out a little sigh of relief at his touch. "Sure."

She followed him and reluctantly placed her belongings on the mound along with everyone else's.

"Don't worry, I promise no one will take your stuff," Joey said, once again reading her mind. Lilah chuckled to herself.

Sebastian grinned devilishly at Lilah. "Well, what do you think? Sick, huh?"

"Um, yeah, it's pretty sweet," Lilah said, trying to sound enthusiastic. "How in the world did you find it?" she asked Sebastian directly.

"I knew you'd like it," Sebastian said, ignoring her actual question.

Lilah opened her mouth to ask more but was blinded again as, without warning, several spotlights throughout the field were turned on high. She, along with most of the others, shielded their eyes with her arms. Screeches and sounds of metal scraping metal could be heard over the voices of everyone waiting to enter. Someone had begun to turn on some rides, and dozens of people emerged from the smaller tents behind the linked chains separating the visitors from those that belonged. Noise erupted everywhere.

Lilah jumped, and Joey and Sebastian laughed.

"Don't worry, you'll get used to the light and the noise," Joey said, and leaned in a bit toward her. She smelled wood and spice. "Lilah, look," he said, and pointed forward past the rope.

Lilah stared up ahead at the rides beginning to move. At the same moment, the concession stands turned on their signs of neon green, yellow, and orange, and the large tent flaps opened with the help of two guys about her age. Both had ponytails and were wearing navy-blue T-shirts. Light from inside the tent materialized as teenagers she had not seen before emerged. The girls were dressed in jeans with neon-colored shirts and matching scrunchies. Some were in lime, some bright orange, and others in purples, blues, and yellows. It was like watching a rainbow.

The other group, mostly guys with expressionless faces, were dressed in what looked like navy polo shirts with their collars up and dark, distressed jeans. The boys reminded Lilah of the popular kids at school. They all had an air of confidence and lackluster expressions on their faces, not needing anyone's approval, too cool to make eye contact. Lilah shuffled to her right to try and see more.

"Well, lookie here at Miss Anxious. Can't wait to get in, Lilah?" Sebastian said, not waiting for an answer. "Told ya, Joe, you don't know your girl as well as you think."

Joey just looked at Sebastian and shrugged.

Lilah shifted from foot to foot. Sebastian was right, she really did want to see more.

Without a word, Sebastian took her by arm and pulled her forward to the edge of the rope. She felt her eyes adjust more to the light. Once they stopped moving, she took her arm away from Sebastian. Joey, oblivious, talked to the girls next to Lilah.

The intense heat was making Lilah's head start to pound. To distract herself from the headache that was forming at the back of her neck and head, she looked up and noticed a flag at the top of the carnival tent up ahead. She squinted her eyes to read it.

"What does that say?" she asked Sebastian, and pointed.

"You don't miss a thing, do you?" he said with a smirk.

"Nolianna."

"Nolianna?"

"Yup, it's what we call this place."

"And what is this place, exactly?"

"What does it look like?" he asked, and looked Lilah square in the eyes.

"A carnival, obviously," Lilah retorted. "But how did it get here?"

"Exactly. We're at Carnival Nolianna. This is a place for us to have the fun we deserve,"

Sebastian replied. "And as far as it not being possible— look around you! It's totally possible! This place is off the hook."

Lilah tried to share in Sebastian's enthusiasm, but she needed a lot more information before she could accept anything he said.

"It's just for people like us, " he declared.

"What do you mean 'people like us'?" she asked, her voice quivering.

"Duh! Think about it." Sebastian let out a pompous snort.

Lilah crossed her arms in front of her and could feel herself becoming shaky and annoyed at his lack of answers. "I really don't know. Just tell me," she demanded. She was getting really tired of the back and forth word games Sebastian played. He loved to string her along and force her to keep guessing. Enough was enough.

Sebastian looked at her and raised his eyebrow. He opened his mouth to speak but was interrupted by a booming male voice over the loudspeaker. The crowd quieted.

"Welcome, everyone. Please join us in the main tent for the opening of night five of Carnival Nolianna!" the modulated, even-toned male voice said.

As if by magic, the world behind the rope came to life in full force. Organ music replaced the voice on the loudspeaker, and dozens of additional people in bright clothing began to emerge from the large tent. They took their places at their prospective rides, attractions, and booths. They all looked like they were having the time of their lives, patting each other on the back with wide grins, joking around. Several waved to the crowd waiting to enter, and many waved back. Conversations all mixed together, and it seemed like everyone was talking at once. The rope was removed by one of the workers, and everyone shuffled into the larger tent. Taking Joey's hand and holding the ring on her necklace with the other one, Lilah followed the crowd.

Chapter 11

☙

INSIDE THE TENT, the large, striped flaps shaded the bright-ness from outside, and single-bulb lights hung from the wooden poles and crossbeams that steadied the structure. The entire area was empty except for a stage and a few chairs set to the side. It was fascinating and eerie all at once, for they could have been in the inside of a carnival tent anywhere. It baffled her that they were supposedly still in Ithaca and yet she knew nothing about it until this evening.

The entire wall behind the stage was covered by a bright, cardinal-red velvet curtain, which masked whatever mysterious thing was behind it. Approximately sixty other teens her age milled around, talking and laughing in the empty space. A six-foot-something guy, probably in his early twenties, with a chiseled jawline, high cheekbones, a crooked smile, and a mess of chestnut brown curls sat with his huge feet dangling over the side of the stage. He too wore a navy-blue collared shirt that had a small, red symbol embroidered just above his heart that Lilah couldn't make out, even when squinting. Next to him were two girls and one guy, she guessed all about the same age, dressed in the same way.

"Welcome to Nolianna! Please join me in up here," the guy yelled, moving his hands in circles for everyone to move in closer. Everyone obeyed.

"Tonight is the fifth night of nine here in Carnival Nolianna," he said. "I'm Matthew, your host. For you newcomers, don't worry! You're going to have a great time tonight. If you have any questions, just stop anyone wearing a piece of clothing with a spider on it." Matthew pointed to the large, embroidered spider on the wall of the tent to his right that Lilah now saw matched the embroidery on his shirt.

Everyone looked up at the symbol and then back at Matthew obediently. Lilah stared at it for a moment and bit the side of her tongue, annoyed that she hadn't noticed it. The mixture of the warmth and unexpected surprises of the evening had thrown her off her game.

"Guests that are returning also know their way around. Please take time and get to know one another. We're a family here. Just enjoy the night, and experience as much of it as you can."

Applause erupted from the crowd.

Matthew laughed and held up his hands again. "Okay, okay. I get it. Let's get this thing going! Please make sure to have something to eat and drink. Our Nolies work hard to make sure you have lots to choose from while you're here."

"We should totally go over and ride the Noli-Drop first," Joey whispered in Lilah's ear.

Lilah's cheeks prickled at the warmth of Joey's breath on her neck.

"The only thing we ask is that you remain on the main grounds. Guests are not permitted in the living quarters or the roped-off areas. Please abide by this rule or you will not be allowed to continue your time with us," Matthew said, expressionless. Softening, he smiled and added, "Thank you for being our guests tonight and we hope you will return in the future." He finished talking, stood up, and hopped off the stage.

Everyone clapped, including those next to Matthew on the stage who had never taken their eyes off him. The crowd dispersed.

Lilah's heart raced. She turned to Joey. "Okay, seriously! What *is* all of this? And what did Matthew mean it's the fifth night?" she asked.

"I'll explain it later, I promise," Joey said, and bumped shoulders with her. She raised an eyebrow at him. He wasn't the greatest at keeping promises so far.

Matthew and Sebastian walked up to them just as Lilah was about to ask more questions.

"Hey, dude," Matthew said, and shook hands with Joey. He turned toward Sebastian and asked, "Who's this?" with a smirk on his face.

"This is Lilah."

"Nice to meet you, Lilah," Matthew said, and looked from her to Sebastian and then back again.

"Hi." Lilah shuddered. Matthew was definitely good-looking, though his eyes were cold. For some reason, they very much reminded her of Abe the first night they had met. Lilah shook her head slightly to clear it.

"I hope Sebastian shows you a great time tonight."

"Oh, she's here with me," Joey piped in, and took a step forward.

"Oh, sorry man," Matthew said, and took a step back, the smile fading from his lips. He glanced at Sebastian and then back at Joey before trying to cover up his reaction and slapping Sebastian's shoulder.

"Sebastian, can you stop over later and fill me in your idea for the new ride?"

"Sure. How about if we do it now? I don't have anything else going on," Sebastian answered, and his forehead crinkled.

"Let's bounce," Matthew answered. "Nice to meet you, Lilah, I hope you have a great time tonight." He completely ignored Joey.

"Cool. I'll catch you two later," Sebastian said, and walked away with Matthew. Joey pulled Lilah closer to him.

"Guess it's just the two of us. I'm so stoked to show you this place. Let's go."

"Okay," Lilah said, and followed in step behind him. She turned slightly to see Sebastian and Matthew still staring at her while they talked. Lilah swallowed hard. There was something about the way they gawked at her that made her skin prickle.

"Hey, you want to go look around?" Joey asked.

"Sure," Lilah said breaking her gaze from Sebastian and Matthew.

They made their way to the back of the tent and outside onto the field. Excited guests scattered in different directions toward various parts of the carnival. Several girls with flowers painted on their cheeks ran by, singing along with the pulsating music that played. The organ music had turned to a thumping rave-like cacophony. Confetti filled the air, and several people carried streamers that danced and waved across the sky. Everything was moving fast, causing to Lilah feel light-headed. Everyone around her talked and joked like they were long-lost friends. Large groups of people made her anxious. She felt lost after everything that had happened in the last few days, but was glad Joey was there to help her. She looked at him, and he grinned ear to ear.

"Who are all those people?" Lilah asked loudly. Joey was moving his shoulders to the music.

"Well, there's us—the guests—and the Nolies, who work and live here."

Lilah pursed her lips. She figured that much out. "What I meant was—"

"Hey, man, good to see you," said a guy with ebony skin and a crew cut walking by. He wore a navy shirt. Lilah let out a sigh.

Joey and the guy clasped hands and hugged briefly.

"Angel, this is Lilah. Lilah, Angel," Joey said. It was becoming increasingly clear that everyone knew and liked Joey in Nolianna.

Angel smiled, and showed that half of his front left tooth was missing. Lilah nodded and bowed her head. When she looked down, she noticed the spider tattoo on the inside of his left arm and a tiny red spider on the side of his sneakers.

"So Joey, did you hear about what happened at the Kat the other night?" Angel asked.

While Joey and Angel talked, Lilah turned her attention to the Nolies working the booths. Several girls wore neon T-shirts with small spiders on the front, some guys wore navy polo shirts with the emblem, and some wore hats with the symbol. She made eye contact with several of them, who smiled back. They all appeared happy and carefree, swaying to the music, laughing, twirling, and smiling at everyone they passed. Something about it made Lilah's stomach hurt, and she didn't look at anyone too long until her eyes settled on a girl with an auburn braid intertwined with a lime-green ribbon that cascaded down to the middle her back. Her face was like an acorn in both shape and color. She had a high forehead with a perfectly smooth complexion. The matching lime-green T-shirt accentuated her big dark-brown eyes that drew Lilah in as soon as she saw them. If Lilah had to guess, the girl had to be close to six feet tall, with a tiny waist, curvy hips, and big boobs. She looked like a model. Lilah's insides turned green with envy. Even from far away, she was smoking hot.

Lilah nudged Joey with her elbow. He stopped talking with Angel and turned his attention back to her.

"Who's that?"

"Who?"

"The babe in the lime-green shirt with the long braid."

Joey glanced toward the girl and said, "That's Ginger. She's in charge of the makeup tent. She's got mad skills. Sebastian doesn't like her though."

Lilah took a slight step forward and cocked her head to the side. There had to be a story behind that, and Lilah wanted to know more. She made a mental note to seek Ginger out.

Realizing Lilah was staring, Ginger gave a little wave.

"Hi. I'm Jayla," a girl with crimped black hair, flawless black skin, and red rosy lips announced and walked up to them carrying a tray of fried cakes. "Want one?"

"Yah, I'm starved. Thanks, Jayla," Joey replied and scooped two off the tray.

"You want one?" she asked Lilah. "They are *the shit*. So good. Made special for all the guests."

"Nah, I'm okay for now," Lilah said. She wasn't a huge fan of fried cakes or anything fried really. Every time she ate something fried, her stomach hurt for several hours afterwards.

"Okay, but make sure to get one later. You won't be sorry," Jayla said, and then walked toward another group of people.

"You ready to head out?" Joey said, placing one hand on the small of Lilah's back and finishing the fried cakes with the other. Shivers surged throughout her body.

Joey didn't wait for an answer and pulled Lilah by the arm toward the open field and rides. Like waiting at the top of the stairs on Christmas morning, the air sizzled with excitement. Lilah felt like she was going to burst—the energy pulsated in her bones. It reminded her of what it felt like to be so happy in the moment and yet not know what to expect next all at once.

Over the next few hours, they flitted from ride to ride. They met a bunch of people whose names escaped Lilah; they all began blending together after about the thirtieth one. It was hard to tell at times who was a guest and who was a Nolie. Luckily, being with Joey made it easier and he knew everyone.

At one point, when Joey was talking with yet another new person, Lilah stepped over the side and watched a giant UFO-like ride with flashing red, white, and blue lights spin round and round. It made her nauseous just to watch it.

"Hi, I'm Asha," said a pink-cheeked girl with a bright red pixie cut. She touched Lilah gently on the shoulder.

Lilah turned. "I'm Lilah," she said in a loud voice over the beeping UFO sounds.

"Hey, Asha, have ya recovered from your ride on the Swirling Marvin?" Joey asked, suddenly back next Lilah.

Asha laughed. "I've never felt so sick in all my life," she shouted. "I can't wait to do it again tonight."

"Asha went on the Swirling Marvin five times in a row—"

"Six, actually," Asha interrupted. "It's a record without throwing up." She beamed and then turned to talk to another guy wearing a white-and-blue Yankees T-shirt to her right.

A girl poked Joey in the shoulder.

"Hi, Joe," she said. Her blond ringlets framed her petite face. Batting her long, painted eyelashes, she gaped only at him.

"Hey, Annabelle," Joey smiled at her. The green-eyed monster stirred in Lilah's stomach and her neck tingled.

"Lilah, this is Mimi, Annabelle, Jack, and Kyle," Joey said, and pointed to the others who had gathered around them.

"Lilah's new tonight, and I'm showing her around."

"You totally have to take her on the carousel," Mimi said.

"And don't forget the bobsled. That's my favorite," Kyle added. "Unless she doesn't want to—then you can go with me, Joey."

Lilah bit her lip, trying to conceal a giggle. *Guess Annabelle isn't the only one who likes Joey.*

"You need to make sure to get some fried dough. Micha, the girl that makes it, is a phenomenal cook," Jack said, and then added, "And not bad on the eyes either." Annabelle giggled and punched him on the arm.

"Bobsled, carousel, and fried dough. Got it. Thanks," Lilah repeated. Everyone sure seemed to like the fried dough. Maybe she would have to try it. "So which ride should we go on next?"

"This one is the Sevendust Starship," Asha said, returning to the conversation. They made small talk for a few more minutes until the line moved forward. Everyone around them went in until it got to Joey and Lilah.

"Sorry. All full. You'll have to wait a few minutes," the bald guy working the ride grumbled. He was the first person she'd met that wasn't exuberant. It made Lilah feel so much better. When he turned around to close the chain gate, she noticed a spider on the back of his left shoulder.

"No worries," Joey replied.

Lilah turned and made eye contact with a guy with a round, florid face and military-short hair holding a clipboard a few feet away. He had deep, green-blue eyes.

He walked right up to her.

"I'm Dublin," he said, and a smile crossed his thin, scarlet lips. "Welcome to Nolianna."

"Thanks. I like your tattoos," Lilah said. Dublin had a sleeve of intricate tattoos, and at the center of his upper right arm was the spider symbol. He had a small scar above his lip that made Lilah wonder how he got it.

"Thanks. They do them at the back of the carnival if you're interested. I can take you later if you want to check it out," he said, and raised an eyebrow.

Joey stepped forward, and Lilah's could feel the burn in her cheeks.

"I'll think about it. Thanks." She'd never considered getting a tattoo, though she loved the art of them. Grandma Pea hated them and made it known that while Lilah was living in her house, she wasn't to get one. Now that she wasn't living with Pea, the option was open.

Dublin shrugged, turned toward to walk away, and said over his shoulder, "You know where to find me," and pointed toward the back of the field.

Lilah giggled. Joey raised his eyebrow. "Seriously? I didn't figure you for a tattoo."

"I guess you've got a lot to learn about me then."

"Guess so," Joey said, and squeezed her hand.

"He's nice," Lilah said.

"They."

"They what?"

"Dublin goes by they. They're nonbinary."

"Oh, okay. Thanks for letting me know," Lilah said, and shrugged. She'd never met anyone non-binary before. "What's the deal with the spiders everywhere?"

"It's the official symbol of Nolianna. It stands for weaving our own destiny, I think," Joey said.

More like a tangled web of secrecy, Lilah thought.

"So what do you think of all of this?"

"Honestly, I'm not totally sure what to think." Lilah examined all around, and her eyes settled on the spinning Starships in front of them.

"Yeah, it's definitely overwhelming at first, but don't worry, you'll get used to it," Joey said.

Lilah's head spun. She opened and closed her eyes a couple of times, looking away so she wouldn't get sick. Spinning round and round was not usually her idea of fun.

"I haven't been to a carnival since I was six. I'm interested in checking out what's here though."

"Good! It's funny, I didn't think you would be interested in a place like this. That's why I never mentioned it to you. That—and I couldn't," Joey said.

"How come?"

"It's one of the rules. This place is only for people like us—"

"Like us?"

"Kids without families of their own. Mostly foster kids or orphans, but runaways too."

Lilah finally understood what everyone meant when they said that. She'd forgotten that she was part of that group now too. Grandma Pea had always made her feel loved and wanted.

"So only kids without families can come here?" She was intrigued by the notion that no adults were allowed in. There had to be a reason it was so restrictive.

"Yeah. There's a lot to it all. For now, let's just enjoy being here. There'll always be time to talk later."

Lilah doubted it. There never seemed to be enough time.

Without her noticing, the ride had stopped, and a massive crowd of people exited the Starship. One girl who was wearing a white T-shirt and light-blue distressed jeans looked ashen, and she covered her mouth with her hand as if she were going to throw up.

"Try not to be like her," Joey chided. Lilah gulped and hoped she wouldn't be.

They entered the ride and took a seat next to each other on a red-and-blue plastic covered seat on the round metal ship and braced themselves as they were whisked into the air and spun round and round.

Lilah's heart soared. The swirling and spinning were almost enough to stop her from thinking of all the questions she needed to ask. Who else knew about Nolianna? Why weren't there any adults milling around? How did it get here? How did she not know about it sooner?

Chapter 12

✤

"**H**EY, can we stop and get something to drink?" Lilah asked after the Sevendust Starship. Her back ached from being thrown around in the air over and over again.

"Sure," Joey and squeezed her hand.

They grabbed two sodas and a fried cake from a vendor and sat at a red picnic table. They moved toward the back of the main tent and were surrounded by colorfully lit game booths and concession stands. All around them, Nolies and guests meandered throughout the grounds. Several danced to the ever-changing music, sometimes stopping to sing the chorus of a well-known song, other times to twirl in circles. It was as if no one cared what others thought and they could just get lost in wherever the music took them. A pang of jealousy arose in Lilah, for she'd never *not* worried what others thought.

"So tell me the truth. Why did you follow me here?" Joey insisted. His brow furrowed and his dimple disappeared. "Did Sebastian tell you about Noliana?"

Lilah jerked her head and shoulders back a bit. His questions surprised her.

"Um, no. It had nothing to do with Sebastian, honestly." Her neck muscles tightened as she spoke. She let go of his hand and picked up her drink to take a sip. "You kept leaving so abruptly from the roof, I wanted to know where you went. So when I heard the whistling, I decided to follow you."

"But how'd you get in? Everyone here is invited, and there's a strict number limit of who's allowed in each night." His eyes widened as he spoke, and wrinkles appeared across his forehead.

"I don't know, exactly. Sebastian saw me following you, and when I got to the falls, he invited me in."

Joey took a deep breath and the wrinkles deepened. "You really shouldn't have come. I told Sebastian that he should just leave you alone." Joey said. His lips turned downward and he wrinkled his nose.

Her insides twisted in knots. She wasn't sure why this sudden change in his demeanor.

"Why not? Aren't you glad I came to be with you?" Lilah reached over and took his hand again. Her insides felt exposed for everyone to see, and her heartbeat quickened. She shifted in her seat.

"Lilah, it isn't that," Joey said, moving his free hand to stroke her face. "I like you. I just don't think you understand enough about this place. You shouldn't come here for me."

"Well, then, tell me about it."

All she wanted was for someone to fill her in on what this place was, how it got here, and why it was such a secret.

Joey scooted toward Lilah and dropped his voice to just above a whisper. "I've only been here four times, including tonight. But Nolianna has been around for years. I'm not sure how it started, but it's only open certain nights of the year and access is restricted."

"Restricted how?"

"The entrance trail is only open nine nights each year to guests, and only those who are invited can come in."

"What do you mean, it's only open at night?" The more details she got, the more uneasy she felt.

"The portal, the trail where we came in, opens for exactly seventeen minutes at 8:30 each night, and then again at 5:47 every morning for everyone to leave. Guests have to go home during the daylight hours, but can come back later that same night when the portal opens again," he explained. "Nolianna is open for nine nights a year to guests. On the ninth night, which happens to be Halloween, new members are welcomed in and several members exit," he said.

"So some guests actually become Nolies, and stay here after the portal closes?"

"Yeah," Joey replied. "Some Nolies can come and go at other times, but I haven't figured that part out yet."

Lilah nodded to show she understood. "So then, how does it work?" she asked.

"How does what work?" Sebastian appeared at their table to answer her question with a question. He sat down across from her, and Lilah's heart sank. She hadn't seen him walk up. Joey dropped her hand and moved over a bit so he wasn't quite as close to her.

"Lilah was just asking about Nolianna," Joey said, and split the fried cake in half. He pushed Lilah's half toward her on the paper plate and started eating his piece.

"Lilah, Lilah, Lilah. You just can't let things go, can you?" Sebastian said, shaking his head. "So what do you want to know?"

Lilah raised an eyebrow and looked back and forth between them. Reaching out, she broke off a piece of the cake and ate it. The fried cake had nothing on Eva's cinnamon rolls.

"Seriously, out with it. I know you're dying to know more," Sebastian said with a sly grin.

"Okay," she said. "Joey said Nolianna is open nine nights a year. How do people find out about it?"

Sebastian laughed. "Nolies invite those they've selected who meet their criteria. About sixty people are invited each year, but by the ninth night, only ten new members are invited to join Nolianna permanently."

"So only ten join. Do they move here?"

"Yup. The ninth night is on Halloween, or what we call Masquarade, and then access from the portal closes until the next time it opens a year from now. Everyone who's inside when it closes is here until next October," Sebastian clarified.

"So the majority of guests here tonight won't be here on the last night?"

"Exactamundo. You're a smart cookie with a flair for details," Sebastian teased.

"And after Masquarade, no one can leave Nolianna for a year?"

"Yup."

"And then what?" Lilah asked her mouth feeling dry.

"Nolianna is closed to the outside world until it opens the next year. It always opens in a different place though. Nolianna never opens in the same place twice," Sebastian replied. Lilah's heartbeat pulsated at the base of her neck. Her mind raced with a ton of other questions.

"I know it sounds crazy, but that's it. See why I didn't want to tell you?" Joey said. "You would have thought I was crazy."

He wasn't wrong.

"So how does someone become one of the ten?"

"The ten are invited and choose to be here. At Masquarade, each new member is matched with a current Nolianna member," Sebastian announced.

"Matched?"

"Everyone in Nolianna is partnered up. Ya know, like me and you for the Perform-a-thon. Not that that matters now."

Lilah stared at him, taking in each word. She'd have to worry about school later.

"So people come here instead of going to college? How long can you stay?"

"No one here is over the age of twenty-two. Pairs must return to the outer world before one of their twenty-second birthdays," Sebastian explained, and took a quick sip out of Lilah's soda. "The best part of being is a Nolie is that we're one family. No adults around to tell us what we can or can't do." He twiddled his fingers and looked past her several times.

"So this place is run entirely by kids our age?"

"Well, kind of," he replied. "No one can join before they turn sixteen, but you have to join before your eighteenth birthday."

"And then what?"

"Everyone leaves by the age of twenty-two, like I said," Sebastian stated, his nostrils flaring. His eyebrows furrowed, and the tone of his voice turned to one of annoyance.

"But—"

"Hey Joey, you wanna go on the Screaming Owl with us?" Asha asked from behind her. Lilah hadn't noticed her come up behind.

"Uh, sure. Lilah, let's go on the Screaming Owl. It'll be fun," Joey said, and ended their conversation.

"Thank God," Sebastian said under his breath. "We'll have lots of time later to talk, babe." He pushed against the red table and stood up. "Everyone else is having fun and you're trying to figure everything out. Go enjoy yourself! Unless you want to stay here and talk with me while Joey's off having fun with Asha."

Lilah flared her nostrils and bit her lip. Sebastian knew exactly what to say to get her riled up.

Joey stood up and grabbed her hand. "Come on."

"Later, gator," Sebastian cackled and walked away.

Joey dragged her toward a pirate boat nicknamed the Screaming Owl that swung back and forth high in the air and then tipped over. Her eyes widened at the sight of them going round and round, up and down. The soda she'd guzzled a few minutes before suddenly didn't seem like such a great choice. The people on the ride screamed in delight—or pure terror, she wasn't sure which.

The wait in line was less than a minute, and within three, they were up screaming their heads off too. It was terrifying and delightful at the same time.

The rest of the night was same. Rides, games, people dancing, singing, eating cotton candy, pizza, and fried dough, and meeting new people. Lilah gave into the carefree spirit of the night and just enjoyed being with Joey. It all felt like a dream, a really good one.

A loud bell rang across the grounds and the announcer's voice came on over the loud speaker. "If all of the guests will begin to make their way to the exit, please. The portal is only open for the next seventeen minutes and all guests must leave. Thank you."

She and Joey walked to get their coats and head out.

"Did you have fun?" Sebastian asked, always popping up whereever Lilah was. He walked right up to her and stood so close their noses almost touched. She took a step back to avoid his breath on her face.

"I did. Joey took me on a bunch of rides. We had a really good time."

A flicker of irritation flashed in Sebastian's eyes before he responded. He masked it with a smirk. "Well, good. That's what Nolianna's all about and why you needed to come tonight."

Matthew's voice came on over the loudspeaker.

"Okay, everyone, it's that time! Please make your way to the arch. We hope you had a great time tonight and look forward to seeing you again. Please remember, Nolianna is our place, our home, and we ask that you refrain from talking about it on the outside. It's for all of our protection."

"Huh?" Lilah whispered to Joey.

"Shh," he responded. "We aren't allowed to talk about Nolianna once we leave. It's one of the rules of being here." Lilah's skin prickled. She didn't like to be shushed, especially by Joey.

"To health, happiness, and family," Matthew cheered.

Everyone cheered and clapped. Lilah found her sweatshirt and hat and put them on. She walked with Joey and Sebastian toward the edge of the field. People in front of her walked forward one by one and disappeared down past the sunflowers.

As she waited to take her turn, the hairs on the back of her neck and arms stood up. She looked around, but Joey and Sebastian were busy talking with others in front and behind them. She glanced left and right—no one was looking at her. She made a full circle, trying to figure out why she felt so strange.

As she circled round, she caught a glimpse of a tall shadow moving in the distance behind one of the trees. She squinted to try and see who it was, but as she did, the line started moving again. She took a few steps and looked back over her shoulder. The shadow was gone. A yawn escaped her mouth. Her lack of sleep had to be playing tricks on her eyes.

"Have fun tonight?" Dublin asked. They smiled, waiting for each guest to exit.

"I did," Lilah said.

"Good, I hope to you see you tomorrow night. Don't forget about my offer," they said.

"Okay, thanks." Lilah's face burned again. They were really cute.

She walked forward toward the iridescent bubble next to the sunflowers covering the opening of the portal and walked single-file down the trail. The light from the field behind her dissolved into darkness, and it was near impossible to see anything in front of her. With each step she took, she carefully placed one foot in front of the other as to not trip or stumble down the steep path. She held on to several low tree branches along the way to help steady her.

Carefully, she made her way past the waterfall onto the familiar rocky ground. The crisp air smelled like evergreen and autumn leaves. Daylight shone through the trees and cast shadows on the ground as dawn broke.

Joey and Sebastian had made it down before her and were waiting.

"Oh, shit." Lilah stopped suddenly and put her hands over her mouth. Joey and Sebastian both looked at her. "I never told Abe and Eva I was going out! They're going to kill me. I've got to go back now!"

Sebastian and Joey exchanged a look.

"Don't worry about it. We'll sneak you in if we need to," said Sebastian in a calm and unwavering voice. "They won't even know. I promise."

Lilah had a hard time believing him, but maybe he knew something she didn't. After all, she'd barely spoken to Abe. This knowledge didn't stop the trepidation from pounding in her ears.

"If you say so, but I got to get back, now." She took off at a half-run and prayed they could make it back to the house without anyone noticing she was gone.

Chapter 13

‿

Lᴏᴏᴋ IᴌAH sʟᴏᴡʟʏ opened her eyes. Her eyelids felt like they were made out of lead. The late-day sun shone through her window, causing pain to erupt behind her eyes. It was all she could do to keep them open.

The rusty mattress coils squeaked beneath her, and her head throbbed each time she moved. Steadying her eyes on the small, chipped dresser, she tried to recall everything that had happened in the past twelve hours. Her thoughts were fuzzy, and details escaped her. Her usual easy recall and astuteness were gone. The frustration about her lack of memory caused her head to spin even more. *Was it all a dream?* She slid her hand down the side of her leg and felt the seam of her jeans. It wasn't a dream, and obviously changing out of her jeans hadn't been a priority upon her return to Abe's.

She'd obviously made it back to Abe's without incident. And she vaguely remembered going in through the front door. Lilah lay still and tried to recall more about the previous night. She remembered following Joey, running into Sebastian, and going up the trail to a carnival. And then coming home. She recalled meeting a bunch of new people, going on several rides, a large white and red flapped tent . .

. but the rest was hazy. Was there a girl in neon green? Did someone offer to give her a tattoo? Did they talk more?

Forcing herself to sit up, Lilah reached for her notebook and pen and wrote down what she could remember, none of it really making a lot of sense. She began doodling and tried to force herself to remember more. All she kept drawing were spiders. *Spiders? What's so significant about spiders?* She'd never liked the creepy crawlers. The thought of their little legs inching up her arm made her squirm. And yet, the image of spiders kept coming to her mind. Large spiders on walls, little spiders on people's skin. It was almost as if they were everywhere.

A loud clang of someone banging pans together in the kitchen startled her from her thoughts, and her stomach growled. Slowly, she got up, threw on a pair of gray sweatpants and a sweatshirt, ran her hands through her unkempt hair, and made her way down to the kitchen. She hoped some food would help her feel a little less groggy and maybe help her remember more.

In the kitchen, the newly washed black-and-white checkered floor glistened in the sunlight. It almost hurt her eyes.

"Well, good morning, sunshine!" a familiar male voice said. "Or should I say, good afternoon. Sleep well?"

Lilah stopped walking. Sebastian sat casually at the kitchen table drinking coffee and reading a newspaper, almost as if he lived there. His freshly washed hair shone in the sunlight and his long face was glowing. He had on a navy blue long sleeve T-shirt and jeans. Forcing how he looked from her mind, she crossed her arms in front of her.

Sebastian chuckled. "Nice hair. Do you always look so well put together when you wake up?"

Catching her profile in a shiny skillet hanging above the counter to her right, she drew in a breath. Her hair sprouted every direction like a lion's frowzy mane. A warmth rose up her neck and into her cheeks. "Yup. Don't be jealous, not everyone can look this good all the time," Lilah replied flatly.

"Well, aren't we just grumpy. I would've thought you'd be a little happier today."

Lilah walked by him and grabbed a glass from the cabinet and poured herself some orange juice from the fridge.

"Eva left some sticky buns on the counter for you. You're lucky Caleb didn't see them. You would've been SOL and left to eat Abe's All-Bran."

"Lucky for me, I like All-Bran. Keeps me regular," Lilah said with a straight face, and looked directly at Sebastian.

They both cracked up. Sebastian's sniggering made Lilah laugh harder.

"Ah, there she is. I knew you couldn't stay all grumpy-pants," he said.

Lilah unwrapped the plastic from the plate of sticky buns and sat down with him at the table.

"Are you going to share?" Sebastian licked his lips and stuck out his hand.

Lilah shoved an entire bun in her mouth. "Nope," she said in a muffled voice, her cheeks puffed.

Sebastian laughed again. "See, that's why I like you. You look all sweet and innocent, but underneath, you aren't."

Lilah guzzled some orange juice and patted her lips with a white paper napkin. "Yeah, well, you're one to talk. You come off all tough guy and arrogant," she said.

"And . . ." Sebastian leaned in.

"That's all," Lilah said flippantly.

Sebastian's whole body shook as he let out a burst of hearty laughter.

Lilah couldn't help but smile.

"Yup, you're not wrong. You call 'em as you see 'em," Sebastian said. He got up and cleared Lilah's dishes. He rinsed them and placed them in the dishwasher.

"I can do that," Lilah said, backing up her chair and starting to stand up.

Sebastian held up a free hand and pointed to sit back down. Lilah did. "I know. I just t10hought I'd help. Eva's

really great and I like to clean up after myself whenever
I'm here."

"Are you here a lot?" Lilah asked, placing her elbow on
the table and cupping her chin.

"Nah, I stayed with them for a bit, but Abe and I aren't
really a good mix, so Mrs. R. found me a place just down
the road."

"Mrs. R? As in Mrs. Reed?" Lilah raised an eyebrow.

Sebastian finished drying his hands on a new lime-green
checkered towel and turned to look right at Lilah. "Yeah,
she places lots of kids around here. You know her?"

"Kinda. She brought me here. I really wanted to stay at
my Grandma Pea's house," Lilah replied, a lump forming
in her throat.

"They aren't keen on asking us what we want, if you
haven't noticed. That's why it's nice we have other options,
ya know?" Sebastian said.

He sat down next to her, his arm close to hers. Lilah
leaned toward him and placed her right hand on his forearm. Sebastian straightened his back.

"Can I ask you some things about last night?" she said
in a low voice.

Sebastian's nostrils flared and his eyes darted around the
room. "You know we aren't supposed to talk about it," he
scolded.

She really didn't remember specific rules, only that
there were a lot of them. "Okay," she said, and then added,
"I don't want to break the rules, really. It's just that I have so
many questions, and I can't remember everything clearly
from last night."

"You're probably just tired," Sebastian said, removing
his arm from her grip.

Lilah drew in a breath and held it. Sebastian shook his
head and looked around the room again. Turning her lips
downward into a pout, she batted her eyelashes ever so
slightly at him.

"Fine. Let's go out back and sit on the swings," he said abruptly, getting up from the table. He opened the red kitchen door that led out to the small backyard and walked outside.

Lilah put on a pair of Eva's muddy pink-and-purple polka dot rain boots that were sitting by the door. She went out to join Sebastian, closing the door behind her.

It was the first time she'd been in the backyard. A chain-linked fence sectioned off Abe's from Danielle's house and the neighbors on two other sides. To the left was a rickety one-car garage with four windows, two of which had broken panes from what appeared to be baseball mishaps, based on the baseball-shaped holes. Next to it sat two plastic swings suspended from a rusted turquoise frame. Sebastian sat on a swing and waited for Lilah. She walked across the brown grass that was covered with random dead leaves and joined him. Sitting down on the cold plastic seat, she placed her hands on the rusty chains to steady herself. The frame buckled for a moment, causing her to pause.

Once she decided that it was going to hold them, she turned and looked at Sebastian. His freshly washed hair curled slightly, and Lilah couldn't help but stare at his broad shoulders and perfectly symmetrical face. Turning to meet her eyes, Sebastian smiled, lips parted. Lilah's heartbeat quickened and she looked away.

Sebastian pushed his swing back a bit with his legs to meet her gaze. "Penny for your thoughts," he said.

The butterflies in Lilah's stomach fluttered. As much as she wanted to dislike him, there was something about Sebastian that drew her in. He was hot. And Lilah found his mysteriousness enticing as much as she hated it.

"Honestly, I just want to know more about last night. How in the world is it possible that we went to a carnival? How did it get there, and why is it hidden?" she asked, all in one breath.

Sebastian cleared his throat. "Look, we really aren't

supposed to talk about this here. Tonight, when you come back, you can ask whatever you want," he said coldly.

Lilah suddenly felt a little more confident and tried not smirk. She wasn't sure she wanted to go back. Not being able to remember the full details of the night made her uneasy, but she also knew Sebastian wanted her to return. She had to figure out a way to get him to tell her more.

"Well, I don't think I'm going back," Lilah declared, hoping Sebastian would bite.

"Now wait, don't be so quick to judge," he said, softening a bit. "You really would be missing out. I think you'd like it there if you gave it a chance."

"That's the thing," Lilah said, and made eye contact again. "I don't know *where* or *what* that is. And all I can remember are random bits and pieces."

"It's what it seems. A carnival, in a field, for teenagers," he said dryly, in just above a whisper.

Lilah leaned in toward him. "But *how* did it get there, and what happens to it?"

"Seriously, Lilah, can't you just let it go and enjoy it?" Sebastian snapped.

Lilah straightened her body and let out a sigh. She pushed back on her heels and let the swing take her. She rocked back and forth several times. Looking toward Abe's house, she wondered if she could really trust Sebastian. He always seemed to show up whenever she was alone.

Interrupting her thoughts, Sebastian reached over and grabbed Lilah's rusty chain, pulling her closer to him. "Look, a long time ago, Carnival Nolianna was a real carnival, in the real world. Then one night it up and disappeared. Now it's only open nine nights a year and only for us. It's our safe haven. The one place in the entire world where we get to make the rules, live as we want, be who we were meant to be. It's a family—my family . . . and it could be yours if you would just follow the rules and have some faith," he said, and let go of her chain.

Lilah swung sideways, nearly losing her balance. She put her feet on the dirt ground to steady herself before speaking.

"So if I decide to join, I'll disappear with them?" Lilah's insides knotted into a tight ball. "Yup."

"And I'd live there?"

"Yeah, we have houses in the back, away from the main field. Everything that's there is closed off from the rest of the world on Masquarade—"

"Masquarade?"

Sebastian held up his hand and glared at her.

"Enough. Seriously," he said sternly, his face muscles tautening. "I know you have a million and one questions, and you can ask them all if you decide to come back. That is, if you think it's worth taking a chance on creating a family that will never leave you."

Lilah wasn't sure how to respond. Being part of a family was something Lilah wanted more than anything, but hers was dead, and no one was going to be able to replace them, no matter how much she wanted them to. Plus, she had dreams of going to college and creating a life for herself. Joining Nolianna would change all of that.

A red station wagon with wood-paneled sides and a dented front bumper pulled into the driveway and cut the engine. Both Sebastian and Lilah looked forward.

The back doors of the wagon opened, and Brody, Eddie, and Caleb scampered out, slamming the doors behind them. They ran straight up to Sebastian. Eva got out of the front car door and shook her head at what Lilah presumed was the boys' boundless energy. She made eye contact with Lilah and gave a quick wave.

"Sebastian, will you play pickle in the middle with us?" Brody asked, pulling Sebastian's arm forward and trying to drag him off the swing. Sebastian smiled and glanced at Lilah. Who was she to stop the boys from having fun? Plus, she could use some time to think over last night's events again. Lilah waved her fingers upward indicating for him to go ahead.

"Sure, dude," Sebastian said, standing and patting Brody on the head.

"Go grab the mitts!" Caleb ordered. Being the oldest, he was used to them following his orders.

"You go get them!" Eddie shouted back while looking at Sebastian. It was obvious from the way he watched every move Sebastian made that he idolized him.

"You suck," Caleb quipped.

"Now boys, please. No more arguing. Remember what we talked about in the car about helping one another out," Eva said, walking toward the house. "Unless, of course, you would rather talk to Abe about it."

The boys stopped arguing, and all three ran toward the garage.

"We'll meet you out front, Sebastian! You're in the middle with Brody first," Eddie said over his shoulder.

"How come I always have to be in the middle?" Brody whined. All three boys went into the garage through the white side door and closed it behind them.

Lilah stood up. "I've been summoned," Sebastian joked.

Lilah shrugged. "Yeah, I'm going to head in and take a shower. I've got a bunch to think about," she said. And she did. Sebastian had answered a few of her questions, but she still had so many more. She wanted to trust him, but as Maya Angelou said, "When someone shows you who they are, believe them the first time". In Lilah's experience, if something seemed to be good to be true, it usually was.

"Okay—and Lilah . . . ," Sebastian said, moving closer to her so only she could hear, "I know you're skeptical, but take it from me, being part of Nolianna will change your life for the better. You'll never have to be alone again. You can trust me on that."

Lilah wished she could.

Chapter 14

AFTER A LONG, hot shower, Lilah was feeling a little more put together and awake. She dressed, did her hair, and made her way downstairs in time for dinner. The dining room was set with white dinnerware, mismatched cloth napkins, and two pumpkin-scented candles in the middle of the room that cast shadows on the dark walls. Eva had invited Sebastian to stay for dinner, and he had enthusiastically accepted.

"Did you have a good day?" Eva asked no one in particular.

"Yeah," Eddie, Brody, and Caleb all responded without looking up from their food. They'd spent part of the day with Mrs. Reed; she'd supervised a visit with their estranged aunt who had come out of the woodwork.

"Did the visit go okay?" Eva posed her question differently, this time directly to the boys.

"Yup. She took us for ice cream," Brody said, before filling his mouth with another spoonfull of mashed potatoes.

Eva's shoulders slumped. "Oh, okay," she replied in a hushed tone, and the corners of her mouth turned downward.

The boys were taking some time getting to know their aunt. Lilah had overheard Eva on the phone with a friend before dinner: Eva worried the aunt might want them and she would have to give them up. The boys seemed oblivious to Eva's worries, and continued shoveling their food in their mouths like they hadn't eaten in days.

Eva passed a basket of rolls toward Caleb. He gladly accepted it and took two.

"We learned about gravity this week in school," Eddie said. "Whatever goes up, must come down."

"Well, maybe whoever threw that ball that came down in my garage window last week might want to fix it before they get in trouble," Abe grumbled. Once again, his dreary personality was shining through. Lilah wondered what he had to be so grumpy about all the time.

"Oh now, you don't know if it was a ball for sure. It could have been the wind knocking down a branch. You know how windy it's been lately," Eva reframed, always the protector of the boys.

Abe moaned and took a swig of his beer.

"What're you two going to do on this lovely Saturday evening?" Eva asked, and looked directly at Lilah.

It was the sixth night of Nolianna, and Lilah hadn't completely decided if she was going to go back.

"Lilah and I are going to hang out with Joey tonight," Sebastian responded, answering for her. "Danielle said he could have a movie marathon with a bunch of us. We'll probably all spend the night."

Abe's eyes darted to Sebastian and then Lilah. Lilah swore he smirked beneath his scraggly, long gray beard.

"Abe, honey, what do you think?" Eva said. "Is it okay with you if Lilah goes? I'm okay with it."

"Uh huh," Abe mumbled and downed the rest of his beer.

"It's fine if you go. Just make sure to get some sleep," Eva said, and simpered at Lilah.

Lilah raised an eyebrow and looked from Eva to Sebastian. Grandma Pea never would've agreed to it. Sebastian flashed a smile.

"Thanks, Eva. I'll take good care of her," Sebastian replied. "Can I be excused?"

"Of course, dear. You two should make sure to dress warmly if you're going outside. We're having an unseasonably cold fall this year," Eva responded. "And Lilah, try to be home at a reasonable hour tomorrow. I'm sure you have some school work to catch up."

"I do, thanks." She definitely had some work she could do, but this whole Nolianna thing brought up a ton of unanswered questions as to whether or not she would be able to do it.

"Lilah, I'll catch up with you in a few. I gotta grab my coat from out front," Sebastian said, and gathered his plate and cup.

"Just leave it, dear, I'll take it to the kitchen," Eva offered.

"Thanks, Eva," Sebastian responded, and gave Eva a quick peck on the cheek as he walked toward the front hallway. Her face turned three shades of red and she let out a giggle.

Not missing a beat, the three boys took Sebastian getting up from the table as their signal to exit also. They scurried into the living room to watch television, and three thumps could be heard as they plopped down on the floor.

"Poor Sebastian. His foster parents are hardly ever home. I'm glad you're getting to know him," Eva directed to Lilah.

"Whatever. He's a suck-up," Abe grumbled. "When I was his age, I had to fend for myself. How's he supposed to be a man if you're always feeding him?"

"Don't mind him, Lilah. He's just cranky as usual," Eva said, and began gathering dishes off the table.

"Here, let me help you," Lilah said, and grabbed her plate and the half-eaten bowl of potatoes.

121

"If I didn't know any better, I'd say that Sebastian has some feelings for you," Eva hinted when they were alone in the kitchen.

Lilah took a few steps back and turned away slightly.

"I see the way you look at him too," Eva added trying to push for a reaction.

Lilah clenched her jaw. Sure, Sebastian was attractive, but Eva was taking her wariness of him to be attraction. She wondered if Sebastian did too.

"Um, uh, maybe. I guess. He's nice," Lilah replied, avoiding eye contact. She didn't want to have to get into it any further with Eva.

"Just be careful. Sebastian's a good boy, and then again, so is Joey. I'd hate to see either of you get hurt by making the wrong choice," Eva said.

Lilah was about to ask what she meant, but the kitchen door swung open, letting in a gush of cold air. Joey walked in and closed it behind him. He rubbed his hands together for warmth. "It's getting really cold out there!" he said. "Hi, Eva," he said flashing her a smile.

"Hi Joey," she crooned. She really liked attention from Joey and Sebastian.

"Lilah. Are you ready to go?" Joey asked. "Eva, is it okay with you that Lilah comes over tonight?"

"Well, that's very considerate of you to ask. Yes, it's fine," Eva said, and began emptying the dishwasher.

"Ready, Lilah? We'd better get a move on. Everyone'll be arriving soon and we don't want to miss the first movie," Joey said.

Both of them turned and looked at Eva. Lilah didn't want to be rude or assume she could leave without helping out first.

"It's okay, dear. I'll take care of the rest of the dishes tonight. You just go have fun," Eva retorted.

"Okay, thanks Eva," she reciprocated. "Thanks again for dinner. It was really yummy. I'll see you in the morning,"

"Bye you two," Eva said.

Joey and Lilah walked through the dining room and stopped in the hallway by the front door. Sebastian sat talking with Abe in the living room. They grew quiet when they saw Lilah and Joey.

"I thought you were meeting me at my house," Joey snuffled. His face grew red and wrinkles appeared across his forehead.

"I hung out with Lilah this afternoon and Eva invited me to stay for dinner," Sebastian said, and stood up to look down on Joey. He was only a few inches taller, but used it to his advantage.

"Cut it, you two," Abe scolded. "I'm trying to watch the news." He motioned with his hand for them to move. Lilah just watched the interaction, thinking Pea would have never talked to anyone like that. An ache of loneliness mixed with longing welled in her heart. She'd give anything to back with Grandma Pea.

"Thanks for dinner, Abe," Sebastian responded, ignoring Abe's demeanor, and walked toward them. He stopped next to Lilah and leaned over her shoulder to get his coat off the hook. His face was almost next to hers. Joey jerked her toward him and she stumbled a bit.

Lilah looked at the two of them and moved to put on her coat, mittens, and hat. Abe returned his attention to the television and the three boys sprawled across the living room floor never even bothered to look at them.

Joey swung open the wooden front door and took Lilah's hand, and the three of them rushed out. They quickened their pace down the street. Sebastian walked ahead of Joey and Lilah.

"If I knew you wanted some company today, I would've been happy to come over," Joey said in a gruff voice.

Lilah looked at him.

"Oh, chill out, man," Sebastian said over his shoulder. "Seriously. Abe asked if I could help move some stuff around in the garage, and Eva left a snack for me when I was done. Lilah woke up and we just sat and talked. No harm, no foul," he huffed.

Joey looked at Lilah and she raised her shoulders a bit and then let them drop.

"Oh, okay," Joey said, though his lips turned downward. Lilah wasn't sure if she should be flattered or upset at Joey's reaction. She'd have much preferred for Joey to come over, but it wasn't up to her. She was still trying to figure out her whole living situation, let alone Joey, Sebastian, *and* Nolianna.

"It's freaking cold tonight," Sebastian said, pulling his collar up around his neck while they walked. "You warm enough, Lilah?"

"Yeah."

"Sorry," Joey mouthed to Lilah, and gave her a quick peck on the cheek. Warmth spread down to her toes despite the cold.

The trip to the falls seemed much shorter the second time, and Lilah only tripped once on a root. Luckily, Joey's strong grip steadied her and kept her from falling. Sebastian ran ahead and met up with the others. Joey and Lilah made their way to the back of the crowd waiting to go on the trail.

Lilah glanced over at Sebastian and felt a burning at the base of her neck. His broad shoulders were illuminated by the moonlight and his curly hair waved in the wind. Lilah whipped around as if she might get burned. Her feelings confused her. She only wanted to be with Joey, but Sebastian drew her in like a moth to a flame, and she couldn't ignore how hot he was no matter how much she tried to convince herself otherwise.

They shuffled forward as people moved along the path.

Sebastian looked down at Lilah and Joey's intertwined hands and frowned. Lilah didn't say a word and looked away from his stare. She couldn't help but wonder if being with Joey was going to be a problem.

Chapter 15

B Y THE TIME Lilah made it up the trail, the carnival was in full swing. The chain had already been dropped and the guests were excitedly moving toward their first attraction of the night. Sweat formed on her lower back, causing her to shed her outerwear again down to her Puddle Dive T-shirt. Guests were already scattered across the field, confetti blowing throughout the air and the music pumping. Several Nolies mulled around the field, opening up tents and arranging garbage cans. Lilah walked forward onto the field and made a mental note to remember the details in front of her.

"Lilah!" Joey bayed, and walked up to her. He touched her on the arm with his free hand. "Ready to go in?"

"Um, yeah, sorry, I must've been lost in thought."

"I hope it was something good, like about me," he whispered. He leaned down and gave her quick peck on the cheek. A giggle escaped her mouth.

"So what do you want to do first tonight?" Joey asked, and put his arm around her waist.

"I'm not sure. I'd love to see some more of the grounds."

"Sometimes you're so strange, Lilah," Joey teased.

"What do you mean?" Lilah wasn't how to take what he said.

"It's what I like about you. You're so different. Everyone else here can't wait to get on the roller-coasters or one of the rides. You want to walk around and observe everything," Joey said.

"Why is that strange? Aren't you curious at all about what's here and what we're getting into?"

"We?" Joey repeated, and gave her slight squeeze.

"Well, yeah. I'm here, aren't I?" she said, and then mumbled, "At least for now."

Joey turned to talk to Luna and Kyle, who they had met last night. Lilah remembered who they were upon seeing them. Funny how she hadn't been able to recall them before. Little details of last night had crept into her thoughts all day, though an accurate array of events and how they transpired never came to her fully. She took a deep breath and moved forward toward the center of Nolianna.

The carnival was alive in front of her. The rides with their colorful neon lights spun, whirled, and swirled. Upbeat music from a band she'd never heard of filled the background, and the multicolored carousel began circling, vintage white and black horses going up and down. It looked way older than any other ride in Nolianna and had ripped, painted scenes of what once was a night sky all around the rounding board at the top. Screeching sounds of metal on metal pierced the air occasionally, though after a while it became mundane and just part of the atmosphere. The ground beneath her was clay-like dirt that dusted her shoes, and brightly colored signs filled the entire fairgrounds as far as her eye could see. She looked off into the distance to try and figure out what was in the surrounding areas, but there wasn't much to see. There was a clearing past the carnival boundaries, some random run-down buildings, but nothing else distinct. She turned to ask Joey about the living quarters but realized he was nowhere to be seen.

"What's up, buttercup?" Sebastian's smooth voice came from behind her.

Lilah held her breath and he walked up next to her.

"Nothing. Just looking around."

"Where'd lover boy go?"

Lilah looked around and shrugged. She let out a sigh. The Disappearing Joey Act had just begun.

"Don't have a cow. I'm sure he hasn't found some other hottie to make the moves on, at least not yet," Sebastian joked, and laughed.

Lilah's nostrils flared. "Aren't you funny."

He laughed harder. "Oh, lighten up. You two barely know each other. There's lots of fish in the sea, babe," he said.

"Yeah, well—"

"Good evening, everyone! And welcome to the sixth night of Nolianna! We're happy you've returned for another night of fun," Matthew's voice filled the air over the loudspeaker. "Please enjoy yourself. Tonight's specialty for all guests is deep-fried Oreos! Please make sure to go over and try them out!"

Cheers erupted throughout the grounds.

Lilah walked away from Sebastian and darted toward the middle of the grounds, hoping to do some exploring before anyone noticed.

"Hey, Lilah. Glad to see you're back." Dublin walked by holding a bunch of rope.

"Hi, Dublin. Good to see you too," she said remembering them all of a sudden, and stopped walking to read the signs on the smaller tents, trying to figure out where she wanted to go.

Sebastian came up behind her and scooped her up off the ground.

"Hey . . . ," she said as he spun her around in his arms. Their cheeks glided against one another and Lilah's cheeks burned.

He stopped spinning and put her down. Dublin disappeared from sight.

"I'll have to try that again some time," he said, and let her go. She frowned at him.

"Lighten up. I'm going to win you over eventually, trust me. Come on," he said, and took her hand. He pulled her forward, past the large carnival tent where there were several games and activities already in full swing.

"Let's start with the games tonight," he said, ignoring the fact that she was dragging her feet, making it harder to pull her along. She didn't really want to spend the time with him and wanted to try to find Joey. Or even Dublin.

Realizing Joey was nowhere to be seen, she sighed and gave in. Refusing Sebastian now seemed just as futile as on the first day of school.

"Let's start with the milk bottles. Maybe I can win you a stuffed bear or something so you can cuddle with it and think of me," he said, and tossed his hair away from him face with the back of his hand.

Lilah rolled her eyes.

They walked up to an area that had about twenty games under several small, rainbow-colored tent awnings. The awnings were smattered with stripes, stars, and colorful patterns that made Lilah happy—their whimsical nature somehow set her insides at ease. There were games like the milk ball toss, pretend rifle shooting, and bobbing for apples. To her right were rides that were pretty standard at any carnival, like teacups, swings, tall and daring roller-coasters, and upside-down pirate ships, most of which she half-remembered riding the night before. She couldn't see all the way in the back, but she was able to see signs that included a picture of a cat, a horse, and a monkey. She had no idea there were animals in Nolianna.

Standing on her tiptoes, she stretched her neck to see more.

"Sebastian, what's back behind the animal signs?"

His neck and face muscles tensed. Scrunching his fore-head, he flashed a sly smile. "Oh, nothing that would interest you."

Lilah raised an eyebrow and took a few steps forward. He grabbed her arm and she stopped in her tracks. Not letting that stop her, she scanned the area in front of her.

"What's the Kat?" she asked, pointing to a small red-and-black, illuminated sign with the word "Kat" flashing. It was at the very back of the field, hidden by several smaller tent peaks and concession stands. One might miss it if they weren't at just the right angle.

"The Kat? It's where all the Nolies gather and everyone hangs out after the night is over," he replied.

Lilah's ears prickled. Shuffling a few steps forward, she wanted to see more.

Sebastian held her in place.

"Sorry, babe. Only Nolies are allowed in. You have to wait," he said with a wide smirk on his face.

Lilah wished she could smack it right off.

Sebastian's face lit up, and he shook with laughter.

"You really need to chillax, Lilah," he squawked and turned his attention to a girl approaching. "There's Kady, she runs the Kat. I'll introduce you, but don't expect much. She isn't real friendly, especially to guests."

They walked up to the girl with stringy white hair with black roots pursing her lips.

"Hey, Sebastian, who's your friend?" Kady asked in a snarky voice. She twirled a finger around her long, unkempt, shoulder length hair. Her black combat boots were scuffed and worn, her black fishnets had gapping holes, and the skintight black halter dress barely covered her malnourished frame. The dress had a small red spider embroidered on the front in the center. Several tattoos were randomly scattered on her arms and neck in black-and-red.

"This is Lilah. She came in with Joey," Sebastian said, and looked at Kady. Lilah looked into Kady's blue, almost black, vacant eyes, and a shiver ran down her spin. They were void of emotion, empathy, or kindness. A pang of pity mixed with anxiety erupted in her gut at the same time. She felt sorry for Kady, and yet wanted nothing to do with her.

"Joey, huh? I thought she was with you. Joey was hanging around here earlier, and it sure didn't seem like he was with anyone, if you know what I mean," Kady said like a hungry feline, waiting to pounce on her weaker prey. Lilah was the mouse, and Kady was obviously ready to devour her.

Little did she know that Lilah wasn't easy devoured. Lilah had met girls like her before, and they were a dime a dozen. She wasn't scared of what this stick-thin girl could do to her. "Oh, no worries. I'm having a great time with Sebastian," Lilah said. She stepped closer to Sebastian and took his arm in hers.

Sebastian ate it up and pulled Lilah closer, enjoying the game. "Be nice, Kady," Sebastian replied in a distinct, forceful tone.

Was he being protective or giving an order? Lilah wondered, but didn't dare ask.

Kady raised a pierced eyebrow and bared her teeth a bit, slowly turning it into a half smile. "Aren't I always nice, love?"

"Sure, we'll go with that," Sebastian said. "Lilah, this is Kady. She runs the Kady Kats tent I was telling you about."

Lilah curled her lips curled into a half-smile of her own.

"Well, I imagine you won't be here long," Kady hissed.

Lilah laughed. "No worries, Kady," she said. Sebastian took a step forward and mouthed something Lilah couldn't see. Kady's eyes grew wide, and she took step back.

"My bad . . . just not all of us are meant to be part of the Kat. Don't go all postal on me!" With a quick roll of her eyes, Kady turned and walked away. As she did, Lilah heard her mutter, "Whatever. Hasta la vista, baby."

"What's her problem?"

"Kady's been around a while. She's only got a few years left here, and can be a total beotch. She's one of those girls who always wants what everyone has and doesn't care about anyone who doesn't benefit her. Just stay clear of her, and you'll be fine." Lilah nodded. "There are very few people in Nolianna like Kady. For the most part, everyone's pretty chill. If Kady bothers you, you let me know. I'll take care of it."

Lilah drew in a breath. She opened her mouth to challenge him, but stopped. "Uh, okay, thanks."

Sebastian stood up straight. "Let's head over to the makeup tents. I think you said you wanted to see more of the area."

"Okay." Lilah held his arm, and they walked toward a set of two white, smaller tents set to the side of the signs for the animals and games. In the distance, Kady stood glaring at her and she stared right back and waved. Kady's nostrils flared, causing Lilah to stifle a smirk.

They walked up to the smaller of the two red tents that had a rectangular, lit-up sign with red-and-white letters flashing "Makeup" in cursive. A woman's voice crooned from the speakers above—some sort of rock song Lilah had never heard before.

"So what's beyond there?" Lilah asked, and pointed past the tents. In the far distance, there were four long wooden houses she hadn't seen before.

"Just a few random buildings," Sebastian replied.

"What—"

"Seriously, can't you just give it a rest?" Sebastian huffed. He pulled her arm toward him and stepped in front of her to go into the tent. "Come on, I'll introduce you to a few of the girls that do makeup, and then we'll go play some games and knock down some pins," he said over his shoulder.

Lilah glanced at the brown building, shrugged, and joined him in the makeup tent. She had no intention of letting it go.

Chapter 16

❧

INSIDE THE TENT stood several collapsible white plastic tables covered with makeup bottles, brushes, curling irons, lights, accessories, and racks of clothing, all packed tightly into the relatively small space. A makeup station with a metal chair, vanity, and rectangular mirror and accentuated with large, clear light bulbs sat in the back of the tent, unused. The warm air was stagnant and made breathing hard. Lilah coughed a few times, trying to catch her breath. Even with the stale air, though, discovering new aspects of Nolianna was a nice distraction from her interaction with Kady and the disappearance of Joey.

"So who works in these areas?"

"Everyone in Nolianna has a job based on their talents and interests. For example, Matthew is the leader this year—he's in charge of all operations, Kady runs the Kat . . . and there's Ginger who manages the makeup and costuming tents."

"Ginger?" Lilah raised an eyebrow. She didn't want to let on that she knew who Ginger was. She remembered her long auburn braid, that she was gorgeous, and that Sebastian had some kind of beef with her.

"You may've seen her. She has really long braided hair

and is usually with at least two other girls who help her dress everyone . . ." Sebastian's voice trailed off at the end and his whole face wrinkled for a split second.

"Wow. Somebody doesn't like Ginger," Lilah teased, trying to get a reaction out of him.

"Why do you say that?" Sebastian said, and his cheek muscles tightened.

"It's just you got a look of something on your face I haven't seen before."

"Everyone likes Ginger. She isn't the brightest bulb, but whatever. She and I had a bit of a falling out, so I just avoid her. No biggie," Sebastian said.

Lilah smirked. "So kind of like a lover's quarrel?"

"Not even close," Sebastian snapped.

"Chillax, I was just kidding." Lilah couldn't help herself from using his words from earlier.

"Yeah, uh, I knew that," Sebastian said, and gave a fake laugh. "You can meet Ginger later. She doesn't seem to be around right now. Let's head over to the games."

"Okay." Lilah took one last glance around. She walked out of the tent and drew in a deep breath. It was still warm, but she could breathe much more easily. They moved on to the games under a blue-and-white spiraled awning and at first watched everyone play. Eventually, though, Sebastian convinced Lilah to throw a few balls.

"Hey, Lilah, try to hit some this time," Sebastian said after her first three failed attempts at knocking anything down.

"Ha, ha," she said, and pictured Sebastian's face on the front bottle. She threw it with all her strength and knocked down eight of the nine.

Sebastian gasped. "Wow, I didn't know you had it in you."

"There's lots of things you don't know about me," she said, and turned to walk to another game. He stayed behind and talked to some of the people running the games.

"Oh, don't let Sebastian get to you so much," a girl with a tan complexion said. She had rosy cheeks and seductive brown eyes and a pretty smile.

"I'm Prisha."

"I'm Lilah."

"It's amazing how he can turn a simple game of toss into a competition or something to pick on people for. He's just kind of like that," she said.

"I was beginning to think it was just me," Lilah commented, and her shoulders relaxed a bit. "Your outfit is really pretty." Prisha wore a striking red-and-gold sari over a pair of jeans. Underneath, she had a red shirt with a spider on it.

"Thanks. I'm a seamstress here. Are you going to be joining us in Nolianna?"

Lilah's eyes scanned the perimeter to see who might be listening. "I, uh, yeah, maybe. I just don't know what I would be assigned to do. I can't sew or design clothes. I'm horrible with fixing things, and I don't really like cooking that much."

Prisha laughed. "There are so many different jobs and things to do in Nolianna. I'm sure you're good at a lot of things. Sebastian talks about you every time I'm around him. He said you've got mad skills."

Lilah's jaw clenched. She wasn't sure how she would fit in here, and talk of Sebastian's interest made her feel uncomfortable and quite frankly, irritated.

"You just have to let your mind be free, and I think you'll fit in here just wonderfully," Prisha said.

Lilah shrugged, unsure of what to say next.

"Come on, let's go ride the Twister," Prisha said, and took her arm. Together, they headed toward the rides. Lilah couldn't quite figure out what it was Sebastian wanted from her—and a piece of her was afraid to find out.

The knots in Lilah's cheeks unclenched and, for the first time in a long time, she felt light. All of the Nolies she'd met other than Kady and Sebastian seemed genuine and kind. Nolianna was growing on her without her even realizing it.

She and Prisha joined several other people and rode the twister, the pirate ship, and the tilt-a-whirl. After the second time on the tilt-a-whirl, Lilah's head started to spin.

"Prisha, I'm gonna get some water. I'll catch up with you in a bit," Lilah said, and meant it.

"Okay, see you in a bit," she said and dispersed with the others to ride the Afterburn, the taller of the roller-coasters that had a straight drop at the end. Lilah was happy to pass on it.

She walked toward an empty wooden picnic table and sat down. A wave of nausea washed over her. Despite feeling nauseous, Lilah couldn't help but feel a little giddy inside. Her whole body relaxed and she was really enjoying the night, even if Joey had taken off again.

She watched people pass or head toward different rides or games. Almost everyone was in a group. Lilah waved to several people that passed. The sick feeling in her stomach went away and was replaced with a hungry growl.

"Hey, whatcha doing?" Sebastian asked, and sat across from her.

"Taking a break. That last time on the tilt-a-whirl did me in," Lilah said, placing her elbow on the table so she could put her palm under her chin.

Sebastian grinned. "Do you want me to get you some something?"

"Actually, that would be great. All of a sudden I'm hungry."

"Sure. What do you feel like?" he asked.

"I don't know. Can we go take a look?"

"Sure, babe, anything you want," he said, and added, "Anything."

"Well, you can start with not calling me 'babe.'"

Sebastian laughed.

"Come on, Miss Always-So-Serious. Let's get you something to eat," he said, and Lilah stood up. He took her arm and steered her toward the concession stands that were placed throughout the field. There was a ton of stuff to choose from.

"I think I want a hamburger and chips. And some water."

"Okay, I'll grab them. Why don't you grab us a table, babe?" Sebastian said, and smothered a laugh.

She rolled her eyes, but let out a little laugh. He was persistent, she'd give him that.

"What do you want on it?" Sebastian asked.

"Ketchup, mustard, pickles."

"You betcha," Sebastian said, and walked up to a stand with a large neon-green sign with the word "Concession" in orange cursive and a picture of pink cotton candy, fried dough, and sodas. She sat down at an empty picnic table and waited for Sebastian to bring over the food. He was surprisingly quick.

Lilah batted her eyelids at him and his eyes sparkled. As much as she wanted to dislike him, she couldn't completely bring herself to write him off. Plus, it was kind of nice to flirt with someone. Joey seemed to have a bunch of admirers, why couldn't she?

"Here you go, enjoy. I brought you a fried Oreo, tonight's special. All of the guests have to have one, er . . . Try one!"

"Thanks," Lilah replied. The hairs on the back of her neck stood up; she didn't like the way he said *had* to have one. Why would she *have* to eat anything in Nolianna?

Sebastian got a burger, too, and they both dug in. Lilah took a few napkins and put them on her lap. In between bites, she asked, "So what's beyond the tent and at the other end of the field?"

"Not letting it go, are you?" he said, and shook his head. "That's just the storage areas, bunkhouses, and places everyone lives when they aren't working."

Lilah strained her head to the left and tried to see beyond the tent. She couldn't see anything but the brightly colored carnival tents, games, and sea of people.

"You can't go back there, though—at least, not yet. I know you'll want to at some point," Sebastian said.

Lilah finished her burger and wiped her mouth with her napkin, ignoring his comment. He was right, though, she had every intention of trying to go back there.

"Here, you have to try this. There's nothing like it," he said, and handed her the Oreo.

"You can have it if you want. I'm so full," Lilah said, and placed it in front of him.

"I've already had three. You go ahead, gotta watch my figure," he said, and patted his mid-section.

Lilah reached over and broke the cookie in half, making him think she was going to eat it.

"Hey, Tommy. Come over here and sit with us," Sebastian called, and motioned to a guy who was standing with two girls. The three of them came and sat down.

"Lilah, this is Tommy, Adira, and Remi," Sebastian said. "This is Lilah."

"Hi," said Remi. "You have the most gorgeous color hair. Is it natural?"

Lilah sat back a bit. "Um, yeah it is. It's gotten a bit darker as I've gotten older. It used to be more orange," she said.

"I wish I had your hair," Adira chimed in.

"No one's *ever* said that before," Lilah said crinkling her nose. It was hard to believe anyone would want to look like her.

"Yep, Lilah doesn't know how pretty she is," Sebastian said. Lilah blushed a deep shade of red to match her hair.

"Hey Sebastian, did you hear about the crazy raccoon who accidently sneaked into Nolianna last year?" Tommy asked.

Tommy wore a navy T-shirt with a picture of spider hanging upside down, but the two girls next to him were in regular clothes, no spiders anywhere. They sat eating fried Oreos.

"Yeah, you want to know what happened?" Sebastian asked with a Cheshire-cat grin.

Everyone moved in closer to him to listen. While Sebastian ate up the attention, Lilah palmed the half of Oreo and placed it in a napkin on her lap.

Distracted, Sebastian jumped into the story about the racoon, and Lilah slowly inched her way to the end of the table. Several others readily took her spot while they listened to Sebastian's story.

"Hey, Lilah, where ya going? I was just getting to the best part," Sebastian said, eying her suspiciously.

At least ten people, most of whom Lilah hadn't even noticed joining their table, turned to look at her and gave her dirty looks for interrupting the story.

"Sorry. I have to pee."

"Okay, but hurry back. We still have a ton of rides to go on tonight," Sebastian said, and then turned his attention back to the growing crowd of listeners.

"Where was I?" Sebastian continued.

Lilah headed toward the bathroom, but instead of going in, she made a quick left and ducked under a rope that was separating the carnival from the rest of the field. She dashed away from the midway toward the forbidden section of grounds, praying no one would notice.

Sliding past some empty, dilapidated buildings, Lilah kept moving until she came to a barn-like structure made out of wood with a blackened tin roof. Metal bars encased the burlap-covered windows, though a light from inside shone through a small crack in a beat-up window. Lilah sidled up to the window and peeked in.

A gasp escaped her mouth.

Inside were hay-filled stalls for animals, but each contained a twin-sized mattress with blankets, pillows, some random navy clothing, and a few personal items. One of the stalls had a small framed sign that read, "Semper Simul." The saying was so familiar to her, but she couldn't remember what it meant exactly and was more concerned with the notion that some of Nolies were actually living in the stalls like animals.

Lilah stumbled backwards and shook her head. It didn't make sense. It's not what Sebastian had told her. Turning to go look at a different building, she took another step and smacked into something large and firm—or rather, *someone*.

Calloused, hard fingers wrapped around her left bicep and yanked her forward. Lilah's body began to shake. Afraid to look up, she took a deep breath and her mind raced, trying to figure out how to explain what she was doing there. She looked up at the giant of a man who stood over her, glaring.

She gulped for air and her lungs burned.

He had to be least 6'6", was bald, and was solid muscle. His jaw had a slight indent, but somehow the rest of his face was off-center and ill-matched. The whole right side of his face was burnt and discolored. Scars continued down his neck. He wore Carhartt work pants and a navy, fitted T-shirt, which accentuated his muscular physique that was caked with dirt. His massive hands were rough, calloused, and tight around her arm. He squeezed so tightly that Lilah could already feel the bruise forming. Her heartbeat galloped at full speed.

He stood, silent.

Lilah squirmed under his grip and continued to stare.

His nose was off-center, and the right side of his lips turned downward. She shuffled a bit to the left and looked into his eyes. She gasped again.

He had one blue eye and one brown eye. She'd never seen anyone with eyes like that, only animals. Without thinking, she moved her free arm upward to touch his face.

He let her touch his cheek gently before stepping back. He yanked her with him.

"Oww!"

A look of concern crossed the left side of his face.

Lilah's insides unclenched a bit.

The guy moved his left hand and pointed toward the main tent. A thin red bracelet on his left wrist drew attention to where a tattoo that looked like the body of a snake or some type of vine went up the length of his arm. Tattoos covered the majority of his body, from what she could see. There were animals, trees, and several words in different languages. There were spiders—lots of spiders. The one tattoo that stood out the most was the word "Ox" that was tattooed on his right forearm. Instinctively, she knew.

"Look, Ox—that's your name, right?" She paused.

He winced.

"Uh, yeah, I know I'm supposed to be over there," Lilah whispered, and motioned backward with her head. She opened her mouth to lie to him and tell him she gotten lost, but something inside of her made her tell him the truth instead.

"Look, Ox, I know I'm not supposed to here. Sebastian said that back here is where everyone lives. I wanted to see it for myself. I didn't mean to pry. I'm sorry."

She told almost the whole truth. She was sorry she got caught, but not sorry she left the main grounds.

Ox reached out with his free hand and touched her necklace that had come out from under the collar of her shirt. She remained still. He turned it over in his large fingers.

"I'm sorry. I won't do it again," Lilah pleaded.

Ox loosened his grip, and Lilah moved her arm a bit.

Without a sound, Ox dragged her toward the rope where she'd snuck in next to the bathrooms. He peered forward and without warning, pushed her under the rope. She was back on the main field with the others without anyone being the wiser.

Lilah turned to thank him, but he was gone.

Turning back around, she stumbled toward a picnic table, sat down, and tried to catch her breath. After a few more minutes, she finally stopped shaking. She breathed a sigh of relief.

Chapter 17

⁂

"**T**HERE YOU ARE!" Joey's voice was music to her unsettled heart. Without a care of who watched, she turned, stood up, and threw her arms around Joey's waist and pulled him tight.

"Hey, you okay? You seem upset," Joey's back straightened.

"I'm fine. Just tired. And happy to see you."

He pulled back slightly. "Uh, okay," he said, and eyed her up and down. "What have you been up to?" he asked. "I just saw Prisha, and she said she thought you were going to catch up with her before the end of the night, but she hadn't seen you."

"Oh, well I wasn't feeling real great after the last few rides, so I took a break," Lilah said, and finally let go of Joey. They took a few steps to the right and sat down at an empty picnic table that wobbled on the uneven dirt when they sat down.

Joey placed a hand on her knee. "Are you okay? You look a little pale," he said, and then added, "And that's saying something."

A shaky laugh escaped her mouth.

"Yeah, I think the last few days are catching up on me," she replied, a lump forming in her throat. "Where have you been? You disappeared again."

"I know, sorry. One of the stages came apart, and I was helping fix it," he said.

"Wow, you don't even live here yet, and you're already fixing stuff," she said, and met his eyes.

"I can't help it. I love it here. And I feel useful. I'm not used to that," Joey said.

"I get it." And she did. What she didn't get was that he never told her where he was off to and that Sebastian always seemed ready to fill his absence.

"I know. That's why I like you so much," he said, and leaned forward to kiss her cheek.

Lilah's cheek reddened.

"Come on, let's head to the arch. It's almost time to leave."

"Good, I've had enough for tonight," she replied.

Joey frowned. "Did you not have fun tonight?"

"No, I did. It's just so much to take in." She debated whether or not she should tell him about her encounter with Ox, but decided it was probably better not to just yet.

"That's my girl." He stretched out his hand and helped her up out of her seat. "Come on, Carrots, let's get you home," Joey said, and they walked toward the front of the tent in silence.

She took a depth breath and let the tension of the past hour go. They arrived at the front of the main tent and arch when Matthew's voice came on over the speaker.

"Friends, the time has come again to part," Matthew said. "Please make your way to the arch. And once again, to health, happiness, and family!"

Lilah could hear cheers throughout Nolianna.

"Thank you for celebrating with us. We're one night closer to becoming a true family. Enjoy your travels back."

Lilah swayed a bit.

"Lilah, are you okay?" Joey asked, and put a hand on her lower back.

"Yeah, I'm just a little lightheaded." Joey handed her winter gear from the pile, and she put it on. Sweat covered her body instantaneously as she joined Joey in line to exit the carnival.

Joey walked in front of her, and she turned to her left and noticed a group of Nolies off in the distance. She squinted her eyes and realized that Sebastian, Ox, and two other large men dressed in navy shirts she'd never seen before stood in a tightly knit circle around someone.

She reached out and touched Joey's arm. "Hey, I forgot my mitten insert. I'll be right back. You go ahead. I'll catch up with you in a minute."

"Okay. I'll wait for you at the bottom," he said, and gave her a peck on the cheek. Making her way to where the clothing pile had been, she kept walking to get a better view of what they were doing. A cloud of dark-brown dust lingered around them. No one else seemed to notice the interaction, including Joey, who had already left and descended the trail.

She got about five steps away from the group when a guy wearing a red trucker hat and polo in the middle of the group fell to the ground with his eyes closed. Ox reached down, scooped him up, and placed him over his massive shoulders. Ox turned to leave, and suddenly the group noticed Lilah. Sebastian bounded toward her, his face muscles taut.

"Lilah, what're you still doing here? You need to leave, now!" he ordered. "And you need to forget what you saw, got it?"

The throbbing veins in his neck popped, and he squared his body toward her, fists clenched at his sides.

She swallowed hard.

Sebastian brushed by, grabbing her by the shoulder, and dragged her toward the bubble and the sunflower-lined trail. The weight of his hands felt like a boulder on her shoulders. In one quick motion, he pushed her forward toward the steep incline. She stumbled, catching a tree branch with her left hand to help steady her and tearing the skin on her palm. She winced.

As she made her way to the bottom of the trail, she felt a sinking sensation in her gut. Her eyes darted all around, but no one waited at the clearing, not even Joey. She clenched her hand and pulled a few pine needles from her palm.

Sebastian appeared behind her. Lilah ignored him and took off toward Abe's. She wanted nothing else to do with him tonight. But Sebastian's long strides let him catch up to her without much effort. Lilah sneered at him, and after walking for a few minutes, Sebastian spoke.

"Look, Lilah, I'm sorry you had to see that. That guy was caught in the living quarters and tried to stay in Nolianna without permission. He wouldn't leave on his own, so we had to make sure that he would leave and not tell anyone else about us."

Lilah stayed silent.

"Understand?" Sebastian reached out and touched her arm. Her arm burned at his touch and she pulled away and then stopped walking. Turning, she looked him dead in the eyes.

"Sure, whatever you say, Sebastian, " she lied. Sebastian peered down at her and a sly smile crossed his face.

"Good. There may be hope for you after all," he said, and continued walking toward Abe's.

Lilah pursed her lips and clenched her fists. Pain radiated in her left hand. She may have been fooled earlier by his charm, but now she vowed to never trust him again.

They made it to Abe's without another word. The sun was beginning to rise over the horizon, and Lilah slipped into the house as easily as she had left. She went straight to her room and frantically wrote down everything she could remember from the night. It took a while for her heart to stop pounding as if it were going to jump out of her chest. She could have just as easily been that guy Ox carried out. Instead, Ox protected her, and she wouldn't forget it, no matter what Sebastian wanted.

Chapter 18

⁂

SUNDAY MORNING came and went. Lilah was awoken several times by the boys who thought nothing of yelling at each other from room to room or even floor to floor whenever they felt like it.

At 3:30 p.m., the sound of metal trash cans being knocked over, set back up, and knocked over again finally made her get out of bed. The boys loved to play trash-can bowling when Abe wasn't home.

She got up and took a much-needed shower. Dirt and black clay still covered her arms and legs thanks to Sebastian pushing her. Just thinking about him made her blood boil. As she let the hot water run over her body, her mind wandered to the night before, and she wondered why Abe and Eva never came to find her or check on her whereabouts the past two nights. Joey had told her they were easygoing, but it was more than that—they really didn't seem to give a shit.

She took her time drying off and then moisturized her skin, which felt strangely leathery. The drastic changes between heat and cold over the past few days had wreaked havoc on her sensitive skin. Her mind turned to Prisha, Ox, and the past nights' events. What happened to the guy? Sebastian was pretty clear she wasn't to bring it up, but what if he was hurt, or worse? Shaking her head, she changed thoughts, not wanting to think that something horrible could have happened to him.

It was amazing, really. Her recall of specific details of her conversations were still crisp in her mind after she woke up, and she could remember the entire night in Nolianna with precision. Her hunch was right—they must put something in the specialty food to blur everyone's memories. No wonder Sebastian refused to eat the Oreos. And come to think of it, she hadn't seen any of the Nolies eating the Oreos either.

Her heartbeat raced. She had to tell Joey. Throwing on some comfortable navy sweatpants, her K-Swiss, a long-sleeve thermal shirt, and a Rolling Stones faded T-shirt, she headed downstairs. The glorious smell of hot cinnamon and sugar wafted in the air, and she followed it to the kitchen where Eva was humming what Lilah recognized as "Sailing" by Christopher Cross.

"Well, hi there, sleepy head. I'm guessing that by sleeping most of the day away means you stayed up most of the night. I hope you had fun," Eva said with a raised eyebrow.

A rush of hot air swept over Lilah's legs from the open oven. Eva was using a toothpick to check several pies.

Lilah stifled a yawn.

Eva laughed and closed the oven door. "Needs a few more minutes," she murmured, taking off lime-green oven mitts.

"Go sit down, dear. I just took some cinnamon rolls out of the oven a while ago. I'll get you a glass of milk to go with them. Just don't let the boys know you got one first. I'll never hear the end of it."

"Thank you, Eva," Lilah replied, and did as she was told.

Eva brought over the rolls and a glass of milk and placed them in front of Lilah on the lime-and-black checkered placemat.

"Joey stopped over earlier and dropped off your book.

You forgot it at his place last night," Eva said, and pointed to the book on the table.

Lilah reached out and turned it over. *Frankenstein.* It wasn't hers, but she figured Joey was trying to tell her something.

"Oh, *that's* where I left it. I was wondering."

Eva walked over to the gray laminate counter and started putting dishes away. Lilah opened the book and saw a folded note on the inside cover. She closed the book and ate her roll in three bites. After gulping her milk, she wiped away her milk mustache and got up from the table.

"Eva, I'm going to head up to my room and read for a bit," she said, and placed her dishes in the dishwasher. "The rolls were delish. Thanks."

"Hmm, hmm," Eva gestured over shoulder, and Lilah briskly exited the kitchen.

"Family dinner's at six. Don't be late!" Eva yelled.

"Got it!" Lilah sprinted upstairs, taking two steps at a time. She threw open her bedroom door and tore open the book. Grabbing the note, she ripped it open, and plopped down on her bed to read.

Carrots, meet me up on the roof at 5:00. X ~ J

Lilah let out a little giggle. The digital alarm clock on her dresser flashed 4:58 p.m. Without wasting a moment, she brushed her hair, ran her tongue over her front teeth, and threw on an extra layer beneath her sweatshirt. She opened her window enough to slip through and pulled it almost closed, wedging *Frankenstein* in between the sill and window. Holding her breath with each shaky step up the rickety metal stairs, she made her way to the roof in a matter of seconds.

"Hey, beautiful," Joey said. He was waiting, leaning back against the house peak with one foot up behind him. Her heart skipped a beat.

"Hey, yourself." He wore a navy-blue sweatshirt, and his hair was tousled from the wind. Tingles ran down her spine at the mere sight of him.

"Come here," he said, motioning to her and drawing her into a tight hug once she was beside him. She pulled back slightly and stood on her tiptoes to brush her lips against his.

"Where were you this morning?" she asked. "You didn't wait for me to walk back."

"The guy who came in after me said you were talking to Sebastian and that he offered to walk you back. I didn't want to get in the way, so I just went ahead," Joey said. His face scrunched at his cheeks and his shoulders tensed. "Should I have waited?"

"No, it was fine. I, um . . . actually, yes. You should have," Lilah sighed, and added, "I just wanted to walk back with you, that's all."

"Sorry. This whole thing is new to me. I love spending time with you, but I also don't want you to feel like I'm trying to keep you to myself."

She leaned in closer to him, placed her head on his shoulder, and inhaled the intoxicating smells of soap, sandalwood, pumpkin spice, and all that was good in the world. He held her tight and after a minute, he let go and moved to their usual spot.

She took a seat next to him and leaned into his shoulder. He put his arm around her and took her hand in his. He brushed her knuckles with his thumb and a tingly sensation ran up Lilah's arm.

"What are thinking about?" he asked.

"Me? Nothing really. You?" The image of the guy in the red trucker hat flashed in her mind, along with Sebastian's reaction. Lilah's hearbeat quickened.

"Oh, I was just thinking about being here with you. It's nice. I can't remember ever being with someone like you," he said.

"What do you mean, like me?" She raised an eyebrow.

He gave her a goofy grin and squeezed her hand. "I mean, I'm comfortable around you. I can be myself. I know we haven't been around each other in a long time, but I feel like I've known you forever. It's not like when I'm around other people, or even in Nolianna."

Lilah leaned away from him a bit. "But every time we get around the other people, you disappear. I just thought maybe you didn't want to be around me."

Joey's forehead wrinkled and it was his turn to pull away slightly.

"It's just that you flip-flop. Sometimes you want to be around me and then you just, well, aren't," she added. Lilah knew she had to be honest and had to figure him out a bit more if she were even going to consider going back to Nolianna. She couldn't just let him off the hook. "At school, and even in Nolianna, certain people expect me to be a certain way," Joey said in a hushed voice. I don't want you to see that side of me. They don't get me like you do,"

His words cut like a knife.

"I don't get it. You're comfortable around me, right?" Lilah asked.

"Yes."

"And yet you don't want me to be around you and your friends?"

"I can understand that that's how you'd take it, but no. I don't want you to see me around some people, and I wouldn't even really call them my friends. But I'm different when I'm with them. It's a guy thing."

"A guy thing?" she asked, and raised an eyebrow at him. "Are you embarrassed by me or something?" Shame and fear tangled in her gut doing an all-too-familiar dance. She'd never been interested in anyone like she was with Joey, but she also wasn't going to stand for being treated poorly.

"No, of course not. Just the opposite. *You* should be embarrassed by *me*. I'm not as smart or as together as you are. You deserve better than me."

Lilah turned her head to look at him. "What about in Nolianna? You always disappear. I never know where you go. One minute you're standing by my side, and the next minute you're gone. I end up spending most of my time with Sebastian."

Joey looked around the roof. "We aren't supposed to talk about that," he said.

"I know, but we need to talk. I only went to follow you, and I keep questioning myself. I wanted to be where you are," Lilah blurted out. She didn't care who heard. She needed some answers, or at least reassurance. Nolianna rules were of no importance to her.

Joey turned his head and locked eyes. His facial muscles softened. "Lilah, I want to be with you too. I want you to be my girlfriend, actually." He paused nervously. "I'm just trying to figure out how it'll work," he said. He leaned forward and kissed her cheek, letting his lips linger for a moment longer than necessary. Butterflies danced in her stomach. "From the moment we met as kids, you've been with me," Joey said.

"Can I ask you something?" Lilah said, and cleared her throat. The words were stuck and she couldn't swallow. Her mind wanted answers, her body betrayed her, and her heart wanted him. "And please, be honest with me."

"Of course I'll be honest with you. You're the one person I feel like I can be honest with all the time," Joey retorted.

"Where do you go when you disappear in Nolianna?" Lilah cringed. She shifted her body weight to the left.

Joey pulled her toward him. He put his hand under her chin and raised her eyes to meet his.

"Remember how I told you I was really interested in carnivals and all that goes on behind the scenes?"

"Yes, I remember."

"On my first night in Nolianna, one of the activity booths lost power and they couldn't figure out why. I've always been interested in how things work, so I helped figure it out. From that moment on, I became really interested in the set-up and running of Nolianna. The guys who work on that stuff took me under their wing and let me help them."

The pent up tension in her stomach let go, and she let out a big sigh of relief. Something inside of her knew he was telling the truth. Her jaw and neck muscles relaxed. Kady was just trying to get her worked up.

"Why?"

"Sebastian introduced me to Kady, and she said it didn't seem like we were together. I wasn't sure how to take it."

"Oh, Kady. . . . I haven't figured her out yet. I met her the first night of Nolianna. She tried to get me to spend time with her, but I wasn't interested. When I told her no, she got mad and told me that I could forget joining and that I wouldn't be matched with anyone. Sebastian told me not to worry about it though. She has no power in Nolianna."

"Matched?" Lilah asked. "I haven't thought about that much. Who is Kady matched with?"

"She was matched to this guy Axel, but he found someone else last year and dropped her. He said Kady was too moody and mean. Kady's now matched with some girl."

"So you aren't interested in Kady?"

Joey looked at her, his face tensed. "Lilah, don't you get it? I'm interested in *you*. Only you. That's why all of this is so difficult. Before you, I was sure I wanted to join Nolianna, but now, I only want to join if you come with me."

A shudder ran down her spine. "So then we want the same thing—to be together. I'm so glad." And she was, except for the Nolianna part. Her heart sank. "What do we do then? I know how important Nolianna is to you, but I'm not sure it's right for me. Plus, there's a good chance we won't both be picked, and even if we are, we might not be matched."

A deep ache pulled at her insides. Joey was all she had in the entire world.

"I don't have many options. I want to join Nolianna, and I want you to come with me. But I also want you to be happy. If you decided to join, that would solve our problem. If you decided not to, I wonder if maybe, when I leave Nolianna in a few years, we could find each other again and continue what we have now," Joey murmured.

"Joey, I don't think I could be apart from you for so long. Too much could happen." A tear rolled down her cheek, followed by others. Joey put his arm around her and kissed her hair.

"I know. I knew as soon as I said it that it wouldn't work. I just don't know what to do. I want in and you don't. I can't ask you to change your mind. It has to be your decision, not mine. I don't want you to resent me," he said.

They sat for a few moments holding on to each other, and her tears eventually stopped. She could feel Joey's heartbeat racing. Thoughts swarmed in her head, and she wanted to tell him so many things but somehow couldn't find the words. A deep sadness in her core expanded to her whole body, much like the one she felt when she lost her family, and then Pea. It was all happening again.

"I'm sorry," Lilah said, breaking the silence between them.

"What are you sorry for?" he asked. "You have no reason to be sorry. This is such a strange mess we're in."

"I'm sorry that I can't just say I'm going to join you. I'm just not sure right now. I need more time. It's all happening so fast and seems so crazy. Can you give me that?"

"Lilah, I'd give you all the time in the world if I could. We still have a few days and nights together. And who knows, maybe tonight you'll feel differently," he said, and squeezed her tight.

"Right . . . tonight. How is that going work? It's a school night."

Joey looked at her and shrugged. "For me, Danielle could care less if I go out or even go to school. As for you, I asked Sebastian that too. He said he told Eva and Abe that he needed help studying and that you were going to come over to help. They said it was fine."

Lilah shook her head. Sebastian had talked to them? They hadn't said anything . . .

"But what happens when I don't get back until the morning? And what about school?"

Lilah turned and looked straight into Joey's eyes. He squeezed her hand.

"Does that mean you're coming tonight?" Joey's eyes sparkled.

"I'm thinking about it," she said, and looked away. He leaned forward and brushed his lips against her cheek once more, stopping close to her ear.

"Good. Try not to worry about the details and tomorrow. We'll figure it out—together," he whispered. His warm breath on her ear caused a shiver to run up her spine. She turned her head and gently kissed him. He returned her kiss.

Suddenly, the faint sound of Eva's voice could be heard downstairs. She'd opened the back door and called out to the boys. "Boys! Dinner! Go wash up!"

Lilah jumped, and Joey laughed. They both stood up. Joey gave Lilah a hug and quick kiss before he walked around the peak to the planks to return to Danielle's.

"Sebastian's going to stop over about 7:45, so be ready, okay?" Lilah tensed. "Yes, Sebastian," Joey added. "I have to help Danielle before I go, and then I told a couple of the guys I'd help them put up some of the lighting near the games tonight. But I'll also try to come and find you. I want to spend as much time together as we can, okay?"

Lilah looked away. "Okay," she said, dropping her chin down toward the ground. Joey took a few quick steps and took her in his arms. Cupping her chin, he brought her face upward toward his. He brushed his lips across hers one more time. She closed her eyes, and the warmth of his lips radiated onto her. Every muscle in her body tingled. They each stepped closer to one another and held each other tight.

Breathless, Joey stepped back. "Just in case you had any doubts," Joey whispered. Lilah felt her skin tingling all the way down to her toes. "I have to go, or I'll never leave. I'll see you in a bit, Carrots." He turned and disappeared behind the peak.

Lilah stood still and tried to catch her breath. She'd fallen for him hook, line, and sinker. Now she just had to figure out what to do about it.

Chapter 19

❧

"WELL, THERE YOU ARE," Eva said. She was standing at the stove, stirring a large metal pot. "Luckily Abe's running late from the lodge meeting. Dinner's a few minutes behind."

"I'm sorry. I lost track of time," Lilah said and she walked in the kitchen to wash her hands.

"I remember what's it like," Eva quipped in an amused voice.

"What *what's* like?" Lilah asked, and turned slightly so she could see Eva better.

"What it's like to lose track of time when you're with someone you really like," Eva said, trying to get Lilah to say more.

Lilah's pulse quickened, and she turned back to the sink. Eva chuckled.

"Wow. You've been busy," Lilah exclaimed, trying to change the subject. Spread out on the kitchen table and one of the counters were ten pie crusts in pie tins.

"It's fine, dear. Happens to us all," Eva replied, ignoring Lilah's statement.

She tried again. "What are all the pies for?"

"There's a fundraiser for the Veteran's Outreach. I agreed to make six pies but made an extra for us to have after dinner."

"They look delish. Need any help?"

"No, I'm all good. Why don't you head in and watch TV or something with the boys? I called them in a few minutes ago, and they already washed up. We can eat when Abe gets home."

"Okay." Lilah didn't wait for Eva to say anything else and walked out of the room. She went into the living room to see what the boys were watching. The three of them were in their usual spots on the floor, sprawled across the rug with plastic GI Joe toys and soldiers all around them. No one turned to acknowledge her when she entered. She walked by them and took a seat on the couch.

She heard the front door swing open and bang into the wall. The small table teeter-tottered, threatening to fall, and the picture hanging above it shook.

"Oh, look, hard at schoolwork, I see," Abe groaned in the direction of the boys.

He slammed the front door and took off his coat and scarf. He threw them on the bench next to the wall and walked into the living room. Taking the remote away from Brody, he turned toward the TV and clicked on the local news.

"In today's news, a sixteen-year-old male wearing a red trucker hat, matching shirt, and blue jeans was found in an abandoned lot on Stewart Avenue early this morning. Additional details are unknown at this time. He has been taken to Cayuga Medical Center for evaluation and treatment. His condition is critical, and there are no suspects at this time," the male announcer said. "The boy is believed to be a runaway from a nearby county. Due to his age, his identity has not been released."

Lilah gasped, and the boys turned to look at her. She put her hand over her mouth and leaned forward to steady herself. When she did, Abe coughed, drawing her attention away from the TV.

"Eddie, turn that off, now. I hate to see that stuff," Abe said. "Time for dinner. Move it!"

Eddie dutifully got up and turned off the television. The other two boys jumped up and headed into the dining room. Lilah looked at Abe, but he followed the boys down the hall into the dining room.

She stood still and felt a lump forming in her throat. Her hands trembled.

"Lilah, dinner!" Eva called from the dining room. Lilah took a deep breath and shoved her shaking hands in her pockets. She'd lost her appetite but knew she had to join everyone else anyway.

She walked into the dining room with her head down.

"About time," Abe grumbled.

Lilah balled her fists in her pockets. She looked up. Sebastian stood holding out her chair for her to sit down. *When did he get here? Did he have dinner with them every night? So much for a reprieve.*

"Look who just came in through the back door! Just in time to eat dinner," Eva said, and put her hands on her hips.

"Well, go on. Sit. I'm hungry," Abe snarled.

The boys were already seated and stared at Lilah. She moved to her seat and sat down. Sebastian guided the chair for her and then sat down.

"Sebastian, why don't you start the potatoes, and Lilah, the meatloaf," Eva said. They did as they were ordered. The boys had already started in with the beans and rolls. Everyone filled their plate and started eating.

"So Sebastian, why *are* you here?" Abe asked, and then added quietly under his breath, "As if we didn't know."

Lilah picked at her food with her fork. She took a few bites but couldn't really eat. The thought of the guy being taken out of Nolianna consumed her as she pushed her food around her plate. Was he okay? What happened to him? Did the Nolies hurt him? Was Ox and Sebastian in on it? Is that how they handled things in Nolianna? Would Sebastian tell her the truth if she asked? She was pretty sure she knew the answers.

Sebastian looked up from his food. "I told Eva I was going to pick up Lilah for studying tonight, and she invited me to come early for dinner."

Lilah looked at Eva, whose faced reddened a bit, and then she looked away.

"Yeah, I'm sure she did," Abe grumbled in between bites of potatoes.

"Boys, why don't you tell us more about your visit with your aunt?" Eva said. She was good at taking the focus off when things got awkward. Lilah assumed it was a skill she learned being married to Abe.

Lilah ate some of her dinner while the boys spoke. Sebastian eyed her several times during the meal, but she didn't acknowledge him.

"Hey, Lilah, we've got to get going. The study group will be at my place in a few minutes. Are you finished eating?" Sebastian asked.

"Actually, I'm not. I was hoping to have some of Eva's apple pie. Plus, I'm not really sure I'm in the mood to study with everyone."

Sebastian dropped his fork, making a loud clanging noise on the plate. "Oh, um . . ."

Lilah bit her cheek to stop herself from smiling.

"Oh, well, I don't think the pies are finished baking just yet, dear. If you want, I can save you some for when you're done studying," Eva said.

"Thanks, Eva. I guess I'll go get my stuff then."

Sebastian let out a loud sigh and his shoulders dropped. "So, you *are* coming?"

"I guess," Lilah said, and stood up. "If it's still okay with Eva and Abe." She picked up her plate and silverware to take into the kitchen.

"Whatever," Abe said.

"I'll take your stuff into the kitchen and meet you by the front door," Sebastian said, his facial muscles relaxing.

Lilah handed him her dishes and grabbed her coat, scarf, and mittens. Sebastian joined her a few minutes later. The two left Abe's and hurried to the falls.

"You had me going there for a minute, Lilah. Not cool," Sebastian said when they were almost at the falls.

"Yeah, well, you seem to just show up whenever you want."

"Most girls would love all the attention."

"Well, I'm not most girls."

"Obviously," he said. "I really don't know what your problem is. I'm just trying to be nice."

"Nice? You do know that I only like you as a friend, right? And that I'm with Joey?"

They had just about reached the waterfall and a group of people were already waiting for them.

Sebastian stopped and grabbed Lilah's arm. "Look, I get it. Joey's a nice guy and it's your choice who you date. But I'm the one who brought you to Nolianna, not Joey. Just remember that."

Sebastian was clueless. It wasn't just about Joey. What about the guy in the trucker hat that Ox carried out of Nolianna? What happened to him? What did they do to him? Lilah wanted to scream and demand answers from him, but knew she couldn't. He wasn't about to give her an inch.

His tone was stern and facial muscles tensed. Lilah could feel the heat from his body and knew he was angry. The thing was, she didn't care. She wasn't sure why she was even going back to Nolianna other than to be with Joey. What Sebastian said or thought really didn't matter much.

"Whatever, Sebastian. I'll see you later," Lilah said, and joined the rest of the group by the waterfall. It was obvious he had feelings for her and wasn't happy that she was with Joey. The thing was, it wasn't his decision who she was with.

Searching the faces, she didn't see Joey and hoped he was either just running late or had already gone up the trail.

Lilah teeter-tottered from foot to foot. She didn't want to think about Joey not being in Nolianna or what had happened to the guy on the news. Over her shoulder, she could feel the weight of Sebastian's glare and swore she heard him say, "Soon you won't have to worry about Joey anymore."

The hairs on the back of her neck and arms stood up. He'd confirmed what Lilah already knew in her heart. Sebastian wanted Joey out and her to join. She couldn't ignore her instincts any longer. Now she just had to figure out what to do about it.

Chapter 20

☙

LILAH WALKED UP the trail and shaded herself from the light at the top. The sunflowers nearest to the bubble drooped a bit and almost looked like they might be dying. Lilah wondered how they even got there. Turning her attention ahead of her, she saw that about thirty other guests milled around, chatting and waiting to be let onto the field. Lilah disrobed from her winter gear and placed it in the pile to their right.

Without warning, someone came up behind her and swept her up into their arms. Lilah drew in a breath and smelled the mix of sandalwood and soap. She let out a giggle.

"I was wondering if you were ever going to get here," Joey said, and put her down gently. He wore a long-sleeve black shirt. His blue-gray eyes pierced a hole right through her heart and her insides melted.

Lilah bent down to tie her shoe and the ring on her necklace popped out from under her shirt. She reached up and touched it. Being with Joey was so bittersweet. He liked her for who she truly was, but being with him made her miss her family and what had been taken from her. It reminded her what it was to have someone who understood and cared about her.

She stood back up and gazed at him.

"You okay?" Joey asked.

Lilah nodded.

"Hey, cutie, welcome to night seven," Dublin said as they walked by carrying some kind of electrical control panel. "Glad you're back," they said with a wide grin.

Her lips curled upward and she bit her lip. Joey coughed.

"Relax, Romeo. We all know she's with you," Dublin said, and smiled as they passed. "Doesn't mean I can't try."

Lilah let out a little giggle. Dublin blew her a kiss and laughed.

She looked over her shoulder and watched they walked away. Joey coughed again, making her laugh out loud. He leaned over and gave her a quick kiss on the cheek. She opened her mouth to ask him what he wanted to do first when two large bald guys with navy T-shirts with spiders walked up. If Lilah met them anywhere else, she'd probably get nervous. They looked shady at best. It was amazing that every time she was in Nolianna, she saw people she'd never seen before.

"Hey Joey! Come help us fix some of the lights and put up wires," one of them ordered with a slight lisp. They both ignored Lilah.

Joey glanced over at Lilah.

"Go. It's fine. I'll find something to do," she said, and Joey kissed her again on the cheek.

Joey beamed from ear to ear. He didn't wait for her to say anything else and walked off with the two guys toward the back of the field.

Lilah took a deep breath and looked around. The carnival rides had started, and the cacophony of people laughing, the metal-on-metal screeching of rides in motion, the sound of switches being turned off and on, the clanking of horseshoes, and other various sounds echoed through the grounds. Confetti and streamers blowing in front of fans made things around her less visible. Looking down, Lilah noticed that a new layer of hay had been put down in several spots on the field. It crunched beneath her feet while she walked. Sweat formed at the base of her back. She liked to be warm, but the heat was almost too much at times. Walking aimlessly, she passed by most of the games and rides, lost in her thoughts and unsure what she felt like doing.

"Are you waiting for your fortune? Madame Mystique is the best. She has a real gift for reading the cards," said a soft, feminine voice.

Lilah looked up and saw Ginger, dressed in a bright neon-orange T-shirt, tiny black spider earrings, and perfectly braided hair with matching orange ribbon woven intricately through it. She waited for Lilah to speak.

Lilah shrugged.

Ginger pointed upward, and Lilah turned her gaze to the faded, hand-painted sign above their heads that read "Madame Mystique, Fortune Teller Extraordinaire" in front of a beige tent. She'd never noticed the tent or the sign before.

"Oh, I didn't know there was a fortune-teller in Nolianna. Does she, like, read a crystal ball and tell me my future?" Lilah joked.

Ginger laughed. "It's so much better! She reads your tarot cards. Tarot is much more exciting and easier to believe for skeptics like yourself."

Raising an eyebrow, Lilah asked, "How do you know I'm a skeptic?"

"You're wearing away the dirt," Ginger said through curved lips.

Lilah looked down at her feet. They were covered in loose dirt, and she'd worn away all the hay in a small circular area several feet wide. She must have looked like she was pacing and trying to decide if she should go in or not.

"It's okay. I'm actually not much of a believer either. Just don't tell anyone. I'm Ginger, by the way," she said, and held out her hand. She wore a thin red bracelet with silver accents, much like the one Ox had around his wrist.

Lilah shook her hand. "Nice to meet you, Ginger." Lilah said, pretending she didn't already know who she was. "I'm Lilah."

"I know who you are, everyone does. I wanted to meet you the other night, but I didn't get the chance. I've been dying to come and talk with you," she said, and added, "I finally have some time 'cause tonight's my night off."

"That's cool. I'll been looking forward to meeting you too," Lilah admitted, staring at Ginger's neck.

"You noticing my tattoo? Almost everyone who works here has one." Ginger turned to the side so Lilah could look more closely. It was a small black spider, with a faint green outline.

Lilah blushed. "Sorry, I didn't mean to stare. I'm still trying to get used to all of this," she admitted.

Ginger patted Lilah's arm. "Seriously. Last year when I came in, I was lost for like the whole week. I totally couldn't believe a place like this existed. But I can tell you for sure it does. And the tattoos are just a symbol of who belongs and who doesn't."

"I figured. That distinction is becoming obvious," Lilah said.

"Yeah, it would seem that way, but you'd be surprised," Ginger said, and then quickly added, "You know, we all blend together."

Lilah raised an eyebrow.

"You're very perceptive. I think we're going to be great friends," Ginger said, and gave Lilah a broad smile.

"So do you like it here?" Lilah asked.

"I do. I'll admit, it isn't for everyone, though. I love creating and picking out all the colored outfits everyone wears. 'The brighter, the better' is my motto," she said, and waved her hands down the sides of her neon shirt with a giggle. "I've always loved color. Nolianna allows me to be who I am; it allows all of us to be who we are." She grinned at Lilah, but the lines around her eyes drew deeper. Lilah opened her mouth to comment and closed it. She was no stranger to the sadness and fear that often showed on her face despite her efforts to conceal it.

"I've seen you around the tent with Sebastian," Ginger continued. "I spent a lot of time with him last year, but haven't seen much of him recently. He seems to fancy you, though," she said with a sigh.

Lilah eyed Ginger. "Between you and me, Sebastian's fine and all, but I'm not into him that way. I have feelings for someone else," Lilah whispered.

Ginger stood a little straighter and her face muscles relaxed. "Don't let Sebastian hear you say that. He won't like that at all." She paused, looking eager for more information. "Who is it? You can tell me."

"Joey. He's new here too. I followed him here. You may have seen him around."

"Oh, he's cute! I've never seen anyone with that color eyes. Does he like you too?" Ginger asked.

"Yes. We're together, but we try not to talk about it too much or be too obvious or anything."

"Your secret's safe with me," Ginger giggled. "And don't worry, I won't say anything to Sebastian. He can be way jealous and kind of a jerk. I would know."

With those words, Lilah felt an instant bond with her. The flap on the tent next to them opened.

"Next," a rough, deepened, female voice called from inside the draped opening.

"Okay, our turn. And just so you know, Madame takes some getting used to . . ." Ginger pushed Lilah forward and added, "We'll definitely have to talk more later. I like you. We're going to get along great, I just know it."

Lilah felt a warmth rise in her upper body. Something deep in her heart knew she could trust Ginger and that they would be good friends. And the bonus of it was that it would probably piss off Sebastian. All the more reason to get to know Ginger.

Chapter 21

LILAH AND GINGER shuffled forward a few steps and ducked under a large, beige flap. A woman sat alone in the middle of the tent. Lilah couldn't see her face or anything else about her, really. The room was dark and bare except for a single lit bulb above their heads, a small wooden table, two empty wooden chairs on one side and the woman on the other side of the table. They stood on a dirty, red-and-brown oriental rug.

"Well, I know Ginger's not here for a reading—so *you* must be," the woman said flatly in a sonorous, monotone voice. "Sit," she ordered.

"Okay," Lilah replied, wringing her hands nervously in front of her. She sat in the chair directly across from the woman and instantly noticed her smooth olive skin and deep-set, almost black eyes. The teller reached forward and took Lilah's hands.

"Name?" she asked indignantly, looking at Lilah square in the face. An eerie feeling of uncertainty made the hair on Lilah's neck stand up.

"Lilah."

"We'll start with your hands, Lilah. They lead me to your heart and your head. For they, like we, are all connected," the woman said. "I'm Madame Mystique. You may call me Madame."

Something from her evasive tone made Lilah think she didn't want her to respond, so she didn't. Madame had some kind of accent, but it was hard to distinguish. Her tone was direct, yet raspy. The one thing Lilah was sure of was that Madame didn't think a lot of Ginger. She'd barely acknowledged Ginger was there and when she did, her stare was so heavy if it were a laser it would have split Ginger in two.

Lilah drew in a breath and tried to focus. She wiggled her hands a bit to make them relax.

"Goddess mother, join us here as we summon your spirit, your kindness, your wisdom, and all-knowing heart. Bring Lilah what she needs on this night. Protect and keep her in your infinite spirit." When Madame finished her opening, she took Lilah's right palm face up in her own and began examining it closely. Her hand was cool to the touch.

"Next," she said, and pushed the right hand away. She took Lilah's left hand, inspected it, dropped it, and took back her right hand.

"Interesting. In my time, I've only seen this in one other. You have three, not the four," she said, and intently stared at Lilah's hand. She turned it over several times, pulling it close to her face, toward Lilah, and then away again.

"Your third and second lines are connected. It's very unusual. Very few have this. Hmmm," she said quizzically and raised her finger to her lips for a moment.

Lilah looked at Ginger. The grip on her hand tightened and loosened several times before Madame continued talking.

"Most believe the eyes are the key to the soul. You believe this, yes?" she asked, not waiting for an answer. "I believe the hands hold the key to the soul. I'll show you."

"Your life and your love lines are one. Not sure what it means exactly," Madame paused. "They are connected as if in one breath, one heart. Your line of family is short—it barely exists. Your next line has to do with prosperity. You have much and will be blessed with money. It is the length and shape of the connected lines that are strange. It is almost as if it is a necklace that entangles you," Madame said.

At the mention of a necklace, Lilah's heart and stomach both lurched forward.

"What does it mean when those lines are connected?" Ginger asked, and pointed to the long line across Lilah's hand.

"That is not for you to know. And we are not there yet," Madame Mystique snapped at her.

"Sorry," Ginger whispered, and cowered.

Lilah watched Madame continue to inspect her hand and wondered if Grandma Pea had the same lines on her hand as well. A pang of sadness rose up in her chest. She would never know.

"Hold out your left hand, palm up," Madame ordered. A few scrapes remained from her fall. Madame drew in a deep breath before continuing.

"Let me explain. These here show what you are born with. There are supposed to be four lines—the heart, the head, the life, and the fate," Madame said. "Each hand tells us something different. On your hands, the lines on the right hand are connected, which gives you three. The ones on the left are not, so four."

Lilah stared at her.

"Hmmm . . ." Madame held Lilah's hands tightly in her own and brought her face very close to Lilah's left palm. Lilah could feel her heated breath on her skin. She shifted in her chair.

"Your hand is long with an oval-shaped palm. Your fingers are long. You're a water sign, less common than some of the others. This tells me you are perceptive and often sympathetic to others. You are moody. You do what you want and use your intuition as your guide. Your creativity is important, though not many recognize this because you believe knowledge is more important. You are wrong."

Lilah twisted her head side to side slightly and shrugged. Madame was spot on. Lilah had learned to rely on what she knew to be true, though she thought of herself as creative too.

"This top line is your heart. It's rather straight and not long. You are one who is less interested in romance and issues of the heart. It is broken in parts, telling me that you have experienced great pain in your life."

Lilah shuddered.

"The next line is that of the head. This shows that you think realistically and have thirst for knowledge. It is straight," Madame said, and pointed at the line.

Lilah sat still and stared at her. Her heartbeat increased, and as much as part of her didn't want to believe what Madame was saying, the rest of her wanted to know more.

"The next line is your life line, which begins near your thumb and travels in a half circle. You have had major life changes, and its straightness says that you're cautious in relationships," she said, and then added, "Above all, you have a strong being and good health."

Lilah pursed her lips and nodded slightly. She was okay despite all that had happened to her.

"The last line does not show for all, but for you, it is prominent. This line is deep, and so you are strongly con-trolled by fate, though breaks are present. You are prone to changes in life from forces outside of yourself. You like to have control, but life provides many circumstances that you must contend with that are not within your power to change." Madame dropped Lilah's hand and moved her chair back.

"Um, okay. Thank you, I guess." Lilah wasn't sure how to respond to all that she had heard. Everything Madame had said was true, though a little vague. Disbelief swirled in her head—and yet, the truth made part of her believe.

"Stay. I will get my cards," Madame said. Without another word, she got up from the table and disappeared. Lilah hadn't planned on getting a reading, but why not? She didn't have anything else to do, and being with Madame meant she didn't have to be with Sebastian.

Lilah turned to look at Ginger, then fidgeted in her chair. Ginger looked all around and when she saw that Madame wasn't in the room, scooted her chair closer so that their legs touched.

"Hey, I forgot. I've got to meet some people at the makeup tent. Will you be okay?" Ginger asked.

"Uh, yeah. I guess. Is something wrong?"

Ginger looked around again. "No, it's just . . . just take a word of advice, okay?"

Lilah gulped.

"Don't tell anyone about your reading . . ."

Madame returned and sat down again across from them. She glared at Ginger. Lilah looked from Madame to Ginger. She needed to ask Ginger more questions but knew she couldn't with Madame in the room.

"Hey, I have to go. I'll catch ya later, okay?" Ginger said. She looked at Madame the entire time she spoke, and Madame nodded in approval.

"Uh, sure, I can manage," Lilah answered, though confused about why Ginger had to leave so suddenly. A minute ago she'd said she was free all night.

"Okay, let's catch up the next time you come back," Ginger said.

Lilah guessed Ginger was confident that she'd be back. "All right. Thanks for coming with me tonight," she said, and with that, Ginger exited the tent.

Lilah got a sinking feeling that she was missing something.

Chapter 22

ONCE GINGER LEFT, Lilah was alone with Madame. Strangely, it felt like the temperature rose about ten degrees. It made it difficult to breathe deeply. She wanted a better look at Madame and needed something to distract from the heat, so she scooted her chair closer to the table. Something was off about Madame, just like Ginger said.

Madame had to be around Lilah's age to live in Nolianna, but the wrinkled skin around her almost-black eyes aged her well beyond her twenties. Lilah squinted to examine her more closely.

The faded tan lines around Madame's mouth made her look more like a middle-aged woman than teenager. Her long, gray-blue hair wisped around her face while untamed curls cascaded down the middle of her back. She appeared haggard, almost sad, and didn't smile—not once. It was as if a perpetual frown was plastered on her lips. When she spoke, her raspy voice reminded Lilah of someone who'd smoked for over fifty years. She wore a long, flowing dress with bangles and all sorts of jewelry up and down her arms. Her fingers were crowded with silver rings. She didn't seem to have any tattoos, and Lilah didn't see any spiders anywhere on her clothing or accessories.

"So, child, what is it you ask of the cards today?" she asked. Lilah shrugged her shoulders. "You want to know, what is the direction your life is taking?" Madame waited, staring until Lilah inched forward in her chair and signaled that she was ready—or at least impatient.

"Yeah, okay. Why not?" Lilah responded.

"Many others have asked the same. This is not simple tarot, but rather the way of Nolianna and traditions around the world. You will see that it seeks more truth than any simple card trick could teach you. Are you ready to see what the cards have in store?"

"Yes."

Madame Mystique waved her long, sinewy fingers over the deck and closed her eyes. She mumbled under her breath and, without opening her eyes, shuffled the cards several times. Her fingers were quick as she laid them out. Lilah picked five.

Dagger-like red fingernails tapped each card after Madame placed them on the table, right-side down. She placed the cards into a "T" shape and slowly turned the cards over one by one to reveal five colorful pictures. Each had words on them, but not in English.

Madame studied the cards. She sighed loudly several times, tapped certain cards, and placed a finger on another. Her eyes darted back and forth. Hunching over at one point, she brought her face so close to one of the cards that Lilah thought she was putting her head on it. Madame's face scrunched and relaxed, scrunched and relaxed.

Great. Once again, I don't understand. The thought was so absurd that it brought a little smirk to her face.

Madame continued her odd behavior for several minutes. Lilah grew impatient and began to squirm in her chair. She traced the circular pattern on the rug beneath her with her foot. It was as if Madame had forgotten she was even in the tent. Lilah shifted several more times in her chair, crossing and uncrossing her legs.

After at least five more minutes, Madame leaned back in her chair, took a deep breath, and broke eye contact with the cards. She clasped her hands in front of her and looked at Lilah straight in eyes.

"Your cards are very interesting," she said, and pointed to the card closest to Lilah. "This is the present," she said. "The first card you have chosen is the Five of Wands. You see, the men, they are diverse and seem to be fighting each other with their wands. This card shows a current battle—for you, it is between reality and dreams. You have a picture in your mind of what reality should be, but your dreams tell a different story. The number five is significant. Does five represent anything to you?" she asked.

Lilah shook her head.

"Something to think about. The number five often depicts uncertainty and change, a deviation from a plan. This is frustrating and confusing. In this picture, the dragon is reality and it takes fire, energy, to follow what is present in one's dreams. Your dreams are not clear, but the messages they tell you are, if you are willing to pay attention. This card is telling you to trust instincts—for secrets abound. Dreams can tell more than reality," Madame said.

Lilah wanted to respond, but didn't. She believed dreams could be messages from loved ones or the psyche trying to figure something out. Nolianna was all about secrets. It fit with what Madame said.

Madame focused again on the cards. She raised her hands above the cards and waved them in circles. She chanted in another language and closed her eyes again. Lilah sat and watched patiently. It was strange—she had already chosen the cards and had seen all of the pictures. Madame probably needed a moment to make up more mumbo jumbo.

"Next, we focus on the future," Madame said, and pointed to two cards. She turned them over.

Lilah raised an eyebrow when she saw the first card. Someone must have told Madame which cards to use. On top of the card in bold was the word "lovers," showing a picture of a man and woman, both naked under some type of deity.

"I see you smiling. You notice the lovers, yes?" Madame Mystique said, fishing for information. "This is the Lovers card."

"Yes."

"There is man and woman, but also the Angel of Air. This card is love and attraction. Often is about finding your other half. This may or may not be about a specific person. You are happy in a relationship, yes?"

"Yes. I mean, I think so. We haven't really talked a lot about it," she said, all in one breath.

"This card represents love, but also communication. The sun is prominent. She brings warmth and security in a land of green, representing happiness. There is a karmic purpose for this one. Though don't be too quick to judge happiness, for there are snakes and pests present," Madame said.

Isn't that the truth? Lilah wanted to say, but caught herself. Her mind raced to the pest Sebastian, images of spiders, and all of the spider tattoos she'd seen in the past few days.

"You must pay attention to clues. This card speaks of balance. You seek balance, yes?"

"Sure." Didn't everyone?

"What's most interesting is that the card is reversed or upside down. This tells that there is a split between you, a wrenching apart. Some aspect of what you love may be split in two. Is there turmoil in a relationship or the possibility of having to part?"

"Well, that's always a possibility," she said, thinking about Joey. He felt like home to her. And yet, Sebastian and Nolianna split them. Was this what the cards suggested too?

Madame let out a deep breath and bobbed her head up and down. "This card's also blocked. Blocked means the

KINDREDS

upright energy of the card is not manifesting itself. This means that although there is love, there is something that prevents the two halves from being united. There's a choice to be made. You often rush a decision purely on inner desires. You must be careful of the conflicts that will arise within you if you make too rash a choice. Again, you must find balance within," she said.

Lilah's eyes grew wide. Was it possible that Madame knew something Lilah didn't and was telling her not to join Nolianna? Wasn't that against the rules?

"This card is one of intensity when paired with the Lovers. See his horns? This is the Devil," Madame said. She pointed at the card, and the lines around her mouth deepened into a scowl. The Devil couldn't be a good card.

"This may not be what you think, though. The Devil is half god and half goat. The Lovers, when right side up, bring out the best in the Devil. But in this case, they are upside down and their energy is somehow blocking the godly good side of the Devil—your deepest desires. The worst of the Devil is in this one. Often the Lovers bring clarity and a deepened relationship to the Devil. In your case, they aid in his cruelty. You must figure out what is blocking truth and goodness. How might you be aiding that which is not good?" Madame asked.

"So let me get this right," Lilah said. Her voice rose an octave while anger came up like bile in the back of her throat. Her fists clenched. Her emotions were beginning to show more than she wanted—she wasn't sure why! She didn't even believe in tarot readings. "I'm doing something to aid in the creation of evil that is going to prevent me from being with someone I love?"

Madame leaned her body forward and her head came in closer. She dropped her voice to ensure no one else could hear her words.

"Child, as we have seen thus far, you are caught in a fog of reality versus illusion. It's the inner world with which you must concern yourself, not that which is around you. The Lovers can only be parted by the Devil if they remain blocked. It is up to you to change the energy of the surrounding situation. Lovers aren't always who we think they are," she said. "But be warned, you may have to part from someone with whom you deeply love. Whether it is permanent or not will depend on you."

Lilah allowed Madame's words to swim around in her brain.

"Let us move on to the next card. Maybe it will help us makes sense of other parts," Madame said, and pointed to the cards on the table.

"This is the Three of Wands. In this card, the man looks out over the cliff and reflects. While you focus on the inside, you must also compete on the outside. The card represents a powerful battle with fierce and worthy competition. You find a moment in the future when you must stand and face one who is as strong and worthy a contestant as you. You overcome the fear of being seen. You can no longer hide behind your silence. Your future depends upon this," she said.

Lilah leaned closer to inspect the cards. She thought for a moment. "Does the competition have to be with a person, or can it be a place?" she asked.

"It doesn't have to have human form. Competition is anything that competes for your attention and focus," Madame said.

That was easy. Her competition was Nolianna. Lilah closed her eyes for a moment. The room around her spun with all of the new information Madame provided—information that Lilah somehow believed. She needed to shut it out, forget it all. While she shut out the visual world, she breathed deeply. Heat and dust filled her lungs and caused her to cough. Lilah opened her eyes. Madame waited.

"Okay, so what's the last card? It looks like a jester or something," Lilah asked.

Madame paused for a second.

"You have drawn the Fool."

Lilah's eyes widened, and then she let out a roar of laughter that shook her whole body. The tension of the past few moments escaped her body. Her head had been so busy analyzing everything that her body had tensed from head to toe. She hadn't stopped to remind herself where she was, who she was with, and who was in charge of everything in Nolianna. *She* was the fool! For a few moments, she'd actually been fooled into thinking that all Madame had said was real!

"The Fool is dressed in brightly colored clothes and is carrying a small pack. He has a small dog with him and they stand on the edge of a cliff. This traveler doesn't know where he's going and only carries a few worldly possessions. He is much like you after the recent death of your loved one. Will the Fool take note of where he is going? Will you? Do you know?" Madame asked, and again she paused and took a deep breath.

Lilah drew in a quick breath and examined Madame. How did she know about Grandma Pea?

"This is card of great possibilities. You have all that you need to make the trek and be whoever you choose. You're at the start of a new beginning, but you must choose your steps carefully. The cliff is deep and vast. A wrong step and you will stay lost. You do not know yet what you are to do, but use your senses. The answers lie within you. You must balance your head and your heart. You will know what you need to know in the right moment. Trust in the world, that you are always together," she said, and then became quiet.

Lilah's insides twisted and she felt sick to her stomach. Her body swayed back and forth involuntarily. The only words she heard were *always together*.

Those were the words Grandma Pea said to her right before she died. That she would be with her, that they would be always together.

Madame's words swam in her brain, and the questions in her head kept coming. Lilah closed her eyes again. Joey's face appeared, then Grandma Pea's, her parents, and Aiden—the five of them. The people she felt closest to throughout her life. Four of them were lost to her. The thought of losing one more was too much to bear, and tears streamed down her cheeks. The roller-coaster of emotions dragged her up and down again, over and over again. Upside down, right side up. The motion wouldn't stop. She couldn't explain it, but she had never before felt so pulled in all directions. Panic erupted throughout her entire body, and a feeling of nausea washed over her for a second time.

Lilah's eyes opened and darted around the room frantically, but she was all alone. An overwhelming sense that the walls were closing in made her tremble on the edge of sprinting away from the tent. She had to get out of Nolianna and go back to Abe's as soon as humanly possible. An overwhelming sense of doom consumed her, and she needed to write everything down she possibly could.

Her brain scrambled and tried to make sense of what was real and what wasn't. The answers had to be there somewhere. She jumped up and tore out of the tent, running through crowds and finally making her way to the trail. *Screw waiting to be dismissed at the end of the night*, she thought, and left without a word to anyone. On the entire run back to Abe's, the only thing she could hear was *always together*, over and over in her brain.

Chapter 23

THE TRAIL from the gorges was still dark, and the moonlight guided her to Abe's. Not a soul was around when she hit the pavement of the street, and she was relieved to be alone. She had made it back in record time and went right to her room as soon as she got to the house. It was still the middle of the night, and no one at Nolianna had even seen her leave, let alone tried to stop her. She hadn't even bothered to get her jacket or other belongings from the pile and was half frozen by the time she got to her room, despite the sweat dripping down her back from sprinting all the way. It didn't matter—she had to get back to write it all down. Pulling out her notebook from the top drawer of her desk, she grabbed a pencil and wrote down every single detail she could remember about the night and her meeting with Madame Mystique.

After she had described every detail, she grew weary of writing and sank back on her bed. Closing her eyes, she drew in a few deep breaths when she heard clanging noises outside and a tap on her window.

Lilah jumped and opened her eyes.

Joey stood outside her window on the small, black metal platform with the winter clothes she'd left behind in

Nolianna. He waved when their eyes met, motioning with his hands to for her to let him in.

She opened her window and he stepped over the paint-chipped windowsill. He stood in the middle of the room and turned to look at her.

"Here, let me take those," she whispered. The last thing she wanted was for Abe to hear Joey in her room.

"Are you okay?" His voice shook.

"Yeah, I'm fine," she whispered again.

Joey took a step forward and looked her directly in the eyes. "What happened to you tonight? I was so worried. I looked for you everywhere. Is everything all right?"

"Everything's fine, really," she said, a bit puzzled that he'd even noticed she was gone. He'd taken off every time they were in Nolianna and never noticed where she was before.

She wasn't about to tell him anything yet. She needed time. Time to process what happened to the guy in the trucker hat, what Madame had said, how Sebastian kept watch on her, and about her encounters with Ox. There was just so much. It made her head hurt.

Joey stepped forward and put his arms around her. Lilah drew in a breath and answered him.

"I was with Ginger for part of the night, and then I went to have my tarot cards read. It was really silly," she said, trying to be flippant. She didn't want him to know how she really felt. She wasn't even really sure herself.

"Um . . . okay. I guess as long as you're okay," Joey said.

She got on her tiptoes and gave him a kiss on the cheek. "Thank you for worrying about me. You're very sweet," Lilah said and tilted her head backward to look up at him. "I think I am just overwhelmed. The past few days have just been so much to process."

"I just don't know what I would do if something happened to you," Joey said, and pulled her in for another hug. After a few seconds, he pulled back and yawned. "If you're sure you are okay, I'm gonna go get some sleep, and you should too," he murmured. "I'll figure something out to tell Sebastian about why we left early. I don't want him to think we aren't interested in joining."

Lilah shrugged.

"Good night, Carrots."

Lilah felt a warmth envelope her. She loved when he called her that.

"Goodnight," she whispered.

Joey turned and went back out through the window. She watched him go, and he gave her a little wave when his feet hit the ground.

Her insides wanted to burst. She wanted so badly to tell him everything. That Nolianna wasn't what it seemed, even if she wasn't sure exactly what that meant. About how Abe never said a word about her coming home every morning, how Sebastian never left her alone for long, and all about Madame Mystique's prediction that she was going to lose someone she loved—and most importantly, how she felt about him. But the timing just wasn't right. It had to wait. She closed her window and took off her socks, jeans, and bra from under her shirt. Exhaustion crept up and her eyes felt heavy.

She needed more time to think, but the allure of sleep drew her in and enticed her into its web. She only had a couple hours until she had to get up for school. She wrapped her quilt around her, and her body relaxed. She wanted to figure out a way to get out of going back to Nolianna. She didn't believe that Sebastian would let her be with Joey there, and she couldn't risk losing him.

At 7:23 a.m., a loud knock on her door woke her from a deep sleep.

"Lilah, dear, you're going to be late for school," Eva called.

Lilah stumbled out of bed and opened the door. "Eva . . . thanks. I must've overslept. I'll get ready quick."

Eva looked her up and down with a raised eyebrow. "Is everything all right, dear?"

"Yes, I'm fine. Thank you for waking me up. I'll be right down."

"Okay," Eva said, and walked away.

Lilah closed the door and got dressed in a heavy, navy-blue University of Michigan sweatshirt and her favorite Levi's. Her head pounded. She pulled on her black, low-top converse and yawned. Her crazy mess of frizzy curls swirled around her head like always, unmanageable and untamable. She ran her fingers through it and pulled it into a bun with several strands poking out in different directions. It was the best she could do in the time she had. She grabbed her backpack off the small desk chair and headed down the stairs, once again missing breakfast.

"Have a good day," Eva said, and handed Lilah a bagel with cream cheese. "You can eat it on the way to school."

"Thanks, Eva. I'm starved," she said, and took it out of Eva's hand, thankful in the moment for her. "Oh, and I may have to stay late to work on a project at school today if that's okay. I'll be home about dinnertime."

"Of course, dear. An education is important for a girl," Eva said. Lilah shook her head from side to side. Eva was just as ancient as Abe in some moments. She walked out the front door and looked over at Danielle's house. Joey wasn't anywhere to be seen. Rather than be late, she started toward school, hoping Joey would catch up if he saw her.

"That bagel looks good," Sebastian said from behind her.

Lilah's jaw clenched. She had to stay calm and act like nothing had changed. "You want some?" Lilah said, and held out the bagel.

"Seriously?"

She laughed. "Yeah, why not?"

"Nah, I'm good. Where's lover boy this morning? Shouldn't you be sharing that with him?"

"Joey? I'm not sure. I haven't seen him since last night."
That wasn't a *total* lie.

"Trouble in paradise? I heard he was looking for you
everywhere last night, and you were MIA." A slight smile
crossed Sebastian's lips.

"Yeah, well, I left early. I wasn't feeling well, so I came
back to Abe's. Joey's great and all, but he's really unpredict-
able. I never know if I'm going to see him or not."

"I'm sure he's just got a lot to do, ya know, with
Halloween coming up and all," Sebastian assured her. He
moved closer so that their hands were almost touching
while they walked. "Why'd you leave early? Everything
okay? Are you having doubts about Halloween?" Sebastian
asked in a calm voice.

"Well, I'm still on the fence, honestly." A nagging sensation rose in her chest as she waited for Sebastian to ask
more, or try to convince her to join, but he didn't.

"Don't worry, that'll change."

She was about to ask why when they arrived at school
and Mr. Sanders, their gym teacher, walked by.

"Hey, Sebastian, you got a few minutes? I could use
some help in one of the equipment rooms."

Sebastian shrugged. "Sure, Mr. Sanders," he said, and
turned to Lilah. "I'll catch ya later, Lilah, okay?"

She smiled at him. "Sure. How about we have lunch
together? We can work on our Perform-a-thon piece."

Caught off guard, Sebastian stepped toward her.
"Really?" She wasn't sure if he was thrown off by her asking
to have lunch, or work on something she knew he couldn't
care less about. It didn't matter. If she was going to figure
out a way to prevent her and Joey from disappearing with
Nolianna, she was going to have to convince Sebastian to
help her. Without him knowing. And that meant spending
more time with him even if it went against what her heart
wanted.

He coughed and cleared his throat. "I mean, sure. That's cool. I'll see you at the cafeteria."

"Great, see you later, dude."

He chuckled and then walked off with Mr. Sanders. She had him exactly where she wanted him. Turning to walk up the main stairs of the building, Lilah felt a tap on her shoulder.

"Hey, Carrots, what was that all about?" Joey asked. The morning sun warmed the air, and Lilah squinted to see his face. He moved a step to his left and blocked out the sun. "Better?" he asked.

"Mm-hmm." She drew in a breath.

"What's up with Sebastian?"

"Nothing. He was just checking in about us leaving early last night, that's all."

"Oh, okay. Come on, I'll walk you to your locker," Joey said, and took her hand. Lilah looked around to make sure Sebastian wasn't anywhere around to see.

"So, have you given any more thought to . . . ya know?" Joey asked.

It was time to be more honest with Joey and drew in a deep breath. "I have. I'm not sure what I want to do. I just don't see the appeal like you do, though I do want to be with you. Tell me something—what is it about that place that makes you want to be a part of it?"

"All my life I've moved from house to house. Just when I get comfortable in a place, I've had to leave. No one has ever really cared about me other than my mom," Joey said and dropped his head a bit. His voice lowered to make sure only Lilah heard him. "In . . . ya know . . . everyone understands how I feel and has felt that way too. Plus there aren't adults who try to make us follow their rules or pretend that we're their family. I want to be able to be who I am, and I think I can there."

Lilah took in each of his words. They reached her locker and dropped hands. She opened the green, metal locker door. Joey leaned against the locker next to hers.

"But what I don't get is why you can't just wait another year or two when you age out of the system? You'll be on your own then and can do whatever you want."

"But that's the thing. I won't be able to do whatever I want. There'll always be someone telling me what to do. I'm not going to college," Joey said, and tapped his foot on the locker. "Plus, even if I were, I can't pay for it. I don't want to be in school, anyway. I want to work with my hands, and I love the idea of learning how to do all the behind-the-scenes stuff. And I found that in Nolianna. It almost seems like it's too good to be true."

Too good to be true, indeed, Lilah thought, and her mind flickered to the guy in the trucker hat. There was nothing good about the way he'd been treated. Her heart ached for him, and for Joey.

Joey continued, "I don't understand how it all came about or why only a select few can be a part of it, but for the first time in my life I'm part of something bigger than me. There's a family that wants me and that I want to be a part of. No more pretending to be something I'm not."

Lilah clenched her fists and had to force herself to look at him. "You say no more pretending, but you had no problem lying to me that day in the hallway and pretending to be in some band. *And* we pretend we're going to watch movies or go study or whatever when Abe asks us where we're going every night," she said through gritted teeth.

"Look, that's different. And not telling you the truth . . . well, that wasn't my fault. There are rules, and I was following them. It wasn't personal," he said defensively.

Her insides tensed. The problem was that for Lilah, it *was* personal. Nothing good ever came of lying, especially to someone you cared about.

"Okay, but answer me this: Let's say I join, and I'm matched with Sebastian and not you. Then what?"

"Lilah, it's no secret that Sebastian has a lot of pull in Nolianna, and he likes you. You both have a lot in common. He always talks about wanting to go to college after he leaves. He comes on strong, but he's really smart. I don't ditch you on purpose when I'm there, I swear. I just wanted to give you some time to get to know others and was hoping that you would feel the way I do. Even if we aren't matched, we can still be together," Joey answered, sounding as if he was trying to convince more than just her.

Lilah didn't follow his logic. She didn't see how Sebastian and her were anything alike. Her heart started to hurt. She had so much to ask him and tell him—about Ox, the guy in the trucker hat, and the argument she witnessed between him and Sebastian. Knowing she would never feel satisfied until she was honest, she opened her mouth to tell him.

The bell overhead rang.

"I gotta go, Carrots. I'll catch you later today." He leaned down and kissed her before running off in the other direction.

She had to come up with a plan to convince Joey that they had other ways of being together other than disappearing with Nolianna. She had to.

Chapter 24

❧

"AND ONCE AGAIN, Lilah, nice of you to grace us with your presence," Abe barked. "You're supposed to be home after school, helping Eva in the kitchen."

"Now, Abe, I told you she was staying after school today to do some schoolwork. She had my permission," Eva explained.

"Yeah, well, I hope you aren't that hungry, 'cause them three ate everything Eva prepared. Maybe next time you can be home on time and not go hungry," Abe said, and threw his napkin on the table.

The three boys sat smiling. Brody had rice in his hair, and Caleb had a milk mustache. Lilah stifled a smile. Abe stood up and left the table. He was obviously done eating, or at least with everyone at the table.

"Eva, I'm sorry I'm late. I lost track of time working studying."

"Don't worry, dear. Abe's been in a bad mood for the last few days. He always is this time of year when his precious Buffalo Bills are losing and the temperatures turn colder," Eva said. "Why don't you come on in the kitchen? I'm pretty sure I have a little extra set aside for you to eat. You boys finish eating and clear the table," Eva ordered.

The boys groaned.

Lilah followed Eva in the kitchen where she handed her a plate with rice, chicken, and peas. "I always keep an extra plate of food just in case," Eva informed her. "The boys ate all the rolls tonight. Sorry, I didn't think to keep one separate." The boys entered the kitchen one by one to and put their dishes in the sink.

"They were *so* good," Brody said. Caleb snickered.

Eva shot him a look, though it was followed by a smile. She loved that the boys enjoyed her cooking so much.

"Eddie, can you please take out the trash?" she asked after he placed his plate in the sink.

"Okay." He dutifully walked over to the trash can.

"And you two, don't go in there and start bothering Abe unless you want to be sent to your rooms, or worse," Eva warned.

"Yes, Eva," the two boys said in unison, and left the kitchen, sulking.

Lilah took her plate and sat down at the kitchen table. Instead of working on dishes, Eva joined her. Eddie came in from taking the trash out and closed the door behind him. He walked straight past them to join the other boys and Abe.

Lilah shoveled her food in her mouth and pushed her chair back as soon as she was finished. She kicked the table by accident when she stood up and her glass shook, threatening to fall over.

Eva scooped it up and handed it to Lilah.

"If it's okay with you, Eva, I'm gonna head up to my room for a bit to read before going to Sebastian's around 7:45. We have to work on our play for Perform-a-thon more and the draft is due shortly before Thanksgiving."

She prayed Eva would buy it. Part of her was sad that she hadn't been able to put much time or effort into writing the play for Perform-a-thon, and would have liked to have worked on it more, but Eva didn't need to know all of that.

"I don't see why not. You sure are working hard on your schoolwork! I'm proud of you. The boys could learn something from you," Eva said. "Did you get done all you needed to tonight at school?"

"I did. I was able to meet with Ms. Denton for a bit about Perform-a-thon, and being a reference for my college essays. I didn't mean to miss dinner."

Eva stopped drying the plate with the checkered towel for a moment and her face dropped, but then continued. "Oh, no worries. I knew you'd be home," Eva said. "Lilah? Before you go, can I ask you something, just between us?"

Lilah's stomach knotted. There was something mysterious about Eva. She seemed nice enough, but there was something below the surface that caused Lilah's heartbeat to quicken. It might have been Eva's tone, or quick changes in her expressions, but whatever it was, Lilah didn't think she could trust her.

"Sure, Eva," she replied uneasily, wishing she could run out of the room.

"Is everything okay between you and Joey?"

It wasn't the question Lilah expected. "Yeah, I think so. Why?" She raised an eyebrow.

"You seem to be spending more time with Sebastian. Danielle said Joey mentioned something about it."

Lilah stopped pacing and looked straight at Eva. The knot in her stomach turned to a pang of uneasiness. She felt the heat spread up her back to her neck and face. Eva picked up on her response and put her hand on her arm.

"Maybe it's nothing, dear. It's just that I know the two of you had something going and I was surprised to hear you're hanging out with Sebastian. Did something happen to the two of you?" Eva asked. "Are you having feelings for him?"

Lilah's mind scrambled while her mouth fumbled for words. "Well, truthfully, Eva," she said, and lowered her voice, "I really like Joey and things were going fine . . ."

She paused and looked around to make sure no one else was in earshot. "But the more time I've been spending with Sebastian, the more I've started to like him too. Joey's great and all, but there's just something about Sebastian that I'm drawn to."

Lilah was lying, hard. Even the words left a bad taste in her mouth. She may have been attracted to him at first, but he was full of secrets and was only concerned about himself.

"I think maybe Joey and Sebastian have both picked up on it," Lilah added quickly. Something registered on Eva's face, and her eyes almost sparkled for a second. Lilah hadn't figured Eva out yet, but she was pretty sure Eva knew more about Lilah and the guys than she was letting on. It was all just too convenient.

"Well, you know, Lilah, the matters of the heart are always complicated. Sometimes we think we want one thing, but then someone comes along and changes everything. Just be true to yourself," Eva said in a motherly tone.

"I just don't want to hurt Joey. I like him a lot," Lilah said. That was the truth.

"For what it's worth, dear, Joey is a kind and sweet boy, but I have to agree, there's something about Sebastian. People are just drawn to him. I think that you two would make a very good couple," Eva said.

Lilah faked a smile.

"Well, just try and think things through carefully," Eva said, and turned back to the sink to wash dishes.

"Eva, is it okay if I go to Sebastian's tonight then?"

"I don't see why not," Eva replied.

"Okay, thanks. I'm gonna run upstairs and get ready," Lilah said. "Thanks for saving some dinner for me, and for listening. It's nice to have someone to talk to that I can trust,"

Lilah lied again. She still wasn't sure how to interact with Eva. She kept asking questions about Joey, but also favored Sebastian. There was something about the way Eva looked at him when he was over that Lilah couldn't quite figure out. At first she thought it was a motherly look, but there was more to it than that. Eva seemed to know more about Sebastian, Joey, and her than she let on, and yet was never direct with her words. It made Lilah's insides uneasy.

"Oh, no problem, dear," Eva said and started humming.

Lilah ran up to her room, grabbed her sweatshirt, and threw on an extra layer to keep her warm. Then she ran downstairs and pulled on her coat, hat, and gloves. She left the house and stepped onto the porch.

"Hi, Carrots," Joey said. He stood to the side of the porch under an umbrella. The rain drizzled around them and the temperature was dropping. It wouldn't be long before the snow followed.

"Were you waiting for me?"

"Always," he said. Her heart skipped a beat. "Here, you'll want this," Joey said, and handed her another umbrella. "Always be prepared." He leaned down and brushed his lips across hers. "Come on, we gotta get moving," he said, and took her hand. The touch of Joey's hand made her warm all over, even through her glove.

They both had to concentrate on their footing, making it difficult to talk. After they passed the last house at the end of the block and got onto the wooded path, she stopped walking. Joey stopped too.

He turned toward her. "Are you okay?" he asked, his voice quivering a bit.

She gazed up at him and pulled his face close to hers. She kissed him, hard. She needed to feel his lips on her, his body next to her. He kissed her back. Her arms wrapped tight around his body and her hands searched his back, grabbing at his shirt, wishing they had more time together. They broke apart after a moment. The moon reflected in his eyes and Lilah felt a little woozy.

"You're so cold, love. You're shaking. Even your eyes are watering," he said, and grabbed her hand again. "Come on, let's get moving. I know a place we can be warm."

He didn't realize that it wasn't the cold that caused her to shake and her eyes to water.

When the waterfall came into sight, Lilah counted the guests waiting—there were twenty-two, all with their eyes on Sebastian, who was holding court. The smaller crowd just reminded her that time was of the essence. Only two nights remained, and only two nights stood between her and the future she wanted. She just had to convince Joey that he wanted it too.

Chapter 25

҉

THE WATER GUSHED down the rock embankment, making it difficult to hear what Sebastian was saying to the crowd. Lilah stood to the side and waited. The group started moving one by one up the trail. Joey started talking with Kyle while they waited.

Suddenly, Sebastian was beside her. He seemed to sense that she was lost in her own thoughts and waved his hand in front of her face and said, "A penny for your thoughts, beautiful." He held up a shiny penny.

Lilah felt heat rise to her cheeks. He may have been devious, untrustworthy, and not what he seemed, but he still had some kind of power over her.

"I was just wondering what we're all going to do tonight when we can go in. I've been looking forward to it all day," Lilah said with a forced smile. It wasn't a total lie. She was wondering about the night and how she was going to get more information about Nolianna.

"Well, there's a new ride opening up, the Thrasher. It's awesome. We don't usually open new rides while guests are still around, but we decided we would open it tonight after the community meeting," Sebastian said. "And sorry

I didn't catch up with you earlier. I had somethings come up."

She tilted her head and batted her eyelashes wanting him to think she was disappointed but also undertood. Needing him to think she was into him, she wondered if she could convince him to help her keep Joey out of Nolianna without either of them knowing.

A sly grin spread across his lips. "And guess who gets to be the first to ride the Thrasher? It will make up for me flaking earlier," Sebastian said, his words a little too obvious for her. He took her hand in his.

Her stomach dropped. "Oh no. I'm not going on that thing," she said, and backed away from him, pulling her hand out of his grip. She was thankful she didn't end up seeing him during the day, though it was surprising given she offered to have lunch with him.

"What's wrong? Is Lilah afraid of a little scary roller-coaster?" Sebastian baited.

She shook her head yes. "Seriously, come on, Lilah. Don't be such a chicken. I get to be one of the first people to ride it, and I want you to come on it with me. It'll be fun," Sebastian said.

She didn't get a chance to answer.

"Sebastian, come on. It's time to go in," said Jason, a guy Lilah recognized from gym class at school. He was about five foot two and had blond hair and a crooked nose. He turned and walked up the trail.

"Think about it," Sebastian said. "I'll come find you, and you can decide then, okay?"

"Decide what?" Joey said, turning toward her after Kyle left.

Lilah drew in a breath. "The Thrasher opens up tonight, and I want Lilah to be one of the first to ride it with me," Sebastian said.

"Oh, that's cool. You should totally do it, Lilah," Joey said, and looked at her.

Great, even he's in on having me do things I don't want to. Seems like no one cares what I want.

"Hey Sebastian, did I hear you say we have a community meeting tonight?" Joey asked.

"Yeah, we're getting close to the Masquarade and everyone has to make their decision if they're interested in joining," Sebastian said. He looked at Joey and then Lilah. "Tonight at the meeting they'll fill you in on all the details. And before we leave, everyone will receive their envelopes and numbers."

"Come on, we should get moving," Joey said, and started to walk toward the trail. He carefully stepped over the pools of water that Lilah usually stepped in. His long legs were such an advantage.

"Yeah, we should go," Sebastian said. He started to step forward, then said, "The best part of Nolianna is almost here—the matching." He winked at Lilah. Her brow furrowed involuntarily in response.

Sebastian seemed to notice her look and asked, a little more quietly, "Why, Lilah, are you thinking of not joining?"

She tried to recover. She smiled and relaxed her shoulders. "Of course I'm thinking of joining. I know I'm hard to read sometimes, and I'm always asking questions, but between you and me . . ." Lilah leaned in a little closer so that her mouth almost touched his cheek and only he could hear her. "I really do want to be part of Nolianna. I'm just afraid of saying it out loud in case something happens. That seems to happen to me a lot, ya know?"

He looked at her skeptically, though something in his expression had changed. He knew her enough that he probably wouldn't buy her act, but she would do her best to convince him. She had to throw him off his game a bit.

"Uh, um . . . well, I'm sure you won't have any problems," Sebastian said, and took a step backwards. "Let's go in."

They both made it up to the top where the others stood waiting. The field was still roped off and nothing had been opened up yet. Sebastian made his way to the front of the group and pulled Dublin, who was waiting on the other side of the rope, to the side. Lilah moved toward the front of the group, but she couldn't get close enough to the front in time to hear what they said or even read their lips. Lilah clutched her hands together to keep them warm.

Sebastian finished his conversation and waited for Dublin to walk away. He then turned to find Lilah behind him. He placed his right hand on her shoulder. Her heartbeat quickened at Sebastian's touch. He leaned in, and she felt his stale breath on her face. He paused for a moment and chose his words carefully.

"Uh, Lilah. Don't worry about going on the Thrasher with me after the meeting. Why don't you just spend the evening with Joey? That way you can have some quality time with him. I have some things to take care of," he said. His expression was stern, and any sense of playfulness was gone. "I mean, after all, isn't he why you wanted to join anyway?"

It wasn't what she'd expected him to say. "I thought we were going to go on the Thrasher?"

"Looks like we aren't going to open it tonight after all."

"Oh, okay." Lilah looked up at him, her stomach knotted knowing she had to make her lies believable. "Sebastian, please don't assume anything. There are several reasons I keep coming back to Nolianna. This place . . . and some people . . . are growing on me." She reached out and grazed his arm briefly. A little bit of vomit started to rise up in her throat at the thought of being with Sebastian.

Sebastian lifted his chin to survey the nearby area before responding. "Lilah, you go ahead. I'll come find you later and we can talk. I like it—you keep me on my toes. We're gonna be great together." Sebastian turned, ducked under the chain, and walked toward the main tent.

Lilah noticed Joey staring at them, and she walked over to where he stood.

"What was that all about? Sebastian seemed pretty intense," Joey said. "I didn't want to interrupt, but is everything okay?"

His endearing face made her heart skip a beat. She dipped her head down so Joey had to move in a bit to hear her.

"Look, Joey, there are some things I've pieced together about Nolianna that I haven't told you about. I know you want me to trust you and join, but I need to know more before I decide, okay?"

Joey opened his mouth to respond, but then closed it.

"I just need some more answers. Sebastian agreed to find me later and talk. It isn't anything to worry about, I promise. I just want to know what life will be like for me here—for us."

"Okay," Joey acknowledged, but the lines of concern around the corners of his eyes told her he wasn't convinced.

"How about after the meeting we hang out together tonight?" Lilah suggested. "Unless you have work to do?"

Joey perked up. "I promised I'd help a bit with fixing one of the rides, but they can get on without me. After all, I'm not a Nolie yet," Joey said, and gave her a quick kiss. They'd agreed to lay low on the PDA, but she was glad for the reassurance.

Prisha and Kyle walked up and unhooked the chain in front of them, both smiling at Lilah and Joey. Matthew's voice came over the loudspeaker.

"Welcome to Nolianna, once again. Night eight! Congratulations! You are one step closer to joining our family." Everyone throughout the fairgrounds cheered. Matthew paused for a moment before continuing.

"There's been a slight change of plans. The community meeting has been postponed until approximately halfway through the evening. All guests and Nolies on shift B must attend."

The crowd went wild. Everyone clapped and cheered even more. Matthew laughed over the loudspeaker and then added, "As I was saying . . . we'll be closing down all of the rides and tents for the community meeting, which will be held in the main tent. We expect everyone to be there!" The hoots and hollers began again. "Now, tonight is a night of fun and is one step closer to our final Masquarade tomorrow night. Congrats on making it this far. Have fun!"

Loud popping noises from streamers being exploded came along with confetti filling the air. Loud, pulsating, celebratory music penetrated the air and all the guests started hugging one another and high fiving.

Joey grabbed Lilah and kissed her. "Come on, Carrots. We're one step closer to being together. Forget your doubts for one night, please. I don't care who sees us. Just have fun with me!" he whispered in her ear and then kissed her earlobe.

Goosebumps exploded on her neck.

"Okay, I'll try—for you," she said, her voice softening a bit. She really wanted nothing more than to just to be able to relax with him and enjoy their time together. The problem was she didn't know who to trust, not even herself.

Lilah turned her head to see if anyone was watching. The last thing she wanted was someone to tell Sebastian they saw them kissing. Luckily, they were all too busy hugging, laughing, and scattering throughout the field.

Joey took her hand and they walked toward the middle of the carnival, which was back in full swing. Joey was almost giddy with laughter, and Lilah couldn't help but feel her heart swell. She wanted nothing more than stay in the moment with him.

She turned her head slightly to one side, and only then did she see Sebastian, Kady, and Ox standing way off in the distance next to some of the large pine trees on the perimeter. They were in an area restricted from guests and had a perfect view of everything that was happening on the main parts of the field. They glared at her and all three had their arms crossed in front of them. Lilah caught their gaze, and Sebastian turned his back to her.

An overwhelming sense of dread engulfed her. So much for being discreet. She'd blown her plan with Sebastian. The only thing left was for her to enjoy being with Joey for the night and regroup.

Chapter 26

✤

T̶HE NEXT FEW HOURS flew by, and Lilah did her best to forget about Sebastian.

"Hey, slow down you two," Sebastian baulked as they ran past him. He was sitting at one of the red picnic tables by himself. He had a plate of French fries and two fried pickles in front of him.

They stopped and stood on the other side of the table. He glanced at their entwined hands and frowned.

"Hey, Sebastian. Sorry. We didn't see you there," Joey said, and dropped Lilah's hand. It was almost as if Joey instinctively knew he couldn't be close to her when Sebastian was around, even if he would have denied it.

"Are you two having fun? Everyone's commenting on what a cute couple you are," Sebastian sneered. He couldn't hide his distain.

If Joey noticed, he didn't let on, and answered, "Yeah, Lilah and I are having a great time. Figured we'd go on all the rides we could tonight. We can't wait until we can be together all the time here." Joey moved closer and put his arm around her. Lilah wondered if he was baiting Sebastian.

Sebastian gritted his teeth. "I'm glad. That's what you're supposed to be doing, having fun and being together, right

Lilah?" His eyes flashed anger. It was obvious that being with Joey wasn't going to fly.

Lilah smiled and replied, "Yes, it's been really great to just be carefree for a night."

"Here, have some pickles. They were made especially for the guests. You have to try them," Sebastian said curtly.

"Thanks," Joey said, and took a bite.

Lilah took a pickle and held it up to her mouth. Out of the corner of her eye, she spotted Ginger at a nearby concession stand talking to a few other girls. "Hey, there's Ginger. I'm going to say hi. Thanks for the pickle, Sebastian, I'm starved," she said, and walked away. She needed a few minutes to process everything and was so thankful to see Ginger.

"I was wondering when I would see you," Ginger said as she approached. "You okay? You look pale, even for you." The other girls turned and walked away. Lilah was grateful.

"No, I'm not. I just don't know what to make of all of this." Lilah looked around and noticed that other guests were watching her.

"Here, sit down. It must be the aftershock of all the rides. If you don't like all of them, why would you go on them?" Ginger said, a little louder than necessary.

Lilah slid past a large green trash can and threw the pickle in it. She sat down on the top of the picnic table. Ginger leaned in and whispered in her ear, "Don't let him see that he's getting to you. After the meeting, come to the makeup tent. We can talk more freely there. Make sure to come alone. Just tell Joey that you want to learn more about working in Nolianna and that I agreed to show you." Ginger straightened back up.

"Oh, hey, Nova," Ginger said to one of the other girls from the makeup tent who walked by. Nova stopped and looked at Lilah. She had long, pin-straight auburn hair and green eyes. Her bright-yellow shirt was neatly tucked into her dark-blue jeans, which had rhinestones on the back pockets.

"Lilah hates rides that spin. I can't believe they convinced her go on them. Talk about crazy!" Ginger looked right at Nova, who stared at Lilah. "Don't worry, she'll be fine in a few minutes. But she probably won't be going on the teacups again any time soon!" Ginger laughed.

Nova smiled.

"Hey, we've gotta go get ready for the meeting. See you in a bit, okay?" Ginger said.

"Okay, sure," Lilah said. "Bye, Nova. Talk to you later, Ginger."

Nova waved, and they both walked off toward the main tent.

Lilah drew her arms around her and took in a deep breath. She scanned the area around her, and in the distance she saw Ox standing off to the side of the main tent. He stood just far enough away that most people wouldn't see him, and he could go unnoticed. Several guests and Nolies were filing into the tent. Lilah watched Ox for a moment and then decided to go in with the others. She walked to the main entrance and entered the tent. The air buzzed and Lilah's skin prickled. Electricity from all of the excitement was almost palpable in the air. Everyone in the tent chatted loudly and settled into several rows of collapsible metal chairs that had been set up in front of the main stage. The large, red-velvet curtain had been pulled up slightly in one corner to let individuals walk out onto the stage.

Matthew, along with seven other people, entered from behind the curtain and took their seat in front of the group. Sebastian and Kady also came in, sat, and faced the crowd. The heat in the tent rose and the crowd grew silent.

An older guy with dark olive skin and a well-groomed dark beard Lilah hadn't seen before stood behind the podium. He was about six feet tall and wore a navy-blue, silky button-down with slim-fitting dark jeans and black motorcycle boots. His shirt was unbuttoned a few buttons to show his dark, curly chest hair, and he wore several leather bracelets on one wrist, much like the one Sebastian wore on occasion. The black ink on his arms caught Lilah's eye, though she was too far away to make out what they were, exactly. He had the whitest teeth Lilah had ever seen—even from a distance she could tell he'd had work done on them. In a way, he reminded her of a younger John Stamos from Full House.

"Welcome again, everyone. Tonight is the night you've been waiting for," a man in a British accent said, and smiled at the crowd. The crowd consisted of about one hundred people, though only twenty-two were guests based on Lilah's count at the waterfall.

"For those of you who don't know me, my name is Elan. I'm in charge of the events and planning here in Nolianna. It's been a year in the making, but once again we find ourselves at the evening before Masquarade!"

The crowd cheered. Elan smiled and held up his hands to shush the crowd.

"It is with great pleasure that I turn you over to Matthew, our fearless mate and leader." Clapping erupted and several hoots and whistles came from throughout the crowd.

Matthew gave Elan a quick hug and turned his attention to the group. The noise dissipated.

"Welcome, all. For the past year, I've been the leader in Nolianna. The leader is always supported by their partner—in my case, the beautiful Nala. . . ." He pointed to a stunning, thin, straight-haired brunette with an angular nose and high forehead who sat directly to his right. She gave him a perfect, squared-toothed smile, and then flashed it at the crowd and gave them a quick wave.

"It is my job to make sure that the daily operations of Nolianna are in working order and to help assign tasks. All members vote on the leader position, and the majority vote wins the honor of leader for one full year in Nolianna. The votes are cast on night eight, which is tonight, by all current members. Whoever the leader is matched with will become his or her confidant and partner in running Nolianna," Matthew explained. He looked at Nala and they exchanged a knowing glance. Several whistles came from the audience and laughter exploded. Lilah didn't quite understand why.

"All right, all right," Matthew continued. "It's been a great honor to serve you, and my time has come to an end. While this will be my last speech before leaving Nolianna, I am excited for what is to come," he said with a smile. He looked at Nala again, and she nodded her head. It was easy to see how well-rehearsed they were. Everyone continued to hoot and holler.

"Thank you for your kindness. Nolianna has been our home for the last few years and we truly love it. We're sad to have to return to the other world, but our time is up. Before we go, we can't wait to invite ten of you to be the next members of our family in just a few short hours."

Wild applause erupted again.

"Tonight, at the conclusion of night eight, ten of you will be invited to join us as Nolies. This is a great honor, and we are very careful about who is invited to be part of our family. You have until the start of tomorrow's festivities, night nine, to make your decision. Plesase know once you join, you cannot change your mind. Not that anyone ever would!" he joked. The crowd roared. Matthew looked at the others on the stage and bowed. Kady rolled her eyes. He held up his hands again to quiet everyone.

Joey squeezed Lilah's hand and beamed ear to ear. Lilah's stomach dropped.

"Okay, in just a few hours, everyone will receive an envelope with a number inside. Numbers one through ten will have the first chance to join Nolianna. Should someone decide not to join, the next consecutive number will be called until ten new members join. You'll have between the end of tonight and the start of tomorrow night's opening to make your decision. If you agree to join, sign your name on the back of the card and return it upon entrance."

The guests all looked around at each other, no doubt wondering who would be here and who wouldn't. Quiet chatter was exchanged between several clusters of people.

"As you know, upon acceptance, the ten will forgo their life with their current foster family and become a permanent member of Nolianna. You may bring one small bag of personal items with you. No electronics will be allowed, including cameras, pagers, or phones. You each will be matched with a current Nolie who will mentor you and become your companion while here."

Lilah made eye contact with Sebastian, who sat with his arms crossed and leered at her. Lilah's stomach churned, and she felt sick. She wanted to yell or scream or do something to stop the uncertainty she felt down to her toes. Gazing at the row of guests next to her and then at Joey, she noticed that no one else seemed to share her discomfort. Hoots, laughs, and clapping filled the air.

Matthew continued talking over the crowd.

"Okay, that's it, my friends! Enjoy this night! We have the rest of the night to play! Have fun, and we look forward to the future together! To . . ."

"Health, happiness, and family!" everyone chanted together. The clapping continued and everyone began chattering at once.

Lilah stood up and turned to Joey, who threw his arms around her.

"Lilah, can you believe it? We've almost made it. I can hardly wait a few more hours! Come on, let's go get something to eat with everyone! It's a night to celebrate!" Joey started hugging several other guests around him. Lilah wished she could join in his enthusiasm, but she couldn't. He simply did not understand that it might not work out the way he wanted it to.

Chapter 27

⁂

AFTER THE CROWD settled down and dissipated, Joey and Lilah went back out into the carnival where everything was in full swing. The music was pumping, people were dancing and singing, one girl was even doing cartwheels over by the concession stands. The cacophony of noise and commotion made pain break out at the back of Lilah's head. The noise of the rides squeaking as they went round and round, people laughing, and the chaos of people moving around made its pulsing more and more noticeable. The overpowering smell of sugar and cinnamon filled her nose, causing it to twitch. She squinted her eyes and rubbed her temples. Lilah could've cared less about going on any more rides. The pain in her head was stronger than her desire to participate in the night's festivities any further.

"Hey, I hope you don't mind, but I'm going to hang out with Ginger in the makeup tent. My head is kind of hurting," Lilah said, and placed her hand on Joey's arm. They were waiting in line under a blue and white striped awning above a concession stand.

"Uh, okay. Are you all right?" Joey asked, wrinkles spreading across his forehead.

"I'm okay. I just need to get out of the light and noise for a bit. I'm going to find Ginger. I want to pick her brain about how she got so interested in makeup and stuff," she said to Joey.

Joey smiled ear to ear. "That's my girl! Ya never know, you might really like something like that," Joey said. "Have fun, and I'll catch up with you later!" He squeezed her hand. Prisha and Asha, who were in line ahead of them, smiled at her.

Lilah walked around several of the booths where guests and Nolies were knocking over milk bottles, shooting balloons with water guns, and arm wrestling. Everyone she passed had a smile plastered on their face.

"Hey, Lilah, me and some of the other girls are going to work on some makeup while we're on break. Wanna come see?" Ginger's voice came from behind her.

Lilah turned. Ginger was talking in a much louder voice than necessary.

"Sure."

"Well, come on then!" Ginger said, and took her by the arm.

They ducked inside the small white makeup tent. It was more crowded than before with racks of brightly colored costumes that lined the tent walls. There were three makeup tables with naked, lit bulbs surrounding the mirrors. The three tables each housed two stations and all sorts of tubes, brushes, and other kinds of makeup Lilah had no idea what to do with.

"Lilah, this is Nova, who you've met. And that's Violet," Ginger said, pointing to the two girls beside her. Violet's spiral, chin-length black hair was pulled back on one side by a pink clip, and her petite frame made her look younger than most of the other people in Nolianna. Lilah recognized both of the girls as greeters at the front of the tent who also worked the concession stands.

"I didn't believe Ginger when she said you were interested in learning more about makeup. You don't seem like the type who's into that sorta thing," said Nova, who had put on bright-yellow eye shadow to match her shirt.

Lilah wasn't sure how to take what she'd said. Was she complimenting her, or picking on her? "Well, I'm always up to learning new things. Seeing as Ginger asked, I figured I'd take her up on her offer."

"Good for you. You need to be open-minded here," Violet said, giving Nova a bit of a strange look.

"Guys like girls who look their best, and makeup sure helps," Nova replied with giggle.

Lilah tried not to roll her eyes. What was it with girls worrying about what the guys thought of how they looked? Even Eva believed women should be submissive to men. It was so 1950s. She took a seat at one of the three tables, and Ginger began pulling Lilah's hair back with a scrunchie.

"We'll start with some basics. I promise, it'll all look natural," Ginger said. She tipped her head to the left and raised her eyebrows to indicate that the girls would be gone in a few minutes.

Sure enough, after a few moments, Violet and Nova waved goodbye and headed out of the tent. Ginger finished playing with Lilah's hair and then started to paint her face while they talked. Normally, Lilah would have protested, but she was more concerned about talking to Ginger.

"We only have a few minutes," Ginger said in a low, hushed voice.

Lilah sized her up in a quick glance. She knew that with so little time, she had to trust her instincts. They hadn't talked much, but something about Ginger's energy told Lilah she could confide in her.

"What do you want to talk about?"

"Do you know if Joey or I are going to be matched?"

"Not with each other, plus you gotta be careful," Ginger whispered, and then added, "They don't often let people in who are couples. Kinda messes with the dynamics of things."

"But why not? Matthew said we're partnered with another person for mentoring and jobs. Why does it matter if Joey and I are together?"

"Because it makes all the difference. When Nolies choose a match, the hope is that it'll be for the rest of their lives. Now that doesn't always happen, but that's the intent, even if no one talks about it. Having a significant other enter with you can only cause trouble. It happens every year that people do change partners, but no one's allowed to leave Nolianna for good on their own. They must leave with their final partner. It's set up so that the first match should be the only match, and it's difficult to change. The truth is that for girls, there isn't usually a choice."

"That's not fair! Why shouldn't we get to choose who we're matched with and if we leave with someone?" Anger erupted in the center of her abdomen.

"Look, I don't have time to go into all the details, but you must know that if you continue to be a couple with Joey, one of you won't get chosen. And I can guarantee it won't be you," Ginger said. She scanned the tent opening as she talked.

"So what are you saying? That I'll be matched, but Joey might not?"

"Yes, that's exactly what I'm saying," Ginger replied.

Lilah felt a bit of relief. If Joey wasn't chosen, then Lilah wouldn't have to join. It would work out perfectly and Joey wouldn't be mad at her for not joining with him—the choice would be taken away from him. It dawned on Lilah though that Ginger was hinting at something else.

"And let me guess—I'll be matched with Sebastian."

"Yup. That's rumor, at least. Usually we don't know, but it's been all the talk around here, especially because I was matched with him before you were."

Lilah looked at her and raised her eyebrow. "What? *You* were matched with Sebastian?"

"That's what I wanted to talk to you about. Last year when I entered Nolianna, I was matched with Sebastian. I thought the match was going well, but then he dropped me, telling Matthew and Nala that he wanted a new partner. No one asked me, but because Sebastian is in line to be the next leader in Nolianna, he can choose whomever he wants. Rumor is that he wants you," Ginger opined.

Lilah's mind raced with everything Ginger had just said. "Ginger, I'm so sorry. Please know, I have no desire to be with Sebastian, now or ever!" she shouted.

"Shhh," Ginger hushed her, and a smile appeared on her face. "I know that now. Originally I was mad and wanted to meet you so I could force you out, but I like you. I can see the connection between you and Joey. No one, not even Sebastian, could break that. That's why I wanted you to see Madame Mystique. She has a gift of some sort. I figured she'd be able to tell you whether or not being here was really right for you. Her tent is the one place in Nolianna where what is said is unknown."

Lilah sat back, eyes wide. How was it that nothing said in Madame's tent was shared with others?

"I'd guess from your reaction that she told you to be careful," Ginger said.

"Yes, but the thing is, I don't want to be here unless Joey is. He's the only reason I'd join."

"I know that, but you can't let others know. If you or Joey ask Sebastian if the two of you can be together once you join, he'll say yes. He'll say something about Nolianna being a place for happiness, and that if your choice was to be together, you would be," Ginger asserted.

Lilah's heart sank.

"The thing is, he's a liar. Sebastian knows that you only want to join because of Joey. He was hoping that once you were here, you'd want to join regardless of Joey, but that hasn't happened. I'm not sure what they're going to do about it," Ginger said.

"They?" Lilah said, and a wave of sadness swept over her. She was trapped and didn't know how to convince Joey not to join.

"Yes, *they*. There are several groups here. Some are less obvious than others, and all of us are trained to follow orders. Usually it isn't an issue, but the truth is that keeping Nolianna a secret and doing what the leaders want is a top priority for all Nolies," Ginger said, and brushed pink blush across Lilah's cheeks.

Lilah didn't know what to say.

"Let me finish your makeup, someone's coming," Ginger said, and reached for an eyelash curler.

Ginger continued to paint Lilah's eyes, cheeks, and lips while Lilah's mind spun with all the new information.

No one appeared, but it was obvious that Ginger was worried that someone was listening.

"Your hair's so pretty, but you always wear it the same way. I think it would look nice straight or in ringlets. And green is such great color on you. It really brings out the color in your eyes," Ginger said in a louder voice than before.

After a few moments passed, they heard footsteps outside the tent.

"Someone will come shortly. I know you have a lot to think about. Take what you know and choose carefully. I know you love Joey, but you'll only be able to be with him if neither of you join. You've got a few hours left to decide. Please know, I'm here to help if you need me," Ginger said in Lilah's ear.

"Okay, thanks," Lilah whispered. She couldn't help but worry that something might happen to her, or worse, to Joey, if she didn't join. "Ginger, will you help me if things go wrong?"

"What do you mean?" Ginger asked, and a look of concern crossed her face.

"If we both join, but then something happens to Joey, I don't want to be here without him. I don't know what will happen exactly, but I just feel like I may need a back-up plan. Will you help me get out if need be? Can I count on you?"

Ginger gave her tight-lipped smile. "Of course. What are you thinking?"

"I'm hoping it won't come to this, but I think I need to come up with an escape plan just in case.

Ginger bit her lip and looked off in the distance for a moment. Lilah's heart galloped in her chest.

"Of course I will! All you had to do was ask!" Ginger remarked enthusiastically. Lilah threw her arms around her friend.

"Thank you so much. I hope it won't come to that."

"You're welcome, but listen, no matter what, you need to remember one thing. Sebastian wants you. He's very dangerous, and once he makes up his mind, he'll do anything to get what he wants." Ginger pulled back and looked Lilah directly in the eye.

"Got it."

Without missing a beat, Sebastian appeared in the doorway, panting for breath.

Ginger turned her back to him and mouthed to Lilah, *"Anything."*

The hair on the back of Lilah's neck stood up straight. She believed her—every word.

Chapter 28

※

SEBASTIAN TOOK A FEW STEPS forward, beads of sweat dripping into his eyes. He tripped and knocked over a clothing rack. Brightly colored shirts and fabric flew in every direction. A pair of purple stockings landed across his face. Lilah giggled.

"I don't think those are your color, Sebastian. Nice way to make an entrance, graceful," Ginger said, not missing a beat.

Sebastian removed the stockings and threw them on the dirt floor. "Be a dear and pick those up for me, Ginger. Thanks," he said flatly.

Lilah balled her fists. Ginger didn't flinch. Sebastian looked at Lilah and his cheeks turned red.

"There you are. I thought you'd be with Joey," he said, and turned away from Ginger and gave all of his attention to Lilah.

"No. I wanted some girl time. Ginger was just giving me some tips on how to be a girl." Lilah laughed out loud in his direction. "Nova and Violet just left. What do you think?"

"You look really beautiful. Joey's a lucky guy," Sebastian said.

"Well, at least for now," she said, and looked away. "Thanks."

It took Sebastian by surprise. He shifted from foot to foot. "I hope Ginger and you are getting along well," he said, and returned to his usual spying self.

"We are. She was telling me all about the makeup that the girls wear here and how she became such a talent. She even made someone as hopeless as me want to learn a thing or two."

"Don't fool yourself, Lilah. Not everyone needs makeup to look good. And everyone in Nolianna possess several talents, some are just more useless than others. Right, Ginger?" Sebastian said, and rolled his eyes at her.

Ginger didn't seem to notice his distain. She fluttered her eyelashes. It was obvious she still very much cared for Sebastian. Ginger began to clean up the mess he made while he stood and talked to Lilah.

"Everyone can use a little help now and then," Ginger said, and looked at Sebastian for a response. He gave none. "I have to get going though. I'm expected to help with costuming in the back for tomorrow night. I'll see you both later," Ginger said, and looked to Sebastian for an acknowledgement of her leaving.

"Yeah, later," Sebastian said without any emotion or even a glance her way.

Ginger left, and Lilah sat still at the table. She was acutely aware that Sebastian blocked the only way out of the tent. Heat exploded up her back.

"So it's just you and me. What do you think of your new look?" Sebastian asked, and smiled.

Lilah hadn't even looked at herself in the mirror because she was so focused on the conversation with Ginger. Glancing upward at the mirror, a familiar face stared back at her. She gasped.

If she hadn't known better, she would have thought it was her mother staring back at her in the mirror, not herself. Ginger had flattened some of the frizziness from her hair, and now it hung straighter, just like her mother used to wear hers. A lump formed in Lilah's throat, and she was at a loss for words.

"Yeah, you look pretty great. Not that you don't usually. Joey's lucky to have you," Sebastian sneered.

Lilah cleared her throat and turned her eyes away from the mirror to focus on Sebastian.

With a serious look on her face, she stood up and got right next to him. She gently put her hand on his arm.

"Look, Sebastian, can I be honest with you?"

"Sure."

"We're alone, right?" She looked around for effect.

"Yeah, no one's around or can hear us," he said. Lilah's stomach turned over. This was her one chance to get Sebastian on her side. If she could convince him to block Joey from joining, she wouldn't have to join and she and Joey could be together.

"I like Joey. He was the first person I saw at Abe's the day I moved in after Grandma Pea died. He's been really nice to me, and things have been moving kind of fast. The thing is, as I get to know him, I realize more and more that he isn't really that deep."

Sebastian looked at her and raised his eyebrow in suspicion.

"Don't get me wrong, he's cute and sweet and all, but I don't see us getting along for the long haul. We have a good time together, but I don't really know him and he doesn't really know me. I worry that if I join Nolianna and he does, too, he'll expect for us to be together. It'll just be awkward for me if he's here all the time. So I was thinking that I'm not going to join."

She kept her eyes laser-focused on Sebastian the whole time.

"But I thought he was your boyfriend? You followed him here to be with him. I saw you kissing earlier. Now you're saying he isn't your boyfriend?" Sebastian said, squinting his eyes in disbelief.

"No, he *is* my boyfriend, but I'm thinking I should break up with him. That way, he's free to join and I won't. I know he really wants to be here, and I think I would too, but I just can't imagine being around him all the time. He's fun and all, but I never intended for it to be anything more than that. I don't know what to do."

Lilah sighed loudly and put her head down. She looked at Sebastian through the corner of her eye.

Panic was flashing across his face and his eyes darted around the room. He drew in a breath and held it. He tried to cover up his reaction and relax his facial muscles without much success.

"So if Joey wasn't here, you'd consider being part of Nolianna? I thought you didn't have any interest in being here. I mean, you have a lot going for you out there. Why would you want to be here?" Sebastian asked.

She shifted in her seat.

"You're right. At first I had no interest in being here, and I did only come because I followed Joey. Since being here I've met some really great people, like Ginger. I think I would fit in well, and I really don't have a lot I would be leaving behind. I have to admit, it's not what I planned, but neither was losing my family."

Sebastian paused and looked at her.

Lilah's eyes misted over. It was easy to access tears even if the reason she was crying wasn't what Sebastian thought.

"Well, we'll just have to wait and see. I think you could be here and have a really great life regardless of what Joey does. I'll let you in on a secret. Ginger and I were matched last year. Did she tell you that?" Sebastian asked, clearly trying to change the subject.

"Really? You and Ginger? I had no idea," she lied. "What happened?"

"We were matched, but we just didn't get along. At first we were attracted to each other, too, but as we got to know each other, we didn't have anything in common. We decided to ask if we could no longer be matched together."

"You both asked to be rematched?" Lilah waited to see if he would tell the truth.

"Yeah, we both asked and were given permission."

Liar, liar pants on fire kept running through her mind.

"See, so even if you and Joey were here together, it doesn't have to be awkward. Just don't let him get to you," Sebastian said. Sebastian's muscles flexed and he stood up straighter.

"Um, okay. I guess. But I still think it might just be easier for me to not join," she said, and shrugged.

"Well, don't be too hasty. Is there anything else you want to know about Nolianna before you have to make your decision? I told you I'd answer your questions for you, and I keep my promises," Sebastian said.

Lilah thought for a moment. She wanted to choose her words carefully.

"I was wondering . . . I know we're matched with someone. What if I don't know that person or don't want to be with them?"

"You'll know the person. You've met most of the people here or will get to know them. Plus, you're matched for your jobs, not personality. That person is like a mentor. It can always be changed," he lied, again.

"But look at Nala and Matthew. They were matched and became a couple. Isn't that what's expected?"

His brow furrowed and he shifted his stance. "Nah, it's great when that happens, but it doesn't always. They're just a good fit."

"What happens when someone leaves? I mean, how does one just reenter the other world after being gone for years at a time?"

"Regardless of when you're here, everyone who leaves is still part of a family. We help each other out. Each year when a group leaves, there's a group on the outside ready to help them create a life. It's actually a really smooth transition. You'll be surprised how easy it is," Sebastian said. "I mean, look at Abe and Eva. They've taken in foster kids and young adults for many years. That's their role on the outside."

"Abe and Eva? They're members of Nolianna? Seriously?" Lilah took a small step back from Sebastian. She'd had suspicion, but didn't think he would just come out and tell her.

Sebastian eyed her and Lilah watched him clench his fists. "Well, sure. Whatd'ya think? How else would they let you come and go as you pleased? I figured someone as smart as you would've put that together early on." Sebastian said flippantly, trying to cover his mistake.

"I sort of thought they might be involved, but I wasn't really sure. It makes sense, though, why they never asked what time I would be back or why I was always going to your house to hang out. So they know I may join Nolianna?"

"Yeah. They both believe in giving kids a chance to build a real family and the space to do that. Nolianna is the perfect place to create family and a sense of belonging we've never had." He took her hand in his before he continued. "The thing is, Lilah, you're special. Most of us come to Nolianna because it's fun and different than the lives we have out there. None of us have family, and most of us don't fit in at school or even in our foster homes. Here we can be whoever we want. Most people can't wait to join. Very few ask the questions that you have. I'm not sure if that's good or bad, but others have noticed. You bring a great deal of analysis to everything you do. That's a skill that can be used in Nolianna. Usually anyone who asks as many questions as you do would be gone after the first or second night, but you're the exception. You're a good fit for

Nolianna and will be an important leader here," Sebastian said.

"Leader? But what if I don't want to be a leader?"

"Every place has leaders. There's a big difference, though, between being a leader and being an authority. People are naturally drawn to you. They want to get to know you and hear what you have to say. I'm not sure you really see yourself that way, but we recognized it the first time you came to Nolianna. We have leaders to help maintain our structure and ensure that every year new members can enter Nolianna. It's an honor to be a leader here. I hope in time you'll agree," Sebastian said.

"I've never seen myself as much of a leader before. I like to keep to myself," she said aloud, to herself more than to Sebastian.

"Come on, Lilah. Some of the best leaders are quiet and strong. That's how I see you. I knew it when I stole your schedule that first day we met," he said. Once again, Sebastian the chameleon was changing the mood so he could flirt and get his way.

"You know, that wasn't very cool. It was hard enough being new, but then to have to rely on someone I didn't know to get around . . . it bothered me."

"You really needed to chill. I was just teasing. I could tell you were all nervous and I thought I'd help you feel less alone," Sebastian said in a calm and sincere voice. She almost believed him.

"Oh."

"You're something special, Lilah. I don't think you even realize it, but I do."

Lilah searched his face for some kind of indication of what he meant. "Let's go out and play some games before it's time to leave. I think you have enough to think about before leaving tonight," Sebastian commented, and put his hands in his jeans pockets.

"Uh, okay." Sebastian's words swam in her head. Once again, she wasn't sure what to believe when it came to him. He seemed to have a caring side, but then his actions showed her otherwise. A piece of her wanted to believe he had her best interests at heart, but her brain refused to accept it.

Lilah walked out into the light again, and her head instantly began pounding. Laughter rang throughout the grounds, and the carnival organ played a joyful, wacky tune. All of the rides swirled and twisted in full motion while everyone ran around playing games, dancing, and eating cotton candy. To anyone else, this was a haven, a place to just play and enjoy being in the moment. To Lilah, it was a headache.

They walked toward the game tents, and Lilah stopped. "I'll catch up in a sec. I just have to tie my shoe," she said to Sebastian, who was five steps ahead of her.

She bent on one knee to tie her shoe when she saw Ox around the side of the tent, carrying a pile of scrap wood. He stopped cold in his tracks when he saw her and stared, emotionless. She smiled slightly to let him know that she saw him.

He didn't respond. A tightness arose in her chest, making it hard to breathe. He always seemed so isolated from the others, to always be off on his own.

She looked down, finished tying her shoe, and stood up to go talk to him, but by the time she looked up, he had vanished.

Sebastian came over by her side. "Hey, Lilah, come on. It's later than I thought, time to go."

Lilah's heart sank.

Chapter 29

LILAH FOLLOWED Sebastian toward the front of the massive red and white striped main tent and archway. His strides were miles longer than hers, and he beat her to the exit where all twenty-two guests were gathering. He held up two fingers to Dublin, who leaned in and listened to whatever Sebastian said. Dublin nodded and walked away. Sebastian made his way in front of the group and held his hands up in the air.

Please don't let Joey get in. Please don't let Joey get in. Lilah shuffled from foot to foot. The air around her prickled her skin, and the anxious chatter made it difficult to concentrate.

"All right, everyone," Sebastian yelled.

Everyone silenced.

"In my hand, I have the envelopes you've been waiting for. As you know, tonight ends night eight, and ten of you will be invited to join us for the remaining ninth night of Carnival Nolianna."

Thunderous applause and screams erupted. Lilah threw her hands up over her ears and turned. A sea of least forty Nolies, some in various neon T-shirts and others in navy blue, stood behind them. Sebastian held up his large hands again. Everyone quieted.

"In a moment, we'll begin passing out envelopes. Inside will contain a number. As you can see, there are twenty-two of you left. Everyone will be given a number. Numbers one to ten will be offered admission immediately. If you receive one of these numbers, you have until entrance time tomorrow night to make your decision," Sebastian orated. He stood with his chin up, projecting his voice so everyone could hear. It was obvious from the smug look on his face he loved being the center of attention. Lilah looked to her left and right; everyone around her was giving him their undivided attention.

"To accept our invitation, you must sign the back of the card, place it in the envelope, and return it to a current member of Nolianna before or upon entrance tomorrow night. If you decide not to join, you're to return the envelope into the black basket on evening nine at the falls or give it to a member of Nolianna without signing it. Once your decision is made, it is final."

"What happens if someone doesn't join?" Kyle's shaky voice came from the back of the group. Several people muttered "yeah" under their breath.

A flash of annoyance crossed Sebastian's face. "I was just getting to that," he continued, and cleared his throat. "If you receive a number between one and ten, and you decide not to join, the person with number eleven will be offered a spot, and so on until all ten slots are filled."

Murmurs and whispers filled the air throughout the crowd. People wondered aloud if they were going to be chosen and what they'd do if they weren't. Two girls were already crying. Lilah couldn't help but roll her eyes.

"Those of you returning tomorrow night can bring one small bag of personal items, no more. All of your wants and needs will be fulfilled in Nolianna, and there's nothing you need to bring from the outside world. Please remember that no phones, cameras, computers, or other electronics are permitted. Your bag will be checked upon entrance. Those who don't have a number under ten, don't worry just yet. Please come on night nine to the entrance of Nolianna, as sometimes there are opportunities to join at the last minute. Okay, let's get started! Please get your winter gear and meet at the edge of the field."

All of the Nolies behind the guests yelled, "To health, happiness, and family!" and then began fist pumping the air and hollering. A sizzle filled the air and all of the guests started hugging, laughing, and chatting noisily.

Lilah planted her feet firmly on the ground, closed her eyes, and drew in a deep breath. The time had come to find out their fate. Never in a million years did she think she would be put in a situation like this. One week ago she was sleeping snuggly in her bed at Grandma Pea's house and contemplating applying to college. Now she was standing at Carnival Nolianna praying she and Joey wouldn't be chosen to disappear.

Opening her eyes, she watched Joey and Sebastian talking together in front of her. She moved to join them, careful not to favor Joey over Sebastian, hoping her talk with Sebastian earlier convinced him not to let Joey in.

"So, here we go," Lilah said and batted her eyelashes.

Joey moved to her side and took her hand. He didn't notice that she focused only on Sebastian.

Sebastian rolled his eyes. Lilah's stomach dropped. "I'll meet you both on the other side of the trail. I have to give out numbers," he glowered and walked toward the shadowy opening by the sunflowers.

"I can't believe it's finally here," Joey said, and kissed her on the forehead. Lilah tried to hide her fear.

Joey paced back and forth. He squeezed her hand so tightly that she was pretty sure she'd have a mark when he let go. She knew how important it was to him to have a number ten or under. And she knew how important it was to *her* for him to have a number over ten.

Dublin, standing in front of them and dressed in tan pants and a button-down navy-blue shirt, said, "Okay, they're asking that all the guys go first. All the guys, please make your way to the trail."

Joey leaned over and rubbed his nose against hers. "I'll wait for you on the other side. Wish me luck!" He rushed forward without looking back.

Lilah stood completely still and watched him disappear down the trail. Several of the girls around her made small talk and bobbed up and down waiting in anticipation of their turn. Needing a distraction, Lilah walked up to Dublin.

"Hey there," they said, and smiled. They had several freckles on their nose Lilah had never noticed before.

"Can I ask you something?" Lilah asked sheepishly. She stuffed her hands in her jeans pockets.

"Sure, shoot," they said.

"Are you the only nonbinary person here?"

Dublin laughed. "Well, that wasn't the question I was expecting."

"Oh, uh, I'm sorry. I was just wondering. It's just that we're always separated into males or females."

Dublin's eyes crinkled in the corners, making their tiny scar disappear. They took a step toward Lilah and put their hand on Lilah's shoulder. She moistened her lips and chewed on her bottom lip.

"I knew I liked you. You pay attention to things other people miss. I went with the guy's side. It's really up to the person to decide. No one here cares what anyone chooses. It just has to fit for that person. You just have to make who you are known."

"Okay, cool," Lilah answered and smiled back at them. "Thanks for letting me ask. I hope I didn't make you feel uncomfortable."

Dublin laughed. "I've been asked a lot more personal questions than that. No worries. Thank you for asking."

Lilah's mouth had gone dry, and she could feel a lump forming in her throat. She wanted to continue talking with Dublin, but knew she had to leave. There was a possibility she wouldn't see them again.

"It's been nice talking with you," was all she could come up with to say.

"You too. Hopefully we'll get a chance to talk more," they said and shrugged. "Looks like it's your turn. Good luck!"

"Thanks," Lilah muttered, butterflies erupting in her stomach. The time had come. She shuffled forward and was the last in line to get her envelope.

"The best for last," Sebastian jested. He held out the envelope. She reached to take it from him and he pulled it way. He crinkled his nose playfully. "Are you sure you want it?"

She stuck her hand out and turned her lip in a pout. She was tired of Sebastian being such a bulldozer. "Please, just give it to me."

"You betcha. Here you go," he said. He grazed her hand with his when she took the envelope.

She took cautiously made her way down the trail, holding her breath the whole time. She held the envelope so hard it wrinkled under her grasp. She walked out from the trail and through the puddle of water from the waterfall. Everyone else was gathered in small groups either hugging or crying. She scanned the crowd for Joey. His back was to her, so she couldn't see his reaction.

"Excuse me. Excuse me," she said, and pushed through several small clusters of people.

When she reached him, Joey turned. He had tears in his eyes. The tension at the base of her neck released. Sebastian had bought it! He didn't get in!

Joey drew in a long, deep breath.

"Lilah. I'm ten. I'm in!" he said. He picked her up and spun her around.

Lilah's whole body stiffened. The tension at the base of her neck returned and made its way to her temples. She had all she could do not to throw up. *How did he get in? What was Sebastian up to? She'd thought for sure she'd convinced him not to let Joey in.* Her heart sank.

"What'd you get? I'm dying to know!" He placed her feet back down on the ground and took her hands in his. They held her envelope between them.

"I don't know. I haven't had a chance to open it. I wanted to wait until I saw you." Lilah's whole body shook. She looked at the envelope and sighed, knowing what it would say.

"Here goes nothing."

She opened it, pulled out the card, and read it.

"Number one. I'm in too."

Joey beamed, his dimples in full force and his stormy eyes sparkling like Lilah had never seen before. Again, he picked her up in his arms, kissed her, and spun her around until they were both dizzy.

"I can't believe it. I can't believe it. We made it! Don't you see, Lilah? We can be together! It's what we hoped for all along!" he said, beaming. He kissed her hard on the mouth.

After a moment, he set her down and she saw Sebastian looking at them. He had a smile on his face, but Lilah recognized the flash of anger in his eyes.

"Congratulations, guys. I knew you'd be excited," Sebastian said, and shook Joey's hand. "Welcome to the family," he said through his fake, smug smile, never taking his eyes off Lilah.

"Thanks!" Joey said, and hugged Sebastian instead. She looked the other way.

The crowd dispersed in different directions and the three of them started walking up the path toward Abe's when the realization of what had happened began to sink in. Lilah's whole body started to ache and the sadness she had been stuffing down began to take over. Hot tears stung the corner of her eyes, threatening to fall. She did her best to stop them, afraid she might not stop crying if she started. If she didn't join, Joey was going to leave her, just like Grandma Pea, and the rest of her family. She'd be all alone in the world once again. Only this time, was there something she could do to stop it? Lilah knew she had a decision to make. Did she go with Joey into Nolianna, or did she let him go without her? Would her heart ever be able to heal if she let him go?

They walked in silence as the morning light began to appear and dawn awakened. Dew covered the grass, and puddles of rainwater were scattered across the road. Before she knew it, she saw Abe's grungy gray house in front of them.

"Night, Sebastian," she said. "See you at school."

She continued walking, not waiting or caring for a response. Joey reached out and touched her arm. "Lilah, give me a sec. I just want to ask Sebastian something," he said. "I'll meet you on the porch in a sec."

She made her way up to the porch and sat on the old wooden swing. Her mind was too tired to race. Her usual million thoughts turned into only one: she had to convince Joey not to join. She would have to tell him everything. They could live at Pea's. He needed to know the truth, or at least what she knew of it. The fact that Sebastian was willing to hurt people who didn't follow the rules like the guy in the trucker hat, and that he kept so many secrets, it only made sense that there was still a lot more he was keeping from her. But she knew in her heart she could convince him if she tried hard enough.

When he was done talking to Sebastian, Joey bounced up the four cement stairs with a single leap.

Lilah drew in a deep breath. Her lungs tightened and her head pounded. She only had a few more minutes before a migraine completely took over.

"Joey—"

"Sorry about that, Carrots. I just didn't want to miss an opportunity." Joey came up next to her and took her hands in his. He sat down on the porch swing next to her.

"No problem. I was hoping we could talk for a few minutes about tonight and the future. *Our* future," she said, with a pit the size of the Grand Canyon forming in her stomach.

"Of course."

Lilah's heartbeat quickened when she realized what Joey had said. "Uh, Joey, what did you need to ask Sebastian just now?" A huge lump formed in her throat and made it hard to swallow.

"I didn't know if Sebastian could take our envelopes, or if we had to wait," Joey said.

A pang in her stomach made her lurch forward.

"Lilah, are you okay?" Joey asked.

She sat up the best she could and looked into his eyes.

"You signed your card and gave it to Sebastian, didn't you?"

"Yeah. I didn't want to wait another minute. I signed it while I was waiting for you and I just gave it to him. I'm now an official Nolie! You can give him yours the next time we see him," Joey said, and squeezed her hand.

Her insides went numb. Tears stung her eyes and the pit in her stomach turned to pain that ran throughout her whole body. She wanted to scream, but when she opened her mouth, nothing came out. Her head throbbed like never before. Joey's words rang in her ears.

I signed it while I was waiting for you.

Was that why they had separated the girls and the guys on the way out of Nolianna? Was it so that she couldn't stop Joey from signing his card?

All she could do was look at him. A look of concern crossed his face, causing his forehead to wrinkle.

"What is it, Carrots?" he asked. "Are you having second thoughts? Please tell me you still want to be with me, and that you're joining Nolianna," he pleaded.

She tucked her thumb safely into his palm and his fingers covered them.

"It's not that," she whispered. "It's just . . ." she wanted to tell him, but it was too late. He'd decided for both of them.

"What is it? You can tell me anything. Please?" he asked.

"Nothing. I just wanted to know what I should pack."

Joey laughed. He leaned forward and kissed her face. "So does this mean you're coming with me? You finally stopped all your analyzing and are going to follow your heart? I can't believe it!"

"I guess . . ."

"Oh, Lilah, you won't regret it. I love you," Joey said for the first time, and kissed her. Her heart wanted to cherish his words, but she already regretted her decision.

"Come on, you'd better get upstairs before Eva or Abe finds us," Joey said, and pulled away from her. "Plus, you look like you're half dead from exhaustion."

He stood up, helped her off the swing, and turned to walk inside.

"Joey . . ."

"Yeah?"

"I love you, too." And she meant it with every fiber of her being. She'd never said that to anyone other than her family, and now he was her family. Being with him was her one solace from losing everyone else. No way was she going to just let him go too.

"You'd better," he joked. "We're going to be so happy together. I'm just glad this whole thing is over. Our decision's made. Nolianna it is, for both of us," he said. "Now hurry up, before we get caught."

He let her go and walked down the stairs to go to Danielle's.

"I'll see you in a few hours, Carrots," he mouthed before walking away.

"See you soon," she whispered, and went into the house. She went straight to her room and collapsed onto her bed. Every last inch of her ached. Tear cascaded down her cheeks.

She did love him, but she had lied. She wasn't joining Nolianna, at least not without a fight.

Chapter 30

THE MORNING SUN shone bright through Lilah's window. She'd tossed and turned, and only slept about three hours when her alarm went off at 9:30 a.m, thankful for late start due to midterms. A bone aching tiredness filled her body and the last thing she wanted to do was get up. The air in her room was warm and stale. She'd forgotten to leave the window open, and the smell of mold had crept in when the heat kicked on. Hopping up, she opened the window to let some fresh air in and got back under the covers.

Her body cracked and a heaviness filled her chest. The hurt was familiar. It had only been a little over a week since Grandma Pea died, but in some ways it seemed like such a long time ago. Sadness lived in her bones. She wished she were happier. Joey loved her, and she him. They had each other. Why wasn't that enough? Why did she have to analyze everything so much? Why did she have to always be so different from everyone else? She wouldn't be in this mess if she could've just been like everyone else.

She sighed and rolled onto her side, hoping sleep would set in again.

"Oww," she said aloud. Something poked her in the hip. She moved over and found a tightly folded paper in a triangle shape. It must have been in her pocket and fallen out at some point.

She sat up and opened it

She took a deep breath and read,

Lilah—

I overheard something tonight I had to tell you. Joey will be matched with me, and you with Sebastian. And they won't take no for an answer for you. I'm sorry. At least we'll be able to spend more time together.

—Ginger

Lilah shuddered. Ginger confirmed what Lilah already knew, that Sebastian would do whatever he could to try and keep her and Joey apart in Nolianna. A wave of relief washed over her; at least if Joey was matched with Ginger, she'd have some chance of spending time with him if they couldn't get out of joining.

Lilah contemplated staying in bed and skipping her study group for midterms. What would it matter if she was going to be gone tomorrow anyway? Instead, she pulled out her notebook and read all that had happened since being forced to live at Abe's: Meeting Joey, he and Sebastian arguing, how strange she felt after first entering Nolianna, how no one else seemed to care what or how Nolianna came to be . . . the more she read, the more questions she had. What would Pea say if she told her that college was on hold because she was joining a carnival? Lilah knew exactly what Pea would say. Don't do it. She'd be crazy to join. But Pea wasn't here anymore. Lilah was alone except for Joey. He was the closest thing to family she had, and she could lose him too if she didn't do things right.

Fighting with her thoughts, Lilah took her time getting out of bed. She changed her clothes, brushed her hair, and headed downstairs to get something to eat. Knowing the study group was useless, she decided to just catch Joey after his first test—if he'd even gone in.

She went downstairs and into the kitchen. The house was unusually quiet, and no one was home from what she could tell. Her stomach gurgled. She grabbed a freshly baked piece of bread off a plate on the counter and shoved it in her mouth. Her head started to pound from the heat in the kitchen. Eva must've been baking before she'd woken up.

Lilah walked over and opened the back door to get some fresh air when she heard Abe and Sebastian's muffled voices coming from the garage. They were inside, so they didn't see her open the door.

She hurried outside and eased the screen door shut without a sound. Taking quiet, quick steps, she rushed over to the side of the garage and crouched behind the dented trash cans.

"Hurry up, you're such a pain in my ass," Abe grumbled. "Eva's going to be home any time now, and she's not going to like any of this one bit. I'm not supposed to be seen with you."

"Look, old man. I've done everything I'm supposed to do. This whole thing is going to be over soon, and it better turn out the way you planned," Sebastian snapped back.

A scraping sound of something heavy on the concrete filled the air.

"Ya know, you could help me out a little."

Sebastian walked out a few steps from the garage and loaded a couple of boxes into Abe's car trunk.

"Looks to me like you can handle it just fine. You're young and strong, Mr. Bigshot-to-be. After all, people will be doing everything for you shortly as long as you stick to it," Abe said.

Abe's words burned her ears. Sebastian was going to be the leader of Nolianna—and if she was going to be matched with him, was she going to be a leader too? She didn't want to be a leader of Nolianna. She didn't even want to join Nolianna. She just wanted to stay with Joey.

Sebastian went back and forth a few times between the garage and the trunk. When he finished moving the boxes, Abe stepped forward.

"You got it all?" Abe asked.

"I think so. The brown boxes all go in, and the stuff in the red box we'll use tonight," Sebastian said.

"Uh huh," Abe muttered.

"And you're sure it's going to work? It won't hurt them, just erase their short-term memory from the past week or two?" Sebastian asked.

"Yup. And the stuff in the other box is the powder with a much lesser dose, just to fog them up for a bit," Abe said.

Sebastian laughed. Lilah's blood boiled. They had been drugging the guests! She'd been right all along.

Fog them up? More like make them forget what they'd been doing! Lilah wanted to scream.

"This is the one you want," Abe said. "Make sure only to use half. It's going to knock him out good. But remember, it's lethal if you give him too much."

"Yeah, I got it. It'll be fine. Joey doesn't suspect a thing. I was worried about Lilah, but she has to join now if she wants to be with Joey. I outsmarted her again. Too bad her little lovebug won't make it to the Masquarade," Sebastian said.

His laugh pierced the air.

The hair on the back of Lilah's neck stood up straight. Her stomach dropped to the dirt ground beneath her feet.

Abe, unimpressed with Sebastian, cleared his throat. "You sure you're good? Not going to screw it up this time, are you?" Abe asked.

"Seriously, I got it. Joey'll black out, and Ox will take care of him from there," Sebastian said in a deep, agitated voice. "He'll be replaced, and no one will be the wiser until it's too late. Ginger will get all dramatic, but I don't care. She's ridiculous anyway," Sebastian said, and started to laugh again.

"If you say so," Abe said flatly, and shuffled some boxes around.

"By the time Lilah figures it out, it'll be too late. Plus, even if she tries to run, Ox'll stop her. It's all good."

"Okay, but what happens if Lilah doesn't join?" Abe asked.

"Oh, don't worry, she will. Lilah will follow him like the lovesick puppy she is. She seems smart, but when it comes to Joey, she's dumb," Sebastian snickered.

A slow growl erupted at the base of Lilah's throat. She clenched her fists, and it was all she could do not to hit something.

"Well, it seems like you've thought of everything," Abe said matter-of-factly. "Let's get the rest of the boxes out of the cabinet and close up for the day. Eva should be home soon. I have to make it look like I came home early for lunch."

Lilah's body shook with rage. The emotion of the past few days rushed into her chest, arms, and head. It was bad enough to lose Grandma Pea and have to move into a new place, but now these people thought they could make choices for her without telling her the truth. They were seriously mistaken.

After peeking around the top of the garbage cans to make sure Sebastian and Abe were back in the garage, Lilah got up and ran to the front of the house, away from the garage. She checked to see if either one had come out. They hadn't.

She made her way into the house through the front door and went straight into the living room. She sat down, grabbed a magazine off the coffee table, and curled her feet under her to make it look like she had been there a while. No more than a minute passed when Abe came in through the back entrance into the kitchen and then into the living room.

"Oh, uh . . . Lilah . . . I, uh . . . I didn't see you there," he said, and avoided eye contact.

He shuffled from foot to foot. He almost looked like a child who'd been caught doing something he wasn't supposed to, not the other way around.

"Did you just get home?" she asked, not giving him an inch.

"Yeah, I forgot my tools and had to come back home. I was in the garage. Skipping school today, are we?"

"It's a late start with midterms for the rest of the week. I got up a few minutes ago. I'm headed out soon." The anger seared in her body and she was becoming overheated. Luckily, Abe wouldn't even look at her.

"Uh, okay. Make sure you aren't late," he said, and walked away.

She waited for Abe to go into the kitchen before she got up. Despite feeling lightheaded, she raced up to her room to grab her bag. She had to find Joey.

Chapter 31

❧

A FEW MINUTES LATER, Lilah tore down the stairs and rushed out of the house. There wasn't a moment to lose and she knew she had to tell Joey everything. It was the only way to stop him from joining.

She stepped out into the street and from behind her she heard, "Hey, Carrots."

Turning, he came into her view. He was wearing a gray hoodie, his hair tousled and wet from a recent shower. A slow, dimpled smile crossed his face. His gray-blue eyes met hers, and her heart melted. He bent and kissed her gently.

"I can't wait 'til tonight. How about you?" he said, stroking her hair.

Lilah caught a glimpse of Sebastian coming from behind Abe's. He was trying to make it look as if he wasn't hurrying toward them. His face was stern, and he half walked, half ran toward them.

"Do me a favor—meet me at lunch in the courtyard in about an hour. Go to the cafeteria first and make up some excuse that you forgot your book or something. Then go straight there. We need to talk. Don't say a word to anyone, especially Sebastian," Lilah blurted out.

Joey looked at her and scrunched his forehead. Sebastian came right up and walked in between them.

"Hey. Joey, I thought you were going to wait for me," Sebastian said, out of breath.

"Sorry, man. I was done with the chores Danielle gave me and thought I'd head out early. Lilah had already left, and I was hoping to catch up with her. And I did," he said, and titled his head in her direction.

"I can see that," Sebastian snarled.

"What's your problem, dude?" Lilah barked back at Sebastian. She moved to Joey's side and took his hand. There was no use pretending that they weren't a couple. She loved Joey, and regardless of what happened, Sebastian wasn't going to change that. Lilah was tired of pretending and trying to appease Sebastian. His bad mood was just going to get worse if she had her way. She smirked and batted her eyes at him.

"Nothing," he said, and looked away. His cheek muscles tightened, and he clenched his fists.

They all walked to school in silence. Joey remained oblivious, and Lilah still hoped her Hail Mary talk with Joey at lunch would work. They got to school and all had to go to their lockers before homeroom. The school had been decorated for Halloween, and several teachers and students were already wearing various costumes and makeup to celebrate.

"Hey, Lilah, we should've dressed up for Halloween. You could have been a carrot," Joey teased.

Sebastian punched Joey in the arm. "Dude, that's not cool," Sebastian defended her without understanding the context.

Lilah started to laugh. "I gotta go to my locker before schools starts," she said to Joey.

Joey pulled her into a tight embrace. She let him hold her for a moment and relished being in his arms. He bent down and gently put his lips on hers.

Sebastian cleared his throat several times. "Look, love-birds, you can do more of that later. Come on, man, I gotta get to my locker," Sebastian said directly to Joey, and kicked the locker next to him.

"No one is stopping you," Joey said, breaking the kiss but not the embrace. He held Lilah for a few seconds longer and then let go.

"I'll see you at lunch in the cafeteria," he said. "Love you." Sebastian pulled him down the hallway.

Lilah beamed. She mouthed, "I love you too," even though his back was turned and he probably didn't see it. It didn't matter. She just had to get through study group, and she prayed that Sebastian wouldn't be able to follow them to the courtyard.

Luckily, no one in her study group cared about going over the class material, so Lilah was able to sit alone at a table to piece together the beginning of a plan in her note-book. She tuned out her group's chattering about some party they were going to for Halloween to force herself to think. It was obvious that they both would join unless she could convince Joey not to, but then Sebastian would have Joey taken out. Disappointment caused her shoulders to drop a bit. They were going to use Ox to get Joey out, just like with the kid on the news. Somehow, she had to stay long enough in Nolianna to make it look like she was going to join, but then get out at the last minute.

Lilah dropped her head down into her hands. How in the world could she pull this off?

And then it came to her. She'd be wearing a mask at Masquarade. All she had to do was get someone to take her place, last minute. But who?

Lilah sat back and placed her hands on the table, causing the chair under her to lift and balance on two legs. And like a lightning bolt hitting metal, the answer flashed.

Ginger!

The answer was there all the time. Of course! Ginger would do it.

A surge of new-found energy mixed with hope filled Lilah's body. Reaching for her pen and notebook, she felt a surge of new-found energy, Lilah feverishly brainstormed several ideas and thoughts.

Her first idea was to try and convince Joey not to join. If she couldn't, they'd go in together. Second, if Joey didn't get taken out of Nolianna, she'd have to join along with him. This thought made her shudder. The last thing she wanted was to give up her dreams of college and creating her own life. She and Grandma Pea worked so hard to make it a reality. Lilah didn't want to disappoint her, even if she wasn't around to see it happen.

Putting the first two ideas aside, Lilah needed to focus on how to escape once she was already there. Abe said Ox would take Joey out, but where would he take him? Would Joey be hurt? The thought of Joey not being okay made Lilah want to throw up. She stopped writing and stared at the paper, her thoughts swarming. Tapping the pen on the paper was all she could do for a moment to try and get the visual of Joey laying on the ground like the guy in the trucker hat out of her mind. Could she convince Ox to take him some place safe? She'd have to try.

Returning her pen to paper, she scribbled down a few more thoughts. Once Joey was out, Lilah would have to find a way to make it out of the portal before it closed without Sebastian stopping her. Biting the inside of her cheek, Lilah wracked her brain.

Thinking through the exact details was difficult because she didn't know exactly how Masquarade worked and whether she'd be left alone long enough to make it happen. A lot of the details would have to be worked out with Ginger when she got there tonight and there was a chance she wouldn't be able to get out in time. Somehow, someone had to switch places with her during Masquarade. The only one she trusted was Ginger, but she was going to be in the ceremony too. How could they pull it off? The thought of being stuck in Nolianna made Lilah want to scream. She was tired of being forced to do things she didn't want to. It was time to make her own choices.

She just had make sure Ginger would go along with it.

Chapter 32

❧

WHILE SHE HADN'T figured out every detail, Lilah was content with what she wrote down. There was a very small margin for error, and getting Ox and Ginger on board was only the beginning. The thing was, she felt drawn to them even though she'd only had a few interactions with them. It wasn't easy for her to trust people given everything that had happened and the secrets swarming around her like a pack of angry bees, but she had to trust her instincts about them if she was going to pull off her plan. Hopefully she could persuade Joey that Nolianna wasn't the place for them and then all of her brainstorming would have been futile. She could hope.

When the bell rang, Lilah stumbled into the hall and rushed to her locker.

"Hey, watch it," a girl dressed as a zombie said when Lilah pushed by her, almost knocking her down.

"Sorry," Lilah mumbled.

"Yeah, right," she said. Lilah grabbed her jacket out of her locker and went into the girl's bathroom. She needed to wait a few minutes until the hallway quieted down.

After a little while, most of the noise was gone, and she exited the bathroom, making her way to the courtyard.

Luckily, it was reasonably warm outside and the sun shone through the clouds just enough for the puddles to shimmer. A slight breeze blew dead leaves across the courtyard. She tapped her fingers on the wooden table as she sat out of view of the window, waiting for Joey. Each time the door opened, her heart skipped a beat.

After about ten minutes, her stomach started to ache. The hope of Joey making it in time to talk was waning.

Just then the door opened and out walked Joey. His mouth turned upward when he saw her, dimples out.

"Hey, Carrots, can I join you?"

"Of course. I was wondering if you were going to show," she replied. He winked at her. Her insides fluttered.

"Oh, ye of little faith. I would've been out sooner, but Sebastian kept trying to make me stay. Luckily, one of the cafeteria workers cornered him. While he was distracted, I snuck out. I'm sure he'll notice, but there's only fifteen minutes left until the bell, so he can't go anywhere, Joey indicated, and then added, "He's in a really bad mood, even for him. I was glad to ditch him."

Lilah sized Joey up. She wanted so badly to just put her arms around him. Instead, she reached her hands out across the table and let out a sigh. He took her hands in his. Tears stung her eyes.

"Hey, what's up? Why do you look like you're going to cry?" He sat forward across the table and squeezed her hands. "Have you changed your mind? Oh my god, are you breaking up with me?"

She shook her head, the tears rolling down her cheeks. "Joey, I love you. I need you to know that," she said, staring at their perfectly entwined hands. She couldn't bear to look him in the eyes.

"Okay, Lilah, you're scaring me. What is going on?" Joey asked, his voice deepening.

"I need to tell you something, and I'm afraid you're going to hate me."

"Okay, now you're really scaring me. What is it?" His voice shook. He sat back a bit and his dimples disappeared.

"I know you have your heart set on living in Nolianna, and it seems like an answer to all your prayers. But you can't join. *We* can't join."

Joey didn't react. "Lilah. You're just having cold feet. It's scary, but we'll be together. That's all that matters."

"No, you don't understand. We *won't* be together. They won't let us," she pleaded.

"They who? Lilah, come on, you don't know what you're talking about," Joey said shaking his head side to side. "It's all just happening so fast. Look, it's one thing if you're having doubts about us, but don't try and convince me that joining's a bad idea. It's my only option. I thought *you* of all people understood that." Joey pulled his hands away from hers and clicked his tongue against the roof of his mouth, producing an unpleasant sound. He pushed against the table and stood up, causing Lilah to lean back uncomfortably to look at him.

"Joey, please don't go! Just hear me out. Abe and Eva are in on it," she revealed, much more loudly than she intended.

He stopped and stared at her. "What do you mean, 'in on it'?" He sat back down with a thud. He put his hands in his hoodie and crinkled his forehead.

"I swear, it's not cold feet. Abe and Eva are part of Nolianna," she explained, and leaned forward, her chin jutting forward. "You remember when I moved in, how weird Abe and everyone was, and they have never once prevented me from going out at night and returning the next morning?"

"Yes."

"That's because Abe and Eva are past members of Nolianna. They want me to join, so they haven't interfered with me coming or going. They're in on it. I don't know exactly how they benefit by us joining, but somehow they do. I overheard Abe and Sebastian talking and Abe confirmed it."

"Are you sure you heard them correctly?" Joey challenged. "I mean, maybe they were talking about something else."

She knew he wouldn't want to believe her. "No. They were talking about Nolianna. And think about it. There's so much we don't know. What happens after Masquarade and we can't leave? What happens after our time in Nolianna is up? I'm pretty sure we don't get a say in it," she blurted out all in one breath. "And there's so much more."

Joey looked at her, his eyes wide.

"Okay, what else," he stipulated in a hushed, restrained voice and tensed his jaw. Joey put his head in his hands for a minute, but remained silent. Lilah took a deep breath and blew it out slowly from her nose. She wanted to give him a minute to let it all sink in.

"I don't understand it all, really, but I don't think we're supposed to. Each night they put some kind of drug in the daily food special that helps fog our memories. Haven't you ever noticed that you can't completely recall all of the details of the night? It's because they don't want us too."

Joey lifted his head, his curls covering his forehead. "So what if they're in on it? At least we can be together." His eyes searched hers, imploring her to get what he wanted: acceptance to join Nolianna.

"But that's the thing, they aren't going to let us be together. Ginger told me I'm going to be matched with Sebastian, and you with her."

Joey shook his head. His face had dropped as she talked, and a red rash she had never seen before appeared at the base of his neck. He didn't say anything, but his fists clenched. "But that's only because we have to be paired to learn about Nolianna. We can switch once we're there for a while. Sebastian told me," he said matter-of-factly.

Lilah could feel the anger radiating down her arms. He wasn't listening, or he didn't want to hear her. "He lies. Don't you see that? Every time I'm in Nolianna, you disappear and I'm left to explore on my own. I met with Madame Mystique and she confirmed that I'll lose someone I love if I make the wrong choice. That person is you," Lilah asserted. She could feel the tears stinging her eyes. "Sebastian, Abe, Eva, and even Kady, they all have it out for us."

Joey cackled in a way Lilah had never heard before. "Kady? Seriously? Kady is just a miserable chick who doesn't like anyone. She's the least of our worries," he replied, dismissing what Lilah was saying.

"You're missing my point . . ."

"No, I'm not," Joey said sternly. "I get it. You're scared about joining. But I'll be there with you. I won't let anyone come between us," he insisted, and reached across the table for her hands. Reluctantly, she reached back.

"No, you don't get it. Sebastian is set on having *me* join, not *us.*"

Lilah searched his face for a sign that he was taking in anything she said and felt a prickling sensation run up her spine when she realized he wasn't. He'd made up his mind long ago. What was the point of telling him anything if he took in nothing she said? He didn't want to truly hear what she had to say, and nothing seemed to change his mind on wanting to join. She didn't even bother to tell him the details of Sebastian and Abe's encounter in the garage, Ox, how Ginger had warned her about Sebastian, the guy in the polo shirt, or even her plans for Masquarade if she needed them. He didn't want to hear her. The crinkling of his face muscles and adamant refusal to accept that joining Nolianna was a bad idea told her all she needed to know.

Joey looked off in the distance and then back at her. "So all this time, I've been thinking Sebastian was my friend, but it's really been about having *you* join. Why you?" he asked in an accusatory tone.

Lilah felt her skin prickle. She hadn't expected him to be so confrontational. It was almost as if he was jealous of her.

"I honestly don't know. I just know that Sebastian's got it in his mind that I *have* to join," Lilah warned.

"Well . . ." he paused. Tears welled up in his eyes. He ducked his head down so Lilah couldn't see, and he placed his elbows on the picnic table. "Why didn't you tell me all of this?"

"I'm so sorry, Joey," Lilah said, and looked away to try and meet his eyes.. He didn't shy away. "I wanted to tell you about my suspicions, but I never really had any proof until earlier when I heard Sebastian and Abe confirm what I thought. I've been trying to tell you ever since," she said.

"Maybe if I talk to Sebastian, I can find more out," Joey proposed, shaking his head.

Her head hurt once once again and the familiar pain seeped in. Joey wasn't going to budge or change his mind no matter what she said. He refused to accept what she was saying.

"No, he can't know what I heard. The thing is, I don't know what we're getting ourselves into if we join. If Abe has been a part of all of this from the beginning, don't you think there might be other things we don't know?" Lilah sniffed and tried to contain the anger that was making her blood boil.

"But maybe you misunderstood," Joey suggested. "The carnival is all I've dreamed of since I was kid. I have to at least talk to Sebastian."

Without her holding back any longer, the pent-up tears spilled onto her cheeks. He had confirmed her worst fear. Joey still had every intention of joining.

"Can't you consider what I've told you and choose the way that we can stay together for sure? Please! I love you.

I don't want to be apart from you. We can run away and move into Grandma Pea's house. We'll be safe there," she begged, and then added, "and together." She scoured his eyes and face, hoping his heart could understand what she was saying. Fear enveloped her whole body and an involuntary tremble erupted head to toe. She was going to lose him to Nolianna—or really, vice versa. It felt as if she were on a sinking ship without a lifeboat.

"I know this isn't what you want to hear. But Lilah, I still want to join," he stated plainly. Her words didn't matter to him. He simply refused to believe that Nolianna wasn't all it was cracked up to be. He was willing to lose her rather than believe what she was saying

Lilah let out a sigh.

"I'm sorry, Lilah, but I think you're wrong and it's all just a misunderstanding, or at most a coincidence that you saw Abe and Sebastian together," he said, and looked down at their hands, which were still entwined. He paused and then looked up again into her eyes. "Come with me, please. I love you. I know you don't trust Sebastian, but you can trust me. You're all I have in this world. I know we've only been together for a short time, but fate brought us back together. I can't do this without you."

Every fiber of her being wanted to trust what he said, but at the same time she wanted to punch him square in the face. He refused to believe that she might be right, and gave her no choice. Joining Nolianna would not allow them to be together, and he rebuffed anything she said. The problem was, she'd already lost so much in her life—she couldn't handle losing him too. Lilah bit her lip, trying to decide if she should tell him the rest. Stealing a quick glance at him and then looking away, she knew the answer was to give in and join with him. Was there any possibility she was wrong and that Sebastian would let both of them stay?

"Okay, I'll join with you—but only if you promise not to tell Sebastian what I just told you," she assented.

Joey raised one eyebrow, and a small smile formed at the corners of his mouth. "Do you really mean it, Lilah? You'd come with me even though it means living in the unknown and going against what you believe about Nolianna?"

She took a deep breath and leaned her head in toward his.

"Joey, you're my family now. Where you go, I will go—but you have to promise me not to let anyone know what I've told you. We'll just have to figure it out once we're there."

Joey leaned forward and placed his forehead to hers. His smile grew and then he tilted his head and kissed her. Her lips quivered under his.

"It'll be okay, Carrots, I promise. I'll never let anyone come between us. I swear," he whispered, and rested his cheek against hers.

She kept her eyes closed, hoping to stop the moment in time.

A bell rang in the distance. They had to go to the gymnasium for testing. Her heart just hoped it wouldn't be the last time they'd have together alone. Joey pulled back and looked at her from across the table.

"I promise you, it'll all be okay. We'll be together," he said. She wanted desperately to believe him.

He stood and held out his hand. She reached for him. They were joining Nolianna.

Now it was all up to her.

Chapter 33

❧

THE REST OF THE AFTERNOON passed without any excitement. Sebastian showed up after her last class to walk Lilah home. He was determined to keep her away from Joey, and it worked. Joey was nowhere to be found.

As they rounded the corner, Lilah spied Mrs. Reed's car pulling out of Abe's driveway.

"Huh. I wonder what Mrs. Reed is doing here?" she said and quickened her pace a bit.

Sebastian kept pace. "She's probably here about the boys. Their aunt has been making noise about taking custody of them," he said nonchalantly. He always had an answer for everything.

"Oh, Eva will be bummed," Lilah said, though she didn't fully believe it was about the boys.

"She'll get over it," Sebastian said callously, and then added, "at least that's what Abe would say."

Lilah knew that it was his sentiment as much as Abe's.

Mrs. Reed drove by in her sedan and waved. Lilah waved back and made her way up the front walk at Abe's.

"Well goodbye to you, too," Sebastian said sarcastically.

"Later," Lilah said without turning around. She went straight up the stairs to her room, only emerging when she heard Eva call her down for dinner.

"Lilah and I were thinking of going up to the park tonight for some star gazing if it's okay with you and Abe," Joey said to Eva at dinner. He'd been helping the boys with their jump shots after he was done with his chores at Danielle's, and Eva had invited him to stay to eat with them. He'd gladly agreed. "It's supposed to be a nice night, and a bunch of our friends are meeting up," he lied.

Lilah's insides wanted to scream. She looked down at the tuna noodle casserole on her plate and pushed it around with her fork.

"That's fine," Abe said, never looking up from his plate.

"Are you going too, Lilah?" Eva asked.

"I was thinking of staying home tonight," she said. Abe dropped his fork on his plate, causing a loud crashing noise. He started to cough.

"But then Joey convinced me I should go, so I guess I will if it's okay with you," she said, and looked at her supposed foster parents with a smirk on her face, glad to make them squirm.

"Yeah, yeah. That's fine, I guess," Abe choked, picking up his fork.

"Well, you two just be careful. I know you'll be smart," Eva said, and looked at Lilah. She smiled. "I think you two are going to have a wonderful time—"

"How come Mrs. Reed was here earlier?" Lilah asked, interrupting on purpose.

Eva's cheeks flushed and her eyes darted between Lilah and Abe.

"Oh, she just had to drop some papers off for the boys. Nothing to worry about," Eva rattled off.

"Lilah, why don't you help Eva clear the table," Abe said before Eva could say anything more.

Lilah's back suddenly felt prickly. She knew there was more to it. There was always more to it when it came to them. Eva was just as much a part of Nolianna as Abe. She wondered if Mrs. Reed was in on it too—at this point, it wouldn't surprise her.

"I can help too," Joey chimed in. He was so happy. He'd smiled ear to ear throughout dinner.

"That's women's work. You can come and help me move the wood in from the front porch for the fire tonight," Abe said.

Good old sexist Abe, always the male chauvinist pig.

"Okay, I guess." Joey looked at Lilah and shrugged his shoulders. They both stood up and attended to their chores. The three younger boys weren't home for dinner. Mrs. Reed had taken them to see their aunt.

Lilah helped Eva clear the table and scraped the food remains from each plate into the trash.

"Oh, that's fine, honey. Thank you," Eva said, and took the last plate from her hand. "I'll finish up. I know you have lots to do tonight," she hummed.

"Thanks," Lilah said, with a little more frustration than planned.

"Is everything okay, Lilah? Is there something you want to talk about?" Eva asked.

A pent-up scream formed in her throat, making it hard to breathe. She took a few shallow breaths. "I'm fine, Eva. Everything has changed so much in the past few weeks, I'm just tired."

Eva moved closer to her and took her hands. "Lilah, I believe things happen for a reason. We might not always know what that reason is, but you're smart. You'll figure it out," she said. "And you're such a lucky girl. It's obvious how much Joey cares for you. Who knows, maybe the two of you'll be like Abe and I someday," she said.

Anger mixed with sadness twirled in Lilah's gut and chest. If it wasn't for Eva and Abe, she wouldn't be in the mess she was in! Lilah missed Pea so much at this very moment. Pea would actually care about her, not try to trick her into doing something she didn't want. For a moment, she'd let her guard down with Eva and had actually deluded herself into thinking she cared about her. Lilah huffed.

"Thanks, Eva. You're right. I think I'm going to go upstairs and get ready for stargazing with Joey."

Eva smiled. Her job was done.

"And Eva, thanks for reminding me how lucky I am," she said, and went upstairs.

When she got into her room, she sat on her bed and looked around at the yellow-brown walls and her posters. All she had brought with her were her books and notebooks, which were scattered around the floor and desk, the handmade quilt from Grandma Pea, and the picture of her family sitting next to her bed. What was she going to do with this stuff? The books she didn't need, but her notebooks, the quilt, and her picture were all too important just to leave behind. If she didn't take them, Abe and Eva would have them. If she did take them, what would she do if she couldn't bring them out with her?

A shudder ran down her spine. A knock on her door startled her.

"Come in."

Joey stood with his backpack slung over his right shoulder and a huge grin on his face.

"Are you ready?"

"Almost. I was just looking around my room one last time. I have to pack up my quilt and a few things. Give me five minutes, and I'll meet you downstairs."

"Okay. Remember, you don't have to bring much. Everything we could ever want is waiting for us after tonight," he reminded her and stepped closer. "Lilah, before we go, I wanted to thank you for coming with me. I know it isn't what you planned, but I love you. I want to be with you, always."

She shuffled toward him and put her arms around him. He smelled like soap, sandalwood, and autumn right before it rained. The familiar feeling of warmth and love engulfed her. He was her family now.

She looked up at him, stood on her tiptoes, and kissed his cheek. "I know. We're going to be fine."

He squeezed her tight and then let go. "Hurry up and grab your stuff. I'll meet you downstairs," he said, and turned to leave the room. He paused, and said, "I can't wait to start our life together. I'll see you in a few."

He turned and left. Lilah grabbed her quilt and folded it. She placed her notebooks and the picture of her family in between the folds in the quilt. Then she put it in her backpack, along with some clothes and toiletries just in case she needed them. The thing was, Joey had no idea what she had planned. She had no intention of being in Nolianna without him.

She closed her eyes and touched the ring around her neck. She didn't talk much to her parents anymore, but in this moment, she needed them more than ever.

Mom, Dad, please help me tonight. You've always watched over me. Guide Joey and me on our path together. Let us be together—always together.

She took the ring off the chain and placed it on her finger. It fit perfectly. She placed the chain back around her neck and a sense of calm washed over her body. Her heartbeat, which had been so erratic over the past few hours, finally slowed.

She grabbed her bag, flung it over her shoulder, and walked out of her room. By the time Lilah got downstairs, Abe and Eva had already left for their night out, and Joey waited at the bottom of the stairs.

"Are you ready for this, Carrots?" he asked.

"I think so." Her stomach flipped.

He took her hand, and they didn't waste any more time. They walked out of Abe's house and made it to the woods in record time. The night sky had gone from blue to black, and stars were beginning to appear. Eight others waited for them in front of the large, cascading waterfall. Lilah recognized four of them: Rosa, Luna, Tomas, and Kyle.

Joey high-fived Tomas. None of the people Lilah had met on the first night she went to Nolianna were there. The other strangers stood in a circle to the side, talking quietly.

Lilah looked around. Sebastian was nowhere in sight. She reached in her back pocket to make sure her envelope was there.

"Dude, can you believe it?" Tomas asked. "We made it! I knew we'd both be here!"

"Thanks, man. I can't wait to go in tonight. This is what we've all been waiting for," Joey said. Lilah smiled and shifted from foot to foot.

"I'm so nervous," Rosa said, stepping over to talk to Lilah. Her black hair was in a perfect ponytail and black, winged eyeliner highlighted her deep-set brown eyes. "I wasn't sure what to bring! I know they said we didn't need anything, but I wanted to bring something with me. I ended bringing socks, a toothbrush, underwear, and a few pictures from school. If anyone opens my bag, they're going to think that I've seriously lost it," she giggled.

"I know. I stood in my room forever, trying to figure out what to bring and what to just leave behind," Lilah said with a smile, knowing that she had to play the part of the excited new Nolie.

"Sure is cold out tonight," Luna said, wrapping her arms around Rosa. She couldn't have been more than 4'9" and seventy pounds. Her newly-dyed blue, pixie-cut hair framed her large face.

"At least we can ditch the gloves and hats when we get inside," Rosa giggled.

"Yeah, we don't have to worry about being cold, that's for sure," Tomas replied.

"Okay, everyone, it's time," a voice yelled over the flowing waterfall.

Lilah looked up. Sebastian had emerged from a trail next to the falls and crossed the puddles in a few quick strides. He smirked and then high-fived and hugged everyone. He walked up to Lilah last.

"I wondered if I'd see you tonight. I wasn't sure you were coming, Lilah," Sebastian said. He grabbed her and hugged her. She half hugged him back. He pulled away, and if he noticed her lack of response, he didn't let on. "You're really going to be happy. I know it was a tough decision, but it was the right one," he said. "Do you have something for me? You're the last one."

Lilah pulled the envelope out of her pocket and handed it to him. He opened it and made sure it was signed.

"Awesome. Okay, so here's the deal," Sebastian said, circling his arms for the group to come in closer. They all moved in.

"Everyone has their number. Once we go in, you have a couple of hours to do whatever you want. Once the announcement is made, we'll all go and get ready for the Masquarade. You'll be split up by gender to get ready. We'll all be dressed in costumes and masks. A little before midnight, we'll hold the initiation ceremony, and you'll be called by number to meet your match. Numbers will be announced in descending order. At exactly midnight, the portal will be closed and all those in Nolianna will be official Nolies for the rest of their lives. Any questions?" Sebastian asked.

"What about our stuff?" Tomas asked.

"You can either put it where the coats usually go, or you can bring it with you. After the initiation ceremony, we'll show everyone where you'll be staying," Sebastian responded.

"Where's everyone else? You know, all the other hopefuls, number eleven and up?" Lilah asked.

Sebastian smirked. "Seriously, Lilah? Do you really think anyone in the top ten wouldn't join? No one would come hoping to get in that wasn't in the top ten. That'd be stupid." A few of the others laughed.

Lilah's heart pounded and she clenched her fists.

"Okay, let's go in," Sebastian said, and walked up the trail.

Joey took Lilah's hand and unclenched it. "It'll be okay. Promise," Joey said in her ear. She leaned against him.

The group took turns going one by one up the trail as they had the previous nights. Lilah and Joey were the last ones at the top. The tops of the sunflowers now drooped almost to the ground, and the opaque bubble that they passed through swirled into a mix of black and grey.

Voices of at least 50 Nolies greeted them as they passed through.

"Woo hoo! Congrats! Welcome!" came at them as they stepped onto the hay-covered field. At least fifty Nolies greeted them. The ten new members passed through the crowd and toward the carnival, which was in full swing. No waiting. No chain to hold them back. The Ferris wheel spun round and round. Its brightly lit colors swirled into each other amidst scraps of paper confetti, streamers, and smoke. Screams and shouts of joy could be heard throughout the fairgrounds. Many of the Nolies were already off having fun. Lilah's ears rang. The smell of sugar and cotton candy filled the air. Every single person here was a chosen one. It was a night of celebration for the Nolies. They had all made it in, and it was time to enjoy and meet their new family—time to become part of something bigger than themselves. At least, that's what everyone around her said.

Lilah plastered a fake smile on her face and walked through the field with the others. For the first time in her life, she was just like everyone else.

At least, for the next three-and-a-half hours.

Chapter 34

❧

"**H**ey, Lilah, how about we go ride a few of the rides before we have to get ready?" Joey asked, his eyes sparkling.

"Sure. Let's start with the Ferris wheel. It's always been my favorite," she said. She wasn't lying—it *was* her favorite. The Ferris wheel was the one ride she remembered going on with her family, so many years ago. Joey and Lilah walked hand in hand toward the giant wheel and waited their turn. It didn't take long. They took the next available car together.

"Can you believe we're here?" He wrapped her tightly in his arms. She leaned into him.

"I can't believe it. If someone had told me a month that any of this would happen, I'd have said they were crazy. And yet here I am," she said, and turned to look at him.

"Here we are," Joey said with a serious tone, and turned to face her. He tipped her chin with his hand and kissed her. His lips were warm against hers and fit perfectly. When he pulled back, she sighed.

"You aren't still having doubts, are you?"

"No, I made the decision to be here with you—*for* you. But it's for me too. I have to see this through. I can't imagine being away from you," she said, and looked at his gorgeous face. She gently touched his cheek. His image burned in her heart.

"Nothing can come between us now. Not even Sebastian," he said. She raised her eyebrow at him. "Lilah, listen, I know Sebastian has had a thing for you. He hasn't exactly been shy about it. We talked, though, and he knows how I feel about you. He promised me that if we joined, he'd leave us alone. He promised to be your friend and that's all," Joey said, his blue eyes darkening with concern.

"I guess we'll just have to see how it all plays out." She knew exactly how it was going to work out. Joey wouldn't listen to her. She loved that he was so trusting, but this time, he trusted the wrong person. It was going to be up to her to fix it.

Joey's dimpled cheeks melted her heart.

"Oh, Lilah, you're still such a pessimist! We're here together! You have nothing to worry about," Joey asserted.

"You're right. There's just so much I don't know. Where are we going to sleep? What are we going to do tomorrow?"

"Tomorrow we're going to be together. That's all that matters," Joey said, and kissed her.

Their lips met and tingles spread from her head to her toes like wildfire. His lips tasted like oranges and sweet cream, and the longer he kissed her, the more she was lost in the moment. How perfect he was! For a second, she forgot everyone and everything. She kissed him back, hard, with every emotion she had left in her.

Suddenly, the Ferris wheel stopped moving, and they were forced to stop.

"Hey, lovebirds, the ride's stopped. Time to give someone else a chance to ride," Tomas yelled from a few feet away at the ride's exit.

"Uh, sorry," Joey said. His face reddened liked a cherry. Lilah laughed.

They both broke into laughter and left the ride behind. The nerves of the night had hit them both hard. The release of laughter felt so good.

"Come on, let's get something to eat," Joey said, still dragging her forward.

"Actually, could we just sit for a minute, first?"

"Uh, sure," he said and walked toward an empty table. Lilah was wary about them eating anything and she wanted a minute to check out the food stands before anyone had a chance to slip Joey anything. She followed him and sat down on one of the benches.

Joey swayed in front of her. His face was ashen.

"Are you okay?" she asked, placing a hand on his forearm.

"I'm not sure. My stomach really hurts. I'm not sure if it's from the Ferris wheel or if I just need food," he replied sitting down. He put his head in his hands. "I'll be okay in a minute."

"Joey, have you had anything to eat or drink since we left Abe's?"

"No." Joey dropped his arms down, crossed them, and placed his head on his elbow.

Alarm bells went off in Lilah's head, but she tried to ignore them. The knot in her stomach wouldn't dissipate though.

"The only thing I've had is some gum Sebastian gave me. It was kind of gross, so I threw it away after a few minutes," Joey commented, never taking his head off his arms.

Lilah closed her eyes for a split second. She wanted to scream and shake Sebastian. Despite her best efforts to watch Joey, he'd drugged him anyway. She hadn't stopped him! What a snake.

"Hey, you two, enjoying the night?" Sebastian walked over, and Lilah opened her eyes at the sound of his voice. Once again, Sebastian's time was impeccable.

"Yes, we are," she said. She clenched her fists and had to mentally stop herself from jumping across the table to punch him.

"Joey, you okay, man? You look green."

"I'm fine. I think I got motion sickness or something," Joey said, unable to lift his head.

Sebastian cackled loudly. "What a baby. Didn't you just ride the Ferris wheel? Maybe you should stick to fixing the rides instead of riding them," Sebastian teased. Joey didn't respond. "Hey, Joey, why don't you come with me. It's almost time to get ready, anyway. You can lie down in the back tent for a while before the Masquarade."

The alarms in her body went off and Lilah jumped in her seat. Sebastian wanted Joey to go with him now. Instinctively, she placed her hands on Joey's arms.

"Don't worry, Lilah, you'll see him at the Masquarade," Sebastian said snidely.

Joey turned his head to the side so she could hear him. "Sorry, bae, Sebastian's right. I've got to go lie down. I'll see you at the Masquarade."

She slowly removed her arms from him and stood up. He held onto the table for support.

"Don't worry. I promise I'll see you in a little bit. I love you," Joey said. He bent down and kissed her cheek, despite not feeling well.

"I love you too. Always."

Sebastian rolled his eyes. Lilah glared at him. Joey turned and walked toward the main tent, and Sebastian put his hand on Joey's shoulder.

"Don't worry, man, you'll feel fine in a little bit. I'll show you where you can lie down."

"Thanks, Sebastian, you're a good friend," Joey said.

It was the last thing she heard him say before they were out of earshot and in the tent.

Lilah sat for a moment and looked around. In the distance, she saw Ox working behind the Afterburn. He was her one chance, her one saving grace. If she could convince him to help her, Joey would be safe, even if she couldn't get out in time. Relying on him was a gamble, but something in her was drawn to him and she had to rely on that knowing.

She got up and walked toward him. Ox disappeared to the side of the roller coaster. She ducked under the chain-link fence surrounding the side of the roller coaster and under the wooden sign that blocked the main electrical panel for the ride and turned to the right, where she literally bumped into him. He raised his arm as if ready to punch her.

"Sorry. I didn't mean to bump into you. Please don't hit me," she said, and ducked. She threw her arm up over her face just in case. He lowered his arm. He didn't say anything, but the stern look on his face made her think twice about what she was going to do.

He stood motionless.

With a deep breath, she reached out her hand and took his left hand in hers. He stared at her hand and then touched the ring on her finger.

"Ox . . ." She took a deep breath and looked at him. She couldn't read the expression on his face. "Ox, I need you to listen to me."

He stared at her and grabbed her arm. In one quick motion, he pulled her behind a large sign that blocked anyone from seeing them.

Lilah winced at his overpowering grip. "I've been going back and forth on what to say to you. I know you're friends with Ginger, but I also know your loyalty lies with Sebastian and Nolianna," she managed to say, her insides quivering as she spoke. "This is my Grandmother's address." She held up a small scrap of white paper folded in half. "It's a safe place that not too many people know about. I want you to have the address in case you ever need it or need to put something or *someone* there," she said, all in one breath.

Ox stared at her. She motioned her hand forward so he would take it. "I'm only giving it to *you*. Please, take it," she said, and then added, "Joey's life may depend on it."

Ox took the paper and put it in his workpants pocket without looking at it.

"Please—"

"Ox, hey, Ox! Come on out! We need your help over at the main tent," a male voice called out.

Ox held his large, crooked pointer finger to his lips to signal for her to be quiet. He moved to the side of the sign and gave the guys a thumbs-up. Ox took a few steps toward them, and they turned to leave.

"That guy is so strange. One minute you think he knows what he's doing and the next he's where he isn't supposed to be. What a doof," one of the male voices said. They walked away and voices faded. Ox pointed for her to leave.

"Okay, I'll go." Before she did though, without thinking, she reached up on her tiptoes and kissed him his scarred, imperfect cheek. "Thank you. You don't know how much this means to me," she said.

She snuck around the sign and walked toward the direction she'd come from. Her walk turned into a run, right to the makeup tent. She threw herself inside and knocked over a table of jewelry. It was quiet except for Ginger, who was laying out dresses and makeup for the night's event.

"What the . . . ?" Ginger started to say, and interrupted herself with a laugh when she saw Lilah. "So I guess you made it after all. Just like Sebastian—you sure know how to make an entrance!" she said. "I was wondering when you were going to get here. Have you decided what you want to do?"

Lilah bent down and picked up the scattered jewelry. She took a few deep breaths. "Is there anyone else here?"

"No, we're alone. We don't have long, though. They're supposed to make the announcement soon, and all the girls will be coming here to get ready," she said.

"Ginger, I don't know if I've done the right thing or not, but I need your help. I need you help me get to the portal during Masquarade before I'm unmasked. Please!"

Lilah took a deep breath and tried to slow herself down. Her heart beat intensified even more than when she'd met Joey. Lilah needed her friendship and support more than ever, or she'd be stuck in a place she didn't belong without the one person she needed most.

"I'm all in, sister," Ginger joked. "Just tell me what to do. I can't wait to see Sebastian get a taste of his own medicine. You'll be the one we all talk about for decades to come, and I'll have had a part in it. Genius!"

Lilah smiled and motioned for her to come closer to hear the rest of her plan.

Ginger moved closer and leaned into Lilah so no one else could hear. The time had come to let Ginger in on the whole thing and trust their connection. Everything depended on it.

Chapter 35

❧

AFTER LILAH filled Ginger in on the plan, Ginger returned to the costuming and make-up tent to get what she needed.

Lilah walked to the main tent and did a double take upon entering. The white-and-red striped tent walls were draped with white linens, and the dirt floor was covered with two massive black-and-gray area rugs with a large spider in the center of each. The rugs were separated by a red aisle. Lilah couldn't help but laugh. The aisle of doom had been set up, and each new Nolie would have to walk down it before the night was over.

Several other new members were sitting down in the first row in front of the stage with about a hundred Nolies behind them. Lilah scanned their faces for Joey. He was nowhere to be seen.

"Aren't you totally excited?" Rosa inquired, and put her arm around Lilah's shoulders. She'd walked up behind her without Lilah realizing.

"Mmm hmm," Lilah said, and nodded. She tried to force a smile, though her insides felt like a volcano about to erupt.

They sat in the end two seats of the first row. Matthew took the stage at the front of the tent. He was dressed in jeans and a vintage Coke T-shirt.

"Attention! Attention everyone. Please settle down," he said. He raised his hand to silence the crowd, and everyone obeyed. "It is with great pleasure that I welcome you all to the start of the initiation ceremony of Nolianna."

The crowd erupted in cheers, howls, and catcalls. Matthew again raised his hands. "It is my honor to welcome the new members to our family. You've all made a great decision in joining us. This will be my last announcement before our departure this evening," Matthew said, and paused. He turned to Nala and reached out his hand for her to join him. Nala, dressed in jeans and a black cashmere sweater, dutifully moved to his side. Her long hair glistened, and she flashed a quick smile to the crowd before turning her attention back to Matthew.

Lilah looked at the others by the front of the stage. She didn't see Sebastian, Ox, or Kady.

"It's been my pleasure to serve as your leader of Nolianna for the past few years, but our time has come to move on. Your new leaders will be revealed at the start of this evening's ceremony. We've considered each of you carefully and believe that the new leadership will be a strong team to continue with Nolianna's traditions and visions for the future," Matthew said, and took a sip of from a red plastic cup.

"For all of you new members, it's now time to bid goodbye to the carnival rides and attractions, as well as your fellow Nolies. All new female members must report to the makeup tent to get into costume. All male newcomers will remain here and will be taken to one of the smaller tents to get ready," Matthew said, and looked at Nala again who hadn't stopped smiling.

"Enjoy this once-in-a-lifetime night when you finally become part of a family for good. We'll see you at the

Celabratio in two years' time—and remember, we're always together," he said, and held up his cup. "To health, happiness, and family!"

Lilah gulped. Celabratio was yet another thing she didn't know anything about.

Matthew placed the microphone on the podium, and he, Nala, and eight other departing members left the main tent. The crowd burst into a standing ovation.

Matthew's words rang in her ears. *Always together.* She twirled the ring on her hand. The words made her heart pound. They were her mother's words, Grandma Pea's words, her family crest—not Nolianna's. Nothing Matthew said would change that.

The five new female members, including Lilah, got up and walked briskly to the makeup tent. Lilah put her hand on Rosa's shoulder, and she turned with a wide grin on her face. "Hey, what did Matthew mean he'd see us at 'Celabratio'?" Lilah inquired.

Rosa giggled. "Oh, that. Every few years, Nolies are invited into Nolianna for a three-day celebration. It's supposed to be epic. Nolies come from all over."

Lilah opened her mouth to ask more, but then closed it. If her plan worked, she wouldn't have to worry about being at Celabratio or any other event in Nolianna after tonight.

"Come on, let's go get ready," Rosa stated.

Lilah took Rosa's arm, and they went into the makeup tent. Ginger saw her and dipped her head. Every inch of the open space was filled with girls, makeup, or costumes. There was hardly room to move. The noise level had increased exponentially, and the heat was stifling.

"Oh my god. I can't believe we did it," Rosa said to Luna, whose eyes seemed even more blue than when Lilah had first seen her at the waterfall.

"I know. And look, these dresses are gorgeous," Luna said. She grabbed one of the gowns off the rack and spun around with it in front her like Cinderella. Lilah smiled at them, but had more important things to think about than the fun of getting dressed up.

"Which one do we wear?" Rosa asked.

Luna shrugged her shoulders. The noise grew louder every second, as did the temperature. Sweat formed on Lilah's upper lip and she wiped it away with the back of her hand.

"Okay, everyone!" Ginger yelled, and she clapped from the other side of the tent. She jumped up on one of the tables. No one listened. "Hey, shut up!" she yelled.

The noise came to halt and all eyes were on her.

"That's better," she said with a huge smile plastered on her face. Lilah hadn't seen her that happy before. "You each will be dressed in a color based on the order of your number, starting with the highest. As you can see, there's a station with each of your numbers on it," she said, and pointed to the station next to her.

A large number one was lit up next to Ginger's station.

"You'll be given an assistant to help you dress, do your hair, and put on your mask. There's exactly sixty minutes to get dressed. You'll then line up by your number, starting with the highest and ending with number one. If you have any questions, please ask your assistant."

Several girls started talking and moving around the tent.

"Wait! One more thing," Ginger said, and held up her hand. "Assistants, please make sure that all masks are fastened correctly and that the hoods are pulled up. They can't come off before it's time! Thank you everyone! Enjoy!"

Everyone started talking at once. The noise level skyrocketed again.

Beads of sweat formed again on Lilah's lip and brow. Ginger motioned her over and pointed her small, battery-powered fan at Lilah. Lilah's hair blew up and out. She raised her hands to smooth it down but gave up when she saw it was a useless battle. "Wow. You really love this, don't you?" she asked Ginger.

"I do. I love seeing everyone get all dressed up. It's so fun!" Ginger said, and then her smile faded slightly. "I only hope it stays that way."

Lilah was about to ask her what she meant but was intercepted by another girl who needed to know where some of the makeup was.

"Lilah, I'll be back in a sec. I've laid everything out for you. Go ahead and start putting your hair back into a ponytail. I'll do the rest in a few minutes," Ginger said, and walked over to another station.

Lilah examined her station. On top of it there was a beautiful, bright royal-blue gown with a black-and-white hood, matching mask, and tiny, black spider earrings. It looked as if all the new Nolies were given a pair to wear upon joining. She took her seat in front of the big mirror, which was illuminated by several light bulbs.

Glancing up as she reached for a brush, she caught a glimpse of Kady casually walking in. Several girls parted to make way for her. She wore her usual black garb, only this time, it was a tight skirt that barely covered her underwear, a black spaghetti-strap tank, all-black combat boots, and black fishnets. Her eyes were painted with gray eye shadow and perfect black wings. She wore a pair of black cat ears in her long, blond hair and a small, black mask that only covered her eyes. Numerous tattoos, usually hidden by clothes, were out for all to see. The noise in the tent decreased to a low murmur.

Kady strolled right up to Lilah. "So you made it in after all. Just couldn't stay away from your poor lovesick puppy Joey, could ya?" Kady said with a smirk on her face. She ran a hand over the blue dress on the station. "Aren't you just going to be a sight out there."

Lilah rolled her eyes. Kady wanted something, and Lilah was pretty sure it was just to make her squirm. She wasn't going to give her the satisfaction. "What do you want, Kady?"

"What, no 'hello'? No 'nice to see you, Kady'? No 'I can't wait to be matched so I can live happily ever after'?" she snorted.

In all of her life, Lilah had never met someone so boldly mean. She may have been outwardly beautiful to some, but to Lilah, Kady was the ugliest human being she had ever met, along side Sebastian. The two deserved to disappear with each other in Nolianna. Lilah sat on her clenched fists so she wouldn't punch her. "And what's wrong with that? Do you have something against happily ever after?" Lilah batted her eyelashes for the full effect.

Kady smiled, but her eyes were dark and full of spite. "I just don't think things always turn out as we think they will," she sneered. "Anyways, enjoy your night. I can't *wait* to see you in the matching ceremony. Ciao!" She walked away without waiting for a response.

Instead of giving into her tangled web of anger, Lilah simply returned to putting her hair into a tight, low ponytail. She tucked it into her collar to hide what she could of it, not wanting any of her crazy, red waves to be seen in her costume.

"What was that all about?" Ginger asked, and began putting gel on Lilah's hair to smooth it out and slick it down. She twisted it into a tight bun at the base of her neck, much like the one Ginger wore.

"Nothing. Don't worry about her. I think she has some personal vendetta against anyone in love. She's jaded. She seems to take pleasure in others being unhappy, just as she obviously is." Lilah stopped sitting on her hands and clutched them together. They were shaking.

Noticing, Ginger gently put her hands on Lilah's and placed them down on the arms of the chair. She ran her fingers over Lilah's hair and tightened the ponytail.

". Just watch your back with her. She's the type to try and hurt people just because she can. Girls should raise each other up, not bring them down," Ginger said. "Come on, we've got to get you in this thing. Are you ready?"

Lilah let out a sigh and shrugged before taking off her T-shirt. She placed it in her backpack.

"Ginger, can you take care of my backpack?"

Ginger's eyes darted around the room to make sure no one was listening. "I'll put it in the green trash can closest to the entrance outside the main tent. Just grab it when you're ready."

Ginger held out the gorgeous, flawlessly sewn blue gown. She unzipped it and held it near the floor so Lilah could step into it. Lilah left her pants and shoes on, which made it easier to step into. The gown was long enough that she didn't have to worry about anyone seeing her sneakers.

With Ginger's help, Lilah stepped into the dress, and Ginger pulled it up around her. It was quite heavy, due to several layers underneath that made the bottom stick out like the dresses in the old Western movies Grandma Pea used to watch. Ginger zipped up the back. The zipper was covered by a row of buttons. Ginger smiled.

"Wow, you really look beautiful," she said. "Here, look for yourself!" She spun Lilah around.

Lilah blinked several times, unable to speak. The beautiful royal blue accentuated her eyes. The high neck on the gown was intentional, and it made her neck look longer than it ever had before. Her waist was cinched and highlighted her curves. She was almost sorry she couldn't keep it.

"Oh, wait, don't forget your gloves. Everyone has them this year, a new addition," Ginger said, her eyes twinkling. She handed Lilah long, white gloves, which had matching blue spiders on the back of the hand. Ginger had thought of everything.

Lilah gazed around and watched the other girls in their costumes. They were magnificent. There wore all shades of dresses: deep red, hunter green, light blue, and bright sunshine yellow.

"Ginger, who made all of these costumes?" Lilah asked. "They're gorgeous!"

Ginger beamed. "I did."

"*You* did? I knew you were a wizard with makeup and hair, but I had no idea you could design and sew!"

"I had a foster mom who used to let me design and sew her clothes. She taught me everything she knew. I've been making all sorts of clothes and costumes since I was little. I fell in love with it, really. I had Prisha help sew a few, but I designed them. I'm lucky that I get to use my talent here in Nolianna. Not everyone does," she remarked.

"Well, you're incredibly talented." Lilah moved closer to her so their faces were close enough to touch. "Thank you, my friend. My biggest regret is that I won't be able to spend more time with you after tonight. It's been a long time since I've felt like I could really trust a girlfriend."

Ginger looked at her with tears in her eyes. "Wait. I almost forgot." She reached over to the small table to her left and grabbed a red and silver bracelet. She placed it around Lilah's left wrist and then lifted her sleeve to show Lilah a matching bracelet.

"There's one for you and one for me. Connected we will always be." They both smiled at each other.

"I felt connected to you the first time I saw you. And the best way I can show my friendship is by doing what's best for my friend," Ginger whispered.

The sound of a loud gong filled the air. Cheers erupted in the tent. Several girls clapped and hugged each other.

"Okay, you all set?" Ginger asked.

"Think so."

"Don't worry. Just leave the rest to me," Ginger said, and lifted the mask with a cloth backing over Lilah's head.

Lilah's face and hair would be completely covered. Once that was in place, Ginger pulled up the large, velvet hood. No one would be able to tell who she was until the unmasking. It was perfect.

"All the new members have a hood this year. That way, you won't stick out," Ginger said. Lilah smiled under her mask and hood. "Okay, girls, line up by your number. The highest number will start at the door, all the way to number one," Ginger announced.

Everyone got into place.

"So here's how it'll go. We'll walk to the main tent and wait outside. The first part of the ceremony will begin with the announcement of the new leaders. Once that's complete, the Masquarade will begin. Each number will be called, one by one. When it's your turn, you will walk down the aisle to the front where you'll be introduced to the crowd. You'll then be given your match. You'll take your partner's hand and wait for the final match to be made. Whatever you do, do *not* take your gloves or masks off until you're told!" Ginger said to the five waiting in line.

The four other masked girls all nodded in understanding.

"After the final match is made, you'll dance with your match. Once that's over, each match will be unmasked, again in order. Any questions?"

"Yeah—then what happens?" Rosa asked, pulling her mask up above her mouth so she could be heard.

"Well, then we party! There'll be dancing and drinking for the rest of the night!" Several of the girls stifled giggles. "Okay, go ahead and line up by the front," Ginger said. The other four masked girls walked toward the tent's opening.

Lilah took a deep breath. The beginning of the end had finally come. She lifted her mask slightly so Ginger could hear her. "Are you sure you're going to be okay?"

Lilah looked directly into Ginger's eyes for any sign of doubt or hesitation. A slight ache arose in her, and she wished Ginger could come with her.

"Lilah, I've been waiting for over a year to get back at Sebastian for what he did to me. I couldn't be more ready," Ginger said, and gave her a quick squeeze. "Don't worry about me. I made my choice to be here, and it's fine for me. I'll see you soon," Ginger said, and hugged her. "I have to go get ready."

Ginger, along with all the helpers and assistants, exited the tent, and only the five were left. No one said a word. After about two minutes, Nova appeared.

"Here we go, ladies. Just follow in line, and we're going to take our places at the back of the main tent."

The line moved forward slowly, and everyone continued to be silent.

Lilah took deep breaths. She was thankful for the few last moments of silence before the ceremony. They walked for a few minutes and arrived at the main tent. All the Nolie girls were dressed in fancy gowns, and the guys had on matching suits with elaborate fabrics and embellishments. Each outfit was intricately decorated, and the members had brightly colored masks, though they didn't have hoods like the new members. The current Nolies made their way toward the front and sat with their coordinating match in several rows of chairs in front of the stage. All the new members sat in the last two rows, males on one side and females on the other, with an aisle separating them.

Two large guys in navy-blue suits and navy-blue Masquarade masks blocked Lilah's view of the five male inductees.

She drew in a breath and held it, praying she could make it through the ceremony without lifting her mask—everything depended on it.

Chapter 36

࿐

"**A**TTENTION, EVERYONE!" Sebastian's voice boomed.
Everyone in the tent turned to the front where he stood smirking and holding a microphone. He wore a royal-blue suit that matched Lilah's perfectly. His face was partially covered with a black-and-white mask. His defining jaw line and hair gave him away without him even having to speak.

Lilah's neck muscles tightened. She turned her head from side to side a few times, trying to ward off the pulsations slowly creeping into her head.

Sebastian held up his hands to quiet the crowd. "Good evening, my fellow Nolies! As you know, tonight is Masquarade—what you've all been waiting for! It is with great honor that I've accepted the lead position in Nolianna. We're a family, and from tonight on, we are one. We take care of one another here at all costs. I look forward to leading the next group of Nolies toward greatness here in Nolianna," Sebastian bellowed. People cheered and clapped. "Now let the initiation ceremony begin!"

A group of four Nolies, including Kady, rose from their seats and joined Sebastian onstage. Kady hadn't bothered to change. She handed Sebastian a scroll. He scanned it and then handed it back to Kady, along with the microphone.

"This year we have an unusual occurrence. Because our new leader will be matched tonight, in order to continue in the usual initiation process, I will be announcing the matches. So everyone, pay attention," Kady barked. She glared at the crowd.

A few murmurs filled the air and several people shushed others. When it was quiet, Kady began. "We begin our ceremony with number ten!"

A processional played on an organ filled the air.

A male from the other side rose, dressed in a royal-blue suit with black and white ruffles and patches on the arms and legs, matching mask, and blue hood. The base color looked markedly close in color to Lilah's, though one would have to look beyond the black and white material to see it. It had had to be removeable. Ginger was a genius.

Lilah held her breath. The guy behind the mask was supposed to be Joey. And yet she knew by his height and heavy walk that it wasn't. He stood in the aisle and waited to be called.

"Number ten, please join your brothers and sisters at the front of the tent." Everyone clapped. He walked down the aisle.

The hairs on the back of Lilah's neck stood up. She felt the stare of someone on her. She looked around from behind the mask and noticed that Ox and two large guys who had been blocking the aisle were standing just a few feet behind her. They all stared at her, arms crossed over their big, muscular chests.

She didn't dare move, and clapped along with everyone else until the guy reached the front of the aisle and took Ginger's hand. Together they turned, faced the crowd, and walked to the side so there was room for others to join them after their numbers were called.

KINDREDS

Next, a guy in a deep red suit went to the front of the stage and turned to face the crowd.

"Number nine, please join your brothers and sisters at the front of the tent to be matched with your mate."

Number nine stood. She was dressed in an alluring deep-red dress, white gloves with glittery spiders sewed on, a red hood, and a matching red mask made out of feathers. She happily skipped down the aisle to meet her match. She took his hand, and they too turned to look outward at the crowd for a moment before joining Ginger and her match. The ceremony continued with each number being called and the matched couple proceeding down the aisle. Finally, it was Lilah's turn.

"Number one, please join your brothers and sisters at the front of the tent to be matched with your mate," Kady said in a sing-songy, fake voice.

Wearing a mask that only covered his eyes, Sebastian smiled when Lilah stood up. He was her match, just like she knew he would be. She slowly made her way down the aisle. "You look beautiful, Lilah," he said. "I've been waiting for this moment since we met." He took her hand. She held it, and they turned to face the crowd. Lilah's insides shook and she pulled her lips tight to stop them from shaking.

The crowd went wild. Cheers pierced her ears, along with confetti, streamers, and bottle caps popped all around them. Everyone jumped to their feet in celebration. Sebastian bowed and waved to the crowd with his free hand.

Everyone jumped to their feet, and within a few moments, the wooden, collapsible chairs were cleared away as the music swelled. The long aisle carpets were rolled up and replaced by one large red-and-black carpet with a gray spider in the middle.

"My lady," Sebastian said, and bowed toward Lilah. The thought of pushing Sebastian out of her way and making a run for it filled her head, but she resisted her urge. There was no way she'd be able to escape.

Sebastian took a few steps forward, and she allowed him to lead her to the center of the spider, which was now the makeshift dance floor. Everyone in the main tent partnered up with their coordinating match and danced to the music. Sebastian held her hand tightly in his and pulled her close, with his other hand at the small of her back. It was all she could do not to step on his feet.

"I know you had your doubts, Lilah, but you'll see. Tonight will be a night you'll remember for the rest your life," Sebastian said.

Vomit rose in her throat and caused her cough. She wanted to hit him, scream, throw up . . . *anything* to get him to stop talking.

"It's all so overwhelming," she managed to squeak out. She needed him to believe that she was happy to be there. Sebastian laughed and spun her around.

Music and laughter filled the air. They danced until the music stopped and everyone bowed to their partner. Within seconds, several people began putting the chairs back into place for the final portion of the ceremony.

"If all of the newest Nolies and their partners would please join me onstage, we can finish what we started," Kady barked.

"Is she ever nice?" Lilah asked, causing Sebastian to chuckle.

"Nope. She won't bother you, though, I promise," Sebastian said, grabbing her hand once again. "Come on, we have to go up to the stage for the final phase of the ceremony." Sebastian pulled her behind him and went up on stage. He walked right up to Kady and swiped the microphone. Kady glared at him.

"We now ask that everyone be seated as we move to the part of the evening we've all been waiting for," Sebastian announced.

The crowd moved and took their seats. There were easily over a hundred people in the tent, and the heat that had risen caused sweat to cover Lilah's body. Several people were sneaking drinks of water under their masks.

Sebastian handed the microphone back to Kady.

"Enjoy what's to come, Lilah," Kady guffawed over her shoulder so only Lilah and a few other inductees could hear.

"Don't worry, Kady, I will."

Kady rolled her eyes and turned toward the crowd. Sebastian and Lilah made their way to the side of the stage with the other eight who were waiting to be announced. They joined the end of the line, as they would be last.

"It's my job to welcome our ten newest brothers and sisters to Nolianna," Kady announced flatly to the crowd.

Everyone clapped while the ten newest matches moved behind her onstage. They stood in numeric order close to a ginormous velvet curtain.

"Okay, let's start with number ten. Number ten, please step forward with your match," Kady said with a smirk on her face, and glanced over at Lilah. Sebastian stood up tall and raised his chin in the air.

Ginger had really outdone herself. To everyone else, her dress looked unique from the others. It was a masterpiece, and one would have to really pay attention to the details to figure out it was almost the same dress as Lilah's. Ginger moved to the center of the stage, holding hands with her match and awaiting their directions. Sebastian squeezed Lilah's hand in his. His grip was hard against hers and crushed two of her fingers. He pulled her toward him.

"Number ten is to be matched with Ginger. Ginger, your match is . . ." Kady paused and looked up.

"Well, this is a surprise, for sure. A last-minute change. Your match is Billy," Kady said, and turned to look at Lilah, a huge smirk on her face.

Billy took off his mask and the crowd clapped and cheered once again.

"No! This isn't fair! You *bastard!*" Ginger screamed, and silence replaced the applause. She ran to the end of the line with her fist raised and right up to Sebastian, but before she could get to him, the two large guys appeared and stopped her. "You planned this! You knew all along I wanted to be matched with Joey, and you couldn't stand it! Now what's your precious Lilah going to say?"

The guys fought off her thrashing body to stop her from striking Sebastian. Suddenly, her screams were silenced, and she fell, limp, onto the ground.

"Oh my god, she's fainted," Billy yelled, who had come up behind her. "Someone do something!" Lilah bit the inside of her lip to prevent herself from laughing out loud. Ginger was playing it perfectly. If Lilah didn't know any better, she'd say Ginger had actually fainted. She was an amazing actor.

Sebastian tightened his grip on Lilah. She twisted her hand and tried to pull away, but he was too strong. Several girls ran to Ginger's side to help. Lilah hip-checked Sebastian and tried to shove him with her free hand, but he caught it and pulled her toward him. "Lilah, stop! Wait! Please listen to me," Sebastian begged, raising his eye mask to his forehead.

Lilah continued to twist her wrist. It wasn't hard for her get in touch with her anger at him and use it to try and pull away from him.

"I know this isn't what you expected, and that you're upset, but Joey just wasn't a good fit for Nolianna. It was his choice to leave, I promise," Sebastian said.

"You liar! Joey wouldn't have left me here without him!" she snarled at him through her mask.

Even though she had known this injustice had been coming, anger engulfed her, catching in her throat and making it difficult to breathe, let alone talk. Lilah turned her head away from him.

"Lilah, please. Don't make a scene. Please, just read what Joey wrote," Sebastian pleaded, and held up a note. "It'll prove to you that Joey left on his own and that he wanted you to stay." He loosened his grip on her and she ripped the note out of his hand with her free hand. Was there any way that Joey had actually written it?

Holding her breath, she shook the folded piece of paper to open it. It was exactly what she expected. It was a hand-written note, but not by Joey.

Dearest Lilah,

I'm so sorry. I had to leave. I realized that I don't belong in Nolianna, but that you do. Please try and understand. I will always love you, but I can't be with you any longer. I want the best for you. Sebastian and Nolianna can give that you.

—Joey

Lilah swayed back and forth. Tears welled. The emotion of the past few hours—days—washed over her. The note was a fake. She knew his handwriting, plus, he would have used her nickname, Carrots. She opened and closed her fists several times, trying to keep the pent-up anger that made her want to rip Sebastian's head off at bay. Not being able to control it completely, she fell to her knees, her head looking down. Sebastian wasn't expecting it, so he had to let his grip on her hand go.

"How could he? Why would he do this to me? I thought he loved me," she said, and looked up to Sebastian. The words burnt in her mouth and she made sure he heard her. He reached down and put his hand on her shoulder.

"Listen, we can talk all about it after the ceremony. I know you haven't always trusted me in the past, but I hope now you'll be able to. I won't leave you, not like Joey did. We're in this together," he said in a low voice so only she could hear him.

The two large guys passed in front of them and carried Ginger to the back of the stage behind the velvet curtain. Lilah looked to the side entrance of the tent and saw Ox standing there looking around the room. She wondered if he was there in case she decided to run and tried to catch his eye, but he never glanced her way. Would he let her escape? Had he taken Joey to Grandma Pea's? Lilah felt a wave of nausea wash over her and had to compose herself. She couldn't lose it now.

"What will happen to Ginger?" Lilah asked.

"She'll recover. She always does," Sebastian said flippantly. "Please, Lilah, get up. Let's finish the ceremony. You're here now, and this is where you belong."

She let a moment pass and obediently stood up. Sebastian had won the battle, but the war was not over.

Cautiously, and with one eye on her at all times, Sebastian moved down the row and took the microphone from Kady.

"All right, everyone, please settle down. Take your seats. We'll now continue the ceremony," Sebastian announced, and returned the microphone to Kady.

Sebastian stopped where Billy was standing.

"Billy, just hang out there and Ginger will be back. You might as well get used to her theatrics," he said with a haughty laugh.

Billy's face had been drained of color, and he didn't say a word. He held his mask in his hand and stood obediently where Sebastian told him to. Sebastian returned to his spot in line next to Lilah and took her hand.

"Let's get this moving," he snapped at Kady.

Lilah's arms shook with rage. Sebastian turned. "Lilah, just be calm. It'll be okay. I promise."

"I know. I trust you," she lied.

"Well, what would an initiation ceremony be without a little drama? Everyone, please quiet down and let's try and finish our ceremony without any more incidents," Kady said, sneering. The crowd settled into their seats, and faint music began playing again in the background.

"Jackson, you will be matched with number nine," Kady announced, and the guy in the red suit and mask stepped forward, holding hands with his partner. "And number nine is . . . Rosa!" Rosa and Jackson took their masks off at the same time and hugged.

Lilah drew in a breath and waited.

Chapter 37

✤

"**O**KAY, number eight."

Two girls in pink moved to the front of the stage. The girls stood eye-to-eye and held hands.

"Luna is matched with number eight, Rachel."

Luna took off her hood and mask and the two girls hugged briefly before moving out of the spotlight.

One by one, Kady made her way down the list, and each match stood in front of the crowd. With each match announced, more and more beads of sweat formed on Lilah's neck and back. Kady rattled off each match: seven, six, five, four, three . . .

"Okay, only a few more left. Number two, would you please step forward and—"

Without warning, the loud tearing of rope snapping filled the air. A large wooden pole by the front flap of the tent teetered and fell. Several people sitting in the back rows fell out of their chairs and onto the ground, the beam on top of them. Screams erupted. People began frantically jumping up and running in all directions.

Ginger had pulled it off.

"Oh my god! Lilah, I'll be right back. I have to get this under control. Don't go anywhere," Sebastian ordered, and rushed to the microphone. He pushed Kady out of the way.

"What the hell, Sebast—" she said, partially into the microphone. She shoved him back and glared at him. A girl with short black hair, who was dressed in a simple black dress, a mask, and cat ears, went up to her. She took Kady's hand and the two exited the stage toward the beam.

"Attention, attention everyone!" Sebastian yelled.

People continued to scatter, either to get away from harm or to help the members who were trapped. The two large guys who were focused on Ginger a few minutes earlier ran to remove the heavy beam and prop up the tent from falling.

Lilah, along with a few others on stage, shuffled backwards, flush up against the large velvet curtain behind them. Sebastian's eyes darted between her and the crowd. The muscles in his face were taut, and Lilah couldn't help but smile under her mask.

Sebastian moved toward Lilah and placed his hand over the microphone. "I have to go back there. I'll be right back," he said, shaking his head and glaring at Lilah. Lilah reached out her hand and lifted her mask so he could see her. She took a slight step toward him. Softening her facial muscles and tilting her head, she let her voice quiver while she spoke.

"It's okay. Please go make sure everyone is okay. I'll be right here." Seeming to believe her, Sebastian dropped the microphone and hopped off the stage. He took off in a half-run toward the back.

Lilah returned the mask to her face and moved so her backside was up against the curtain. Everyone around her was busy talking with their matches. No one bothered with her.

Someone lightly grabbed her ankle. Holding her breath, she ducked down as if to fix the bottom of her dress and scurried under the curtain. The satin material of Ginger's dress brushed the top of her head as she went under.

Without wasting a second, she stood up, pushed her hood back, and whisked off her mask.

The back of the stage was dark, and she scanned all around her. She was all alone as Ginger had promised. Standing perfectly still, her ears perked, she listened and prayed Ginger would remember to crouch down a bit so they'd be the same height and not give away their secret.

"Everyone, please! Remain calm. If everyone can please be quiet, we can assess the damage," Sebastian's deep voice boomed in the distance and then paused.

Lilah held her breath and chewed on her lip.

"Okay, as you can see, the beam is being removed, and luckily no one was really hurt," he declared. "We have a few Nolies working on stabilizing the tent so that we can continue our ceremony. Everyone, please—take your seats! We will start back up in just a few moments."

Lilah didn't waste another second. She took off at run toward the edge of the tent where Ginger had drawn a black X marking her way out of the tent in case it was dark, as promised. She rushed under the tent flap and made her way around the outside of the tent. It was imperative that she get to the front of the tent without being seen in order to make it to the portal. About fifteen yards from the front of the tent, she stopped for a second and leaned her head to the side to listen again. Everyone was so focused on what had happened inside that no one was stationed outside the tent.

The commotion inside had settled down, and sounds of chairs clanking together and people chatting and moving around while taking their seats to finish the ceremony replaced the chaos. Lilah drew in a deep breath and ran to the garbage can where Ginger was supposed to have put her clothes.

"All right already!" Kady's annoyed voice came over the loudspeaker. "Let's get this going *finally*."

Lilah reached into the can and felt the smooth nylon. Scanning the grounds around her, she grabbed it and took a few steps back. She unzipped her dress and disrobed. She balled up the exquisite gown and threw it and the gloves into the trash can. She grabbed her T-shirt out of the pack and pulled it over her head as Kady's voice filled the air again.

"And, Justin is matched with . . . Kyle." Applause filled the air.

Not wasting another second, Lilah threw her backpack over her shoulder and looked behind her. Her breath caught in her chest. Dublin stood off in the distance watching her.

Lilah stopped cold and stared at them. They locked their eyes on hers and, unexpectedly, tilted their head in the direction she was going. They weren't going to stop her. They were on her side!

Lilah mouthed the words *Thank You*, and raced by. Behind her, Kady's cool voice filled the air once again.

"Well, this is the one we've all been waiting for. Number one. You've been chosen not only as a sister of Nolianna, but will be matched with Sebastian, our leader. And our number one is . . . Lilah," Kady said apathetically.

A moment passed. Gasps were heard throughout the tent.

Sebastian's angered voice pierced the air, followed by Ginger's laugh. Both had been picked up on the microphone and broadcast throughout Nolianna.

"Where is she?" Sebastian screamed. "You idiot. What have you done? Guys, go find her *NOW*!"

Lilah reached the edge of the field just as Sebastian finished his orders. The iridescent black bubble was only a few steps away, yet had changed to a fast swirling orb that made Lilah pause before going through to the drooping sunflowers. She'd made it—only three more steps and it would all be over. Her legs moved to take the last few steps when a large hand grabbed her from behind.

She screeched to a halt, her arm wrenched behind her. A pain shot up into her shoulder blade and rotator cuff.

"Ox," she pleaded, knowing it was him before even seeing his face. She looked up at him straight in the eyes and could barely breathe from the pain twinning with fear ripping through her body

"Ox, please, I have to go now if I'm going to make it! Please!" she begged. She looked at his face and without thinking said, "Come with me! You can live with us. You don't have to stay here. You can be with Joey and me and live at my grandmother's house. *Please.*"

She didn't know why she said it, but she'd never meant anything more in her whole life.

Ox looked at her and loosened his grip. He took her hand and placed it in his palm. He touched her ring with his free hand and then leaned down to kiss it.

"Ox! Ox! Make sure she doesn't get away," Sebastian yelled from behind Ox as he barreled toward them.

An unbearable ache consumed her entire body. Tears welled in her eyes, and her insides shook uncontrollably. Then, without warning, Ox let go of her hand and pushed her, hard. Lilah fell back and lost her balance as she went through the swirling orb. She wiped out several sunflowers, hit the dirt and rolled down the steep incline, bouncing and scraping into the pointy branches all the way down until she hit the hard ground at the bottom.

Gasping for air, she lay still for a moment, her body aching, though not seriously hurt. Her heart raced and she stared at the trail, expecting someone to appear at any second. Scampering backwards, she brought herself to her feet and ran across the puddles to the dry dirt. She glanced around her and then off in the distance, hoping someone would appear to help her. A light, powdery snow had fallen, and everything around her was white, new, and untouched. The waterfall gushed, and small icicles formed near the top. Her hands burned from her fall and she rubbed them together.

She closed her eyes and waited. Her legs were too shaky to carry her and she wanted to see if by chance Ox would make his way out. She shuddered at the thought of what Sebastian might do to him, wishing he had chosen to come with her instead.

Only the sounds of the waterfall surrounded her. Hot tears of relief escaped her eyelids. Taking a deep breath, she opened her eyes and she saw that she was alone. All alone. It had to be after midnight. Nolianna was closed, and for once, Sebastian wouldn't be showing up. Night nine had officially ended and the portal was closed for the next year. Lilah was so relieved and yet, the shakiness intensified. What if Joey didn't make it out? What if he was hurt or worse . . . Lilah joggled her head from side to side. She had to find out for herself. She refused to speculate on what might have happened.

Still a bit dazed, she slowly brushed herself off. Pain radiated in her shoulder and back. She took a moment and got her bearings. Her backpack had fallen a few feet away from the trail and she walked over guardedly to get it. Snatching it from the entrance, she crossed back over the puddles to safer ground. She grabbed her coat out of her bag and put it on to keep warm, though she was still sweating.

Step-by-step, she steadily walked across the dirt path and toward the opposite direction than when she came from Abe's. She'd watched others use the other trail that came from a different part of town and knew it would take her towards Grandma Pea's. It was lined with tall pine trees and overgrown with large, billowy branches.

It was a much longer walk to Grandma Pea's than Abe's, and it was hard to see in the darkness. Luckily, the moon shone bright above her, and her eyes adjusted. Walking cautiously yet moving as fast as she could, she navigated the terrain, avoiding stray branches and random roots that sprouted up to trip her. She made her way to the top of the unfamiliar trail to a clearing in a parking lot. Realizing she was only about a half mile from Pea's, her heart raced. Madame Mystique's words rang in her head. *You may have to part from someone with whom you deeply love. Whether it is permanent or not will depend on you.*

Madame was wrong! She had to be. Joey got out. Lilah was going home to him. He had to be okay. Everything in her wanted to believe Ox was on her side. Even though he didn't speak to her, he'd protected her every time he could have turned her in. She just prayed her instincts were right.

Chapter 38

❧

HE CLOCK FLASHED 9:57 A.M. Lilah sat in the pink, upholstered chair in the corner of her old bedroom and watched Joey. Nothing had changed except that the few books and pictures she had taken to Abe's were missing. The faint, familiar smell of Estée Lauder's "Beautiful" filled the air. Grandma Pea had given it to her last Christmas and Lilah wore it on special occasions.

Joey lay on the twin bed under a blue, faded blanket. He hadn't woken up since she arrived at Grandma Pea's house a little after 1:00 a.m. She'd never considered that he might not wake up. She did her best to push that idea from her mind.

She'd fought sleep on and off throughout the night, each time awakening with a start. Every time she woke, she'd stared at Joey lying in bed, peaceful and breathing. Relief would wash over her body, and her muscles would relax until she fell asleep again. She didn't dare leave his side for fear of him waking up alone and not knowing what happened.

Lilah inhaled and exhaled slowly. Waiting made her stomach turn. She sat forward and rubbed her eyes, her gaze catching on her ring. The corners of her mouth turned downward momentarily. Missing her parents more than usual, a feeling of sadness swept over her. Out of the corner of her eye, she noticed Joey's fingers moving up and down as if typing. Forgetting her own pain, Lilah jumped up and rushed to his side.

Tapping his fingers a few more times and licking his lips, Joey began to mumble. Lilah leaned in closer over the bed.

"Joey," she whispered, tears burning the corners of her eyes.

He opened his eyes slowly and blinked. He looked at her and pulled himself up to sitting position against the pillows. He returned her stare.

His stormy, gray-blue eyes pierced hers. Lilah's heart felt like it was going to leap out of her chest.

His eyes clouded over and Lilah held her breath.

"Where am I?" Joey asked.

"You're at my Grandmother Pea's house. You're safe. We're safe now."

"Okay . . . but who are you?" His magnetic eyes searched hers. His words cut through her like a knife to her heart. Bile crept up in her throat.

"I'm . . ." is all she could say before the long-built-up sob escaped her throat. The lump in her throat blocked any other words. Her tears spilled on to her cheeks, one by one.

"Please don't cry. It's okay," he said, and a smirk crossed his lips. Joey shifted his body and pulled her hand onto the bed with him. He held it softly and touched her cheek. Lilah stopped her sobs and looked at him.

"I know who you are, Lilah," he assured her. "I'm okay."

All she could do was stare at him. It took a moment for his words to register. She pulled her hand back from him and scowled. "You ass! Don't mess with me like that! Do you have any idea what I've been through in the past twelve hours?" Her voice continued to tremble.

Joey grabbed her arm and pulled her closer to him. He wrapped his arms around her and stroked her hair. Lilah pulled back to look at him to make sure he was real.

"Honestly, I have no idea what you've been through." His voice was soft and apologetic. "I should've listened to you, but I wanted to be a part of Nolianna so badly. I didn't trust you and what you were saying all along. I'm such an idiot. I hope you can forgive me."

She leaned forward and tightened her arms around him. "It's okay. I do forgive you."

He pulled back and touched his finger to her cheek. "I've never been so happy to see you. You have to tell me how we got out—all of it," he said. "And this time, please don't hold anything back."

He knew she hadn't told him everything before. She smiled at him, despite the shudder that ran down her back. Shifting her weight on the bed, she placed her head on his shoulder and recounted everything that had happened from the moment he left her at the picnic table to the moment she saw him lying on the bed.

"Holy crap. It's all so crazy. The last thing I remember is throwing away the gum Sebastian gave me, and then waking up here, with you."

Lilah thought for a moment about Abe and Sebastian in the garage.

"I'm glad I didn't chew it much longer. Can you image what might've happened if I did?"

Lilah sighed and pushed thoughts of what could have happened out of her mind. It still didn't add up how it all came together so flawlessly and only with Ginger's, and possibly Dublin's, help, but Lilah would have to try to figure that out later.

"Please don't ever keep secrets from me again. Okay?" he pleaded. She shook her head in agreement. "And Carrots, thank you for getting me out of there."

She pulled back to look at him. "So you aren't mad at me?"

Joey eye's twinkled and his dimple appeared. "Of course not. This whole time Sebastian was using me to get to you and he had no intention of letting me in. I'll kill him if I ever see him again." Joey's muscles tensed throughout his body and his face flushed. "Why didn't you just tell me everything before?"

She wasn't sure how to respond. "Well, I did tell you some of it, and . . . well—"

"Just say it. Whatever it is, just tell me."

"You didn't want to hear it! I tried to warn you about Sebastian and Abe the other day at school, but you were so set on joining. I didn't think anything would change your mind."

Joey paused and his eyes darted around the room for a moment. He let out a sigh and his body slumped. "You're right. I didn't want to believe you, so I just figured we could handle whatever came our way. I was obviously wrong. I knew Sebastian was set on having you join, so I had to go with you. But I should have listened to you. I'm sorry." Joey choked up on the last few words. Tears formed in the corners of his eyes. "I couldn't let him hurt you, and I knew he would if that was what it took to get you in Nolianna. I had to join with you."

Lilah opened her mouth to respond, but nothing came out. She hadn't even considered that Joey would join for her.

"I thought that once we joined, we'd be together. I just hope you still want to be with me," he said.

"After all we've been through, I hope you know that I belong with you. You're my heart. You're my family now. I told you, wherever you go, I will too. It's the only reason I even considered joining Nolianna." To prove it to him, she leaned in and kissed him softly on the lips. She felt the warmth of his breath on her face and tingles shot all the way down to her toes. Relief mixed with desire washed over her. She pulled away from him abruptly.

He coughed and laughed at the same time. Flustered, she sat back and moved all the way to the edge of the bed.

"I have to stay away from you so we can finish talking," she said in a low voice.

"Okay, okay," he said, "I have a question for you. How did you know the note was a fake?"

"Because every time you've written to me in the past, you've called me Carrots. Whoever wrote the note addressed it to Lilah. Plus, I knew you would never change your mind unless you were forced to," she said.

Joey smiled. "Who would've thought 'Carrots' would save us?" he said.

"Yeah—and, of course, Ginger, Dublin, and Ox."

"Yeah, Ox. That guy is one strange dude," Joey remarked.

Her body tensed. "He isn't strange. Don't say that."

Joey's eyebrows furrowed.

"I know he's a Nolie, but he also helped me get away. I'll never really know why. I owe him my life, *our* lives. I tried to get him to come with me and live here with us, but he wouldn't."

"You what?" Joey asked, his eyes wide and smile gone. He leaned heavily back on his pillows, causing the air to puff out of one.

"At the last moment before I left Nolianna, I felt a connection to him. He could've let Sebastian catch me and make me stay in Nolianna, but he didn't," she said. "And he was the one who saved you too."

"So *he* brought me here?"

Lilah nodded.

"Wow. I can't believe you trusted him and he did what you asked. He must be in all sorts of trouble in Nolianna now."

Lilah shut her eyes and tried to block unwanted images from her brain. The last thing she wanted was to get Ox in trouble, or worse, hurt.

Joey's words interrupted her thoughts. "Well, it's over now, thank god. We don't ever have to go back or deal with any of them again."

Lilah drew in a quick breath. She wasn't so sure that Sebastian would give up that easily. Luckily, the entrance to Nolianna was closed and they had at least eleven months before it opened again somewhere else. For tonight, Lilah wasn't going to let Sebastian steal another moment from being with Joey.

A small grin crossed Lilah's lips. She moved closer to him and placed her head under his chin to snuggle in close. For the first time since Grandma Pea died, she felt at home. Lilah sat for a while and listened to the sound of Joey's heartbeat. He fell into a deep sleep and Lilah let her thoughts drift back to Madame Mystique's words. Madame was wrong. She didn't lose Joey. Nolianna would never come between them again.

Chapter 39

☙

ONCE JOEY was really asleep, Lilah needed a few minutes to herself and snuck off the bed, careful not to wake him. The events of the past week were beginning to catch up with her, and she was bone-tired. A few minutes of refuge in the bath was exactly what she needed to let the tension subside. She walked to the linen closet and grabbed a clean, pink towel, still perfectly folded from before Grandma Pea died. The familiar creak of the closet door made the corners of her lips turn upward. Nothing had changed at the house. She was so thankful Grandma Pea had left it to her and had made all of the arrangements to ensure it stayed in Lilah's name. The house was all hers now, and Joey's. If Nolianna taught her anything, it was that she didn't need another family to take her in. She could make her own.

Closing the linen hall closet, pictures of her family caught her eye. A familiar warmth enveloped her, and she felt their love surround her. They'd protected her and brought her back home. Turning the ring on her finger with her thumb, she searched the Pepto Bismol pink wall in front of her. Grandma Pea loved every shade of pink and Lilah hadn't realize how much she missed it until now.

She looked at the yellowing pictures that hung in their mismatched, wooden frames and was struck by how much she looked like her mother. It wasn't until Ginger had done her makeup that the realization hit her. Her mother was beautiful, and Lilah had never considered that she could be too. Gazing at a picture of her parents just after they were married, she wondered what they would have been like as parents now. Lilah barely remembered them other than their love for each other, and for her and Aiden. Grandma Pea didn't approve of their marriage, so they ran off to California to some little town outside of Los Angeles to wed. They looked so happy.

Next to that picture was one of Aiden at age six and her dog, Bubba. A deep yearning crept up in her stomach, and her heart grew heavy. It was amazing how much she still missed them and yet at times felt like she couldn't remember much about them. She glanced back and forth between the pictures.

A lightning bolt of pain seared her head. Bubba's real name was Oxnard. Her parents had named him after Oxnard, California, where they got married and rescued him.

She grabbed her parent's wedding picture off the wall, knocking down several smaller frames and sending them crashing to the floor. Behind them in the picture was a sign that read "Welcome to Oxnard, California." Her dad had called the dog "Ox," even though everyone else called him Bubba.

She stared at the dog, her blood pumping so hard she could hear it in her eardrums. Bubba's two different-colored eyes stared back at her. It was so strange. Ox had one brown and one blue eye too. A shudder ran down her back. She'd felt connected to Ox from the moment they'd met— kind of like her connection with Ginger, only stronger and without him ever talking. They'd both known it. And he'd brought Joey to Grandma Pea's. Despite being a Noli, he was on her side.

Thoughts swirled in her brain, and her body swayed back and forth. She leaned her head and body against the cool wall for support. Another set of pictures caught her eye.

There was a double-sided picture frame of Aiden and her at age eight in matching red shirts, taken shortly before the accident. On their shirts were hearts and the letters X and O. Kisses and hugs. The frame was made out of metal, and etched all around were intertwined X's and O's. O and X? Ox's tattoo. To her it read OX, but to him, it would have been XO..

Lilah felt nauseous. The room started to spin, and she slid to the floor. Tears welled in her eyes. It couldn't be.

She looked back at the picture again. She and Aiden both wore their rings on their necklaces. At the bottom of both pictures, the words "Always Together, XO" were engraved neatly in calligraphy.

She racked her brain. Again, the pain seared. Ox's tattoos were vines, but she hadn't seen any words or letters that she clearly remembered. Then it hit her.

In the bunkhouse, on the wall, she remembered seeing a wall hanging. It was hand-written, and at the time she couldn't translate what it said. It said "Semper Simul"— *always together*. Her father had always used the Latin. Why didn't she remember that until now?

The room continued to spin around her. Her head pounded as Madame Mystique's words came back to her. "You may have to part from someone with whom you deeply love. Whether it is permanent or not will depend on you."

Her words weren't about Joey. They were about Ox, rather, Aiden.

The clues had been in front of her the whole time and she'd never stopped to put them together. She thought he was dead, but he was alive and living in Nolianna.

Aiden must have somehow survived the accident all those years ago and now lived in Nolianna. She didn't know how, but it made sense. There were so many signs. He couldn't talk, but he gave her every sign possible for her to see it. He'd sacrificed himself for her so she could get out. He'd always taken the heat for her, even when they were little.

She gasped for air. Her insides were on fire. She'd lost him for a second time.

Not wasting another second, Lilah dropped the pictures in the hallway, causing several glass panes to break. She ran to find her sneakers and coat in the front room.

Hearing the crash, Joey ran into the front room. "Lilah, are you okay? Have they come for us?" Joey's words mirrored her own fear that they would.

"Joey, I have to go. I can't talk now but I'll explain later. Please, go to Abe's and ask them if there's any way to get back into Nolianna," she said in one breath. She knew it was a risk, but was desperate for answers.

"Are you serious?"

"Please, for me," she begged. "After everything we've been through, we deserve answers. And Abe has them, please."

Joey bit his lip and reluctantly nodded.

"I'll meet you at Abe's in a little while and will explain it all then!" she yelled. "Just be careful and wait for me. We'll confront them together! Just please, meet me there in a little while."

Tears stung her eyes, and bile crept up into her throat. Enormous grief and physical pain all but knocked her over. Her mind raced. How could her brother still be alive? How did she not know from the moment she saw him again?

She ran as fast as her legs would take her out the front door and onto the street. The trail to Nolianna was too far away, and she didn't want to waste time walking. She remembered that she had an old ten-speed bike in the garage. Running around the house, she threw open the shed door. Luckily the bike was still there and the tires had air. She threw her leg over the seat and peddled hard. It was still early enough in the day that not too many people or cars were out on the road.

The road was icy and her tires slipped. She focused all her energy and strength on staying on the bike, pushing her legs as hard as she could. Retracing her steps to the parking lot and trailhead, she made it to the tree-covered path that led to the waterfall in no time. She jumped off the bike and sprinted to the waterfall. She tripped several times and had to pick herself up to jump over several icy spots in her path.

Panting for what air she could take in, she arrived at the waterfall. She dashed through the water, but the trail opening was gone. She searched the wall of trees. The visible path that had been there all week had disappeared. Nothing. No opening, no trail. She hit the large pine tree in front of her several times so hard her hand started to bleed. In desperation, she even kicked it a few times, only to hurt her toes.

A pent up scream escaped her lungs. She continued to scream until her lungs burned and she was completely out of breath. Then she fell to the ground and wept.

It really was over. She'd lost Aiden for a second time. And worse, there was no guarantee Sebastian wouldn't punish him for helping her. All of the anguish and grief of the past week was almost too much to bear. She cried and cried, and had no idea how long she lay there, as if the car accident that took him from her the first time had just happened all over again.

When her tears began to cease and her adrenaline faded, exhaustion set it. There wasn't anything she could do about Nolianna, but she could go to Abe's to confront him.

At this thought, her whole body convulsed again. She tried to get up but slipped on a rock and fell to the hard dirt. Hitting the ground, her sobs came once more. She had nothing left but tears. Everything in her body hurt and was on fire at the same time. It was freezing outside, yet she burned. She tried to scream again but was unable to make a sound. Time was yet again her betrayer.

The sun began to climb high in the sky above, and a ray of light shone through the trees. The beam illuminated the waterfall. This time of year was cold in Ithaca, but the sun often shone and brought unprecedented beauty. Her sobs dissipated. She had to get to Abe's, worried though of what she would or wouldn't find there.

The one thing she knew though was that she wasn't afraid of him anymore.

Chapter 40

٭

IT TOOK HER what felt like forever to get back to Abe's. She walked the familiar trail once more and when she finally turned onto Abe's street, she saw Joey on the front steps. He was wrapped up in a winter coat with a black beanie on.

Her heart sang as she remembered the first time she saw him. His stormy, gray-blue eyes

had captivated her heart and still did every time she looked at him. He was even more gorgeous today than when they were first reunited. His heart and his goodness made her fall even more in love with him than she thought possible. She had to hold on to that.

She walked toward him and noticed the frown on his face. She looked past him and noticed there were no cars in the driveway.

"They're gone, aren't they?" She didn't need him to answer.

"Yeah. They're gone. It doesn't make sense. They were here just last night!"

"I want to go inside," she said, passing by Joey, needing to see it all for herself. Joey didn't stop her.

She walked inside and searched the bottom floor. All that remained inside was some mismatched, old furniture, but nothing else.

"I don't know how they did it, but they obviously packed up and left quickly," Joey said, and reached out to take Lilah into his arms. She pushed him away. The pain was too raw and the anger too intense. Joey's eyes clouded.

"I'm sorry. There's so much more to this than you know," she blurted out.

"It's okay. Any idea what all of this means?" Joey asked.

"I have no idea, but there are so many questions I need to ask and now I can't. They're gone. Is there any indication of where they went?" Lilah felt the energy draining from her body and did all she could do to keep herself from breaking down into sobs.

"No. They took everything. You know, they never received mail here. I thought it was strange, but Abe had a PO box. So there isn't even the chance of finding out their forwarding address," Joey said.

They stood for a few moments in silence and glanced around the house. After a few moments passed, Lilah went upstairs to her room and found her belongings untouched. She packed the few things she wanted to bring to back to Grandma Pea's.

Just as she had finished packing and stepped into the hallway, Joey emerged into the hallway and smiled. Finally their timing seemed to be good. They walked down the three flights of stairs in silence. The old house creaked and shuddered as the wind howled outside. They made it downstairs and into the front hallway before either of them spoke again. Joey broke the silence.

"So you still haven't told me why you ran back to the falls and then came here to ask Abe how to get back in. Why in the world would you want to do that? I thought you were finished with Nolianna?"

The corner of Lilah's lips turned upwards slowly into a half smile. "I promise I'll explain everything as we walk back to our house, but you aren't going to believe me," she said.

"Oh, Carrots, I'll believe just about anything you tell me right now. Try me," Joey said, and returned her smile. He had no idea of the bomb she was about to drop on him. He looked at her and caressed her face. "Okay, let's go and I'll tell you as we walk," Lilah said.

Joey took her bag and put the strap over his shoulder. He took her hand in his, her thumb tucked in, and she followed him toward the front door. Her legs felt like they were moving through molasses and her heart was broken in a million pieces.

She reached for the front door and it swung open, knocking into a small cherry side table hidden behind it. It jiggled and fell over. She let go of Joey's hand.

He laughed. "Always making a ruckus, aren't you?" he said, and stepped onto the porch. Lilah went behind the door and placed the table upright. She looked up and noticed a medium-sized oil painting of a field in an ornate gold frame. In their haste, Abe and Eva must have forgotten to take it with them. Wedged in the corner of the frame was a postcard with a picture of carousel in Nolianna, only without all the wear and tear of years gone by.

Lilah reached forward and grabbed the postcard. She moved her face closer to inspect it. At the bottom, written in Eva's handwriting, were the words, "Olympia, Washington.".

The hairs on the back of Lilah's neck stood up. She turned it over and there was an address with the name "Aldras Ambers" in the left-hand corner. Could it be that Aldres Ambers was an alias for Abe Anderson? Was it possible that Abe and Eva changed their names each time they moved? Lilah grabbed the card and shoved it in her jeans pocket.

Replacing the painting on the wall, she walked out of the house, slamming the door behind her. She strolled down the front steps to catch up with Joey and a slight smile crossed her lips. All hope wasn't lost. She couldn't wait to tell him about Aiden. And that they had eleven months to get to Olympia, Washington.

CPSIA information can be obtained
at www.ICGtesting.com
Printed in the USA
BVHW032313270221
601161BV00001B/69